Kate Ellis was born and brought up in Liverpool and studied drama in Manchester. She has worked in teaching, marketing and accountancy and first enjoyed literary success as a winner of the North West Playwrights competition. Keenly interested in medieval history and archaeology, Kate lives in North Cheshire with her husband, Roger, and their two sons. *The Blood Pit* is her twelfth Wesley Peterson crime novel.

Kate Ellis has been twice nominated for the CWA Short Story Dagger, and her novel *The Plague Maiden*, was nominated for the *Theakston's Old Peculier Crime Novel of the Year* in 2005.

The Blood Pit

Kate Ellis

PIATKUS

PIATKUS

First published in Great Britain in 2008 by Piatkus Books
This paperback edition published in 2008 by Piatkus Books

Copyright © 2008 by Kate Ellis

The moral right of the author has been asserted

A CIP catalogue record for this book
is available from the British Library

ISBN 978-0-7499-0881-2

Typeset in Bembo by Palimpsest Book Production Limited,
Grangemouth, Stirlingshire
Printed in the UK by CPI Mackays, Chatham, ME5 8TD

Piatkus Books
An imprint of
Little, Brown Book Group
100 Victoria Embankment
London EC4Y 0DY

An Hachette Livre UK Company
www.hachettelivre.co.uk

www.piatkus.co.uk

PROLOGUE

The small figure lay on the sand gulping in salty, seaweed-scented air as the twisted face descended slowly, closer and closer.

The watchers had been egging on the tormentor, braying like donkeys. Relentless, mocking. But suddenly they fell silent and began to back away, as though an evil spell had been broken. Then, after a few frozen, expectant seconds, they fled the scene, leaving the victim alone with the powerful one, waiting for the cruel laugh and the final blow.

There was no pain when the blood started to drain away into the thirsty sand. And as the victim looked upwards, the stars and the towering cliff face silhouetted against the midnight sky began to blur and fade. The end was near. This was death.

Savouring the moment of supreme power, the bringer of death sat back and smiled. But when a sound cracked like a gunshot through the gloom, the tormentor fled into the shadow of the cliff and the victim was left alone, life blood gushing away like a stream, staining the sand a rusty red.

FIFTEEN YEARS LATER

Annette Marrick turned the car into the drive of Foxglove House, narrowly avoiding the couple who were walking past the gate – a man and a woman, not old, not young; out for a saunter in the late afternoon sun with their cheap supermarket clothes and plastic carrier bags. As Annette swung the steering wheel, they scurried out of her path and she smiled with satisfaction before continuing down the drive, bringing the car to a halt in front of the house with a crunch of gravel beneath her wheels.

Charlie's new Range Rover was there, parked thoughtlessly at an angle as usual, and as Annette opened the front door, she couldn't help feeling discontented and a little angry. But she often felt like that these days – especially when he was up to what she thought of as His Little Tricks.

She noticed that the lounge door was shut, which was unusual. Perhaps he was in there, she thought . . . entertaining. Tentatively, she turned the handle and listened for sounds of hurried, embarrassed dressing. But when she stepped into the room, all she could hear was the faint sound of birdsong from the garden trickling in through an open window.

Three months ago, she had had the lounge decorated to her own taste. Cream carpet; white leather sofa; white walls and ceiling; cream drapes at the French windows with the occasional splash of cool green to relieve the monotony.

And red. There were splashes on the walls and ceiling. Scarlet in places; rusty in others where it had begun to dry. The white sofa was now a deep, glistening scarlet and he lay slumped there, staring at her accusingly.

'Charlie,' she whispered, hurrying over to him and touching his arm with the tips of her fingers. When he didn't move she looked down and realised that she was standing in a pool of blood, thick and sticky. She froze for a few moments, wondering what to do, before backing away, her eyes fixed on her husband's dead face.

She took off her stilettos at the door and tiptoed into the hall in her bare feet, her heart pounding. When she reached the huge mirror that hung by the staircase, she stared at her reflection in horror. Her white skirt was stained with Charlie's blood so she unzipped it frantically, only to find that the red had seeped through to her underskirt. She stepped out of that too and stood in her white lace knickers, staring at her half-naked image in the mirror, telling herself to stay calm. There was some way out of this.

Then she rushed to the kitchen and plunged the skirt and underskirt into the sink. She had to be clean. No blood must be found on her hands.

CHAPTER I

Dear Dr Watson or may I call you Neil? Yes I'll call you Neil
– it sounds more informal. Friendlier.

Did you know the monks of Veland Abbey were bled every
couple of months and that they regarded it as a great treat –
a holiday almost? It was their only chance to eat decent food
in the warmth away from the daily grind of hard physical
work and those interminable prayers.

I feel I know all about you, Neil, and I feel you'd under-
stand. You see, I'm scared I might do something terrible. And
I'm scared the bleeding won't stop like it did for those monks.

Neil Watson stared at the letter and frowned. It had been
waiting for him in his letterbox at the entrance to the flats,
between an electricity bill and an offer of a credit card at
amazing rates from a company quite unaware of what archae-
ologists actually earned. As it had promised to be the most
interesting item of correspondence, he'd opened it first. And
now he turned it over, as though he expected to find some
sort of clue on the back of the sheet of A4 paper. The letter
had been printed on a computer. Times New Roman. And
the envelope was the plain white self-seal type with a
computer-printed address. All standard stuff. Apart from the
content.

He realised his hand was shaking. He was an archae-ologist; not the sort of person who received anonymous letters. And the thought that someone out there was watching him was unnerving. The writer knew what he did. And where he lived. He could be watching now . . . somewhere in the shadows. Waiting.

Neil put the letter down on the small dining table that doubled as his desk. Perhaps he should ignore it. There were a lot of peculiar people about and his recent appear-ance on local television had probably lured one of them out of whatever woodwork he or she had been lurking in. He'd raised his head above the parapet; maybe even become a bit of a local celebrity of the very minor kind. Neil had never considered himself the celebrity type but then someone – he couldn't remember who – had once observed that everyone has their fifteen minutes of fame. Although he had to admit that he hadn't particularly enjoyed his.

Fame, in Neil's case, had crept up unexpectedly when he'd agreed to take charge of the Archaeological Unit's first training excavation at Stow Barton – a puzzling collection of medieval ruins on land once owned by a Cistercian abbey two miles to the west. Members of the public could, for a price, take part in a dig, supervised and instructed by professional archae-ologists. The powers-that-be had told him that it would spread the word to the masses. And it would raise some much needed funds into the bargain.

However, from the very beginning, Neil had had an uncomfortable feeling that the enterprise would end in disaster.

He re-read the letter again before screwing it up into a tight ball and aiming it at the waste-paper basket in the corner of his cluttered living room. It was rubbish. The work of a nutcase with nothing better to do.

But half an hour later he retrieved it and flattened it out.

He had an uneasy feeling he might need all the evidence he could get.

The hooded figures on the littered recreation ground that lay on the edge of Morbay's Winterham Estate had their own rituals, strict and unchanging. The circling on bicycles like some tribal round dance. Then the solemn drinking of the strong cider or lager – whatever they could get their hands on. Then, as darkness fell, the furtive communion with their shaman – Daz the dealer who hung round the estate in anticipation of their needs – their alternative emergency service. Then the escape to their tawdry ecstasy of enlightenment – the high point of their day. The thing they mugged, shoplifted and burgled for. The temporary oblivion they craved for want of anything better to do.

At six thirty, after a hard day avoiding the security guards who patrolled the shopping centre in Morbay, Carl Pinney felt thirsty. His mates decided to go to the chippy but Carl, knowing his mum had bought some diet coke from the supermarket the day before, broke away from the tribe, saying he'd see them later, and made for home. He fancied some coke before Chelsea, his stupid bitch of a sister, drank it all. And, besides, he had seen his favourite pizza being shoved in the freezer. And pizza, in Carl's opinion, trumped the Fat Friar's soggy chips any day.

The maisonette he called home was in sight. Built in the 1950s in the utilitarian council-house style, it had grubby net curtains at the windows and an old fridge – once the property of the neighbours – stood on the patch of scrub that his mum optimistically referred to as a lawn. Pathetic really, Carl thought. But his mum had always had big ideas . . . until Dad had walked out and the pills and booze got to her.

Carl was making for the front door when he saw something glinting on top of an open bin bag by the front gate.

The thing caught the light amongst the ready meal packaging, sparkling like a jewel in mud, and Carl leaned over the bag of rubbish to get a closer look.

The blade looked vicious. Thin and sharp and stained with something brown. The handle and the top of the blade looked brand new and as Carl reached down and picked it up he realised that the stain on the blade wasn't rust. It was something far more thrilling and his heart began to beat a little faster.

He stood gazing at it for a while before walking round to the back of the building, to the little flagged area Mum called the patio. The key to the tumbledown shed was in his pocket – he always kept it with him – and as he undid the padlock, the door opened with a creak. All his things were in here – the precious things he kept away from Chelsea and his mum. His private things. He opened the wooden box on the top shelf – the box his dad had given him when he was little – and placed the knife inside carefully before retracing his steps.

When he entered the house he found that Mum was out of it as usual, snoring gently on the settee, a half empty vodka bottle squatting on the coffee table, and Chelsea was nowhere to be seen. So he made himself a pizza before revisiting the shed.

One of the young constables in the patrol car who'd answered the initial 999 call had been sick in the rhododendron bushes lining the drive that lead to Foxglove House on the edge of the village of Rhode, halfway between Tradmouth and Bereton. Detective Chief Inspector Gerry Heffernan had taken pity on him and put him on the gate to keep away the press and the curious. The crime scene had already been preserved with blue and white tape, draped around the front door like welcoming bunting.

It was a pleasant evening, positively warm for early June

and Heffernan was sitting in front of the house on a wrought-iron garden bench, enjoying the late sun while he waited for the Forensic team to complete whatever mysterious rituals they performed on such occasions so that he could make his own examination of the scene. He was wearing a white crime-scene suit which strained around the belly because he'd already had a brief look inside the house. Death was never pretty but this one was enough to turn the strongest stomach.

He heard the growl of an approaching car engine and when the vehicle appeared round the bend in the drive, crunching the luxuriant gravel beneath its tyres, he stood up. Wesley. Just the man he needed.

'Your mobile was off,' Heffernan said accusingly as DI Wesley Peterson climbed out of the car. 'Where have you been?'

Wesley glanced down at his jeans and white T-shirt, not his usual working garb. 'I told you I was taking the afternoon off. It was Michael's school sports day then we all went for something to eat. Pam would have skinned me alive if I'd been called out. It was more than my life was worth to keep my mobile on.'

Heffernan knew that this was the time to bluster a little, to make Wesley feel guilty for his lack of dedication to duty. But somehow he couldn't manage it. He knew exactly how Wesley felt.

'So did he win, then, your lad?'

'Third in the egg and spoon race,' Wesley said with a shrug of the shoulders. 'He's more the cerebral type.'

Heffernan smiled. The kid was clearly a chip off the old block, he thought. But he said nothing.

Wesley looked across at the open front door. He could see figures in white overalls huddled in the hallway, deep in concentration. The police photographer and a couple of Forensic officers emerged from the front door, their faces solemn and businesslike. There was none of the usual banter. Wesley knew that this was a bad sign. 'So what's the story here?' he asked.

Heffernan didn't answer. Instead he called over to the Forensic officers and asked if it was okay to go in. When they answered in the affirmative, Wesley donned a paper suit and plastic gloves and the two men began to make their way to the house.

'Nasty?' Wesley asked.

'You could say that.'

Wesley took a deep breath, preparing himself for the unpalatable. He came from a family of doctors but the genetic strong stomach had somehow passed him by.

Gerry Heffernan led the way into the hall and pointed to a half-open door to his left. 'In there.' The way Heffernan said the words made Wesley feel nervous. He hesitated before taking a bold step across the threshold.

The sight that greeted him made him freeze. There was blood everywhere, pooled on the floor and splashed up the walls, and three white-clad figures were crowded around something lying on the sofa. Wesley recognised one of the figures as the pathologist, Colin Bowman, intent on his work and deep in concentration. Wesley didn't greet him. He had caught the metallic stench of blood in his nostrils and his stomach was beginning to churn. He stepped out of the room quickly. He'd leave them to it for now.

Gerry Heffernan was waiting in the hall at the foot of the wide staircase, carpeted in cream to match the lounge. 'Not a pretty sight,' the DCI observed.

'Who was he? Or was it she?'

'It's a he. Wine merchant by the name of Charles Marrick.'

'Could it be suicide? Or an accident?'

Heffernan shook his head. 'No note and no sign of a weapon.'

'Who else lives here?'

'Only the wife. She found him. She's in the conservatory at the back of the house with Rachel.'

Wesley nodded. If anyone was going to get anything out of the grieving widow, it was DS Rachel Tracey. She had a talent for that sort of thing. A gift. And, to top all that, she had a good ear for a lie.

'How's the wife taking it?'

Heffernan thought for a second, searching for the appropriate words. 'I get the impression she's not exactly heartbroken.'

'Think it could be a domestic?'

'My first thought when I saw the body was that a woman couldn't have done it. But I have to admit that I've known some pretty scary women in my time.'

Wesley looked at him curiously, wondering if he was about to be the recipient of some interesting confidences.

But Heffernan didn't elaborate on his last statement. 'I suppose we'd better make Mr Marrick's acquaintance,' he said with a sigh.

Wesley nodded. It couldn't be put off any longer.

The two men entered the lounge gingerly, stepping over the Forensic team's metal plates, put down to preserve any evidence that might lie on the floor. Dr Colin Bowman was blocking their view of the thing on the sofa and when Heffernan greeted him, he looked round and smiled.

'Come in, come in,' he said like a genial host, beckoning to them to come closer. The lady of the house must have favoured cream and white, Wesley thought, and the overall effect was airy and light – or it would have been if it weren't for the dark stains on the walls and fabrics. At first he thought the deep-red sofa was a dramatic interior design statement. Until he saw the body of Charles Marrick.

Normally Gerry Heffernan would have indulged in a bit of idle chatter, small talk to relieve the tension, but today he stayed silent as Colin moved aside to give them a better view, like an artist showing off his handiwork.

The corpse of Charles Marrick lay slumped against the cushions, staring at the ceiling with sightless eyes. The expression on the dead man's pallid, almost white, face – a desperation, as though he was pleading for help which never came – made Wesley take a step back. Then his eyes were drawn to the neck. Blood must have gushed like a fountain from the pair of neat wounds, close together and perfectly aligned like a vampire's kiss. Most of the blood had been absorbed by the sodden sofa but some had splashed on to the surrounding walls and furnishings and trickled down on to the creamy carpet below.

'There are two neat stab wounds close together and both of them pierced the artery,' Colin pronounced with inappropriate cheerfulness. 'Either lucky or he or she knew what they were doing.'

'There's so much blood,' Wesley observed quietly. Then he felt a little silly at having stated the obvious.

Colin Bowman cleared his throat. 'Who would have thought the old man to have had so much blood in him?'

Heffernan looked up. 'You what?'

'Shakespeare . . . the Scottish Play.' He turned to the corpse. 'What I can't understand is why there are no defensive wounds. He was a youngish man and fairly fit, I should think. Why didn't he put up a fight? And why didn't he call for help? He probably didn't die instantly and there's a phone on the table by the window.'

'Unless he was restrained or knocked out somehow,' Wesley suggested. 'Any sign of a head wound?'

Colin Bowman shook his head. 'Nothing obvious. But something might come to light when I get him on the slab. And there's nothing to suggest he was tied up.' He glanced across at the windows. One of them was open and the white voile drape, spotted with dried blood, billowed gently in the breeze. 'Lovely evening,' he observed absentmindedly.

'Not for him,' Gerry Heffernan replied before marching out of the room.

The feeling of the knife in his hand gave Carl Pinney a sense of power. And the blood on the narrow blade meant that it had been used before – blooded like a warrior's sword. Proved. Carl hadn't washed the blood off – he hadn't fancied it, watching the water in the basin turn red as it floated off in russet clouds. Instead he had dropped it into a thin super-market carrier bag. It'd be safe there.

Somehow he didn't feel like company so he hadn't gone to meet the others. But he needed something to blot out reality. He still had some of the stuff him and Nathan nicked from the vet's surgery in Tradmouth left but he was keeping that for a rainy day. Besides, he fancied something stronger and that would cost money. He felt in each pocket but found nothing but the unfruitful scratch card he'd nicked from the newsagent's the previous day. Daz would have what he needed – but Daz didn't give credit so he had to get hold of cash and fast. He could always go back home to see if there was anything in his mum's purse – she'd be in no fit state to stop him. Or he could try his luck in Abbeyside. There were a lot of upmarket flats and houses in Abbeyside, some owned by well-off single people who'd soon be arriving home after an evening in the pub. Ripe pickings.

He pulled his hood up, concealing his acne pitted face, and slouched down the street. The no man's land between the Winterham Estate and Abbeyside was a small district of small terraced houses, some rundown, some newly gentri-fied by optimistic first-time buyers who'd convinced themselves, despite all evidence to the contrary, that the area was on the up and that the Winterham Estate was improving daily. There were shops and takeaways on the main road but these didn't welcome the likes of Carl. The shopkeepers kept wary vigilance and regularly called the police who responded

with half-hearted boredom. Their hands were tied unless a
crime was actually committed. And hanging round in a threatening manner didn't constitute a crime. At least not yet.

But Carl had no intention of drawing attention to himself
that evening. He had been to Abbeyside many times before:
he had watched the new young residents talking on their
mobile phones, carrying their laptops in black padded cases,
their wallets and handbags stuffed with cash and credit cards.
As far as Carl was concerned, they were easy prey. Asking
for it.

He slipped into a narrow alley that ran between a dry
cleaner's and a Chinese takeaway and stood quite still, waiting,
like a hunter, for his quarry to come into view, striding
confidently, unaware of any danger. He felt in the carrier
bag and touched the cool metal of the knife handle. When
it was over he'd go straight to Daz. His head was hurting
and his mouth was dry. He needed something to blot out
the world and he needed it soon.

Carl waited hours – or it might only have been five
minutes; his sense of time had gone completely haywire –
before he heard footsteps. One person walking quickly down
the street towards his hiding place. Instinctively he crouched
a little, making himself invisible, coiled and motionless, waiting
to pounce. The knife was in his hand but he couldn't
remember taking it from the carrier bag. The footsteps were
louder now, getting nearer. Then a shadow crossed the alley's
mouth, blocking out the evening light, and Carl's muscles
stiffened. This was it. Prey. Time to move.

It happened quickly. Carl leaped out just as the figure had
passed. Later he was unable to recall the exact words he used.
Highwaymen of old used to say 'stand and deliver' but Carl's
opening line was almost certainly smattered with four-letter
words starting with F and lacked the elegance of a bygone
age. He came up behind his mark and pressed the knife against
the side of his throat, expecting the victim to freeze with

terror and hand over all his worldly goods meekly, without a word of protest.

His victim was a man, five ten and dark haired, wearing a soft black leather jacket that must have cost a fortune. He looked young and fit and, what was more important, he looked as if he had money. In a fair fight, he'd beat Carl no problem. But nobody argues with a blade: weapons are the great leveller . . . like death.

But things didn't quite go to plan. The victim swung round and pushed Carl to the ground, sending the knife clattering into the gutter. Then Carl was hauled upright. A pain shot through his body as his right arm was wrenched into an arm lock. He was forced to the ground again and he flinched as a punch landed on his face.

As he lay helpless and groaning, his captor made a phone call and a few minutes later a patrol car sped to the scene, blues and twos blaring. Carl's nose was still streaming with blood when he was pushed into the back seat.

The intended victim, who had introduced himself as Detective Constable Steve Carstairs when he made the arrest, grinned with satisfaction as he picked the knife out of the gutter. Then he climbed into the police car and sat beside Carl, leaning towards him so that Carl could smell his aftershave and the faint whiff of garlic on his breath.

'Not your lucky day, is it?' Carstairs said in a gloating whisper.

The only suitable response Carl could think of was to spit in his face.

CHAPTER 2

The life of a monk was essentially sedentary, spent in cloister, refectory or choir while the abbey's servants did most of the hard physical work. Periodic blood-letting had long been practised in monastic communities for the benefit of the brothers' health. At first the procedure took place in the abbey's infirmary and the usual disciplines of monastic life were little relaxed. Gradually, however, it became the custom for monks to be bled every six to eight weeks in some outlying country manor house owned by the monastery. This became known as the seyney house (from the Latin for blood). Here they would be bled with a lancet from a vein in the elbow then they would recover in some comfort for five or six days. Each recuperating monk was allowed a gallon and a half of beer daily, two good-quality loaves and other victuals. Servants attended him and the normal regime of religious observation was much relaxed. In short, the seyney (or minutio as it was sometimes called) was a holiday.

But for some, it became a nightmare. A horror.

The writer read the words on the computer screen. It was best to stop there and stick to the facts. There would be plenty of time for the real truth.

Neil Watson hadn't felt like driving back to Exeter after

work. He'd visited the pub near the dig with some of his colleagues, putting off the evil moment when he had to return to his empty flat. But an evening on the orange juice rather than his customary bitter had soon lost its appeal so he'd left after the first drink and driven to Tradmouth. The letter was on his mind, nagging like a headache. And the only person he could think of to share his burden with was Wesley Peterson. He could trust Wesley to put the problem into perspective.

Tradmouth was only five miles from the dig but by the time Neil parked his yellow Mini outside Wesley's modern detached house on the hill overlooking the ancient port, it was getting dark. Neil was glad to see that Wesley's car was there. And Pam's.

It was Wesley who answered the door. He looked pleased to see him. But, at the same time, he had the look of a man with things on his mind.

'Haven't seen you for a while,' were Wesley's first words.

'I've been busy organising this training excavation. It's been a nightmare sending out the forms and taking the bookings. Wish I'd not volunteered to take charge but it seemed like a good idea at the time.'

Wesley smiled sympathetically. 'How's it going?'

'Not too bad. But it's early days yet.'

'I saw you on the telly.'

Neil felt his face turning red. 'Yeah. Was I okay?' he asked self-consciously, smoothing his unruly hair. Wesley allowed himself a smile – he'd known Neil since his university days and never once had he imagined that his friend would become a victim of media adulation.

Before he could answer, Pam emerged from the living room. She gave Neil a shy, enquiring smile and asked him if he'd like a drink. He said a coffee would be great before following her and Wesley into the kitchen, wondering how to tackle the subject of the anonymous letter. Here in the warmth of the Petersons' house, it seemed so trivial . . . silly even.

Pam looked up from filling the kettle and caught his eye. 'I've been meaning to ask you if I can bring my class to your dig. I know they'd be interested and I'll see that the troublemakers are well supervised.' The words came out in a rush.

'I'm sure we can arrange something. Give us a week or so to get things going and . . .'

'Thanks,' she said, pouring coffee into the cups – strong for Neil; weakish for Wesley and decaffeinated for herself because she'd been having problems sleeping of late.

Pam took her drink into the living room but Neil lagged behind. He wanted to talk to Wesley alone. He put his coffee down on the worktop and cleared his throat. 'I've had this strange letter.'

Wesley was tired after a day spent getting to grips with Charles Marrick's murder. But Neil's odd pronouncement grabbed his attention.

'What kind of letter?' Neil was someone who'd class a communication from the Inland Revenue as a threatening letter.

'It went on about monks being bled and it said he was scared he'd do something terrible and the bleeding wouldn't stop. Really weird.' Now he'd put it into words it seemed even stranger, more threatening somehow. As though he'd given the idea a power it hadn't possessed when it had been confined to paper.

'When did you get it?' Wesley asked, the mention of bleeding reminding him of Charles Marrick's murder.

'It was waiting for me when I got home last night.'

'No signature, I presume.'

Neil shook his head, gratified that his friend was taking his little problem seriously. 'He said he felt he knew all about me. Could he have been watching me or what?'

Wesley noticed that Neil looked strained, as though this thing was getting to him. Or perhaps it was just the burden of dealing with a load of enthusiastic amateurs on his new project. Never work with children, animals or the general public, he had once heard Gerry Heffernan say. The trouble was, as a police officer, he didn't usually have much choice in the matter.

He tried to think up a few words of comfort, something to put Neil's mind at rest. He didn't want to mention Charles Marrick's death and alarm him even further – after all, there was probably no connection. 'You were on the telly . . . on the local news talking about the dig. I bet that's where this character's seen you and he's taken a shine to you.'

'Can't you do something about it?'

Wesley assumed the apologetic expression he used at work with victims of petty crime when he knew the culprit was unlikely to fall into the hands of the police. 'He's not actually threatened you, has he? And it's only one letter.'

'So far. What if he sends more? What if he starts stalking me. And I don't like all this talk of blood.'

Neither did Wesley, especially after what he'd witnessed that day at Foxglove House. He looked at his old friend. 'I'd never had you down as the nervous type, Neil.'

Neil looked embarrassed for a split second then he shrugged his shoulders. 'It just gave me the creeps, that's all.'

'Let's see it then. I presume you've brought it with you.'

Neil shook his head sheepishly. 'Yeah – I suppose I should have but . . . well . . . I didn't want to carry the bloody thing around with me. Like I said, it gave me the creeps.'

Neil wasn't normally this sensitive, Wesley thought. But if someone was out there, watching him – someone he couldn't see – it was hardly surprising. 'Look, Neil, why don't you let me have a look at the letter and I'll tell you what I think.'

'Yeah, good idea. Can you come to the dig tomorrow? I'll have it with me then.'

Wesley thought for a moment. 'That should be okay. It's not far from our crime scene,' he said, trying to sound casual. The letter had mentioned blood and Marrick's body had been drained of the stuff – so with the possibility, however remote, that it could be linked to the Marrick investigation, he wanted a look at that letter. Neil looked as though he could do with a change of subject – something closer to his heart. 'What do you know about the site so far?'

'Not much yet. The farmer suggested we investigate the place 'cause he's always been puzzled about some ruined outbuildings and lumps and bumps in the ground at the end of one of his fields. It's obvious that a lot of the stones were reused in the present farmhouse – recycling's nothing new. But we've given ourselves the job of finding out what the buildings were originally used for.'

'Barns?'

'Oh no. We've found some fine dressed stone and the remains of mullioned windows. These buildings are definitely high status – fifteenth century or thereabouts. If you want to bring your trowel tomorrow . . .'

Wesley smiled. Unless they made an arrest in the Charles Marrick case pretty soon, there'd be no time for archaeology . . . or much else come to that.

Neil glanced towards the living room door. 'Pam okay?'

'She's fine.' He lowered his voice. 'I'm planning a surprise for our anniversary next weekend – nice dinner and a night in a country hotel near Honiton. I've cleared it with Gerry and booked Pam's mum to stay the night here and babysit.'

'Great,' Neil said as though he meant it. He looked at his watch. 'I'd better get back. I might look for somewhere to stay nearer the dig 'cause I'm sick of the drive. Trouble is, the holiday season's almost upon us and everywhere's booked up or charging top prices.' He looked at Wesley hopefully but Wesley ignored the hint.

The phone began to ring and somehow Wesley knew it

would be for him. Some new development in the Marrick murder perhaps. He sighed as he picked up the receiver and recited his number.

He wasn't surprised to hear Gerry Heffernan's Liverpudlian accent on the other end of the line. 'Get down here quick, Wes.'

'What is it? What's happened?'

But the chief inspector didn't answer. 'Just get down here, will you?'

The line went dead.

'Sorry, Neil . . . got to go.'

'It's not me you should be apologising to, mate,' Neil replied, glancing in the direction of the living room where Pam was waiting for them.

When Wesley arrived at Tradmouth police station it was almost ten thirty and as he entered the CID office he sensed a strange atmosphere. Some of the investigation team were at their desks and DC Trish Walton looked up as he entered and gave him a wary smile. Something was up. He'd assumed it was something to do with the Marrick case but now he wasn't so sure.

He found Gerry Heffernan in his office and DS Rachel Tracey was with him. Gerry was wearing what Wesley always thought of as his 'I'll have his balls for cufflinks' expression; the one he wore when one of his team had erred and strayed from Gerry's interpretation of the path of righteousness.

'What's up?' he asked.

'Sit down.' The words were said quietly. No bluster. No wisecracks.

Wesley obeyed. He glanced at Rachel but her expression gave nothing away. She sat on the edge of her chair, her lips pressed together like a disapproving schoolmistress.

He looked at Heffernan expectantly, unable to bear the suspense. 'Well? What's going on?'

Gerry Heffernan sighed and looked at Rachel who pressed her lips together tighter. Her blonde hair was scraped back into a severe ponytail. It didn't suit her, Wesley thought.

'Steve Carstairs has made an arrest. Young lad tried to mug him and got punched for his efforts.'

'By Steve?' So far it didn't sound too alarming.

Heffernan nodded.

'So? I presume the culprit put up a fight.' Wesley had no cause to defend Steve Carstairs – when he'd first arrived in Tradmouth Steve had given him a hard time because of the colour of his skin and even now there was an undercurrent of resentment which made Wesley uncomfortable on occasions – but a suspect getting a bloody nose in the course of an arrest was nothing unusual. Some people just didn't like being arrested.

'Steve went down to the cells – told the custody sergeant he wanted to check something. Half an hour later the suspect was found lying on the floor. He's been rushed to hospital with head injuries.'

Wesley mouthed the word 'oh' and sat back in his chair. 'I find it hard to believe that even Steve would be that stupid,' he said after a few moments. 'What's he got to say for himself?'

'He says when he left the cell the lad – name of Carl Pinney – was fine. He reckoned he fell and banged his head after he'd gone.'

'Or Steve banged it for him,' said Rachel. 'He's been on edge recently, have you noticed?'

The two men shook their heads. They'd had other things on their minds.

'Trish says he's got personal problems.' Rachel didn't sound exactly sympathetic . . . but then she didn't like Steve Carstairs any more than Wesley did.

Gerry Heffernan sat forward. 'Haven't we all? What problems has Steve Carstairs got? Can't decide which aftershave to use?'

Rachel didn't smile. 'I think it's something to do with his father. His parents got divorced when he was young and his dad went up north – apparently he's just come back and got a job in Tradmouth. I don't know much more than that but I sense there's some bad feeling.' She sounded disappointed that the office grapevine hadn't worked with its usual efficiency. 'According to Trish, Steve's been under a lot of stress.'

'And that's an excuse for beating hell out of a suspect, is it?' Gerry Heffernan growled, shooting Rachel a hostile glance.

'No, sir . . . of course not. I was just saying . . .'

But the chief inspector wasn't listening. 'Anyway, he's suspended from duty pending enquiries. The chief super's doing a very good imitation of a volcano about to erupt and we're a DC short on this Marrick enquiry. He put his head in his hands as Wesley caught Rachel's eye. 'What have I done to deserve this?' He groaned rhetorically before muttering a detailed and colourful account of what he'd do to Steve Carstairs if he ever met him alone down a back alley.

Wesley gave Rachel an almost imperceptible nod and they both got up. They'd leave Heffernan to his private grief and return when he'd calmed down a bit. They left the DCI's office, closing the door gently behind them.

'How's Mrs Marrick?' Wesley asked once they were outside.

'She insists on staying at the house.'

'Someone's with her, I take it?'

Rachel nodded. 'A WPC's staying there.'

'Can't she go to relatives while . . . ?'

Rachel shook her head. 'She says she's got nobody round here. But she has got a daughter . . . name of Petronella.'

Wesley raised his eyebrows. 'Really?'

'She's called her but she doesn't know if she'll come. I get the impression there's something not quite right there.'

'Maybe they've fallen out.'

Before Rachel could reply, Wesley heard the boss calling

his name so he turned round and retraced his steps. When he re-entered the office, Gerry Heffernan looked up and sighed. He seemed to have recovered from his despondency – but then Gerry's moods were like the British weather, changeable and unpredictable.

Heffernan looked at his watch. 'You'd best get home, Wes. There's nothing more we can do tonight. We'll just have to see how Carl Pinney is in the morning and what he says in his statement.'

Wesley said nothing. He had the beginnings of a headache and he felt exhausted. And things wouldn't get any better tomorrow. In fact they'd be worse.

When he finally got home Pam had gone to bed. Neil, she told him, had left soon after he'd been called to the police station – and he hadn't seemed his usual self.

It looked as if Wesley wasn't the only one with problems.

Petronella Blackwell – she'd often wondered why her adoptive parents, had given her such an elaborate first name – inserted the CD into the slot, keeping her eyes on the road. After a few seconds the cello began to weep out the notes of Bach's Suite Number One and she felt hot tears trickling down her cheeks. She wiped them away with an impatient fist, telling herself that she was a grown woman. Annette and Charlie shouldn't have the power to hurt her any more.

She tried to concentrate on the tree-shaded road, following the white lines that kept blurring behind her tears and asking herself why she was making the journey. Perhaps she shouldn't have set off for Devon as soon as she got the message. After all, what did she owe Annette? Nothing. All Annette had done was given birth to her – dropped her like some farm beast. Annette had been sixteen when she'd become pregnant after a brief encounter of the sexual kind with a boy or man she had never named, and she had left it too late to get an abortion. Twenty-nine years ago, she'd given birth by default. Then she'd put on her clothes and left her daughter, crying and hungry in a plastic hospital crib. She'd walked out; abandoned her baby in the hospital while she swanned off to resume her life. End of story.

Only that hadn't been the end. Two years ago, at the age of twenty-seven, after the death of her adoptive father from cancer – her adoptive mother had died some years before in a motorway pile up – Petronella had found herself without a family and newly split up from her long-term boyfriend. It was at this vulnerable stage in her life that she had felt an irresistible, almost primal, urge to trace her biological mother. Her adoptive parents had done everything by the book – bequeathing to her their love of music and animals, particularly horses – and, on the advice of the adoption agency, they had never made any secret of her background. But it wasn't until her comfortable world had fallen apart that she had begun her quest for Annette. And eventually she had found her.

At first it was all tearful reunions and invitations to stay at Foxglove House for as long as she liked so that they could get to know each properly. Then, gradually, she'd discovered that, rather than being the mother of her dreams, Annette was a selfish, manipulative bitch who made her boredom only too obvious once the novelty of having a long-lost daughter had worn thin. Annette's husband, Charlie, had been charming at first – good looking and fun. In her naivety, Petronella had liked him. But when she'd realised the truth, she'd got away from Foxglove House as quickly as she could.

Now, after almost two years of silence, the call had come. Annette needed her.

Charlie was dead. He'd been murdered. And ties of blood are hard to break.

★

Heffernan was in a better mood next morning. In fact when Wesley arrived in the office he seemed positively chirpy. Wesley deduced from this that either Carl Pinney was on the mend . . . or that he'd decided not to make a formal complaint.

'Come in, Wes, come in.' Heffernan said impatiently, consulting one of the crumpled scraps of paper that cluttered his desk and then discarding it, repeating the process until he found the right one.

'You look cheerful,' said Wesley.

'Do I?' The DCI grinned. 'It's good to have our Sam home, that's all.'

'How's his new job going?'

'He's loving it – and the surgery's in Tradmouth so it couldn't have worked out better.' He shook his head. 'I can't believe he's a qualified vet. Doesn't seem two minutes since he was little and . . .' He sighed and looked at the piece of paper in his hand. 'Colin's doing the PM this afternoon so let's get down to Rhode and have a word with the Widow Marrick.' He looked at his watch.

'What about our little problem? Steve's . . .'

'I rang the hospital first thing. Pinney's on the mend. He's had brain scans but I don't know if they managed to find one.' He grinned at his feeble joke. 'He must be better 'cause he's saying he wants to make a statement. And he's demanding a solicitor which isn't a good sign. But if anyone's head's going to roll about this, Wes, I'm making sure the buck stops with Steve.'

'Quite right,' said Wesley with feeling. Some nasty little demon inside him kept saying that he hoped Steve Carstairs got everything that was coming to him. But then he felt slightly ashamed at his vindictiveness.

'I've asked Rach to call me if there are any developments.'

Heffernan stood up, fastening the top button of his purple shirt – a present from his musician daughter, Rosie, who thought that her father should be more sartorially adventurous: Gerry hadn't had the heart to disappoint her.

Ten minutes later they were on their way to the village of Rhode, Wesley in the driving seat as usual. He steered the car up the hill out of Tradmouth and took the left turn at the roundabout. Once past the high school and the leisure centre, they were out in open country with the sea down below to their left. A few distant, white-sailed yachts were skimming like toys over the smooth water and a tiny container ship trundled across the horizon. After a few minutes they reached civilisation in the shape of a postcard-pretty village, with pastel cottages and a narrow main street more suited to the horse than the motor vehicle. Wesley's eye was caught by a fountain of bright flowers tumbling from the balcony of a handsome whitewashed pub. Rhode was the sort of place visitors came to Devon to see. But nowhere is immune to violent death.

Wesley wondered whether to mention Neil's strange letter to his boss but he decided to wait until he'd actually seen it. It was probably a coincidence, but the letter's mention of blood, just as Marrick's body was found, made him uneasy.

Foxglove House stood at the end of the lane that ran by the thirteenth-century village church, crooked to accommodate the contours of the ancient churchyard.

'I'm surprised Mrs Marrick wanted to stay here,' Wesley said as they rounded the bend in the drive and the house came into sight.

'So am I, Wes, but apparently she insisted. If my living room looked as if I'd hired Count Dracula as the interior decorator, I'd be miles away.'

A patrol car was parked outside and the entrance was festooned with crime scene tape. Wesley climbed out of the driver's seat and followed Gerry Heffernan who was marching with determination towards the house.

DC Trish Walton answered the door, standing almost to

attention as they passed. Wesley wondered how much she knew about Steve's suspension. Steve and the sensible, if plodding, Trish used to be an item . . . before Trish came to her senses, as Heffernan put it. However, Wesley sensed that there was still a slight spark of attraction between Trish and Steve, even though it had never exactly been a relationship made in heaven. Now Trish shared a house with Rachel Tracey who would probably keep her on the straight and narrow as far as Steve was concerned. But Trish and Steve were opposites . . . and sometimes opposites can be drawn to each other against all the odds: look at magnets.

'How is she?' was Wesley's first question.

'The doctor gave her something to help her sleep and she seems fine this morning,' Trish replied, sounding rather puzzled. 'She's more worried about how the decorators are going to get rid of the bloodstains.' She shuddered. 'She's even started ringing up specialist cleaners.'

'Already?' Heffernan frowned. He'd come across a good few widows in the course of his career but this was the first one who didn't even wait till her husband's body was cold before removing all trace of him.

'Where is she now?' Wesley asked.

'In the kitchen having coffee. Her daughter arrived last night. Petronella her name is. She's in there with her.' Trish hesitated. 'It's all a bit odd if you ask me. The daughter doesn't seem in the least bit bothered. Mind you, he was only her stepfather – and, reading between the lines, I don't think they got on.' She leaned forward and lowered her voice. 'Apparently Annette Marrick had her when she was sixteen and abandoned her in the hospital. Petronella was adopted and she only traced her biological mother a couple of years ago. Annette's been married twice since she had Petronella but there're no other children. She was fourteen years older than Charles Marrick.' Trish raised her eyebrows and Wesley wasn't quite sure what he was expected to say.

But Gerry Heffernan stepped into the breach. 'So he was what is commonly known as a toy boy. Maybe he had a younger model waiting in the wings. Do you see this as a crime of passion, Wes? Older woman marries younger man. He gets fed up with her and takes up with someone else. She loses control and stabs him in the neck. I know she claims to have an alibi and we've found no blood-stained clothing yet, but it's possible, don't you think?' He watched Wesley for a sign that he approved of his theory.

Trish interrupted. 'Sir, how's that boy Steve was supposed to have . . . ?'

'It looks like he's on the mend,' said Wesley with a re-assuring smile. 'But Steve's suspended from duty.'

She looked Wesley in the eye. 'Steve always was an idiot.'

There was no answer to that. Gerry Heffernan had begun to lumber through the hall, making for the kitchen.

Wesley was about to follow him when Trish touched his arm. 'Steve's been having problems.'

'Rachel mentioned something.'

'His parents are divorced and he last saw his dad when he was twelve. Now he's come back to Devon and made contact again.'

Wesley raised his eyebrows. 'Is that bad?'

Trish shrugged. 'I don't know. I think it's upset Steve a bit. Unsettled him, if you know what I mean.' She gave him a weak smile. 'Actually you might have met his dad. He's manager of that sandwich shop on the High Street . . . the one near the Boat Float.'

Wesley thought he knew the man Trish was talking about – there was a new boss there, a middle aged man with greying hair and an ingratiating smile who always liked to banter words with any reasonably attractive female who happened to cross the threshold. Now he thought about it, he could see a resemblance to Steve – a similar-shaped chin; the same mouth; a likeness around the eyes.

'I think I know who you mean,' he said. 'Time to have a word with the merry widow, I suppose,' he added before making for the kitchen.

Gerry Heffernan had already made himself at home at the kitchen table. A tall young woman in her late twenties with short brown hair and large, pleading eyes, stood at the other end of the kitchen, waiting for an electric kettle to come to the boil. She looked up at Wesley as he entered the room, her eyes registering surprise for a split second. Then she asked him if he wanted a coffee and when he said yes, she took another mug from a nearby cupboard. If this was Annette Marrick's daughter, she was certainly nothing like her mother.

The older woman sat opposite Gerry Heffernan. She had immaculately cut shoulder-length blonde hair, a sun-bed tan and a body that had spent a lot of hours in the gym. Mrs Annette Marrick had put in a lot of effort to keep her younger husband. But she didn't seem too upset by the fact that she'd lost him.

'I'm very sorry for your loss, Mrs Marrick,' Wesley said as he took a seat beside his boss. 'It must have been a great shock for you, finding him like that.'

'Yes it was,' she said but somehow the words didn't sound very convincing. She began to examine her glossy blood-red nails, almost as though she was bored and when the younger woman placed the coffee cups in front of them, the two policemen thanked her but Annette Marrick made no acknowledgement. If Wesley had been in a charitable frame of mind, he might have put this down to grief. But instinct told him it was sheer bad manners.

Wesley addressed the younger woman. 'I presume you're Mrs Marrick's daughter.'

'Yes, I'm Petronella Blackwell,' she said, taking a seat at the table beside her mother.

'I'm sorry about your stepfather,' Wesley said automatically.

She looked away. 'I hardly knew him.'

Her manner implied that she hadn't wanted to know him. There was definitely animosity there. When Wesley caught Gerry Heffernan's eye, he knew that he'd noticed it too.

Heffernan turned to Annette. 'Right, love. I understand you discovered your husband's body when you returned home yesterday. By then he'd only have been dead an hour or so, according to our pathologist. Where had you been?' Annette's apparent lack of grief made him speak more brutally than he would normally have done to a recent widow. And besides, there was a hardness about the woman that he didn't like.

'I'd been out to lunch with friends,' she said with a cool glance at Petronella who was staring into her coffee mug, her face expressionless.

'According to your statement you got home at five thirty. That was a long lunch,' Heffernan said. Wesley could hear the scepticism in his voice – or was it some inborn dis-approval of ladies who lunch?

'We were planning a charity dinner. There was a lot to arrange.'

'Who were you with?'

'I've given the names to that little policewoman.'

Wesley assumed she meant Trish, although, at five foot eight, he wouldn't have described Trish as 'little'. Maybe the word was used to denote status rather than height. 'I'm sure you won't mind telling us again,' he said with a businesslike smile.

She squirmed in her seat and repeated the two names, neither of which meant anything to Wesley or the DCI. But then they didn't mix in those circles.

'Do you mind telling me if you noticed anything was missing?'

'You mean a burglary? You think he disturbed a burglar?'

'We're not sure yet. Is anything missing?'

Annette shook her head. 'Not that I'm aware of.'

'And do you know anything about your late husband's movements yesterday?'

'He'd been into the warehouse in the morning and he planned to come home after lunch to catch up on his paperwork. That's all I know.' She pressed her lips together as though that was all she was willing to say on the subject. Wesley looked at Heffernan who gave a small shake of his head. Leave it for now.

Wesley turned to Petronella. She looked rather nervous, out of her depth. 'What about you, Miss Blackwell. Where were you yesterday?'

'At home in Bath. I took the day off work – I had some holiday owing. Annette called me and I drove straight down.'

'What do you do?'

'I'm a secretary for a marketing company.'

'Is there anyone who can confirm where you were yesterday afternoon?' Wesley made the question sound casual.

She shook her head. 'I'm doing an Open University degree. I was working on an essay.'

Wesley smiled at her and she smiled back shyly. He had no reason to disbelieve her story. She had become entangled in events that had nothing to do with her because of an accident of birth. But he still had to find out about her relationship with Charlie Marrick . . . if she'd had one.

Gerry Heffernan looked Annette in the eye. 'Right then, love. Have you any idea who'd want your husband dead?'

The answer was a shake of the head.

'Had he quarrelled with anyone recently?'

Annette hesitated for a few moments and Wesley knew that she was making some sort of decision. Eventually she nodded. 'He had as a matter of fact,' she said warily before falling silent again.

'Who?' Gerry Heffernan sounded impatient.

'Fabrice Colbert. He owns Le Petit Poisson in Tradmouth.'

Heffernan caught Wesley's eye. They'd both heard of Le Petit Poisson but neither man could have afforded to eat there on the policeman's salary. It stood discreetly on the road leading to the castle and catered for the wealthy owners of the sleek white yachts which bobbed at anchor in the marina. And they knew of Fabrice Colbert too – the chef-proprietor was famous for his cuisine and his volatile temper and he wasn't afraid to display both on national television. Colbert could swear fluently in French and English and Wesley, for one, wasn't exactly looking forward to bearding this particular dragon in his den.

Annette hesitated again. 'Fabrice came storming round here on Monday. They had a big row.'

'What about?' Wesley asked.

'I wasn't involved in Charlie's business dealings. He never confided in me.' She sounded slightly bitter about her late husband's failure to communicate. 'I suggest you ask Fabrice,' she added in a tone that made Wesley suspect she knew exactly what the two men had argued about but she wasn't telling. Perhaps, he thought, it was something personal – a dispute over money, maybe . . . or over a woman.

'Yes, we'll do that,' he said. 'You didn't overhear what they were saying?'

'I'm not in the habit of eavesdropping on private conversations,' she answered self-righteously. Wesley didn't believe a word of it.

'Did your husband have any other enemies?'

Annette took a sip of her coffee before answering. 'He was successful. Successful men have enemies. People can't stand success in this country, have you noticed that?'

Wesley, assuming the question was rhetorical, didn't answer.

'They resent people like Charlie,' she continued. 'And Charlie didn't suffer fools gladly.'

Heffernan leaned forward. 'How do you mean?'

Annette waved her hand in a vague manner. 'You know. People who worked for him and all that.'

Wesley caught on quickly. 'Has he sacked anyone recently?'

'He was always sacking people,' Annette said, as though people being deprived of their livelihoods was an insignificance.

He glanced at Petronella and saw that she was staring into her coffee, looking as if she'd rather be somewhere else. And he saw something else on her face – embarrassment. She found her biological mother embarrassing. He wondered why she'd come down. But then a mother is a mother and there's no time of need like sudden widowhood.

'We'll need names.'

Annette gave another vague wave of her manicured hand. 'You'll have to ask at the shop . . . and the warehouse.'

'Would that be the shop in Tradmouth? Marrick and Company, Vintners?'

She nodded.

Wesley knew the shop. It was the expensive place near the market that specialised in vintage clarets – all the usual chateaux; Margaux, Mouton de Rothschild, Petrus, etcetera. Wesley had found himself in there by mistake when he'd first arrived in Tradmouth and he'd gone through the humiliating experience of searching desperately for the cheapest bottle in the shop under the sneering eye of a haughty assistant. Nowadays he bought his liquid sunshine at the supermarket.

'We know where that is but we'll need the address of the warehouse.'

Annette rose slowly and picked up the notepad that lay beside the telephone. She wrote something down and shoved the paper over the table towards Heffernan who looked at it before shoving it into his trouser pocket.

'What kind of man was Charlie?' Wesley asked gently as the widow sat down again.

'As I said, he didn't suffer fools gladly.' She shot a swift, almost imperceptible, glance at Petronella. 'And he liked his own way.'

Petronella sat, still and silent. She didn't look at her mother and showed no sign of contradicting this harsh assessment of her stepfather's character. Wesley wondered, for the second time, what had brought on this animosity. Had something happened between Petronella and Charlie? They were around the same age. Perhaps there had been a sexual attraction at one time. He had no doubt that he'd find out in due course. But in the meantime he'd take things slowly.

Annette's comments had aroused Gerry Heffernan's curiosity. 'What do you mean, liked his own way? Would you describe him as a bully? Did he bully his staff?' He looked her in the eye. 'Or you?'

'He expected the best of the people who worked for him,' Annette said defensively. 'There's nothing wrong in that.'

'And what about your relationship?'

'That's none of your bloody business,' she hissed after a long silence.

'I'm sorry, Mrs Marrick, but in a murder enquiry we have to ask intrusive questions,' said Wesley smoothly, trying to rescue the situation. 'It would help us to catch Charlie's killer if you'd answer them as honestly as you can. We're not here to judge, just to find out the truth.' He felt quite pleased with this little speech but one look at Annette's face told him that it hadn't had the desired effect. She turned her head away and drummed on the table impatiently with her fingers.

Both men sensed that they weren't going to get anywhere with the Widow Marrick. It would be wise to leave it for now . . . and maybe have a word with Petronella on her own. But that would have to wait: time was marching on and Charlie Marrick's postmortem was booked for two o'clock that afternoon.

It was Heffernan who stood up first, telling the two women he'd want to talk to them again, making the simple statement sound more like a threat than a promise.

'What do you think?' Wesley asked as they climbed into the car.

'That Annette's hiding something,' Heffernan stated bluntly. 'Probably the fact that she killed him. Most murders are domestic.'

Wesley didn't reply. He was keeping an open mind. It was almost midday and they decided to call in at the police station to see whether the team had come up with anything useful in their absence.

Wesley started the engine. 'Mind if we call at Neil's dig on the way back? He came round last night.' He paused. 'He's had a strange letter.'

Gerry Heffernan suddenly looked interested. 'How do you mean, strange?'

'Anonymous . . . about monks.'

'Monks?'

'That's what Neil said.'

'There are some strange people about,' was the DCI's verdict.

'And blood. It mentions bleeding. I'm thinking of Charles Marrick.'

'Why should the killer write to Neil?'

'I don't know. Unless that TV appearance he made's brought some lunatic out of the woodwork.'

'Have you told him about Marrick?'

Wesley shook his head. 'He's jumpy enough already,' he said as they turned on to the road leading to Neil's dig.

After a few hundred yards, Wesley spotted an open farm gate and a group of mud-splashed cars parked just inside the entrance to a field. He slowed down to a crawl and saw a trio of green awnings in the near distance flapping lazily in the gentle breeze . This, coupled with the handwritten sign hanging on the gatepost saying 'Welcome to the DCAU Training Excavation', told Wesley he'd come to the right place.

'Where is he?' Heffernan asked impatiently as he got out of the car, testing the ground to satisfy himself that the earth was solid beneath his feet.

Wesley could see Neil talking to a group of earnest-faced young people who seemed to be hanging on his every word. He must have said something amusing because they laughed dutifully before returning to their trenches and starting work again, scraping at the earth with the dedicated concentration of the learner.

When Neil saw the two policemen he waved them over and led them to a tumbledown farm building with a corrugated iron roof at the far end of the field. 'It's a cow shed,' he explained when he saw Gerry Heffernan's puzzled frown. 'It's got a tap and there's even electricity in the form of one bare light bulb so we're using it as a site office. The farmer provides us with flasks of boiling water for the tea and at least we can wash the finds. I've worked in worse places.'

Gerry Heffernan tried to look impressed but failed miserably.

'Have you brought the letter?' Wesley asked, suddenly impatient.

Neil opened the bottom drawer of the rusty filing cabinet in the corner and took out a crumpled envelope. Wesley read the note inside without comment.

'*I'm scared I'll do something terrible. I'm scared the bleeding won't stop.*'

He passed the note to Gerry who read it in silence and gave it back. Wesley could tell he was thinking the same as he was. Charlie Marrick had bled to death and the author of the note had hinted that he might do something terrible. Had he planned to kill Charlie Marrick and felt an urge to confess all to Neil Watson for some inexplicable reason? The idea, Wesley thought to himself, was quite preposterous. But stranger things had happened.

'Mind if I keep this?' he asked.

'Help yourself,' Neil replied. 'I'm glad to get the thing off my hands. Want to have a quick tour of the site?' he asked as Wesley put the envelope carefully into a plastic evidence bag.

It would have been bad manners, Wesley reasoned, to refuse Neil's invitation. Gerry Heffernan said nothing as he followed Neil and Wesley outside, glad of a break from investigating Charlie Marrick's murder . . . just as Wesley was.

As Neil led them from trench to trench, the diggers – who were mostly young apart from a few middle-aged enthusiasts – glanced up but quickly looked down again. Two men in suits meant officialdom – probably some bureaucrats from the Council checking on Health and Safety.

Wesley looked at what had been uncovered; substantial stone walls and a section of tiled floor which he recognised as medieval. Here, in the middle of nowhere, someone had gone to considerable trouble to build a high status building and his first thought was that it might have been the manor house attached to some abandoned and long-forgotten village.

Neil, of course, had done his homework and had consulted local documents and ancient maps. The site, he explained, had belonged to the Cistercian Abbey of Veland a few miles to the west – until Henry VIII had cast his avaricious eyes over the nation's monasteries and closed the abbey down, stripping the place of its wealth and its roof of its lead. The abbey itself had been bought by a wealthy landowner and converted into a handsome country pile while the mysterious cluster of buildings at Stow Barton had decayed and crumbled so that now only a few walls and tumbled stones were left above ground.

Neil's guess was that it had been a monastic farm, a grange.

Or perhaps a luxury retreat for the abbot, an escape from the day-to-day chore of running the abbey – the equivalent of a Russian dacha for high-up officials of the old Communist Party. The old maps he'd seen referred to it as the site of a manor house. But, like Wesley with his murder enquiry, he wasn't leaping to any hasty conclusions.

Wesley looked at his watch: they had been there half an hour and it was time they moved on. As they trudged across the rutted ground to the car, Gerry Heffernan commented that Neil's discoveries looked interesting and he wouldn't mind having a go at this digging lark himself. This left Wesley speechless as he drove back to Tradmouth for Charlie Marrick's postmortem. Gerry had always seemed to find the fact that Wesley had spent three years at university learning how to dig things up mildly amusing. Perhaps Neil's new tactic of reaching out to the public was having the desired effect in the most unexpected places.

On their way back to the police station, they bought a couple of sandwiches from Burton's Butties, the shop where Steve Carstairs's father worked. Wesley found himself looking out for Steve's father, intrigued to see the man who had produced such a son, but he was nowhere to be seen. When they reached the CID office they found it was almost deserted as most of the team were out pursuing enquiries. But this was how Gerry Heffernan liked it – sitting like a lord in his castle while his vassals were out hunting down information to bring back and lay at his feet.

Taking advantage of the rare oasis of peace, they made themselves comfortable in the DCI's cluttered office, eating their sandwiches from the packet and washing down their impromptu lunch with two plastic cups filled with a boiling liquid from the machine in the corridor that was alleged to be tea.

Wesley took Neil's letter from his pocket. 'Worth sending this to Forensic, do you think?'

He pushed it across the desk and Heffernan studied it carefully.

'Bit crumpled,' he said after a few moments.

'Neil said he chucked it in the bin then thought better of it.'

'The envelope's postmarked Neston so it must be a local nutter. But there's no actual threat is there? He's just saying he's scared he might do something. When did Neil receive it?'

'A couple of days ago. It was certainly posted before Charlie Marrick was murdered if that's what you're thinking.'

Heffernan read the note through again and shook his head. 'Neil gets this and Marrick's found bled to death. Is it a coincidence or not? Whoever wrote this says he's going to do something terrible . . . maybe he did.'

'I'll get it sent to Forensic,' said Wesley, taking the letter from his boss. 'Interesting that the writer's showing off his historical knowledge to Neil . . . almost as if he's trying to make himself feel important.'

'Perhaps that's what it's all about – some poor inadequate wanting to feel significant.'

Wesley smiled. 'You could be right.' He paused. 'Perhaps that's why he killed Marrick – to make himself feel powerful. The ultimate power.'

'After a job as a psychological profiler, are we?' the chief inspector said with a sigh, looking at his watch. 'Ready for the PM? If we're lucky we might get a cup of Colin's Earl Grey . . . which is a darned sight better than this muck.' He tapped the empty plastic cup before picking it up and flinging it contemptuously into the waste bin.

Tradmouth Hospital was within walking distance of the police station and Wesley was glad of the exercise. It was another fine day – the sixth in succession – and the river was teeming with yachts, their sails raised to take advantage of the breeze. Gerry Heffernan gazed at the scene longingly: Charles Marrick's murder meant that it would probably be a while before he had the chance to take the *Rosie May* out to sea again.

When the two men arrived at the hospital mortuary, they pushed open the swinging clear plastic doors and made for Colin's office. He was expecting them.

As usual they were greeted with offers of tea and biscuits and polite enquiries about their health and that of their respective families. To someone who didn't know Colin well, it might seem as though he was touting for business, like an undertaker instinctively noting a new acquaintance's height and build. But the two policemen had known the pathologist long enough to know that the enquiries were made out of genuine concern. Colin seemed particularly interested in Sam Heffernan's new job. It turned out that he knew the senior partner at the Cornvale Veterinary Clinic quite well – Heffernan had observed more than once that the professional men of Tradmouth had their own version of the Mafia.

When the Earl Grey had been drunk and appreciated, Colin led the way to the postmortem room. Heffernan walked by the pathologist's side, chatting but Wesley hung back. No matter how many times he entered this place of death, he never became hardened to what he knew he was about to witness. Heffernan knew how he felt but said nothing. For which Wesley was eternally grateful. Some bosses would have used it as a cue for snide remarks and teasing . . . like his former guvnor at the Met had done.

Charles Marrick was lying on the stainless steel table in the centre of the white-tiled room. There was a time when Pam had hankered after a kitchen in the same materials but when Wesley had told her what it brought to mind, she had opted for something more homely.

Marrick looked strangely peaceful, considering how he had met his end. The flesh was pallid as wax but the livid wounds on his neck provided a shocking dash of colour.

'Well nourished male in his early thirties,' Colin announced as he made his preliminary examination of the body. 'Good muscle tone – he kept himself fit. No sign of injury apart from two wounds in the neck which appear to have pierced the artery causing major blood loss undoubtedly leading to death.' He looked up at the two policemen. 'In my opinion the wounds were made by some sort of sharp, narrow blade. Stabbing rather than slashing.'

'Not a vampire then,' said Gerry Heffernan with a grin.

Colin chuckled. 'Can't rule anything out at this stage, Gerry, but I'll opt for a thin sharp knife.'

Wesley looked away as Colin made the initial incision into the chest, keeping up a chatty commentary into the microphone which dangled above the corpse – it saved making notes in an awkward situation.

As Colin worked, Wesley studied the tiled floor, glancing up occasionally to ask an intelligent question. He avoided the sight of the internal organs being taken from the body and weighed and the stomach contents being emptied into a bowl and examined, although he caught a strong whiff of garlic and whisky mingling with the scent of air freshener and formaldehyde, which rather put paid to Gerry's vampire theory.

The stomach contents, Colin told him, indicated that the dead man had eaten a hearty lunch a couple of hours before death. Some sort of game . . . quail perhaps, Colin guessed – he was a man who enjoyed the good things of life – accompanied by a some sort of fancy potato dish with garlic. He had drunk a small amount of red wine and he had washed the whole thing down with coffee and a quantity of whisky.

Colin Bowman believed in doing a thorough job and it was half an hour before he delivered his final verdict. 'The cause of death was loss of blood through those neck wounds. But he didn't put up a fight, which I find a little puzzling. The angle of the wounds suggests that his attacker was facing him so I'm surprised he didn't raise his hands to defend himself.' He picked up the corpse's right arm and examined it closely, shaking his head. 'No defensive wounds. And there's no sign that he was restrained in any way – no rope or tape marks anywhere on the body.' He looked at Heffernan. 'You sure we're not talking suicide here, Gerry?'

The DCI shook his head. 'No note and no sign of the weapon.'

Colin nodded. 'Mmm. Come to think of it, the angle of the wound's wrong for suicide. I can see from the mark where his watch has been that he wore it on his left wrist which suggests he was right handed. If that's the case, he'd most likely have swept a knife across his throat from the left to sever the artery.' He demonstrated with his hand.

Colin studied the corpse for a few moments then he suddenly took a magnifying glass off the trolley by his side. After making a close examination of the left arm, he looked up. 'There are some scars on the arm – only faint. Probably old cuts or deep scratches.' He put the magnifying glass down. 'They could even date back to childhood so I think we can forget about them. I'll send the stomach contents off for a toxicology report. Taking a blood sample's a wee bit difficult as he's not got much left in him but I'll do my best. And if you want to come back to my office for another cup of tea, I'll make a sketch of the type of knife the killer used.'

'Thanks, Colin,' said Heffernan. He lingered by the table for a while, staring at the corpse of Charles Marrick as though he was expecting him to sit up and tell all. Wesley hung back, focusing his eyes on the microphone . . . on anything but the remains of the victim, the reason why they were there.

Colin nodded to his assistant to indicate that he had finished and began to make for the door, Wesley and Heffernan following in his wake. Then he suddenly turned to face them. 'Do you know, gentlemen, I'd say this was the very opposite of a frenzied attack. I'd say that whoever killed Charles Marrick took a great deal of care to puncture the neck in exactly the right place. It's a neat job . . . there's no tearing around the wounds. Straight in and out.' He looked at Wesley for a reaction.

'He might have been incapable of defending himself . . . drink or drugs maybe.'

'It's possible. The tox report'll tell us that.'

Wesley thought for a moment. 'Or it could be that the victim knew his killer and co-operated in his own death.'

Colin sighed. 'Your guess is as good as mine, Wesley. But I'd say that was a distinct possibility.'

Sam Heffernan folded his new overalls carefully and placed them in the boot of Simon Tench's Land Rover along with his unworn wellingtons and his shiny new medical bag.

'Ready?' Simon asked, unlocking the car door.

Sam nodded.

'Should be a straightforward calving. Nothing to worry about,' Simon said reassuringly as Sam climbed into the passenger seat wondering how long it would be before he shed the mantle of 'new boy'.

He liked Simon, the junior partner at the Cornvale Veterinary Surgery. Simon didn't make him feel foolish when he made a mistake like some would.

'Have the police been in touch again about that break-in?' Sam asked, making conversation as Simon turned the key in the ignition.

'No. Maybe you should have to have a word with your dad. No use having friends in high places if you don't make use of them.'

Sam didn't answer, unsure whether to take the comment seriously. His dad had enough on his plate at the moment without being troubled by kids smashing a window and pinching drugs from a vet's surgery.

As Simon swung the Land Rover left on to the main road, Sam noticed a figure step back into the shadow of the tall laurels by the surgery gate as they passed. He had a strong sense that there was something malevolent about the person, whoever he or she was, but he told himself he was imagining things. Perhaps it was the monk-like hood that shrouded the figure's head on such a fine day that gave him the creeps.

Or perhaps it was the uneasy feeling that the figure had no face.

CHAPTER 3

I have dreams about monks – bad dreams. And in those dreams they're swimming through rivers of blood. Hot blood, flowing through the passages and cloisters of their abbey, sweeping into their great church and carrying away the costly ornaments and the painted statues of their saints.

On the TV you said that you wanted to know more about the history of the abbey and I will find out all I can for you. I know that Veland Abbey was a Cistercian foundation built in the late thirteenth century. The Cistercians – or white monks – usually built their establishments in isolated locations and sustained themselves by working the land. Some of the houses eventually became very wealthy and I wonder if the devil wormed his way into the hearts of the monks of Veland through the sin of avarice. You see I know the end of Brother William's story but I don't yet know how the terrible events began. The worm in the bud that grew into mortal sin and resulted in death.

It must be so good to be like you, Neil, and know that there's a point to it all.

I will write again soon.

Wesley and Heffernan were silent as they left the hospital, taking in the implications of what Colin Bowman had told them. From what they had learned from his widow, Charles

Marrick had hardly been the sort to lie back meekly and allow someone to kill him. It didn't make sense.

Le Petit Poisson was their next port of call. They hadn't warned Fabrice Colbert of their impending visit. Gerry Heffernan always liked to take his witnesses unawares . . . before they had time to perfect their story. The restaurant was within walking distance of the hospital so it made sense to make the journey on foot. Besides, Gerry Heffernan claimed that he was in need of the exercise – Joyce, his lady friend, had begun to drop hints about his weight.

Le Petit Poisson was a turreted folly of a building perched above Battlefleet Creek, half a mile up the steep street leading to Tradmouth Castle. Wesley had heard that the restaurant's view over the river was spectacular – not that, on a policeman's salary, he had ever sampled its delights himself.

'Wonder if garlic spuds are on the menu,' Heffernan mused as they approached the gleaming glass door.

The place reeked of quality. There was no ostentation here, nothing flashy about the discreet Michelin stars displayed above the sparkling white menus housed in a glass case beside the entrance. Wesley began to read the beautifully printed bill of fare. It sounded good. And the figures by each dish told him at a glance that the price matched the food. Top quality.

'Can't stand the snooty waiters you get in these places,' Heffernan mumbled, shifting from foot to foot like a Victorian tradesman who'd just realised he'd rung the front door bell of the big house instead of going round the back to the servants' entrance.

Wesley rang the bell again and this time a young man appeared, dressed in sleek black with hair to match. He mouthed 'Sorry, we're closed' without looking very sorry at all and he was about to disappear back into the bowels of the building when Wesley held up his warrant card. There followed a frantic unlocking of the door and when it opened the young man stood there, looking nervous.

'We'd like to speak to Monsieur Colbert if we may,' Wesley said politely. There was no point in alienating potential witnesses unnecessarily.

There was no mistaking it, the young man's expression changed from nervous to terrified. 'Chef's busy,' he said, almost in a whisper. 'He doesn't like to be disturbed.'

Wesley gave the young waiter – he was certain he was a waiter – a sympathetic smile. He'd worked for a chief inspector like that when he'd first started in CID in the Met. 'I'm afraid we have to talk to him. It's important.'

The young waiter looked dubious. Chef wouldn't be best pleased about being disturbed for some trivial police matter like a speeding ticket – and Chef found it almost impossible to stick to the speed limit in his Porsche. 'I'll tell him you're here,' he said, preparing to scuttle away.

'Tell him it's about the murder of Charles Marrick,' Wesley said to the man's disappearing back.

The waiter turned, his eyes wide. 'Murder?'

'That's right, mate. Murder,' Heffernan said with inappropriate relish.

There was no more argument. The waiter disappeared through a swing door, leaving the two policemen to wander into the restaurant.

The reports hadn't lied. Two walls of the room were taken up by massive windows which gave a spectacular view over the river. The tables by the windows would be the most desirable and Wesley wondered if the diners were charged a premium for them. Probably. But then anyone who could afford to dine at Le Petit Poisson probably didn't care too much about a few extra pounds. The tables were well spaced out and swathed in white linen straight out of a washing powder advert. Nothing cheap and cheerful here. In fact it was all a little too perfect for his liking. He'd have felt awkward eating here.

The young waiter appeared in the doorway. 'Chef will see

you now,' he said in a hushed voice, like a royal flunky about to show someone into the presence of the Queen herself.

They were led into a huge kitchen which looked as though it had been designed by the person responsible for Colin Bowman's postmortem room. The white tiles were polished to a dazzling shine and you could use the stainless steel surfaces as a mirror in an emergency. White-clad acolytes were scattered around, chopping vegetables, mixing sauces and attending bubbling stockpots, and seated on a stool at the end of the room, flicking through a file, was the great man himself. Average height with luxuriant locks and a pristine white jacket with his name embroidered on the right breast, Fabrice Colbert looked the part. King of his kitchen. And a hard taskmaster.

He stood up and addressed one of the sauce makers. 'Damien. How many times have I told you? Taste the fucking thing. How can you get the seasoning correct if you do not use your sense of taste?'

'*Oui*, Chef,' barked the terrified Damien like a rooky private answering the sergeant major.

'Imbecile,' Colbert muttered to nobody in particular. 'Why must they always send me incompetent monkeys?' He swung round to face Wesley who instinctively took a step backwards.

'You wish to speak with me about Charlie?' He pronounced Charlie the French way.

Wesley cleared his throat. 'Yes, sir. Is there somewhere we can talk in private?'

Colbert made a vague Gallic gesture with his hands and began to march towards a door marked 'Private'. Heffernan gave Wesley a nudge and they followed. It wasn't often Gerry Heffernan looked overawed but it seemed that Fabrice Colbert had rendered him speechless. Wesley, however, told himself firmly that he wasn't one of Colbert's kitchen hands and there was no way he was going to be intimidated by a jumped-up cook. He kept this thought in his mind as he entered what he assumed to be the chef's office and sat down without being invited. After a few moments of hesitation, Gerry Heffernan did likewise.

'I assume you've heard about Charles Marrick's death?' said Wesley.

'*Oui*. I hear it on the news this morning. *C'est terrible.*'

'Indeed.' He glanced at Heffernan who was staring at the chef as though he wasn't quite sure what to make of the man. 'When did you last see Mr Marrick?'

The chef didn't look so sure of himself now. 'Er . . . it must have been *Lundi* . . . Monday. Yes, Monday. I go to his house.'

'Mrs Marrick told us that you and Mr Marrick had an argument.' Wesley looked the man in the eye, waiting to see how he'd react.

The chef swallowed hard. '*Oui. C'est vrai*. We quarrelled.'

Gerry Heffernan leaned forward. 'What about?'

There was a long silence. Colbert had been standing up, as though he hoped to get rid of his visitors as soon as possible. But now he took his seat behind the large oak desk covered with receipts, lists and menu plans.

He picked up a pen and turned it over in his long fingers for a while before he finally spoke. 'Charlie Marrick was a crook. *Un voleur* . . . a thief.'

This captured Heffernan's interest. 'What do you mean?'

'I mean what I say. He was a thief. He stole from me.'

Wesley glanced at his boss. 'Can you be a little more specific, Monsieur Colbert? What did he steal?'

'My money . . . and my good name. My reputation.'

This was like pulling teeth. Wesley tried again. 'Can you tell us the details? What exactly did he steal and when?'

Another long silence. Wesley wondered what the man was up to, dangling a piece of juicy information in front of them then refusing to elaborate. But eventually the chef spoke.

'He tricked me. We order wine from his warehouse . . . the best vintages . . . we have a discerning clientele here at Le Petit Poisson. We use his warehouse before and we never have trouble, but this time . . .' He gave an expressive shrug.

'Go on,' Wesley prompted. He looked at Gerry Heffernan who was sitting attentively like a child being read his favourite bedtime story.

'My customers order expensive vintages. When they taste they send them back. My sommelier he changes the bottle . . . the same thing. The wines are not what they claim to be on the label. The Chateau Margaux tastes like a *vin de table*. The Chateau Margaux is a *vin de table*. That Charlie Marrick . . . he swap the labels.'

Wesley gave a low whistle. 'So you order expensive wines and he sends you cheap plonk with expensive labels.'

'That is correct. I am upset. My reputation – the reputation of Le Petit Poisson – is at stake.'

'You have proof of this? It wasn't just a bad bottle or two or . . . ?'

'Oh non, Inspector. This is deliberate. Every bottle we open is the same.'

'Perhaps it was just a bad year,' said Heffernan, trying to sound as though he knew what he was talking about.

Colbert gave him a contemptuous look before shaking his head vigorously. 'If you do not believe me ask my sommelier, Jean-Claude. He will say the same as I do. Charlie Marrick was a crook.'

'You didn't report it to the police?'

For the first time Fabrice Colbert looked embarrassed. 'Maybe I should have told the police but . . .'

'You took the law into your own hands?'

'No . . . I . . .'

Wesley sat back and took a deep breath. The chef was on the defensive for once. Not a situation that he imagined arose very often. 'You have a blazing row with him on

Monday. On Wednesday he's found dead. Murdered. Where were you yesterday afternoon?'

'I was here at Le Petit Poisson. Everybody will tell you . . . all my staff.'

'All afternoon?'

Colbert frowned in an effort to remember. 'I go out once. To Varney's Vintages in Neston with my sommelier to order wine. We used to use Varney's but Charlie offered a better discount. I do not wish to deal with Marrick ever again. Not after he tricked me. I could never trust him again so I return to Varney's.'

'Understandable,' said Wesley. 'I suppose your sommelier will confirm all this?'

There was a split second of hesitation, of uncertainty. Then the mask of confidence reappeared. 'Of course. Please ask him.'

Wesley doubted whether Colbert used the word please too often – it certainly hadn't been in his vocabulary during the making of his TV series – and he felt a small glow of achievement. He stood up and Gerry Heffernan did likewise. 'We may need to speak to you again.' He walked towards the door then he turned. 'By the way, do you have quail and garlic potatoes on the menu at the moment?'

Colbert looked quite offended and shook his head vigorously. 'The *pommes de terre* with the garlic, yes. But quail is not in season and I use only the freshest of ingredients. I hope you do not suggest I am using the frozen game. For a chef such as I . . .'

'Of course not, Monsieur,' said Wesley quickly, wondering whether the chef's ruffled feathers were all part of an elaborate act.

As they left the office Wesley couldn't help feeling that there was an unease behind Fabrice Colbert's arrogant bluster. He didn't bother seeing them off the premises – this job was left to the young waiter who had greeted them when they'd first arrived. But when they walked out through the kitchen, Wesley noticed a trio of chefs chopping vegetables with sharp, vicious-looking knives.

Charlie Marrick had been killed with a thin, sharp blade. And Fabrice Colbert's kitchen was full of the things.

Wesley and Heffernan walked back to the police station and Heffernan spent much of the journey telling Wesley about his son, Sam's, new job as a junior vet – how he was enjoying the work, particularly travelling round the farms. Wesley could tell the boss was bursting with pride at his son's achievements. His daughter, Rosie, however, was another matter – she was still doing casual work, making no effort to find herself something permanent and getting under his feet.

As they walked down the High Street towards the Boat Float, Wesley couldn't resist peeping into the sandwich shop as they passed. Burton's Butties offered – according to the freshly painted board outside – bespoke butties to the customer's specification. The lunchtime rush was long over and it looked as if the staff were cleaning up for the day. Wesley scanned the faces to see if Steve Carstairs's father was amongst them. But he couldn't spot him. Perhaps he was in the back. Or somewhere else, sympathising with his son about his suspension from duty – telling him his superiors were just a load of wankers . . . that he had done nothing wrong beating up Carl Pinney. Wesley walked by quickly. He preferred not to think about Steve just then . . . or at any other time, come to that.

When they arrived at the office Heffernan assigned two large and clumsy uniformed officers to go to Le Petit Poisson to take statements and Wesley knew that the DCI found the idea of a couple of plods tramping through the restaurant's hallowed portals mildly amusing. He'd noticed the boss's belligerent attitude to up-market restaurants before – probably stemming from the time he'd been refused service in a particularly snooty establishment because he had forgotten to put on a tie.

Wesley took off his jacket and was about to put it over the back of his chair when a flash of white paper sticking out of his inside pocket caught his eye. He took it out and saw that it was Colin Bowman's impromptu sketch of the type of knife that had killed Charles Marrick. Long, slim and sharp. A lethal weapon or an innocent tool to cut up food. Take your pick.

He stared at the sketch for a moment. Colin was no artist but he had caught the basic shape of the thing. He stood up and made his way to the office where Gerry Heffernan was wrestling with his paperwork before assembling the team for an afternoon briefing.

He poked his head round the door. 'Gerry, where's Carl Pinney's knife?'

Heffernan looked up. 'It'll be in the evidence cupboard. Why?'

Wesley placed Colin's sketch on the desk in front of his boss. 'This is Colin's drawing of the type of knife that killed Marrick.'

Heffernan studied the sketch and shook his head. 'You trying to say that little toe-rag Pinney murdered Charles Marrick? Nah. Not his style. And according to Marrick's Merry Widow, nothing's missing so it wasn't a burglary gone wrong.'

'He could have panicked – left the scene without taking anything.'

Heffernan shrugged his shoulders. Anything was possible. 'The whole place has been dusted for prints. If Pinney was there, we'll get to know about it.'

Wesley left the DCI's office and made for the evidence cupboard that stood next to Trish Walton's desk. When he took the plastic bag containing the knife off the middle shelf, he spread Colin's sketch out beside it.

'Bingo,' he muttered under his breath. He looked up at Trish who was sitting watching him, curious. 'Trish, can you make sure this is sent off to Forensic right away. I want the stain on this knife matched with Charles Marrick's blood.'

Trish looked surprised. 'The murder victim? You don't think that kid . . . ?'

'I don't know what to think yet,' he said as he handed her the bag.

Petronella Blackwell washed up the elegantly shaped black mugs. There was a dishwasher, of course, built into the sleek white kitchen units but she wanted something to do. Something that would occupy her hands and mind so that she didn't have to think what to say to Annette. She could hardly bring herself to call the woman her mother, even though she had given birth to her. Annette wasn't – or had ever been – the motherly type. But Petronella had still come at her call. She hadn't been able to help herself. Blood is strong.

The presence of the young policewoman who'd been sent round to see they were all right, irritated her. She was sitting with them now, pretending to watch the TV that chattered softly on the granite worktop. Even though the woman was pleasant and sympathetic and near her own age, Petronella could never get the thought that she was there in an official capacity, to watch and report back, out of her mind. She had heard the WPC referred to as 'family liaison' – officialdom in a smiling, caring mask.

She didn't want anyone to overhear what she had to say to Annette. It was embarrassing at best and dangerous at worst. So when Annette put down her glossy magazine and stood up, Petronella hurriedly dried her hands on a tea towel and followed her casually out of the room, smiling at the policewoman as she passed.

Annette walked ahead and when Petronella caught up with her she took hold of the older woman's arm.

Annette swung round. 'What do you want?' she asked in a whisper, looking down at her daughter's clutching hand as though it was something dirty. But Petronella still clung on.

'I'm going to tell the police about Charlie.'

Annette moved nearer so that they were face to face. Petronella could smell alcohol on her breath. As she hadn't seen her drinking, she must have done it secretly, slyly.

'They should know what sort of a man he was.'

Annette stared at her for a few moments. 'You're lying.'

'I'm not. Why do you think I left the first time?'

Annette raised her hand and gave her daughter a stinging slap across the face which echoed like a gunshot in the spacious hallway. 'Charlie wouldn't have fancied you if you'd been lying naked in front of him with your legs wide open. If you know what's good for you, you'll keep your mouth shut,' she said before sweeping up the stairs.

A tear ran down Petronella's stinging cheek and as she watched the woman who'd given birth to her disappear into the bathroom off the landing, she felt a burning, frustrated rage welling up inside her.

'Mum,' she called out. But the word echoed back to her in the silence.

DC Steve Carstairs walked slowly down Tradmouth High Street looking in shop windows, killing time.

He'd never been suspended from duty before, even though he'd often sailed very close to the hostile wind. The truth was, he didn't know what to do with himself. He could look upon it as a holiday but somehow that didn't seem right. Or maybe he should think of it as sick leave . . . after all, the thought of Carl Pinney's smug, smirking face made him want to vomit.

He stared into the window of a menswear shop, hardly registering the clothes on display, clenching his fist so tight that his flesh began to hurt as the resentment welled up inside him. He had seen others bend the rules from time to time. Gerry Heffernan didn't do things by the book if he thought he could get away with it and even Peterson ignored procedure occasionally. Carl Pinney was scum. He thought nothing of using violence on those he robbed of their wallets or mobile phones . . . but when he was given a dose of his own bitter medicine, he whinged to the authorities.

He looked at his watch. Five o'clock – almost time for Burton's Butties to close. He'd never given the shop a second thought until he'd come face to face with his father there. Robbie Carstairs had vanished from his life seventeen years ago when he'd abandoned him and his mother for some little typist at the car showroom where he'd worked. He'd gone up north somewhere but it might as well have been the North Pole as far as Steve was concerned. For a few years there had been Christmas and birthday cards with a fiver stuffed inside. Conscience money his mother had said. Then, from the time he'd reached sixteen or so, there was nothing. Nothing until the phone call to his mother saying he was back.

When father and son met again, they'd managed to maintain a fragile façade of polite, laddish bonhomie. The thing that hung between them like a whale in a fish tank was never mentioned and Steve was no wiser as to why his father had abandoned him now than he was seventeen years ago. Over the years he'd fantasised about his father's return – sometimes imagining some subtle revenge for the pain he'd caused, sometimes thinking how they'd be reunited, his father full of tearful remorse, determined to make up for the lost years. But the reality had been neither of these things. Just awkwardness and stiff embarrassment.

As Steve arrived outside Burton's Butties he could see his father through the plate-glass window, standing in front of the empty shelves, talking to one of the young female assistants. His body language signalled that the conversation wasn't only concerned with business matters and Steve watched him for a while, his heart numb. Then he knocked on the window and his father looked round guiltily, as though he'd been caught committing some crime. But the guilt only lasted a split second. A casual smile was swiftly plastered on his face as he raised his hand in greeting.

'Hello, son,' said Robbie Carstairs as he opened the shop door. 'Good to see you. Come in, come in.'

Steve stepped inside, his heart thumping. He didn't know why he felt nervous. It wasn't like him at all.

Robbie nodded towards the young woman. She was around Steve's own age or maybe a little younger; a natural blonde – or at least that's how it looked – with delicate features and bright blue eyes. Her hair was scraped back into a ponytail, giving her a startled look.

'This is Joanne,' Robbie said, giving the young woman an appreciative glance. 'She started working for us a couple of weeks back, didn't you, my love? This is my lad, Steve, I was telling you about.'

Steve smiled at her and she smiled back. 'Your dad says you're a policeman.'

Steve shuffled his feet nervously. There was no way he was going to admit to his suspension in front of a desirable female. He had his image to think of and she was good looking – just his type. He straightened his shoulders. 'That's right, love. I've not seen you round Tradmouth before . . . I would have remembered.'

She looked him in the eye as though she knew a clumsy chat-up line when she heard it. 'I only moved down here from Bristol a few weeks ago. And I don't make a habit of getting arrested so you won't have met me at work.'

Steve liked her style. And the challenge in her eyes. He glanced at his father who was looking on approvingly. Maybe he hadn't been interested after all. 'You been to Morbay yet? If you're not doing anything on Saturday night . . .'

Joanne picked up her handbag which was lying on the counter. 'Okay. You're on. Give us a ring. Your dad's got my number.' She turned to Robbie. 'Got to go. See you tomorrow.'

As she let herself out of the shop, Steve watched her with approval. Maybe things weren't all bad.

After Robbie had checked all was as it should be, he set the burglar alarm and locked up the shop. And as Steve walked with his new-found father to the Tradmouth Arms for a swift after-work pint, he decided not to mention the trouble he was in at work just yet. Why spoil things?

Wesley Peterson looked at his watch. Six o'clock.

The strange letter Neil had received was lying there on his desk beside a pile of witness statements and as he picked it up and read it through again, the mention of bleeding reminded him once more of Charles Marrick's murder. Surely there couldn't be a connection. And yet the remote possibility provided him with an excuse not to dismiss it out of hand. He bagged it up to be sent to the lab . . . just in case.

Carl Pinney's knife was also on its way to the lab. It was a long shot but it was stained with something that could be blood and Pinney had claimed that he'd found it a short time before his abortive attempt to rob Steve Carstairs. There was a possibility that he was telling the truth. Or that he was trying to disclaim ownership for some reason . . . maybe because he knew exactly how the blood had got there. The knife fitted Colin Bowman's description of the weapon that had killed Charles Marrick, but Wesley found it hard to believe that Marrick wouldn't put up one hell of a fight if the likes of Pinney came at him with a knife.

They were still awaiting the statements from Fabrice Colbert's staff but the chef had seemed confident that they'd back up his story. Wesley had a vague feeling that Colbert, who had a good reason to hate Charles Marrick, and had access to all those sharp knives, was hiding something. But it was only a feeling. A gut instinct. And he'd been in the job long enough to know that you shouldn't ignore such things.

Wesley stood up and reached for his jacket. His sister, Maritia, and her husband of almost a year, Mark, were eating with them that evening and Pam would be wondering what was keeping him. He thought of the hotel booking he'd made for their wedding anniversary on Saturday night and smiled to himself before looking through the list he had made of tomorrow's tasks. But as he made for the door, he knew there was something he was missing . . . if only he had time to think what it was.

Neil Watson was working late. The amateur diggers had knocked off at five, some keen to go, some reluctant, and now he was left with a couple of colleagues to clear up and make a quick assessment of that day's finds. Neil sat in the cow shed cum site office, surrounded by black plastic buckets, trowels, mattocks and kneeling mats, staring at the stack of trays containing finds to be processed and washed.

There had been one particularly interesting artefact – a small, thin piece of corroded metal, not much larger than a pen, encased in rust and earth. Neil had sent it off to be x-rayed, hoping that it might confirm his suspicions about the use of the site. A picture of Stow Barton's past was starting to form in his mind, hazy and incomplete. But perhaps the letter was sending his thoughts in the wrong direction completely. He had to keep an open mind and follow the available evidence.

The papers in front of him were smeared with mud – it was hard to keep the stuff out – and Neil searched through them, looking for the list of diggers. When he eventually found it, he stared at the names, wondering if one of them could be his mysterious letter writer.

There were two professional archaeologists apart from

himself – Diane Lowe and Barbara Smith. Then there were ten students working on the site, all of whom seemed to fit the profile of the species – more interested in drink, food and sex than tormenting the project supervisor with tales of monks and blood. There were two retired people – Muriel and Norman – who were taking part out of genuine interest and somehow didn't seem the anonymous letter type. Muriel was a retired nurse and Norman had been a history teacher at some public school near Littlebury on the coast beyond Millicombe – nice professional people. Then there was a middle-aged housewife who was intending to study archaeology as a mature student. And there was Lenny.

Lenny was what Neil's mother would have described as a free spirit. He'd been everywhere. Done everything. Travelled in South America, joined a New Age commune in Neston, worked in a variety of jobs and had even had a book published. In Neil's opinion, Lenny thought he knew it all and came out with some absolute crap with the certainty of holy writ. According to Lenny, Neil had got the site all wrong. It was on a ley line and the fact the building they were excavating was on a raised mound meant that it was a burial mound – an ancient ritual site, possibly linked with druid sacrifice.

As the man was paying for the privilege of taking part in the dig, Neil had used all the tact he could muster to point out that the raised ground was a geological feature rather than a burial mound. But, in the face of the man's determination, he didn't bother to correct him a second time. Lenny also hadn't liked the idea of the site being monastic – his preference being a hefty dose of pre-Christian mysticism.

His thoughts were interrupted by a rustling sound, the movement of someone wearing a cagoule against the unpredictable Devon summer. 'Neil. Can I have a word?'

He looked up and saw his second-in-command on the

project, Diane Lowe, looking at him expectantly. She was small with curly dark hair and Neil had noticed that she was pretty.

He pushed his list to one side and stood up. 'Yeah, of course. What is it?'

'Barbara's gone home. She's not feeling well.'

Barbara was the other qualified archaeologist on the team, a quiet woman, introspective and intense, who didn't talk much to the paying volunteers. He was afraid he'd made a mistake taking her on without an interview but he was new to this game. Dealing with the public was an unknown country . . . to be explored carefully and full of pitfalls and snares for the unwary.

'Right,' Neil said. 'Everything cleared up out there?'

'Yes.' Diane hesitated for a moment. Neil could tell by the look on her face that she had something out of the ordinary to report. 'Could you have a look at something in trench three? I'd like your opinion.'

Neil followed her out into the open air. It was starting to drizzle, a fine, soft mist, but he didn't bother about going back for something waterproof. Trench three was on the edge of the site. The sort of place a midden would be found filled with discarded rubbish. Archaeologists can discover an awful lot through examining the rubbish of previous generations and Neil had located the trench carefully. So far it had yielded a good harvest in the form of animal bones, oyster shells and broken medieval pottery. Today it had been extended and Diane led him to this new area.

'What do you make of that?' She pointed to a circle of rough stones, about two feet across. 'I thought it was some sort of well at first but the deposits inside seem all wrong.' The earth inside the circle was a deep reddish brown, almost black, contrasting with the rich pink earth in the rest of the trench.

Neil squatted down and studied it for a few moments.

'Haven't a clue. Too small for a filled in well and it doesn't really look like burning or a post hole, does it?'

'It's on the edge of the site near the midden. Could it be some kind of pit they used to dispose of waste from some industrial process or . . .' Diane suggested nervously, as though she wasn't sure of herself.

'Got a trowel?'

Diane produced one from the pocket of her cagoule. It was a large, kangaroo-style pocket which held a multitude of items. Neil took the trowel and traced around the edge of the circle. Then he started to scrape away the soil very carefully. But after a while he stopped. 'It seems to go down a fair way. I think you should record it first thing and then you and Barbara can dig further down tomorrow. Get Muriel and Norman to help.'

'Lenny was working in this trench.'

'Not Lenny,' Neil said quickly. 'Put him in trench one.'

Diane raised her eyebrows. 'You're the boss.'

Neil didn't feel like making explanations – he wasn't really sure why he'd made the decision to exclude Lenny from this new find himself. Until now he'd hardly dared to acknowledge his suspicion that Lenny might be the author of his strange letter. It was just his style. Dramatic. Self-important.

And if the pit was what Neil suspected it was, he didn't want Lenny anywhere near it.

Without further discussion he helped Diane cover the open trenches with plastic sheeting to keep the rain out before climbing into his Mini and heading back home.

Wesley woke up early. Five thirty. It wasn't often he surfaced before the children but today the sound of the milkman clattering the bottles by the front door disturbed him and he lay there thinking, his mind too active to return to sleep.

The previous evening, Maritia and Mark had called round

for a meal – a lasagne Pam had made during the school holidays and stored in the freezer for just such an occasion. But Wesley hadn't been able to give the family reunion his undivided attention. He had the murder of Charles Marrick on his mind, waking and sleeping. He'd even dreamed about it – seeing the dead man grinning at him, blood gushing like a fountain from his throat.

At six thirty Wesley climbed out of bed and went down-stairs to make a pot of tea and some toast. By the time he was creeping upstairs with the tray, the children had started to wake, Michael emerging from his bedroom in his Bob the Builder pyjamas wiping the sleep from his eyes.

All peace gone, they had breakfast as best they could and Wesley left the house just before eight, kissing Pam, who was still half asleep. He'd promised Gerry Heffernan he'd call in on the way to work to go through what they had so far away from the pressure of the incident room. It would help to retrace their steps. To see whether there was anything they were missing.

It was raining so he zipped up the Berghaus coat he wore over his suit. The sky was steel grey and the rain looked set in for the day, but here on the coast you could never really tell for sure. Weather here changed like the expressions on a child's face. From sadness to joy. From rain to bright sunshine.

The wet pavements glistened as he made his way down-hill to the centre of the town. He could see the river ahead of him. Some intrepid sailors were already out on the water and the ferries were scuttling to and fro from one bank to the other. Queenswear rose up on the opposite bank, a town of pastel-painted toy houses clinging to the steep hill. The sight of it and the view over Tradmouth's crazy scrum of rooftops lifted his spirits. But he knew that even here there was evil. Evil that could pierce a man's throat and leave him to bleed to death, helpless and alone.

He took the short cut to Gerry's house on Baynard's Quay, down narrow flights of steps between the huddled shops and houses. As he passed the Tradmouth Arms an impudent sea gull landed near his feet. He ignored the creature and made straight for Gerry's front door, the salty scent of seaweed in his nostrils. The quay was quiet at this time of day. If the weather cleared up later on, it would be filled with tourists drinking *al fresco* outside the Tradmouth Arms from plastic glasses.

The door of Number One Baynard's Quay, a cottage that leaned against its more impressive neighbours like a sleepy child, was opened by Sam Heffernan who greeted him with a wide grin.

'Wes. Good to see you. How are you doing?' The young man, having spent the last few years at Liverpool University, had acquired a faint Liverpool accent like his father's. He was tall with dark hair, newly shorn for his entry into the world of full-time employment. He stood aside to let Wesley in.

'How's the job going?' Wesley asked.

'Great.' Sam looked at his watch. 'I've got to be out in ten minutes. Lucky I've not got far to commute.'

'The Cornvale Veterinary Clinic on the Neston road, isn't it?'

'That's right. I'm off to an equestrian centre with one of my new colleagues today. In fact he was on telly the other night. Did you see him? Simon Tench his name is. Him and his wife were in this property programme . . . looking for a cottage to renovate.'

'Him and a thousand second-home owners,' Wesley said with a hint of bitterness. 'Pam was watching it – she likes that sort of thing. She said something about it being local but I wasn't taking much notice.'

Sam grinned again. 'I wouldn't normally have watched it but Simon told me it was on so I felt obliged. I'm the new boy so I've got to ingratiate myself.'

'Too right,' Wesley said with a laugh as Sam slipped his jacket on.

He looked around. Gerry Heffernan's house was normally as neat and tidy as his desk at the police station was chaotic. Even though Gerry always claimed this was a hangover from his days in the Merchant Navy, Wesley had always wondered how a man could behave so differently at home and at work. But today there were unwashed dishes on the coffee table and yesterday's newspapers scattered on the floor. Even the piano was graced with an empty pizza box. Gerry's children were home. And they didn't share his tendency to keep things shipshape.

Gerry himself appeared from the kitchen. 'Sit down, Wes, if you can find somewhere,' he added pointedly, looking at his son who was making a speedy getaway.

Wesley pushed a cardigan – obviously Rosie's – to one side and sat himself down on the sofa.

'What are we going to do about Steve Carstairs?' Heffernan asked unexpectedly as soon as Sam had gone.

'I know what I'd like to do,' said Wesley. He wasn't normally a vindictive man but sometimes Steve had pushed his tolerance to the limit.

Gerry sat down heavily in an armchair opposite Wesley with a loud creak of leather. 'Even if he's cleared of this accusation, I'm going to recommend he's returned to uniform. It's not that he's bad at his job but . . .'

Wesley said nothing. It was the DCI's decision. 'Do you think he beat up Carl Pinney?' he asked after a few moments.

'Pinney was certainly punched in the face when he resisted arrest but the doctor says the head injuries he got in the cell could be consistent with a fall. But whether Steve did or he didn't, we'll have an internal investigation on our hands. And the one thing I don't want is for it to bugger up this murder enquiry.'

'Think Pinney could have killed Charlie Marrick?'

'There's no evidence that he did . . . except his knife was the same as the murder weapon. But if Forensic come up with a match . . .'

Wesley nodded. It was a long shot but they had to make sure. 'What about our celebrity chef?'

'He's got the motive. But he's also got an alibi. There's Marrick's widow of course. She hardly seems heartbroken. And I get the impression her daughter didn't have much time for her stepfather – there's something odd there.'

'She says she was in Bath when it happened. On her own, so no alibi.'

'She could have driven down and killed him, started back then turned round when she got her mother's phone call. She's certainly not out of the frame . . . if we can come up with a motive.'

'And if Pinney's knife isn't the murder weapon. I can't see her going to Morbay specially and wasting valuable time dumping it on the Winterham Estate, can you?'

Gerry Heffernan scratched his head. 'Probably not. Mind you, it'd be a good way of throwing us off the scent. Has your mate Neil had any more funny letters?'

'Not that I know of.'

'You think there could be a connection with Marrick's murder . . . the mention of blood and all that?'

Wesley said he had no idea but he thought it unlikely. Neil had been on TV and had probably attracted the attention of someone who was disturbed. The most unsettling thing, in Wesley's opinion, was that whoever it was had Neil's home address. But anyone determined enough could find it out from the electoral register.

They walked to the police station in amicable silence and when they arrived Heffernan gave his customary morning briefing. One wall of the incident room was taken up with photographs of the victim, alive and dead. One of the photographs showed Charles Marrick in a bar with friends, good looking, smooth and prosperous, the life and soul of the party. In the other he was posed against the ruins of Machu Picchu with a smug expression on his face, arrogant as any conquistador of old.

In contrast, the police pictures of Marrick's corpse, taken from various angles, showed the shell of the man. No self-satisfied smile. No life at all – that had drained from him with his blood. Wesley stood there during the briefing, staring at the images. He wanted to know more about Marrick. He wanted to know what had driven someone to plunge a knife into his neck and leave him there to die. And he wanted to know why he hadn't put up a fight.

He was lost in his own thoughts when he heard the DCI mention Steve Carstairs's name. A formal complaint had been made, he said, and if anyone knew anything about the incident they were to come forward. But nobody made a move. Rather the whole team looked mildly embarrassed and shuffled their collective feet. Only Trish Walton looked as though she wanted to leap to Steve's defence. But she had no information to offer so she kept silent.

Once the briefing was over and everyone was assigned their tasks, Rachel Tracey marched up to Wesley, brimming with untold news. She perched on the edge of his desk and leaned towards him. He could smell her perfume, light and floral. She smiled, showing a set of perfect white teeth.

'Good news,' she began.

'What is? Steve's suspension?' He couldn't resist saying it.

She ignored the remark. 'Some fingerprints were found in Charles Marrick's bedroom. They don't match the wife, the stepdaughter or the cleaner. I'm having them matched against the database.'

'Good. Let's hope it's the breakthrough we need.'

'And everyone at Fabrice Colbert's restaurant was interviewed yesterday. When we had a close look at the statements we found some inconsistencies.'

Wesley sat up, taking notice. 'What do you mean?'

'The wine waiter . . .'

'Sommelier. He's called the sommelier at Le Petit Poisson.'

'The wine waiter,' she began again defiantly, 'said he was with Colbert all afternoon. He said they visited a wine merchant's in Neston – Varney's Vintages.'

'And?'

'It didn't tie in with a statement from one of the young chefs. He said he was looking for Colbert that afternoon because there'd been a phone call for him. He said he asked the sommelier where he was and he said he'd just been to Neston with him but they'd split up because Colbert had to go somewhere and he'd be back in half an hour.'

'So they told the truth about the Neston trip but after they'd been to Varney's they split up?'

'That's about it. He's the only one who mentioned the discrepancy. Mind you, it was his day off and he was interviewed at home. Nobody had time to get to him and tell him the authorised version.'

Wesley thought for a few moments. 'Are you sure he's not mistaken? Are you sure he hasn't got the day wrong or . . .'

'It's always a possibility. But if you want my opinion, I think we should get Fabrice Colbert in here fast.'

'With any luck he might give the cooks in the station canteen some tips.'

'I'm being serious, Wesley.' She pressed her lips together.

'So am I,' he replied, feeling defiantly flippant – sometimes Rachel's serious nature affected him that way. 'I'll tell the boss. I'm sure he'll be up for another trip to Le Petit Poisson. If we time it right, maybe we'll get a free lunch. If there is such a thing.' He grinned at her and she shook her head.

'You've met Colbert. Do you think he could have done it?' she asked.

'Have you seen his programme on the TV? All that shouting and swearing.'

Rachel nodded.

'Pam always said it was an act . . . that nobody could behave like that at work and survive. But she's wrong. That's exactly what he's like. His staff are terrified of him. Gerry Heffernan at his very worst is a pussy cat compared to Colbert.'

'So he killed Charles Marrick in a fit of rage?

'You know me, Rach. I never jump to conclusions.'

As she walked away, Wesley stared at the picture of Colbert that had just been pinned on the notice board to join their gallery of suspects. Most murders were simple. And this one probably wouldn't be any different.

Annette Marrick stared at the lounge door. It had been closed since the police Forensic team had left and she wasn't quite sure whether she was allowed in there. But, on the other hand, it was her house. They couldn't tell her what to do in her own house.

They had taken fingerprints – left everywhere covered in a mess of grey powder, even the bedrooms. And she was afraid. If she'd thought, if she'd kept a clear head, she could have wiped everything before the police arrived. The horror of Charlie's death had driven all practicalities from her mind. But from now on she'd be far more careful.

She felt a sudden urge to enter the room, to break that invisible seal that had formed on the bland white door and to see the scene of Charlie's death once more. The room would have to be stripped, of course, and the sooner the better. All trace of him would have to be removed. All trace of the man who was a cheat, a bully and a brute.

She walked to the door and placed her right hand on the handle. This was it. Courage.

'What are you doing?'

Annette swung round. Petronella was standing there, her eyes full of contempt.

'Do the police know that you wanted to get rid of him

like you got rid of me?' she said in a heavy whisper. She walked up to Annette and put her face close to hers. 'That's what you do isn't it, Mummy?' The word was almost spat with hatred. 'You get rid of people who are inconvenient.'

Annette stood, stunned, for a few seconds before rushing up the stairs and slamming the bedroom door behind her.

But if she'd turned she would have seen the tears streaming down Petronella's face.

Gerry Heffernan was unavailable. He had to see Chief Superintendent Nutter about the Steve Carstairs situation. Carl Pinney had gone home to nurse his wounds and his solicitor was talking about prosecution and compensation. Gerry rather suspected that Carl Pinney was more concerned with obtaining the latter than the former.

At eleven o'clock Wesley decided that he couldn't put off his visit to Le Petit Poisson for much longer. He asked Rachel to go with him because he trusted her judgement. Besides, he felt the Frenchman might respond better to an attractive female. Or maybe he was just indulging in racial stereotypes.

It was raining quite heavily – a depression coming in from the Atlantic – so Wesley decided to drive. Arriving to interview a potential suspect soaking wet would hardly bestow on him an air of authority. When they reached the restaurant it seemed busier than it had on his last visit. He looked at his watch – they'd be preparing for the lunchtime rush. If there would be a rush at those prices. But then the rich are always with us, thought Wesley, racking his brains for who had said that first, and the white-trousered yachtsmen on the river had been denied good sailing that day so they were in need of some consolation.

He pushed the door open and went in, Rachel following, looking around. She came from a farming family who never visited those sort of places and she herself had never thought it worth stretching her budget just for something to eat. On special occasions she went to the Tradmouth Castle like most other locals. Le Petit Poisson was a cut above.

They were met by the young waiter who had greeted Wesley and Heffernan on their last visit. He looked worried. 'Chef's busy,' he said when Wesley asked to speak to Colbert. 'Can you come back around three?'

Wesley gave him a sympathetic smile as he explained that murder enquiries didn't tailor themselves to Chef's convenience. He needed to speak to Fabrice Colbert and he needed to speak to him now. But from the fearful look on the young man's face he was starting to think his insistence might be a mistake. An infuriated Colbert might be hard to handle.

Suddenly he had an even better idea. He made a great show of reconsidering his request. 'Well perhaps my word with Monsieur Colbert will keep till this afternoon. I wouldn't want to upset the smooth running of the restaurant.' He gave the young waiter what he considered to be an understanding smile. 'But as we're here, I'd be grateful if I could have a word with your sommelier – Jean-Claude, isn't it? I won't need to keep him long.'

The relief on the waiter's face was clear. Jean-Claude, the sommelier, obviously didn't inspire as much abject terror as the chef. In fact when Jean-Claude Montfort appeared, he was wearing an expression of wary curiosity – an expression Wesley usually saw on the faces of innocent men.

Somehow Wesley had expected the sommelier of a Michelin-starred restaurant to be tall, dark and superior with sleek hair and a disdainful manner. The sort of man who sniggered silently if you failed to observe the rituals of the establishment and sneered if you chose the cheapest wine on the list. But Jean-Claude Montfort was small with thinning ginger hair and a tendency to smile. He invited Wesley and Rachel into the restaurant and the three of them sat down at one of the corner tables.

'Would you like a coffee?' he asked. 'I know you police-men . . .' He looked at Rachel and smiled, radiating Gallic charm in her direction. 'I apologise – police *persons* cannot drink while you are on duty.'

Rachel felt herself blushing. 'Thank you. A coffee would be nice.'

Wesley nodded in agreement. Coffee would oil the wheels – make things more relaxed. And he wanted the man to be at his ease. Off his guard.

Once the waiter had brought the coffee with long prac-tised unobtrusiveness, Wesley gave the sommelier a businesslike smile. 'Nothing to worry about, Monsieur Montfort. Just a chat really. I understand you've been having some problems with your wine supplier.' He took a sip of coffee and waited expectantly for the answer.

Jean Claude hesitated for a few moments before replying. 'Yes,' he began. 'I wanted to call in the police. After all, it is a fraud, is it not, to put expensive labels on cheap wine bottles? Of course when Chef and I select the vintages, we taste all the wines and I assure you what we tasted were wines of the best quality and at first all was well. The problem came when the last order arrived. Everything seemed as it should be until the customers began to complain. And when I tasted the wines for myself . . .' He let an expressive shrug of the shoulders finish his sentence for him.

'What did you think of Charles Marrick?'

'He seemed very charming and I know that he and Chef were friends at one time but I . . . He was rather – how do you say it – sure of himself. That English public school confi-dence with no substance beneath.' He looked Wesley in the eye. 'Do you understand what I am saying, Inspector?'

Wesley nodded. 'I think so. Yes. You say he and Monsieur Colbert were friends?'

'*Oui, c'est ca.* They drink together. They go out to night-clubs together.' He looked Wesley in the eye. 'One does not cheat one's friends, Inspector. But Charlie Marrick did. I do not care even if he was in financial difficulties, you do not cheat your friends.'

'Indeed you don't, Monsieur,' said Wesley with feeling. The more he was finding out about Charles Marrick, the more he was starting to dislike the man.

'I understand you've now found a new supplier for your wines?'

The sommelier nodded. 'We have returned to our old supplier, Varney's Vintages. A very old established firm in Neston with a reputation second to none. The discounts are less generous but they are reliable.'

And you can add the increased cost to the bill, Wesley thought. But he didn't put his suspicions into words. He merely nodded politely. 'You visited Varney's on Wednesday afternoon, I believe.'

'*Oui*. Chef and I went over there to taste some wines and discuss our requirements.'

'One of my officers contacted Varney's. They said you and Monsieur Colbert left around three thirty. He'd told us you were there all afternoon.'

For the first time Montfort looked uncomfortable. He poured himself another coffee from the cafetière after asking Wesley and Rachel if they required more with practised politeness. It was difficult, Wesley thought, to interrogate someone who was so anxious to please . . . but who could still be telling huge porkies to defend his chef . . . and his job.

'I really can't remember,' the sommelier said unconvincingly. He wasn't a good liar.

'It's not that long ago, monsieur. Please try to think. It might just be a mistake on Monsieur Colbert's part. He's a very busy man and busy men aren't very good at remembering details like that. My boss is exactly the same,' Wesley added smoothly. Strike up a rapport. Get the man on your side.

'It might have been three thirty. It might have been later. I was back here in good time to prepare for the evening opening so . . .'

Wesley leaped on the personal pronoun like a cat on to a hapless mouse. 'I? You mean you came back here on your own. Monsieur Colbert wasn't with you?'

Montfort swallowed hard. He was cornered. 'I . . . I came on ahead. Chef wished to call at a shop. He told me to go back and make sure everything was as it should be in the restaurant. Our new maître d' has only just started. He is very experienced – he was at one of the big London hotels – but he is still finding his way about, if you understand me.'

Wesley nodded. He understood only too well. 'So what time did Chef get back from his shopping trip?'

Montfort shrugged. 'I do not think he look very long. He was not late back.'

Rachel leaned forward and smiled. 'So you left Varney's Vintages in Neston at half three and you saw Monsieur Colbert what . . . ? Five o'clock?'

'I cannot be sure. You must ask in the kitchens. He will have gone straight to the kitchens.'

'Thank you, we will,' said Wesley, glancing at Rachel. It was time to go. They'd learned all Montfort had to tell them. And now, just before the lunchtime rush, was no time to intrude on the kitchen. They'd send someone over that afternoon to take statements. Without doubt there'd be someone in that kitchen willing to dish the dirt on Chef.

And at least now they knew that Fabrice Colbert's alibi for the time of Charles Marrick's murder was as brittle as the crust on one of his famous crème brulées. Remarkably easy to crack.

'Dr Watson, I'm a bit pissed off. Why have I been moved out of trench three?'

Neil looked at Lenny and searched desperately for a

plausible explanation. Why had he moved Lenny out of trench three? A hunch? A gut feeling? If Neil's suspicions about what he and Diane had found last night were correct, Lenny was bound to interpret the scene as a place of human sacrifice. What is it they said? Never let the facts get in the way of a good story . . . or a version that suits your own peculiar view of the past.

Lenny stood there, sulky as an overgrown teenager in the wide brimmed hat that he probably thought made him look like Indiana Jones. He wore three strings of ethnic beads around his neck and both ears contained a fair amount of metalwork. He stared at Neil, making him feel uncomfortable. His eyes were pale blue. Cold.

'I . . . er, want to give everyone a wider overview of the site,' Neil said. He thought the answer was rather a good one, considering he had thought it up on the spur of the moment.

Lenny didn't look convinced but he headed towards trench one without further protest. A small victory for Neil in what he was afraid was going to turn into a long battle. Lenny was booked in for another three weeks.

Neil strolled over to trench three, trying his best to look casual. Muriel and Norman were scraping away earnestly at the bottom of the trench, their faces a study in concentration as Norman poked the point of his trowel carefully underneath the edge of an oyster shell. Diane was there at the other end of the trench, kneeling on the foam pad she guarded jealously, her trowel gently scraping at the strange feature they'd uncovered the previous night. He asked her permission to enter the trench – archaeologist's etiquette – and when he'd found a spare pad he knelt down beside her.

'What do you make of it?'

For a few moments she didn't answer. Then she looked at Neil, a slightly concerned expression on her face. 'It looks as though a hole's been dug to dispose of something . . .

some liquid or . . . It's no casual rubbish pit . . . look at the stones around the edge.'

'Any ideas about this dark deposit inside?' Neil poked his trowel into the darker earth. 'It's not excrement. In fact I've not seen anything like it before.'

Before Diane could reply, something made him look up, a movement caught out of the corner of his eye. Lenny was standing at the edge of the trench, staring down at them. Neil was tempted to order him back to trench one but he stopped himself – this man was paying for the privilege of taking part in the excavation. He couldn't speak to him like a naughty schoolboy.

'That's where the blood drained away. I told you it was a ceremonial site, didn't I?' Lenny sounded smug. Norman and Muriel, busy at the other end of the trench looked up at him, all ears.

Neil took a deep breath. The worst thing was that Lenny could be right. Tests could prove that the dark deposit was blood – gallons of it, poured into the pit over a period of many years.

He counted to ten before he replied. 'I'm going to send some soil samples for testing.'

'Then maybe you'll believe me.' Lenny smirked down at Neil who was still on his knees. He looked triumphant. The man who was about to be proved right.

'Lenny, you didn't send me a letter, did you?' he asked as Lenny turned to go.

Lenny turned back to face him, his face expressionless. 'A letter? Why should I send you a letter?' he said quickly.

Norman, the retired schoolteacher, looked up from his digging, a worried expression on his gaunt face. 'Is something wrong, Dr Watson?'

Neil forced himself to smile. 'No, Norman, it's nothing. How are you getting on?'

As Norman gave a detailed description of his discoveries,

Neil noticed him glance over at Lenny warily. Almost as if he was afraid.

The coffee at Le Petit Poisson had given Wesley Peterson an appetite so he picked up a sandwich from Burton's Butties on the way back to the police station.

As he entered the shop he almost collided with a fair-haired young woman who was carrying a large wicker basket filled with sandwiches over her arm. She wore a name badge that said 'Joanne' and smiled shyly as he made his apologies.

He was served by a man wearing a man wearing a badge that told the world he was 'Robbie – Manager' – Steve's father himself. Wesley kept the conversation to a minimum, wondering whether Steve had mentioned that there was a black inspector in his department who thought he was God's gift to detection – and that would be the good version. Wesley left the sandwich shop with his tuna mayonnaise baguette, as anonymously as he'd gone in.

When he got back to the station, climbing the stairs rather than taking the lift, he found a report on his desk. It was from Colin Bowman and as soon as he'd read through it, he abandoned his lunch and made straight for Gerry Heffernan's office. He'd want to know about this.

The DCI's office was glass fronted. A goldfish bowl for a publicity-shy goldfish. On several occasions Heffernan had threatened to bring a set of net curtains to give him more privacy as he sat with his feet on his cluttered desk, contemplating the workings of the criminal mind.

He looked up, saw Wesley approaching, and signalled him to come in. Wesley was clutching Colin's report to his chest and he placed it in front of his boss with a flourish.

'Remember Socrates?'

'Didn't he play for Manchester United?'

'The Greek philosopher.'

'Bit before my time, Wes. What about him?'

'He poisoned himself with hemlock.'

Heffernan sat back in his mock-leather executive swivel chair and it emitted a loud groan. 'And?' He wished Wesley would get to the punch line.

'Hemlock was found in Charles Marrick's body.'

Heffernan sat for a few moments in stunned silence. 'Hemlock? You mean he was poisoned then someone stabbed him in the throat? Why didn't they just leave him to die of the poison?'

'Belt and braces? They wanted to make sure?' Wesley said the words but he wasn't really convinced. If you went to the trouble of poisoning someone, why not just let the lethal substance do its job? Why risk detection by hanging around and getting yourself covered with blood? It didn't make sense.

He took the report off Heffernan's desk and began to re-read it. He hadn't taken in the details the first time and now he noted every point. 'Colin's given us a useful list of the effects of hemlock.'

Heffernan scratched his head. 'Go on.'

'Its effects are similar to those of curare although it's slower acting. It paralyses the muscles.'

Heffernan held up his hand. 'Maybe that's why there were no defensive wounds. Colin was puzzled about that, wasn't he?'

'It says here that the symptoms of poisoning can take a while to appear and the victim can take several hours to die. There's a gradual weakening of the muscles resulting in paralysis and eventual failure of the lungs but the victim's mind remains clear until death occurs.'

'So when he was stabbed he would have known exactly what was going on. Whoever did this must be a sadistic bastard.'

'Colin makes one interesting observation. Did you know that quail can eat hemlock seeds and be immune to the poison? Then, if someone eats the contaminated meat, it can kill them.'

Heffernan raised his eyebrows. 'Wasn't Marrick's last meal quail or something like it? Do you think that's what happened? Do you think he ate contaminated quail? Perhaps the killer called and found him there helpless and took the opportunity.'

Wesley considered this scenario for a moment: it was a possibility. 'But whether or not this quail theory's correct, we need to know where Marrick ate lunch on the day he died. I'll send someone round all the local eating places with a photo.' He paused for a few moments. 'Fabrice Colbert seemed most offended when I suggested he was serving quail at the moment. Apparently it's out of season and all the ingredients he uses are fresh. But if he happened to have a quail stuck away in his freezer . . .'

'He might have treated the man he knew had cheated him to a free lunch.'

Wesley smiled. 'And we all know there's no such thing, don't we?'

They were interrupted by a knock on the door. DC Paul Johnson was standing there with a sheet of paper in his hand. And he looked excited.

Heffernan gestured to him to come in and Paul opened the door. 'Fingerprint reports are back, sir.' He looked from one man to the other, his eyes keen as a gun dog, anxious to make a good impression.

'Well?' said Wesley, wondering when Paul was going to let them into his secret.

'There's two reports here. First one concerns a letter sent to a Neil Watson – standard computer paper, self-seal envelope and a few smudged prints but nothing that matches our records.' He paused as if he was saving the best till last. 'And the second is from the Marrick murder – Foxglove House.'

Paul placed the sheet of paper on the desk in front of the DCI. 'There were several clear prints that didn't belong to family members or cleaners, sir.' He paused for effect. 'They belong to a Darren Collins. He's from London and he did three years for a post office robbery fourteen years ago.'

Wesley and Heffernan looked at each other. This brought a whole new dimension to the case. And it muddied the waters that were just beginning to clear.

'Has this Collins got a history of violence?' Wesley asked.

Paul considered the question for a moment. 'He held up a post office with a replica gun but he's had no form since then.'

'So where is he now?' Heffernan muttered rhetorically. 'Is there a photo of this Collins character?'

Paul produced an old photograph and placed it on the desk beside the report. Wesley picked it up and stared at it. The young man who stared out at him was around eighteen with close cropped hair, resentful eyes and a small tattoo of a spider on his neck. There was something familiar about him but Wesley couldn't think what it was. Maybe he had just seen too many like him before. Young tearaways out of control, terrorising a postmaster or off licence assistant for a handful of notes from the till that would keep him in drugs till the money ran out again.

But, according to police records, this particular young thug hadn't continued his career of crime. Unless he just hadn't been caught.

Wesley passed the photograph back to Paul. 'Find out all you can about this Collins character, will you? See if you can establish any connection with any unsolved local crimes . . . or with Charles Marrick. Check on the staff in his warehouse. And get someone from uniform to go round all the local pubs and restaurants to ask if Marrick ate lunch there on the day he died – and, if so, was he with anyone. Look for places with quail on the menu.'

Paul was about to leave the office when Gerry Heffernan spoke. 'While you're at it, Paul, ask Rachel to go round to

Le Petit Poisson and chat up the staff – check exactly what time Fabrice Colbert got back on the afternoon of the murder. Okay?'

The tall, thin detective constable nodded wearily. For the first time in his career, Paul Johnson was starting to look as if the workload was getting him down.

Annette Marrick was doing her best to play the grieving widow. While the police were still hanging around the place like flies round a piece of rotten meat, she had to keep up the pretence. The pretence that she and Charlie had been a devoted couple. That he'd not betrayed her with other women. And that she'd been the model of fidelity.

Living a lie made her restless. Made her want to kick out and shout the truth in their smug, pious faces. Charlie was a lying, cheating bastard. Charlie was cruel and liked inflicting pain. And if she sought solace elsewhere, she couldn't be blamed. Anyone would have done the same.

She stood in the huge dining kitchen that was serving as a living room now the lounge was out of action, with her back to the door. She needed privacy. There was something she needed to do.

Petronella was around somewhere but there was one place Annette knew she wouldn't go and that was the lounge. The place still reeked of blood – that rotting, faintly metallic stench she couldn't get out of her nostrils – and the splashes on the walls had dried to a rusty brown. The carpet had been taken up and the sofa removed on her instructions. She had seen no point in keeping things as they were to remind her of that awful day.

Annette shut the door behind her and stood there, thinking about what she'd say. She'd be casual . . . call in a favour. After all, she'd do the same for them if the situation ever arose. She listened for a while before picking up the phone and pressing out the number. The ringing tone seemed to last for ever and she was about to abandon the call when Betina answered.

'Darling,' Annette whispered. 'I'm going to ask you a great favour.' She was about to outline what that favour was when she heard a sound. She watched with horror as the door-knob turned slowly. 'I'll call you back,' she hissed into the phone before hiding the thing behind her back just as the door swung open.

It was Petronella who stood there framed in the doorway, fidgeting nervously with a strand of hair. 'Who are you calling?'

'None of your bloody business.'

'Betina. That's one of the cronies you told the police you were with when Charlie died, isn't it?'

Annette felt a tear tickle her cheek. 'I expected a bit of loyalty from my own daughter.'

Petronella snorted. 'You mean the same sort of loyalty you gave to me when you left me in that hospital?'

As Petronella shot out into the hall, Annette threw the telephone across the room. If all else failed, she might have to break the habit of a lifetime and tell the truth.

She wished at that moment that she hadn't summoned Petronella – but she'd needed someone and her daughter was her own flesh and blood. That was why she hadn't smoth-ered Petronella at birth. That was why she'd left her there in the warm safe hospital.

But she hadn't known then that your sins always come back to haunt you.

CHAPTER 4

The second letter should have been delivered that day. Neil Watson would find it at his flat when he arrived home and the writer wondered whether reading it would make him feel sad . . . or angry. Or just curious. Or perhaps the subject of blood would frighten him.

The writer began to type. The story had to be told. Little by little. Until everything was clear.

> *I saw you on the television around the same time as I learned what had happened to Brother William. I knew then that you were the one to help me. It was meant.*
>
> *I could tell you all about the ruins at Stow Barton and what happened there in 1535 – but I'm sure you'd prefer to find out for yourself. Think of it as a kind of game. The blood game. I've made my first move and you've not responded. But I'm near you. I could reach out and touch you. I could even make you bleed.*

There was more to say. There had to be more. But it could wait for a while.

Perhaps this was a dangerous game. Perhaps it would be best to stay silent. It wasn't too late to stop. The writer stared at the words on the computer screen and considered the question.

★

According to the kitchen staff at Le Petit Poisson, Fabrice Colbert had returned to terrorise them at approximately four fifteen on the day of Charles Marrick's murder. He had just had time to kill Marrick but not much time. He had come into the kitchen with a carrier bag bearing the logo of a Neston health food shop so it seemed he'd been telling the truth about the shopping trip. But of course nothing was certain. He was still very much in the frame.

Wesley sat at his desk considering what he knew so far. Marrick had enemies and common sense told him that one of these enemies had killed him. He had cheated Colbert and, no doubt, he had cheated others. And his widow hardly seemed to regret his passing. Perhaps there was a lover somewhere with good reason to get rid of Marrick. And Annette's alibi hadn't been checked out thoroughly yet. He'd send Rachel off to interview the ladies who lunched. She would be bound to give an honest and unbiased opinion . . . or maybe not unbiased.

His thoughts were interrupted by Lee Parsons, a new DC who looked so young, he was frequently asked to prove his age in pubs.

'Sir,' Parsons said nervously. 'A report's just come in from Forensics. You asked for a match between the blood on the knife found on that Carl Pinney and the blood of Charles Marrick. There's a match. They're the same.'

Wesley's heart began to beat a little faster. 'What about the knife itself?'

'Available anywhere – supermarkets and . . .'

'Not an expensive chef's knife then?'

Parsons shook his head.

Wesley thanked the young DC and hurried to Gerry Heffernan's office. He'd want to know right away.

This could change everything.

Neil Watson opened the door of his flat, yearning for a hot shower to wash away the dirt of a day's digging. But when he saw the letter lying on his doormat, he felt the blood drain from his face. He recognised it at once. It was exactly like the other one. He stared at it for a while before bending down to pick it up and tearing the envelope open.

He read the letter inside. There was no actual threat this time, just strange stuff about monks. And blood. Monks swimming through rivers of blood. The whole thing was bizarre. And unnerving in view of what they'd just found at the dig.

He'd show it to Wesley as soon as possible. He needed someone to share it with. Living alone, these things preyed on the mind. And the images in the letters disturbed him.

He considered the identity of the writer. Lenny fitted the bill, showing off his knowledge, trying to get one up on the professionals. But it was going to be hard to find out for sure without a confrontation and Neil hated confrontations unless they were of the professional variety with developers or the local planning department. Besides, there was no evidence it was Lenny – just a hunch and maybe prejudice against the cocky man's arrogance.

He was re-reading the letter, trying to make some sense of it, when his mobile phone began to ring.

After a short conversation, he stood for a moment, feeling rather flattered. They wanted him again, the TV company. They wanted him to give an update on the dig on the local news programme. The feedback from their viewers had been good and there was a lot of interest in history at the moment.

Then suddenly apprehension crept in, taking over what should have been a moment of professional triumph. There was always the possibility that one of those interested viewers might be his letter writer.

If he made another appearance on TV, he would be sticking his head above the parapet again. And people who did that put themselves in danger.

★

First thing the next morning, Rachel Tracey asked the question that was on all their minds. 'This Darren Collins's prints were found in Annette Marrick's bedroom – but where is he now?'

Gerry Heffernan shrugged his shoulders. 'That's the six million dollar question, love. When we find that out, we might be nearer to cracking the case.'

Rachel decided to forgive her boss the 'love' just this once. He was under pressure after all.

Wesley Peterson considered the six million dollar question for a few moments. 'Of course all it really indicates is that Collins has been in the Marricks' bedroom at some stage. It doesn't prove he was there when Marrick died. He could be a handyman who did some work there.'

Heffernan grunted. Trust Wesley to put a dampener on things. Not that he wasn't right. Collins might be their man. But on the other hand, he might not.

The picture of Collins, taken so many years ago, had been pinned up on the notice board along with the crime scene pictures and the names and photographs of all the people involved in the case – the possible suspects and those whose paths, through no fault of their own, had crossed Charles Marrick's near the fatal time. Wesley walked over to the board and began to examine the faces, one by one.

After a couple of minutes, he turned to the DCI. 'Gerry, have a look at this. Tell me if you think I'm mad.'

He pointed to the picture of Collins then to another photograph. Heffernan frowned and peered from one image to the other.

'Nah, Wes. Couldn't be. Anyway, he hasn't got a tattoo.'

'Tattoos can be removed.'

'No. You're barking up the wrong tree there.'

'Fingerprints would settle it.'

Heffernan laughed. 'Rather you than me, mate. We'd have

every lawyer from here to Timbuktu on our backs if we tried that one.'

Wesley smiled. A secretive smile. 'He doesn't necessarily have to know.'

Gerry Heffernan pretended to look shocked. 'Wesley Peterson wash your mouth out with soap and water. Have you never read the Police and Criminal Evidence Act?' A grin spread across his chubby face. 'When shall we do it then?'

Rachel Tracey looked concerned as she usually did when things weren't done by the book. 'You sure it's a good idea?'

'He won't even know it's happening,' said Wesley with an innocent expression on his face. 'Fancy coming with me?'

Rachel considered the question for a few seconds. Then she gave her answer. 'Wish I could but I'm going to see the ladies who lunch – the ones who've given Annette Marrick her alibi. A Betina Betis said that she'll be at the boutique she runs in Foss Street all morning. Then I'll see the other one – Celia Dawn – separately to see if she comes up with the same story.'

'You do have a suspicious mind,' said Gerry Heffernan. He sounded cheerful this morning and Wesley wondered why. It wasn't as if they were any nearer finding out who killed Charles Marrick. In fact the case was becoming more confusing by the day.

'We need another word with Carl Pinney. He's a thug and he was found with the murder weapon, although he claimed he found it.'

Heffernan snorted. 'I wouldn't trust him if he said sea gulls shat on chimneypots. Let's bring him in again.'

'After his little triumph over Steve, he'll be on to his solicitor as soon as the police car appears at the end of his road.'

The DCI knew Wesley had a point. At that moment Pinney would consider himself untouchable. Invincible.

'Then let's pay him a quiet visit.' He grinned. 'A courtesy

call. Present our compliments and ask him to go over his story again.'

Wesley looked happier about this proposal. Tact and diplomacy were required in this case. Even though the little toerag was hardly worth it. 'The Pinney residence first, then,' he said, putting on his jacket.

'Yeah. Then we'll pay a call on you know who . . . just in time for coffee.'

Steve Carstairs had never imagined that he'd miss work. He'd dreamed many times of a life of idleness, preferably somewhere hot near a bar and a swimming pool in the company of a couple of bikini-clad blondes.

But the day-to-day reality of enforced sloth was starting to get to him. He had tidied his flat but that hadn't taken long. He had visited his mum, telling her that he was taking some leave rather than the truth that he'd been suspended from duty pending enquiries for allegedly beating up a suspect. He often lied to her to keep the peace . . . and to stop her worrying as all mothers did.

At first he'd decided not to tell his father the truth . . . then later he'd changed his mind. Somehow it had seemed right to relate the brutal facts to the man who'd let him down all those years ago. He'd also told him that he was innocent . . . that Carl Pinney had been lying through his crooked, rotten teeth. And Robbie Carstairs had seemed unconcerned . . . which probably meant he believed him. Or that he didn't give a damn.

In his unfilled hours, he found himself wondering what his colleagues in CID believed. Whether Gerry Heffernan would give him the benefit of the doubt. Or Wesley Peterson. He'd given Peterson a tough time over the years they'd worked together because of the colour of his skin.

Steve knew that Peterson owed him no favours – that he'd probably be there in the front of the queue to condemn him

– and his resentment began to rise like yeast, fuelled by his feeling of helplessness. He'd only done to Carl Pinney what anyone would have done – the little bastard had only got what he deserved. He was innocent. It was unfair. And he was starting to think of himself as the victim.

He felt he had to get out of the flat. And he had a sudden desire to see his father so he drove out to Tradmouth, taking the car ferry across the river.

There was a fine drizzle in the air, casting a gossamer veil over the town as the ferry chugged across the grey water. The clang of the ferry docking at the slipway shocked Steve back to reality and he drove off automatically, circling the streets until he found a free parking space.

But as soon as he arrived at the open doorway of Burton's Butties, he knew that his journey had been a mistake. A long queue snaked to the counter and his father seemed to be rushed off his feet. As was Joanne Beeston who had abandoned her basket for the day and was serving behind the polished glass barrier – sandwich delivery orders dried up on Saturdays; for most office workers it was a day of rest.

When Joanne spotted him she gave a shy wave and whispered something to Robbie who glanced over without a smile. Steve's heart lurched. His father, so long lost to him, looked irritated that he'd turned up unannounced. He experienced a few moments of indecision, considering what to do, before mouthing to Joanne that he'd meet her in the Flying Pig at eight and leaving the shop. He shouldn't have come. He knew that now.

He thrust his hands into his pockets and returned to the car, numb and hurt. It was no use telling himself that his father had reacted that way because he was busy – the expression on his face had told him otherwise. The novelty of having a son was wearing off . . . and the fact that that son was in trouble didn't help.

As he walked with his head down, eyes on the pavement,

he heard a familiar voice saying hello. He looked up and saw Trish Walton.

'Hi,' he said. 'How's things?'

Trish gave him an embarrassed smile, unsure what to say. Should she discuss work? Nobody had told her she wasn't supposed to talk to him. 'Okay,' she said warily.

'How's the Marrick case going?' He was trying to sound casual, to keep the anxiety out of his voice.

Trish hesitated. Then she decided that it wouldn't do any harm to share what she knew. After all, Steve might be cleared . . . and then he'd have to take up where he left off.

'Forensic reckon the knife Carl Pinney used to attack you was the one that killed Charles Marrick. They found traces of Marrick's blood on it.'

Steve swore softly under his breath. 'So he bloody did it.'

Trish shook her head. 'He claims he found the knife. The boss and Inspector Peterson are going round to interview him this morning.'

'He got bail?' The leniency hit him like a kick in the teeth.

Trish nodded. 'The accusation against you didn't help.'

'I didn't do it, Trish. I didn't beat up that little piece of shit. I'd have liked to but . . .'

Trish made a great show of looking at her watch. 'Sorry, Steve. I've got to go.'

'You believe me, don't you?'

Trish didn't answer. She turned and walked away.

He watched her go. If she felt like that, she could go to hell. At least he had his date with Joanne that evening. And he clung to that pleasant thought for the rest of the day.

Wesley Peterson wasn't answering his phone. Neil had tried to ring him the night before – the night he'd sat up brooding about the latest letter he'd found when he got home from work – but the phone had been engaged. He'd spent the

evening in his flat alone, thinking, with a couple of bottles
of beer for company. Someone out there had chosen him
as the recipient of their sick ramblings. And this made him
nervous.

Even though it was Saturday, he knew Wesley would probably be working. But Pam would be home and he felt a
sudden need to speak to another human being. Things had
been awkward between him and Pam for a while, ever since
he'd discovered that she'd had a short-lived fling with another
man. Perhaps it was time he made an effort to mend things
and he had the perfect excuse. It was her wedding anniversary and he knew Wesley had booked a meal and a hotel
room for that night. He'd call round to offer his congratulations.

Before he set out, he called Annabel, his contact in the
archives, to see whether she'd discovered anything more about
Stow Barton. He already knew that the site had belonged
to Veland Abbey and, after Henry VIII had grabbed all the
country's monasteries, that all the abbey's lands had been
sold to a family called Pegram – thrusting nouveau-riche
members of the king's court. New men who had been the
future back then. But, in view of the letters and the strange
pit he'd found, he wanted to know more – and to discover
whether a Brother William had featured in the abbey's history.

But all he got was Annabel's disembodied voice on her
answering machine and he suddenly remembered that she'd
told him she'd be away for the weekend, probably indulging
in some country pursuit – Annabel tended to hang round
with the hunting and shooting set in her leisure hours. It
would have to wait till Monday.

An hour later, Neil arrived at Wesley's house and Pam
answered the door, looking wary, as though she didn't quite
know whether she'd been forgiven. But when he asked if
he could come in, she offered tea.

'I believe you and Wes are off out tonight,' he said as he

slumped down on the sofa, avoiding eye contact with the two young children playing near him on the floor.

She smiled. 'Yes. My mother's even promised to stay the night with the kids . . . which is a first. Things are looking up.'

He nodded, slightly envious of the decent meal and hotel room Wesley would be enjoying that night, painfully aware that he himself had nobody to share such treats with even if they were available.

When Pam left the room to make the tea, he made an awkward attempt to help little Amelia with a jigsaw which seemed rather advanced for her tender years, and felt rather pleased with himself when her elder brother Michael, addressing him as Uncle Neil, asked him what he knew about castles and he was able to give the lad some pointers for the model he was making at school. But all this intellectual activity was brought to a halt by Pam's arrival with a couple of mugs filled with steaming tea and he was relieved. He'd never felt entirely at home with children.

'Did Wes tell you I'd had an anonymous letter?' he said as Pam handed him his drink.

'He mentioned something.'

'I found another one when I got home last night. I tried to ring Wes but I couldn't get through.'

'My fault. I was on the phone most of the evening trying to persuade my mum to babysit tonight. She kept coming up with excuses. Have you brought the letter with you?'

He had stuffed the plastic freezer bag containing the letter into the inside pocket of the combat jacket he was wearing. He handed it over and Pam read it in silence.

'Well? What do you think?'

She considered her answer. 'I don't really know. Whoever's written it seems to have a thing about monks . . . and blood.'

'A weirdo.'

She shook her head. 'It's literate . . . well thought out. The subject's important to him . . . or her.'

'Think it could be a woman?' Neil sounded incredulous. He'd always thought of his tormentor as a man . . . as one man in particular. Lenny. He told Pam about Lenny and his strange view of the world.

'I wouldn't jump to conclusions if I were you,' she said after considering the facts. 'Does your site have any connection with monks?'

'It does as a matter of fact. It was owned by Veland Abbey.'

'And blood-letting?'

Neil pondered the question. 'Monasteries often sent monks to outlying houses to be bled . . . a sort of holiday, just like it says in the letters. Stow Barton might well fit the bill but that's only one possibility among several and I need to be sure before I say anything . . . especially as it's going to be all over the TV. I don't want to make a fool of myself professionally.' He felt his cheeks redden. 'The TV people want me to do another slot on the local news. They say there's been a lot of interest.'

'Good.'

A silence fell between them, an amicable silence between old friends. After a while Neil spoke. 'There could be some evidence for the blood-letting theory. We found a metal object, very corroded but it might be a lancet – I've sent it for x-ray. And there's a pit on the edge of the site with a dark deposit inside. I've done some research myself and found out that in York barbers who did blood letting got into trouble for dumping blood in the streets. They had to get rid of it somewhere, didn't they?'

'A blood pit?'

'I've sent samples off to the lab in Exeter and if the material in the pit does turn out to contain human blood . . .'

'The monks went there for their holidays.'

She handed the letter back but he returned it to her, asking her to give it to Wesley. Then, after an awkward pause, he looked her in the eye. 'You've not seen that Jonathan again have you?' he asked in a low whisper, glancing at the playing children.

Pam shook her head vigorously. She never wanted to see Jonathan again in her life. Her whole being shrivelled with embarrassment at the very thought of her brief lapse from the straight and narrow.

Neil took her hand and squeezed it. 'Give Wes my regards, won't you?'

He gave Pam a swift kiss on the cheek and left.

Carl Pinney lounged on the sagging Draylon sofa and grinned unpleasantly. Up till now he had enquired about Steve Carstairs's whereabouts, peppering the conversation liberally with references to 'his brief'.

Both Wesley and Heffernan could have cheerfully punched the smirk off his pale, spotty face. But that wasn't what they were there for. They knew they mustn't rise to the bait.

Attack is probably the best form of defence — and at that moment Wesley reckoned they needed all the defence against the likes of Carl Pinney and his 'brief' that they could get. 'We sent the knife you used in the attack on DC Carstairs to the lab for tests.'

The expression of contempt on Pinney's face said 'So what?', but Wesley let the concept of the forensic tests sink in for half a minute before he spoke again.

Pinney scratched his crotch in a virtuoso display of boredom and contempt. Then he yawned and slouched back on the sofa, closing his eyes.

'The tests confirmed that your knife killed a man called Charles Marrick in Rhode, near Tradmouth. Someone stabbed him in the neck and he bled to death.'

Wesley watched Pinney's face carefully. But his expression still gave nothing away. The only thing he saw was what had always been there. Studied boredom and utter contempt for the police.

It was Gerry Heffernan who spoke next. 'What happened, Carl? Did you go to the house to rob Marrick? Did you threaten him . . . ask for money? Then things got out of hand, didn't they, Carl? You lashed out and stabbed him in the neck and he started to bleed. The bleeding wouldn't stop and you got scared, didn't you? You did a runner back to Morbay and . . .'

Pinney snorted. 'How did I get out to Rhode? It's miles away. And I ain't got wheels, have I? Use your bloody brains. I found the knife, didn't I?'

'We've only got your word for that,' said Wesley leaning forward. 'And I'm sure lots of your friends have access to cars . . . or aren't afraid to pinch them. Let's face it, Carl, in the exalted circles you mix in, nicking cars is a skill learned in primary school.'

'Reading, writing, arithmetic . . . taking without consent,' Heffernan said. 'All part of the curriculum on the Winterham Estate, isn't it, Carl? The excuse that you don't have a car hardly applies around here, does it? If you want one you just smash the driver's window, hotwire the thing and Bob's your uncle.'

Carl Pinney looked from one man to the other, quite unconcerned. 'You can't prove nothing.'

'What was it like, killing a man? How did it feel, Carl? Why don't you tell us?' Wesley watched his eyes and saw a flicker of something that looked like excitement. 'I bet it was good killing that rich bloke. Watching him bleed to death . . . seeing the fear in his eyes when he saw your knife.'

The two policemen watched for a reaction. But Carl pressed his lips tightly together. He was staying silent. They couldn't prove he didn't find that knife just like he said. They couldn't prove anything.

'We'll need the clothes you were wearing on the night of Charles Marrick's murder.'

'They've been washed, haven't they?'

'What about your shoes?'

'Chucked 'em out, didn't I?'

'Why?'

'They got a hole in. Mum put 'em in the rubbish.'

'That's very convenient.'

Pinney shrugged his shoulders.

'Did Marrick offend you in some way, Carl? Did he deserve all he got? Or did he have cash that you needed for drugs? Did he refuse to give you any?'

Carl Pinney shifted his body until he was sitting up, stiff and straight. He looked Wesley in the eye. 'No fucking comment,' he spat before folding his arms across his chest and slumping back.

While Wesley and Heffernan were encountering the low life on the Winterham Estate, Rachel Tracey and Trish Walton were living the high kind in their quest to confirm Annette Marrick's alibi. First of all they'd called at Betina's – an exclusive little boutique on Foss Street set amongst the art galleries, bistros and expensive gift shops. Foss Street was narrow, quaint and pedestrianised. And it was where the well heeled shopped.

Rachel had hovered outside the shop for a while, looking in the window, coveting a saggy handbag made of leather soft as silk. But she had never spent a three figure sum on a handbag in her life and her thrifty upbringing on the farm ensured that she didn't consider the option seriously now. Besides, the rent on the cottage she shared with Trish was due . . . and the electricity bill.

She tore her eyes away from the temptations of the window as Trish opened the shop door. A bell jangled somewhere in the back and a woman appeared. She was stick thin and her leathery skin suggested that she'd spent too much time on sunbeds over the years. Her coarse, dead straight, blonde hair was a couple of shades lighter than Rachel's own. But then Rachel didn't have to resort to the bottle. It was hard to guess her age, but there was no doubt that she was older than she'd like to be.

She looked at the two policewomen enquiringly with a smile that bordered on the obsequious. But the smile disappeared when they introduced themselves, asked her if she was Betina Betis and said they'd be grateful for a word in private.

Betina whispered a few words to her assistant – a girl in her own image but with twenty years advantage – before leading Rachel through to the back of the shop, past racks of colourful designer dresses to a neat little kitchen. There was a small melamine table and Rachel and Trish were invited to sit. The woman's manners were stiff but impeccable. Rachel wondered what she was hiding.

When it was clear that tea or coffee wasn't going to be offered, Rachel came straight to the point. 'You'll know that Annette Marrick's husband was found murdered on Wednesday?'

'You can't really avoid it, can you? It's been on every news bulletin. It must be awful for poor Annette.'

'You've spoken to her since it happened?'

Betina shook her head. 'You don't know what to say, do you? I sent her a sympathy card.'

Betina Betis wasn't a good liar. Somehow Rachel knew that she wasn't telling the truth when she said she'd had no contact with Annette.

'Tell me about Charles Marrick,' she said, tilting her head to one side. 'What kind of man was he?'

Betina gave the question some consideration. Then she said, 'I must admit, I didn't like him very much.'

'Why's that?'

'We mustn't speak ill of the dead, must we? Bad manners and all that . . . or bad luck . . . can't remember which. And to be truthful, I hardly knew him. Only met him a couple of times.' She gave Rachel a small, apologetic smile which suggested that she'd said all that she was going to say on the matter.

'In a murder enquiry, we do need people to be honest with us,' said Trish, speaking for the first time. 'If we get to know the victim, it can help us find out who killed him and why.'

This didn't seem to go down well with Betina. She shook her blonde head and kept her mouth tight shut. She either couldn't or wouldn't dish the dirt on Charlie Marrick. And all Rachel's instincts told her that there was a lot of dirt to dish.

'Where were you on Wednesday afternoon?'

Betina was prepared for this question. She answered it with all the confidence of a child reciting a poem she'd learned by heart. 'Annette and I met for lunch then we went to Celia's yacht. We shared a bottle of Chardonnay – or two – and discussed a charity dinner we're organising.' Her eyes darted from one woman to the other, anxious to be believed.

'What time did Annette leave?'

'I can't really remember. We had a lot to discuss. It must have been just before I did . . . around four thirty . . . five. Something like that. Sorry I can't remember exactly.'

Rachel forced herself to smile, hiding her irritation. 'Perhaps Ms Dawn will remember.'

There was a flash of something that Rachel suspected was alarm in Betina's eyes, there for a split second then gone. 'I don't think she'll be able to tell you any more than I can. Really I don't.'

Rachel knew she had to speak to Celia Dawn. But doing it before Betina had a chance to contact her to get their story straight might be a tall order.

They left the shop and made straight for Burton's Butties. They'd grab some lunch and make straight for Celia Dawn's place.

*

'I feel like a regular customer,' Gerry Heffernan said with satisfaction as Wesley parked the car outside Le Petit Poisson.

'But hardly a valued one,' Wesley replied, looking at his watch. It was almost eleven o'clock. 'Maybe we should have come here before we went to see Pinney,' he sighed. 'They'll be getting ready for lunch.'

Heffernan gave a wicked grin. 'Flustered . . . that's just how I want him.'

Wesley smiled and shook his head. There were many ways of catching suspects off their guard . . . and Gerry Heffernan knew all of them.

'You ready for your jaunt tonight? What is it? Romantic meal for two and a night in the honeymoon suite?' He gave Wesley a nudge and winked theatrically.

'Something like that. Pity I've got to turn in for work tomorrow.'

'Aye. It was inconsiderate of Marrick getting murdered like that. Take your time tomorrow, eh Wes. I'm sure we can cope for an hour or two,' Heffernan said with a benign grin.

When they finally arrived at Le Petit Poisson, they were told that Chef wasn't there but he'd be back that evening for the Saturday night rush. Wesley felt a little annoyed with himself for not considering this possibility. As a young child he'd gone through a phase of believing that his teachers actually lived at the school and, in the same way, he'd assumed that the great chef spent all his waking hours in his kitchen. Perhaps the fact that his home life and family were never mentioned on his TV programme had helped this assumption. But now they'd been given his home address they turned the car round and drove back through Tradmouth then out to the small village of Ashworthy – a tiny settlement that in times gone by had been considered too small to deserve a church or a pub.

The Colbert residence was a converted farmhouse acquired by the chef when the resident farmer, traumatised by the foot and mouth outbreak, cashed in his remaining assets and retired to the seaside. Modernised to a high specification, the rambling old house set in the rolling Devon fields with its huge modern kitchen, gleaming paintwork and gravel forecourt where the farmyard had once been, had shed its slurry pits, oily tractors, smelly livestock and acres of land to become the sanitised version of the farmhouse, fit for city folk to live in. There were so many houses like this now in the south-west – snapped up by downsizing Londoners or the simply rich who had no roots in the rich Devon soil. Rachel Tracey, Wesley knew, resented the newcomers. And if Wesley had come from a family like hers, he might just have felt the same.

The door was answered by a slim woman with glossy black hair and a slightly oriental appearance. She wore tight-fitting jeans and a white T-shirt and she was beautiful enough to render Gerry Heffernan speechless. When Wesley asked if they could have a word with Monsieur Colbert, she led the way into a cavernous kitchen with an Aga against one wall and a monumental steel fridge against the other. The cupboards were hand painted and expensive and Fabrice Colbert was sitting at a breakfast bar in the centre of the room, sipping a cappuccino and reading a tabloid newspaper. When he saw the two policemen enter, he slid off his tall stool and asked them if they wanted a coffee. Marie would get them one. No problem.

The chef seemed more relaxed than he had done in his restaurant. Perhaps he didn't know that what he thought of as his cast-iron alibi had, like all cast iron, a tendency to develop cracks.

Wesley and Heffernan accepted the coffee. They both felt they needed a rush of caffeine to stimulate the brain. Marie wasn't introduced to them so they were a little unsure of her status – whether she was wife, partner, friend, mistress or up-market domestic help. Wesley wondered whether to ask but, before he had a chance, his boss began to speak and the moment was lost.

Heffernan came straight to the point. 'We've checked out your alibi for Charles Marrick's murder. Not very satisfactory is it?'

Colbert, still relaxed, gave a classic Gallic shrug. 'You tell me. If I'd known I was going to need an alibi I would have been careful to get a good one. But as I am innocent and I did not know Charlie was dead until the next day . . .'

Heffernan asked him to go over his story again, looking for discrepancies. There were none which meant either he had a very good memory for what he'd told the police before or he was telling the truth.

It was Wesley who asked the next question. 'Have you ever heard of a man called Darren Collins?'

Wesley watched the man carefully and saw a flash of something that looked like panic flicker in his eyes, swiftly suppressed.

'No,' Colbert replied. He made a great show of thinking for a few moments. 'Did he work in my kitchen? Some of the staff do not stay for long and I cannot be expected to remember their names. And we have washers-up and . . .'

'So the name means nothing to you?'

The chef shook his head. 'As I said, someone of that name might well have worked in my kitchen for a short time but . . . No, the name means nothing to me.'

Wesley felt he had to fill the time, to justify their visit, so he asked him again about his relationship with Charles Marrick, going over old ground, listening for any slip that digressed from the authorised version. But Fabrice Colbert was word perfect. And calm. There was no tempestuous kitchen devil here – he had been left behind at Le Petit Poisson. Wesley had suspected from the beginning that the whole thing was an elaborate act. The punters expected a temperamental French chef and that's exactly what they got.

Their coffee cups were empty and there was no sign of Marie to provide a refill. Wesley stood up. 'I think that's all for now, sir. Thanks for your co-operation.' He glanced at Heffernan who was smiling benignly as he admired the view from the kitchen window. 'Er . . . I know this is a bit of a cheek but you know that recipe for crème brulée you did on your last TV show . . . ?'

Colbert nodded. 'What about it?'

'Well my wife took it down and now she can't find it. I just wondered if you'd be good enough to write it out for her. I'm sorry to trouble you but . . .' He took a chubby pen wrapped in a sheet of folded paper from his inside pocket and passed them to Colbert.

Wesley made suitably grateful noises as Colbert scribbled down the recipe. Then, as he rolled the recipe up carefully around the pen, he thanked him again. With an ego such as Colbert's a bit of humility never came amiss. The man would end up thinking he had the local police in his pocket. And that's exactly what Wesley wanted him to believe.

By the time they took their leave, Fabrice Colbert was all smiles. And Wesley had the recipe – together with the pen Colbert had used to write it – safe in his pocket.

As they drove off, Fabrice Colbert watched as their car disappeared down the drive before picking up the telephone receiver and dialling a number he knew off by heart.

While his father was consorting with prominent chefs, Sam Heffernan sat in the passenger seat of the Land Rover. He glanced at the man beside him in the driver's seat. At thirty-one, Simon was the youngest partner in the practice. He was dressed for the countryside as usual in an ageing Barbour and brown corduroy trousers and Sam knew his overalls and wellingtons were in the back of the car, along with Sam's own. Fashion went by the board when you were standing in some manure-ridden barn with your arm up a cow's backside.

Simon turned the vehicle on to a dark lane lined with a wall of tall, impenetrable hedges, relieved only by the occasional passing place and the odd farm gate that gave a glimpse across the rolling green fields. Being used to the terrain, he drove with confidence along these narrow, snaking thoroughfares that frightened the life out of the tourists.

'So where are we off to now?' Sam asked.

'Tradington — mare's been in labour for a while and it doesn't seem to be going well. All good experience for you.' Simon was taking his responsibility for training up the new boy seriously. Not that Sam was objecting — he was willing to learn. And besides, Simon was an amiable companion . . . when he got off the subject of house hunting.

'So how do you like large animal work?'

'Great,' Sam replied. 'It's what I've always wanted to do.' He tried to sound suitably enthusiastic.

'You're living back at home, aren't you?'

'Yeah. With my dad. He's a widower so I reckon he's glad of the company and buying my own place is out of the question for a while — houses are so expensive round here.' As soon as the words were out of his mouth, he knew he'd said the wrong thing. Any mention of the property market would set Simon off on the subject of his recent TV appearance on *House Hunters*. Sam decided a quick change of subject was called for.

'I don't suppose the police have got anyone for that breakin at the surgery?'

'Not yet. Maybe you could have a word with your dad . . . chivvy them along a bit.'

'I've not seen much of my dad for a few days. He's busy with this case — the murder in Rhode. Have you heard about it?'

He glanced at Simon and saw that he had turned quite pale. For a while he fell uncharacteristically silent but by the time they reached the farm he seemed to be back to his old, cheerful self.

Sam couldn't help wondering what was bothering him – the break-in at the surgery . . . or the murder in Rhode. But new boys can't really ask questions.

Rachel Tracey found herself a free bench on the esplanade and ate the smoked salmon and cream cheese sandwich she'd just bought from Burton's Butties. She gazed out over the river, watching the yachts glide by and the passenger ferry chug to and fro over the water, and when she closed her eyes for a few moments Wesley Peterson popped unbidden into her mind. But she was strict with herself and banished him from her thoughts. She'd been down that road before and it had led nowhere. Not only was Wesley married but he was probably the faithful type, brought up by strict Christian parents from Trinidad – his only sister had even married a vicar. She should find someone who was available. The trouble was, decent available men were in short supply and even when she'd thought she'd hit the jackpot with a man called Tim from Scientific Support, he'd turned out to be married. Perhaps she would follow her mother's advice and start attending Young Farmers' socials again. She'd done so up till a couple of years ago and she considered it a backwards step. But beggars can't be choosers, she told herself.

When she'd finished her lunch, she stood up and the crumbs she had unwittingly scattered on the ground were swooped up by a hungry sea gull who brushed her legs with its soft wing. Trish, who had gone off to do some emergency shopping at Winterlea's, was walking towards her and she raised a hand in greeting.

When Rachel had looked up the address in her notebook, just to make sure she'd got it right, the two women made their way up to Celia Dawn's cottage on one of the steep, narrow streets that meandered upwards, away from the river.

Celia's house was pristine pink with fresh white paint-work. There were sheer white Roman blinds at the windows, pulled down for privacy and window boxes overflowing with primulas and pansies. The place had a prosperous look, well cared for. But if she was a friend of Annette Marrick's who went in for charity dinners, Rachel was hardly surprised. When Rachel had been a child, most of these cottages had been occupied by locals – fishermen, boatyard workers, shop staff, teachers, firemen, the occasional impoverished artist or writer – an eclectic and lively social mix. But now many were either second homes or belonged to city people who'd retired or downsized to what they hoped were more peaceful surroundings.

A teenage girl answered the door. Dark, sulky and painfully thin. She said her mother was on the yacht – the *Daisy Lady* moored at the Marina. Rachel couldn't miss it, she was assured. Rachel – unlike Gerry Heffernan who would have spent every waking moment aboard his yacht, the *Rosie May*, given half a chance – was a little nervous of boats as they seemed so insubstantial and so vulnerable to the whims of nature. But she walked back through Tradmouth with Trish until they arrived at the Marina.

The thin daughter had been right – the *Daisy Lady* was easy to find. She was the largest yacht in that particular part of the Marina, bobbing above her neighbours like a mother duck amongst her ducklings. Rachel, unsure of the etiquette involved, wondered how they were going to get aboard. But as they walked down the wooden jetty they saw a woman on the deck, slumped on a sunlounger, sipping a drink with a slice of lemon floating on its surface that looked suspi-ciously like gin or vodka. Rachel called to her, asking her if she could have a word – reluctant to mention the word police because there were people in life jackets busy on one of the neighbouring boats – and the woman motioned her aboard with a lazy arm gesture.

Rachel took a deep breath and walked up the gangway, clutching the rails to steady herself, Trish following behind.

The woman wore dark glasses even though the sun was behind a cloud. It wasn't really the sort of day for sunbathing but this didn't seem to bother Celia Dawn. Like Betina she was bottle blonde but Celia Dawn's hair was curly and she was a little on the plump side. She wore an orange vest top and a pair of shorts brief enough to reveal a glimpse of cellulite. She must have given birth to the sullen teenager very early in life because she was considerably younger than Annette and Betina – perhaps close to Rachel's own age – although smoking and too much sun had just begun to ravage her face. She sat up when the two women approached and took off the sunglasses. Rachel was surprised to see the remnants of a black eye – now fading to a sickly yellow. She invited them to sit.

'I need to ask you a few questions about Charles Marrick's death,' Rachel said, coming right to the point.

The woman nodded meekly and took another sip from her glass.

'How well did you know Mr Marrick?'

Celia looked her straight in the eye. 'I was screwing him,' she said bluntly. She sounded sober. And a little angry.

Rachel was rather taken aback. She'd expected evasion – friends covering up for each other. But she hadn't expected this.

'Tell me about him.' She had a feeling that the woman wanted to talk.

Celia took another sip from her glass. 'He could be very charming . . . but basically he was a bastard.'

'Was he violent?' Rachel indicated the eye.

'He liked it rough if you know what I mean. But he didn't do this.' She pointed to her eye and glanced at Trish nervously. 'This was an accident. Cupboard door.'

'Did Annette know what was going on?'

'God, I hope not. We were very discreet. And she never gave me any indication that . . .' Her lips turned upwards in a knowing smile. 'Not that Annette was as pure as the driven snow. What's sauce for goose and all that . . .'

'What do you mean? Was Annette having an affair?'

The woman shook her head and said nothing.

'Considering Charles Marrick was your lover, you don't seem too upset by his death,' Trish observed, watching the woman's reaction.

Celia stretched out her tanned legs. 'Look, Charlie Marrick was exciting in bed. Our relationship was purely physical, can you understand that?'

Rachel glanced at Trish and nodded, assuming a 'woman of the world' expression. But, being a bit of a romantic beneath her sensible exterior, she didn't really understand the appeal of men like Charlie Marrick.

'Look, I'm a single parent and I need a bit of male company from time to time. Charlie was ready, willing and very able so . . .' She shrugged. 'But that doesn't mean I liked him.'

'Have you spoken to Betina today?' Rachel asked innocently.

Celia shook her head. 'No. Why do you ask?'

'I'm trying to establish everyone's movements on the day of Charles Marrick's murder. Where were you on Wednesday afternoon?'

Celia thought for a few moments. 'Wednesday? I usually work on Wednesdays but . . .'

'What do you do?' asked Trish, curious. Celia didn't look the working type.

'Market research – interviewing people. But last Wednesday I was with Annette and Betina. We were here on the *Daisy Lady*. We're organising a charity dinner and we had a lot to discuss.'

'What time did Annette and Betina leave?'

She shrugged. 'I left to go to an appointment at three

thirty. They were still here then but they'd gone when I got back at five.

'What sort of appointment?'

'Hairdresser's. Snippers and Curls.' She looked at Rachel and smiled a mirthless smile, challenging her to prove she was lying.

Rachel knew she wasn't going to learn any more. She handed Celia her card. 'If you remember anything else, ring me,' she said.

But she wasn't holding her breath.

When you're ten years old Saturday is a day of freedom from the tyranny of school and the pointless nagging of grown-ups.

Of course it helped that Daniel's and Nathan's mums worked on Saturdays and their dads were just distant memories, having left for pastures new when they were small – something that had created an unspoken bond between them at primary school. On Saturdays the two boys were left to their own devices and – being too old for toys and too young as yet for the sex, drugs and bottles of strong cider on offer outside the village pubs and phone boxes – they roamed the lanes around the village of Whitely on their bikes when the weather was fine.

Today their mothers had gone to work as usual, in a bakery and a pasty shop respectively, and the boys had left the small council estate on the edge of the village to cycle out to the woods next to Sunacres Holiday Park. From the edge of the wood they could spy on the holidaymakers, sniggering as they watched the self-conscious adults playing ball games or basking like seals on sunloungers outside the wooden chalets. During the school holidays they'd hide in the trees and jeer quietly at the kids playing football with their fathers, hiding their painful envy behind the disdain.

But today there were few holidaymakers about so the boys

went in search of other entertainment. After hiding their bikes in bushes, they scuttled away into the depth of the wood, scratching their bare arms on brambles and bravely ignoring the stinging nettles that grabbed at them from either side.

They trudged on through unexplored territory, stopping now and then to answer a call of nature against a tree, until they came to a small clearing. To their right a thicket of tangled branches formed a rough tunnel, perfect for their purpose. This would be a den to end all dens. A palace amongst dens. Quite magnificent. A fine and private place where the unreliable adult world could never touch them.

Daniel led the way as they pushed through the undergrowth. Then suddenly he stopped.

'Go on,' Nathan snapped, almost falling over his friend.

There was a long silence. 'Nath. Let's go.'

Nathan pushed his friend out of the way and looked down at the ground where the scattered bones lay, pale against the brown of the earth. He held his breath for a moment, taking in the skull, the cavernous eye sockets and the teeth that grinned cheerlessly upwards at the overhanging tree branches.

Daniel began to back away, his eyes on the bones as though he expected them to rise any minute, reassemble themselves and chase the intruding boys out of their secret place.

Their hearts racing, the boys ran back to their bicycles and rode home as though the devil himself was on their tail.

CHAPTER 5

You've seen the pit — the place where the brothers' blood was poured. And no doubt, if you have any intelligence at all, this find will confirm the true purpose of the buildings at Stow Barton. But I wonder if you will discover the rest. I wonder if you'll ever find out the truth about what happened to Brother William. I like this blood game. My wits pitted against yours, Neil.

Did I say it was a game? Perhaps it is and perhaps it isn't. Can a game cause so much pain?

The writer switched off the computer. Why had Brother William's story come to light just as the excavation at Stow Barton was about to begin? Why had its discovery dragged the terrible memory back into the daylight now, when it had been dammed up for years behind a wall of normality? Why had the whole thing returned like an evil-smelling flood?

At four thirty Wesley was thinking of home and the evening ahead — a leisurely meal followed by a spot of hotel luxury. Pam had had to face yet another Saturday on her own with the kids and he felt a little guilty that he hadn't been there to give her time to prepare for their anniversary evening. But at least he had the recipe for crème brulée, written in Fabrice Colbert's own hand, to present to her as a peace offering. He had sent the pen Colbert had used to write it down to Forensic – but as it was the weekend, he wasn't holding his breath for a speedy result.

Gerry Heffernan, beaming like a fairy godfather, had told him to go, saying that they'd done all they intended to do and unless anything new came in, he might as well go off and enjoy himself. Rachel had reported back on her meetings with the ladies who'd lunched with Annette Marrick on the day of her husband's murder, concluding that Annette's alibi was flimsy to say the least. She wouldn't have trusted either of those women, she announced judgementally. But she believed Celia Dawn's revelation that she'd had an affair with Charlie Marrick who liked to add a spot of violence to his love life. The man must have made enemies and the list of suspects probably stretched into infinity. This particular Charlie was nobody's darling.

With this comforting thought in his head, Wesley reached for his jacket which was hanging on the coat stand. He was just about to put it on when the telephone on his desk rang. The desk sergeant sounded apologetic as he informed Wesley that a lady was waiting down in reception with a couple of kids. She was talking about a skeleton in some woods. Was someone from CID available to have a word with her?

Wesley put the phone down and took a deep breath. He put on his jacket and made his way to Gerry Heffernan's office. He'd want to know. He might bluster and complain but he'd still want to know.

In the end they sent Paul Johnson down to see the woman. Somehow neither of them could face it just at that moment and they both trusted Paul to get at the facts. But after ten minutes Paul returned with a solemn look on his long face. The kids had come across some bones in the woodland next to the Sunacres Holiday Park. According to the woman it had frightened the life out of them – but the kids had looked as though they were enjoying every minute.

It was Gerry Heffernan who made the decision. 'Okay, Paul. You and Lee Parsons go up there with her. It'll be nothing – probably a dead sheep or something. But if it turns out to be human, you know what to do.'

Wesley felt relieved. He'd promised Pam he'd be back early. The last thing he wanted was for work to interfere with their special evening.

He walked home. The sky was bright and the weather forecast was good. Even though tomorrow was Sunday, Wesley knew he'd be needed at work again. But Gerry had told him not to arrive till after lunch – his token anniversary present to Wesley and Pam.

When Wesley arrived at the house, Pam rushed out into the hall to greet him. And the expression on her face – something between embarrassment and disappointment – told him that all wasn't well.

'It's my bloody mother – she's let us down. Some friend's turned up out of the blue and she called about an hour ago to say she can't look after the kids. The friend's male of course.'

Wesley put a calming hand on her shoulder. He'd known Della was a selfish bitch but this topped everything. 'Have you tried Maritia and Mark? Maybe . . .'

'They're visiting Mark's mum in hospital – won't be back till late.' Tears were forming in her eyes. 'I've rung the hotel to cancel.'

Wesley clenched his fist. His mother-in-law was becoming more irresponsible than most of her teenage students – and she was getting worse with the years. He would have felt differently if she'd had a genuine reason for ruining her daughter's anniversary, but a date with some man . . . He wouldn't forget this in a hurry.

He looked at Pam. She was taking it remarkably well – or seemed to be.

'If we can't get a babysitter, we'd better have a takeaway,' she said calmly. 'Are you going to ring the Golden Dragon, or shall I?'

Wesley tried to hide his anger. Takeaways were commonplace – the thing he always suggested when he wanted to ease the domestic burden. But tonight they had little choice.

The phone call came just after he'd ordered the food. 'Wanted to catch you before you went off gallivanting,' said Gerry Heffernan's voice on the other end of the line sounding inappropriately cheerful.

'The gallivanting's off,' said Wesley miserably. 'I'll explain when I see you.'

'Oh . . . er . . . right,' blustered Heffernan, unsure what to say. 'Well I just thought you'd like to know that Paul's reported back. The bones in the wood were almost certainly human.'

Wesley glanced at Pam who was watching him expectantly. Perhaps some things were just meant to be.

All in all Simon Tench had had a bleak day. The foal he had been called out to deliver had died but at least he and Sam Heffernan had managed to save the mother. The promised new life had turned to grim death and the incident left Simon feeling depressed. Professional failure and the look of disappointment – sometimes even grief – on his patients' owners' faces, always did.

When he arrived back at the cottage he and Emma were renting just outside the village of Stokeworthy, he found Emma wearing her uniform, car keys at the ready. She kissed his cheek and asked him what was wrong – she was always sensitive to his moods; that was one of the things he loved about her. But as soon as he'd outlined the problems of his day, she'd had to rush out: she'd changed her shift at Tradmouth Hospital and she'd be working all night. She'd have liked to be there for him in his hour of need, but sometimes these things couldn't be helped.

When she'd gone, he sat down and flicked through the

estate agents' brochures lying on the coffee table. They'd have to find somewhere soon. He'd had high hopes of the TV programme – that the company could somehow produce the perfect property for them out of nowhere – but it hadn't happened. Nothing they had been shown had had the right feel and the only one they'd made an offer for had been whisked out of their grasp by a second-home seeker with a city bonus to spend. They were still looking and local prices were still rising. But he and Emma had enjoyed their half hour of fame. Taking part in a TV property show had meant a change of routine and a brief brush with a more glamorous world.

Simon contemplated making himself something to eat. But he wasn't really hungry. He kept seeing the dead foal lying on the straw, still and perfect . . . like a work of art, a beautiful sculpture. The mother had nuzzled it, urging it to stand, to spring to life. Simon buried his head in his hands. He mustn't let it get to him.

He needed a distraction, some mindless noise to fill the room and drive out the gloom. He had just picked up the remote control to switch on the TV when the doorbell rang, piercing the silence.

He stood up. Perhaps it was Emma. Perhaps she hadn't been needed at work after all and she'd forgotten her house keys.

But when he opened the door he saw that it wasn't his wife standing there. But he still greeted the caller with a smile. And after a short conversation, he invited the newcomer in.

Pam had told Wesley that if he didn't go and see what was going on, it would only be on his mind all evening. And she wanted his undivided attention.

So, after making earnest promises that he wouldn't be long, he joined Gerry Heffernan in the woodland near the Sunacres Holiday Park. Colin Bowman was already there, examining the bones. And after a few minutes, he delivered his verdict. 'Well the bones are definitely human – probably those of a mature male – and they've been here quite some time. They're scattered around – most likely disturbed by animals – but more than that, gentlemen, I can't really tell you until I've had a chance to examine them more closely.'

Wesley and Heffernan looked at each other. 'Had they been buried or . . .'

Colin shook his head. 'They might have been in a shallow grave but there's no evidence of it. It's more likely that the body was just left in the undergrowth and the animals got to it. Not a nice thought but . . . nature red in tooth and claw and all that. It's pretty overgrown here. They could have lain undiscovered for years.'

Wesley nodded. 'How old was he?'

Colin looked up. 'You know as well as I do, Wesley, that these things aren't always easy but I'd say he was probably in his thirties of forties. Fortunately we have the skull.' He asked the photographers if they'd finished and when the answer was affirmative, he picked the skull up, Hamlet style, and gazed at it for a few moments. 'There are a few fillings which may help with the identification.' He sighed. 'Any idea who it might be? Have you had a chance to look in your missing persons files yet?'

'When for?' Heffernan chipped in. 'You haven't told us how long he's been there yet.'

'I might know more when I've done a full examination, Gerry, but I can't promise anything.' He looked round at the line of uniformed police officers who were combing the ground in the hope of finding something – anything – that might provide them with some clue. Until they had something they were working blind. The bones could have been there for fifty years or five.

Gerry Heffernan looked at his watch. 'Not much more we can do here, is there, Colin?'

'Got plans for tonight, Gerry?' Colin asked casually.

Wesley saw his boss's face redden. 'Oh . . . er, just going out for something to eat . . . er . . .'

Colin gave Wesley a wink. He'd heard all about the DCI's lady friend, Joyce, who worked in the register office in Morbay. If Heffernan thought he could keep his private life secret in Tradmouth nick, he was sadly mistaken.

'I think Gerry's right,' Wesley said. 'We'll get the area sealed off and we can start a fingertip search first thing in the morning.' He looked down at the sad pile of bones. 'If he's been there for a while, a few more hours won't make much difference.'

'So what happened? Why aren't you at the hotel?' Heffernan whispered as they made their way back to the cars.

'Della happened. She promised to babysit – stay the night – but she had a better offer.'

The DCI shook his head. 'Oh Wes, Pam must be gutted.'

'I'm not too pleased about it myself.'

'I don't know what to say.'

Wesley gave his boss a sad smile. 'We'll just have to have a quiet night in with the proverbial takeaway. There are worse ways of spending your wedding anniversary, I suppose.'

He drove home, thinking of the unknown man who had lain alone amongst the trees for years. He was somebody's son or father or brother. Somebody must be missing him. Unless he was a loner – a tramp – who just lay down one day and died. Some things were too sad to contemplate.

Steve Carstairs had hoped he was on a promise when he'd turned up to meet Joanne Beeston at the Flying Pig – one of Morbay's flashier bars. His father had told him that Joanne seemed keen, whispering the words with a nudge and a wink. She'd mentioned him that very afternoon at work and said she was going home to the small flat she was renting near Bloxham harbour to have a shower and get changed.

It sounded good. Attractive girl. Unattached detective – albeit one who was temporarily suspended from duty. Steve's instincts told him he couldn't go wrong.

When Joanne was half an hour late he began to wonder if his confidence was misplaced as he sat in the soft black leather sofa in the corner of the bar, tapping his feet to the beat of the music and taking occasional swigs from his bottle of lager. But eventually she arrived, breathless and apologetic, fresh from the shower and looking beautiful. Steve got her a drink and she sank into the sofa beside him with a coy smile.

'Sorry I'm late,' she said, touching his arm lightly. 'I had things to do and I lost track of the time.'

There was an awkward silence while they studiously consumed their drinks, searching for something to say.

It was Steve who spoke first. 'Did my dad say anything . . . after I'd been in today?'

Joanne smiled. 'Robbie says a lot of things. He's got the gift of the gab, your dad. Talk the knickers off a nun, he could.'

'About me? Did he say anything about me?'

She hesitated. 'He told me you'd been accused of beating up a suspect. Is that true?'

Steve nodded, annoyed with his father for betraying his confidence – but then Robbie had betrayed him before so it was nothing new. 'I don't always do things by the book but I never touched the little toe-rag. Not that he didn't deserve a good beating. He murdered that bloke, you know. The one in Rhode . . . the wine merchant.'

Joanne's eyes widened in surprise. 'Really? I didn't think they'd got anyone for that yet. It's not been on the news.'

'I met someone I work with.' He shuffled his feet. 'An ex-girlfriend actually,' he added almost proudly. 'She said the knife he tried to use on me was the one that killed that Charles Marrick.'

Joanne gave a theatrical shudder. 'You had a narrow escape then.'

Steve sat back and considered what she'd said. 'Yeah,' he said after a while. 'I suppose I did.' He grinned at her. 'Anyway, we've got him.'

He saw the look of relief on her face and wondered whether he'd said the right thing. A killer at large would have given him the chance to play Sir Galahad, to see her home, to check her flat, to insinuate himself into her life under the guise of protecting her. He felt suddenly annoyed with himself for missing this opportunity. Next time he'd think before opening his mouth.

'So it was really you that caught him?' She sounded impressed. Perhaps things weren't so bad after all. She was starting to think of him as some sort of hero and that suited him fine.

'Yeah. I suppose it was – not that I got much thanks for it.' He thought it wise to change the subject before he started to rant against what he saw as his unjust treatment. The last thing he wanted to do was to bore her . . . and he felt the injustice so strongly that he didn't think he could help himself. 'How long have you been down here in glorious Devon then?' He edged closer to her, his arm draped round the back of her seat.

'It'll be almost three weeks now.'

'Do you like it down here?'

'Bit quiet after Bristol.'

'So what brought you here?'

She shrugged. 'Fancied a change, didn't I? And I knew it from when I was a kid.'

'You came here on holiday?'

'Mmm. What about you? Lived here all your life, have you?'

Steve detected a note of mockery in her question. Mummy's boy. Never been away from home. 'I'm thinking of going to London . . . joining the Met. I fancy a change . . . just like you.' He smirked. 'How do you like working at Burton's Butties?'

'It's okay.'

'And that's the summit of your ambition, is it . . . a sandwich shop?' He immediately regretted his sarcastic tone. 'Not that there's anything wrong with . . .'

'It's all I could get at short notice. It's a job. I did a computer course in Bristol so maybe I'll be able to move on soon. And I've done a bit of interviewing work . . . that was really interesting.' She took a sip of Bacardi Breezer. 'I'm keeping my options open.' She paused. 'I like your dad. He's good fun.'

There was a long pause before Steve replied. 'He walked out on me and my mum,' he said simply. 'But like you said, he's good fun. What about your family? What does your dad do?'

She gave a dismissive grunt. 'Did. He's retired.'

'What did he do before he retired?' Steve suddenly became aware that he was interrogating the woman. But he was curious. He wanted to know all about her.

'Nothing glamorous. He was a caretaker. Want another drink?'

Steve liked a woman who stood her round. But when he gave her a lift back to Bloxham, she didn't invite him in.

Some things needed time.

When Emma Tench returned from her shift at the hospital at seven forty-five on Sunday morning she sensed something was wrong. Simon's Land Rover was parked outside, just as it should be. And the curtains were still drawn across – he was never an early riser on a Sunday. But everything seemed too still – the birds too quiet in the fields around the cottage – as if the world was holding its breath.

The door swung open and she stepped inside. As the curtains

were still drawn the room was fairly dark, but she could see the glossy estate agents' brochures strewn on the coffee table in an untidy heap. She walked in, intending to straighten them. But as she put her hand out to touch the brochures, she saw him out of the corner of her eye, slumped in his usual armchair. For a split second she thought he was asleep and opened her mouth to speak, to scold him for having too much whisky and passing out before he could get upstairs.

But when she saw the blood she stood for a few seconds paralysed before saying his name, tentatively at first. Then with the heartrending despair of a mother seeking a missing child.

As her eyes grew accustomed to the dim light, she saw the drying blood splashed on the walls and floor and spread out around Simon's body like a rusty aura.

He was dead, staring with horrified eyes at the ceiling, and even Emma's medical training couldn't bring him back to life. She sank to the floor, her skirt touching the pool of blood on the bare wooden boards, and screamed.

Wesley Peterson took his wife's hand tentatively, as though he feared that she would snatch it away. 'I'm so sorry about this.'

Pam let him hold on to her hand for a few seconds then she withdrew it. She kept telling herself that being married to a policeman meant that he could be called away at inconvenient moments; that she should be glad he wasn't in the pub with his mates or spending time with another woman or – like some husbands – in the bookie's gambling their meagre savings on the favourite in the three thirty at Newton Abbot. Wesley was only doing his job. And, besides, it was all her mother's fault that she wasn't waking up in a hotel bed with crisp white sheets and having a leisurely shower and a full English breakfast. It was Della who had ruined their anniversary . . . but she still felt a little resentful that Wesley wouldn't be there for Sunday lunch.

'It sounds similar to that murder in Rhode,' said Wesley, hoping that if he confided in her a little, made a point of sharing that part of his life, she might come to understand.

'It'll be a serial killer then,' Pam said flippantly. 'In which case I won't be seeing you for a while. You'd better leave a photograph so the kids don't forget what their dad looks like.' She saw the hurt expression on Wesley's face and immediately regretted her words. It isn't his fault, she told herself, repeating it in her head like a mantra. It isn't his fault. She remembered what had happened last time she'd felt this pent-up fury. And she recalled her fall from grace with shrivelling embarrassment . . . tainted with a frisson of excitement.

'I'd better go,' Wesley said, kissing her forehead with a tenderness that surprised her.

She put her hand on his arm. 'I almost forgot. Neil called yesterday. He's had another letter. I promised to tell you but with my mother and everything, it went completely out of my mind.'

'Did he leave the letter?'

She nodded. 'I put it in the drawer so the kids couldn't get at it.' She opened the drawer and handed it over. 'It's all about monks and blood. Pretty revolting.'

Wesley read it with a frown. The mention of the blood made him uncomfortable. Could the writer have known about Charles Marrick's death? Is that what the letters were about? He put it carefully into his pocket. 'I'll give him a call when I've got a moment,' he said.

He left the house just as little Amelia began to cry for attention. He felt bad about leaving. But he had no choice so he climbed into his car and started the engine. It was time to face the reality of violent death.

He was to meet Gerry Heffernan at the murder scene and when he arrived there he found him pacing up and down like a caged animal outside the confines of the police tape that hung around the boundaries of the cottage's small, gravelled, front garden. Wesley parked some way away, by the entrance to a field full of Friesians, and the chief inspector greeted him with a gruff 'Hi'. He wasn't a morning person.

'So what have we got?' Wesley asked.

'A nurse came off night duty and found her husband lying dead in the lounge.'

Heffernan paused. And Wesley knew there was more . . . something that the DCI – the man with the strongest stomach at Tradmouth nick – found disturbing.

'Trouble is,' he continued. 'I know the victim. Well, I don't know him exactly – I've never met him – but I know of him. He's our Sam's new boss.'

'A vet?'

'Yeah. One of the partners in the practice. Name of Simon Tench. Our Sam's mentioned him quite a bit. He took him round with him to the farms . . . showing him the ropes. Our Sam liked him. He's going to be gutted.'

Wesley nodded, unable to think of anything suitable to say.

'There's no sign of a break-in or anything missing so it's not a robbery gone wrong. And there's another thing, Wes.'

'What?'

'The MO. It's exactly the same as the other one . . . Charles Marrick.'

'You've been in?'

'Took a peep. I tell you, Wes, it's exactly the same. Two wounds in the neck. No defensive wounds. Bled to death. It can't be a coincidence. We're looking for the same killer. I'd put money on it.'

Wesley raised his eyebrows. 'A dodgy wine merchant and a popular local vet. What can they have in common?'

'Search me.'

Wesley felt in his pocket. 'Neil had another letter – blood and monks again. Could there be a connection?'

He handed the letter to Heffernan who scanned it quickly. 'No harm in sending it to the lab, I suppose.' He looked up and saw the police photographer emerging from the front door. 'I suppose we should take a look. The wife's being comforted by a neighbour. Rachel's with her and Colin's inside doing his bit. He'll be demanding overtime at this rate.'

Wesley followed Heffernan to the front gate where both men donned white overalls.

As they entered the house Wesley looked around. The front door led straight on to the living room. Cream walls, wood flooring, pale modern furniture. This was a rented property designed to appeal to the young professional market. Neutral. Inoffensive. Apart from the blood.

Neither man spoke and even the normally jocular Colin Bowman looked subdued. The body of Simon Tench sat slumped in the cream armchair, now stained a deep rusty red. Blood had gushed from two wounds on his neck and splashed on to the walls and the low white ceiling before running down on to the chair and the stripped wooden floor.

Wesley put his hand to his mouth. The smell of blood was strong here and a couple of flies were buzzing around in search of sustenance.

'Nasty,' was the first word Colin greeted them with. 'I met him recently, you know, at a Rotary Club do. He seemed a really nice chap and I know his wife from the hospital. Where is she now, by the way?'

'Being looked after by a neighbour,' Wesley answered quietly, staring at the dead man's face which bore an expression of horrified surprise.

'They got married eighteen months ago and rented this place,' Heffernan said. 'They were looking for somewhere to buy. In fact they were on that property programme on the telly – House Hunters. He was full of it, our Sam said . . . being on telly like that.'

'So Sam reckoned he was a nice bloke . . . not the type to have enemies?' Wesley said quietly, almost whispering in the presence of the dead.

'Oh aye. Opposite to that Charles Marrick.'

The pathologist looked up. 'Bad business, Wesley. Terrible.'

'Would you say Tench and Marrick were killed by the same person?'

Colin nodded. 'It looks that way. But why?'

The two policemen looked at each other. They didn't have an answer for that question. Yet.

'How long has he been dead?'

Colin took a deep breath and looked at his watch. Normally he kept a professional distance from his cadavers . . . it went with the job. But standing there next to the corpse of Simon Tench, he seemed genuinely upset. 'It's only an estimate but I reckon about twelve to sixteen hours. So that means he died yesterday evening . . . any time between seven and eleven. Maybe I'll have a better idea when I've done the PM.' He looked at Gerry Heffernan. 'That boy . . . the one you arrested – I presume he's still in custody?'

'Afraid not, Colin. He tried to mug DC Carstairs but unhappily our Steve took it upon himself to punch the little bugger in the cells. Place crawling with solicitors – they move like arthritic snails when you're buying and selling your house but, boy, do they shift when the likes of Pinney snaps his dirty little fingers. The little toe-rag knows his rights. He was released the next day.'

Colin Bowman gave Heffernan a meaningful look as if to say 'If you'd held on to him, Simon Trench might still be alive'. Heffernan couldn't think of anything to say. He was thinking the same himself. And he was blaming Steve Carstairs for making it so easy for Carl Pinney. He'd played right into his hands.

'I suppose we'd better pick him up again,' said Heffernan with a sigh.

'There's no sign of a struggle. If Pinney had attacked him . . .'

'Perhaps he'd fallen asleep in the chair. Perhaps he didn't have a chance to fight his killer off. We'll have to see if anything's missing.'

Wesley nodded in agreement then he suddenly remembered something. 'Colin, have you had a chance to look at those bones from the wood yet?'

The pathologist gave him a rueful smile. 'Sorry, Wesley. I'll get round to them as soon as I can. In the meantime, I'll book this PM for tomorrow morning. That suit you?'

The chief inspector grunted in the affirmative as they left Colin to his work and made a swift tour of the small house.

Gerry Heffernan broke the silence when they'd reached the living room again. 'Tell you what, Wes, you go and have a word with the wife . . .'

'Widow,' Wesley corrected automatically. Meeting Emma Tench wasn't something he was looking forward to. But he had no choice. He needed to find out what she knew. To gather any clues he could about the dead man's background or associates that might lead him to the killer. Unless, of course, the attacks were random. That was a possibility that couldn't be ruled out.

Gerry Heffernan had picked up a DVD that had been lying on the coffee table. The case bore the words '*House Hunters* – our episode' in neatly printed letters. He dropped it into a plastic evidence bag and stuffed it into his jacket pocket.

The two men parted at the front door. Gerry Heffernan cadged a lift back to the police station in a patrol car, leaving Wesley to face Simon Tench's widow. The nearest cottage stood about fifty yards away and Wesley walked up its crazy-paved path, bordered with an untidy array of bright flowers – an English cottage garden, in stark contrast to the minimalism of the Tenches' home. The paintwork of the front door was faded green and there were old-fashioned net curtains at the small, leaded windows. This was an old person's house, Wesley guessed. But he had learned long ago never to underestimate the powers of observation of the average senior citizen. They had time to take in details unnoticed by the young with their hectic, overstretched lives. Perhaps he would be on to a winner here. He certainly hoped so.

Rachel Tracey answered his knock on the door and gave him a shy smile as she stood aside to let him into the tiny, dark hallway.

'She's very upset,' was the first thing she said. 'But she's a sensible woman . . . a good witness. Not that she's been able to tell me anything much. When she left the house to go to work she says Simon was upset about some foal dying, but apart from that everything seemed normal.' She leaned forward. 'I think she suspects it was suicide.' She said the words almost in a whisper.

Wesley raised his eyebrows. 'Really? Was he depressed then or . . . ?'

Rachel shook her head. 'She didn't mention anything like that. But she said he was sensitive . . . took the death of any animals in his care very hard. She said he found professional detachment far more difficult than she does. She hasn't talked about suicide in so many words but I can tell it's on her mind.'

'Well, I can put her mind at rest then. There's no sign of a weapon and, unless it's a remarkable coincidence, it looks identical to Charles Marrick's murder.'

Rachel looked surprised. 'Are you sure?'

Wesley didn't answer. 'Is she up to having a word with me?'

Rachel nodded and put a hand on his arm. 'I knew him slightly, you know. Met him at a Young Farmers' do and he's been to my parents' farm to treat the beasts. He was a really nice bloke. Everyone liked him.'

Wesley didn't reply. She led him through into a small cluttered living room, all faded chintz and old hunting prints.

A young woman in a pale blue nurse's uniform with a blood-stained hem, was seated next to an elderly lady with white hair, bent back and sharp pale blue eyes. The old woman's liver-spotted hand was resting on her companion's – a gesture of comfort.

'This is Detective Inspector Peterson, Emma,' Rachel said gently. 'He'd like to ask you some questions if that's all right.'

The young woman gave a weak smile and nodded, giving Wesley a long, assessing look.

Wesley addressed the elderly lady. 'Do you mind if I sit down, Mrs . . . er . . . ?' He knew manners counted a lot for her generation.

'Mrs Crimmond. Please do.' The voice was clear and decisive. 'Where are you from?'

Wesley considered the question for a moment. 'Originally from London but I studied at Exeter University. My wife's from Devon and we moved here a few years ago.' He looked into her eyes and knew that he hadn't answered the question satisfactorily. 'My parents are from Trinidad. They came here to study medicine. My sister's a doctor too. She works as a GP in Neston.'

The old lady nodded, satisfied at last. Some would have taken the implication of her questioning as slightly racist, but Wesley guessed that Mrs Crimmond was of an age when she could disregard political correctness in order to ascertain exactly who she was dealing with.

Wesley turned to Emma and gave her a sympathetic smile. 'I'm very sorry for your loss, Mrs Tench. I'm afraid we have to ask you some questions. Are you feeling up to . . . ?'

Emma Tench looked shell-shocked as she drew her hand away from the old lady's and nodded her assent. She'd answer any questions he wanted. But it was clear from her expression she didn't expect the first one he asked.

'Did you or your husband ever have any dealings with a man called Charles Marrick?'

Emma's mouth fell open for a moment. Then she took a deep, shuddering breath. 'I knew him. He was a patient of mine. He was rushed in with a burst appendix last year. I saw it on the news that he'd been found murdered. But what's that got to do with Simon?'

There was a long silence while Wesley decided how much to reveal to her. She was a sensible woman, he thought. And a discreet phone call to the hospital earlier had confirmed that she'd been on duty and was therefore in possession of an unbreakable alibi. He decided to take the risk.

'There are certain similarities between Mr Marrick's death and that of your husband. We think there might be some connection.'

Emma Tench closed her eyes. Wesley could hear her breathing against the background of muted birdsong that seeped in through Mrs Crimmond's old, ill-fitting windows.

'How exactly?' It was Mrs Crimmond who asked the question, cocking her grey head to one side like a curious bird.

'As I said, there are, er . . . certain similarities.' He turned back to Emma. 'Can you think of any link at all, however tenuous, between Mr Marrick and your husband?'

Emma looked up. 'Only what I've already told you . . . that I nursed him once.' She paused. 'I didn't like him much and I can assure you he had nothing in common with Simon. Nothing at all.' There was another long silence then Emma spoke again. 'I was scared Simon might have killed himself, you know. He felt things very deeply and he lost a valuable foal yesterday. It wasn't his fault but he was the type who always blamed himself. I thought . . .'

Wesley could see tears welling up in her eyes. He reached out and touched her arm gently. 'We're pretty sure he didn't take his own life, Mrs Tench . . . Emma.'

She began to cry, taking in great, gulping breaths. Rachel rushed to her side and put her arms around her while Mrs

Crimmond clucked comfortingly, stroking her hair as if calming an animal. Wesley guessed there was some relief in her tears – relief that Simon hadn't chosen to abandon her. Suicide, he knew, was the hardest thing for relatives to come to terms with – that a loved one could choose death over a life spent in their company. But Wesley was certain Simon Tench hadn't chosen his exit from this world. Someone else had chosen it for him.

'Are you feeling up to giving DS Tracey here a statement?' he asked when the sobs had subsided a little.

Emma nodded. 'There's nothing much I can tell you but . . .'

Wesley thanked her and asked Mrs Crimmond if he could have a word in private. The old lady led the way into the kitchen, shuffling along in a pair of men's slippers, supported by a stick.

'It's so terrible,' she said once they were alone. 'I've become quite fond of Simon and Emma, you know. I know they only rented the cottage and they were looking for somewhere to buy but it's nice having a young couple next door. And they're thoughtful . . . not like some. Emma does bits of shopping for me and . . .'

'I know, Mrs Crimmond. It must be a terrible shock for you.' He knew he had to come to the point before she rambled on for hours about the virtues of her late neighbour and his wife. He smiled encouragingly. 'It would help us catch whoever was responsible for Simon's death if you could recall anything unusual you heard or saw last night. Anything at all.'

Mrs Crimmond sat herself down heavily on a folding stool that stood next to the sink. 'I've been thinking but I'm afraid I can't help you. I saw nothing and I heard nothing. But then I am a little bit deaf.'

'You didn't look out of the window and see a car outside at any point in the evening?'

The old lady looked at him sharply. 'Do you think I wouldn't have mentioned it if I had? There's a passing place down the lane. If someone wanted to visit next door unobserved they could have parked there.'

Wesley made a mental note to get uniform to check the side of the road there for tyre marks. The Tenches' cottage was fairly isolated, well on the outskirts of the village. If someone had murder on their mind, it would be easy to park well away from the house and walk.

'I don't spend all my life spying on my neighbours, you know.' The old lady sounded quite offended. 'I have better things to do. I've joined the silver surfers at the library and last night I sent some e-mails before watching a repeat of Inspector Morgan on the television. I need the volume on quite loud so I wouldn't have heard any sounds outside, I'm afraid.'

Wesley forced himself to smile. It was just his luck to find a silver surfer who had abandoned the pleasures of net curtain surveillance for high technology.

Simon Tench was a popular and blameless man who, as far as anyone knew, hadn't an enemy in the world. But someone had killed him. And the last thing Wesley Peterson and Gerry Heffernan needed was a motiveless crime. They were always the most difficult kind to solve.

As they returned to Tradmouth police station, Heffernan made a call on his mobile. Carl Pinney was to be picked up and brought in again. He'd be summoning his solicitor, of course, but that wouldn't stop them. He'd been in possession of the knife that had killed Charlie Marrick and he'd been on the loose when Tench was killed. At the moment he was number one on their list of suspects, even though Wesley wasn't convinced the murders were his style at all. As to their number two, Fabrice Colbert might have had a grudge against Marrick but there was absolutely nothing to connect him to Simon Tench . . . yet.

Gerry Heffernan felt in his pocket. 'I found a DVD of that property programme at the Tenches' place. Thought it might be worth having a look at it.'

Wesley said nothing. He couldn't really see how the Tenches' half hour of fame would be relevant. Unless the killer had seen it and chosen Tench as his next victim for some twisted and unfathomable reason. But then Charlie Marrick, as far as they knew, had never made it on to TV.

'I'm going to ask someone to have a word with the owner of the horse Tench treated,' Wesley said. 'There might be some sort of bad feeling there or . . .'

Heffernan shook his head. 'Sam didn't say anything about the owner taking it badly. These things happen. But I'll ask him . . . get the details.'

Wesley said nothing. It was a long shot. And probably irrelevant. He pulled into the police station car park and suddenly remembered Neil Watson's strange anonymous letters and their mention of blood. The murders of Charles Marrick and Simon Tench and now the discovery of the bones in the woodland next to Sunacres Holiday Park had driven Neil's little problem from his mind. But he wanted to have a closer look at those letters when he had a moment. With their mention of blood, they might have some connection to the case. But on the other hand, they might be completely irrelevant. Another long shot.

They entered the police station, nodding to the sergeant on duty, and climbed the stairs to the CID office. The fact that it was a Sunday made no difference – it was buzzing with purposeful activity like Fabrice Colbert's kitchen.

Wesley found a report waiting for him on his desk – eagerly awaited news from Fingerprints. He smiled to himself as he read it and half walked, half ran to Gerry Heffernan's office.

Heffernan looked up as he entered. 'Nothing from missing persons on that skeleton yet,' he said. 'I've asked for a list of all men of that age who've gone missing in the area over the past fifty years.'

Wesley said nothing. The skeleton had been there a long time by the looks of it so a week or so would probably make no difference. But it was possible that the person who'd killed Marrick and Tench might decide to kill again. That was their priority for now.

'The list might be a long one,' Heffernan continued. 'There must be lots of blokes over the past fifty years who've decided to up and leave. I can think of a couple it could be – men who've disappeared without explanation – but . . .'

Wesley nodded. The boss had a point. And of course it was always possible that the dead man hadn't been reported missing in their area. He could be from anywhere. 'Once we've sorted out these murders we'll make this skeleton our priority,' he said optimistically. 'I've just had an interesting report from Fingerprints.' He smiled. 'I asked them to do it urgently but, as it's the weekend, I wasn't expecting such good service.'

Heffernan looked up, curious. 'Go on. Don't keep us in suspense.'

'Those prints I lifted off the pen Fabrice Colbert used have been checked. And my little bit of rule breaking's paid off. They match the ones found in Charles Marrick's bedroom.'

Heffernan frowned. 'But weren't they . . . ?'

The grin on Wesley's face widened. 'From the fingerprint evidence it looks like our Frenchman's a phoney. Fabrice Colbert is Darren Collins.'

Heffernan's eyes widened with disbelief. 'You've having me on.'

'The prints match. I wondered why that picture of Collins seemed so familiar. He was much younger . . . and thinner . . . and he had less hair – and a bigger nose. But when I studied it again I could definitely see the resemblance. With a bit of plastic surgery . . .'

'You said Collins had a tattoo.'

'Tattoos can be removed. Especially if you want to start a new life.'

'As a Frenchman? There are French staff in his restaurant – that wine waiter for a start – wouldn't they twig? You might be able to fool an Englishman with a fake French accent but a Frenchman . . .'

Wesley had to acknowledge that the boss had a point. His own schoolboy French – although considered quite good in his time – would never convince anyone east of Kent. But he wanted to see Fabrice Colbert and find out the truth . . . whatever that was.

'We could always have Sunday lunch at Le Petit Poisson . . . in the interest of our enquiries, of course,' Gerry Heffernan said with a hungry look in his eyes.

Wesley trusted he was joking. Neither of their bank balances would run to it. They'd have to make do with a quick bite at the Fisherman's Arms to feed the inner detective before their rendezvous with the great chef. If he wasn't who he said he was, he was back as joint top of their list with Carl Pinney. All they had to do was establish some link with Simon Tench. Perhaps he'd eaten at Le Petit Poisson and complained about the food.

'I've just been thinking about the quail,' said Wesley. 'We've had people asking round all the local eating places and we still don't know where Marrick had lunch. If the quail was the source of the hemlock, it's always possible that a contaminated meat was kept frozen and used for the purpose. Colbert got all huffy when we suggested he used frozen food but people have been known to lie to us from time to time. If he did use the quail to poison Marrick, it makes a brilliant murder weapon, don't you think?'

'If he'd left it at that. Why all the blood? Why mess up his neat little MO.'

'To put us off the scent? Or sheer sadism? I'll be interested to see whether any hemlock's found in Simon Tench's body. There were no defensive wounds there either . . .'

'So you reckon our Great French Chef could be a villain who's changed his identity and does a nasty little sideline in hemlock takeaways delivered to the doors of Charles Marrick and Simon Tench?'

Wesley didn't answer. When it was put like that, it sounded far-fetched.

'We'll have a word with him anyway . . . see if he's got an alibi for Tench's death. Let's hope for his sake it's a better one than he rustled up last time.' He paused. 'Anyone heard anything from Steve Carstairs?'

Wesley shook his head. The last thing on his mind was DC Carstairs. And he wanted it to stay that way.

Sunday had never been Neil Watson's favourite day. Sundays usually meant not working and to Neil a day without work – without digging up the past or writing reports about it – was a day wasted. He sat alone in his flat on the ground floor of a large Victorian house which stood on a leafy road not far from the centre of Exeter. It was a spacious flat with high ceilings, ornate cornices and an original fireplace in each of the main rooms. He loved it, loved its airiness.

The one thing it lacked was another human being. This didn't normally bother Neil as he was usually working or socialising with his archaeological colleagues. But sitting there at his old pine table, that bore the rings left by a thousand coffee mugs, with his books and papers spread out before him on a quiet Sunday listening to the distant bells of Exeter Cathedral drifting in through the open sash window, he felt lonely and suddenly envied Wesley Peterson his growing family. But he'd had his chance with Pam when they were at university and, fearful of involvement, he'd let things drift. There had been women since but all his relationships had fizzled out somehow like fireworks in the rain. What woman, he always wondered, could compete with his trenches and artefacts and the camaraderie of the dig? But the training excavation at Stow Barton felt different somehow. He didn't know whether it was the strange letters he'd received, but he felt uneasy about it and wished he had someone to discuss it with . . . someone to share the load.

He'd rung Wesley but there'd been no answer. But then he remembered their planned anniversary treat – the meal and the night in the hotel – with a twinge of envy. He walked into the small kitchen, took a frozen meal for one out of the freezer and popped it in the microwave. When it was ready, he switched on the TV and ate his meal on his knee in front of a repeat of *House Hunters* – a wealthy gay couple from the Midlands in a quest for a mansion to call their own and house their extensive collection of objets d'art. Neil ate hastily, taking in sustenance rather than taking pleasure in the taste and texture of the food, and when he'd finished he returned to the table and opened a book he'd bought in a secondhand bookshop. A battered volume without a dust jacket that had cost him five pounds. A book about medieval monasteries.

He flicked through the pages until he came to the section on monastic medicine. The monks, the book informed him, were bled every six to seven weeks and the purpose of this blood letting was to prevent them from falling ill. He read on, thinking how his mysterious letter writer had been spot on with his facts. The monks had indeed enjoyed the experience of being bled and they'd looked forward to it as a holiday from the daily grind of work and prayer.

Monastic houses, it said, often had manor houses well away from the main complex where the brothers could go to be bled and live the comfortable life for a few precious days. In 1334 the Abbott of Burton, according to the book, granted five days' indulgence from the blood-letting 'from mid day on Easter day until vespers on the fourth day after in that place known as the Seyney House with increased allowance of bread and beer beyond the usual corrody.' Rest and extra beer. Sometimes, the author told him, the monks took the relaxed régime of the seyney house as an opportunity to indulge in lax behaviour and idle gossiping. No wonder they liked it.

He switched on his laptop and brought the pictures he had taken of the site at Stow Barton up on the screen. He studied the ones he had taken of the strange pit and smiled. He had sent samples off to the lab but he was as sure as he could be that he knew exactly what it was. It all fitted. It had been used for the disposal of blood. Human blood. Blood from the monks who had come to Stow Barton for their six-weekly treat.

The trouble was, his letter writer had known all this before he did. And he wondered how.

Ten minutes passed before his reading was interrupted by the urgent ringing of his doorbell. The sound made him jump and set his heart thumping against his chest. He hadn't been expecting company.

He rushed out of the flat into the communal hallway and when he opened the door he saw his colleague, Diane standing there with a bottle of white wine and a shy smile. As he stood aside to let her in he caught a whiff of her perfume. Things were looking up.

The lasagne Wesley had eaten at the Fisherman's Arms lay rather heavy on his stomach as he drove out to Le Petit Poisson. It was two o'clock and he reckoned the Sunday lunchtime rush at the restaurant would be past its peak by now. Time for the chef de cuisine to abandon his knives and ladles and answer some pertinent questions.

It was Jean-Claude Montfort who met them at the entrance and ushered them discreetly through to the back out of sight of the diners who were enjoying their desserts and coffee in the restaurant. He couldn't have looked more uneasy if they'd been from the Environmental Health Department. Wesley found himself wondering whether he knew the chef's secret. Maybe he'd ask him later, depending on how the interview with Colbert – or was it Collins? – went.

The kitchen at Le Petit Poisson was still as active as an ants' nest with each white-clad chef focused on his – or in one case her – appointed task. Gerry Heffernan observed in a whisper that Colbert ran a tight ship. And with those words the captain himself appeared, striding across the tiled floor, hands behind his back like Captain Bligh on the bridge of the *Bounty*.

He didn't look pleased to see them. Ignoring their presence, he picked up a spoon and tasted the contents of a pot bubbling away on the massive stove while the pot's youthful guardian looked on in trepidation. He pulled a face and barked 'more salt' like a military order.

'We'd like a word, Mr Colbert,' Gerry Heffernan said to his disappearing back, shooting the words out like a shot across the bows.

The chef turned. 'Very well. In my office.' If this man really had been Darren Collins in a former incarnation, Wesley thought, he certainly kept up the pretence well. His French accent was convincing . . . not just a parody like the cast of *'Allo 'Allo*. Wesley suddenly feared that a mistake had been made somehow. He could see Colbert's neck and there was no sign of a tattoo. In fact he didn't look much like the photograph of the youthful Darren Collins at all. He nudged Heffernan who looked slightly more confident than he felt that they weren't going to make colossal fools of themselves.

When they reached the chef's office he invited them to sit, his expression a blend of wariness and impatience. 'What can I do for you gentlemen?' he asked.

Gerry Heffernan gave Wesley a discreet nod. It was up to him to broach the subject and he suddenly felt apprehensive.

'Monsieur Colbert. Would you mind if your fingerprints were taken? For elimination purposes of course.'

Colbert stared at him as if he'd made an offensive remark. 'This is ridiculous. This is police harassment. You think that because Charlie tricked me with the wine labels that I kill him. I tell you, I did not. I have a better punishment for him . . . to tell the world he is a crook. His reputation would be nothing and his business, it will fail. For a man like Charlie who likes the good things in life, Inspector, this is worse than death.'

Wesley nodded. Fabrice Colbert certainly had a point. Revenge, he had heard it said, was a dish best served cold and Colbert was more than capable of serving up this particular dish from his vast freezer and finishing Marrick's reputation in the West Country for good.

Gerry Heffernan didn't favour the subtle approach. He leaned forward, looking Colbert in the eye. 'You don't half look familiar. You're the spit of a villain called Darren Collins – did three years for a post office robbery in London years ago.' He watched the man's face carefully. 'You and him could be twins.'

There was a long silence. It was as if Colbert had gone into a trance. Or perhaps his past was just coming back to haunt him.

He shuffled restlessly in his chair. 'Er . . . look. I don't want this to get out. I'd be grateful if it stayed in these four walls.' He spoke quietly but the French accent was gone, replaced by a London twang. 'If I give you my prints, you're going to find out sooner or later so I'd better come clean.'

Wesley glanced at his boss. He hadn't expected it to be so easy.

'When I was young I was a bad lad – did some things I regret. I got in with a bad crowd. You know how it is. Anyway, I was persuaded to do this post office. Got caught, didn't I?'

'So let me get this straight,' said Wesley. 'You're not French at all. It's all an act.'

Colbert shrugged his shoulders dramatically. He was so accustomed to playing the part that old habits were hard to break. 'When I got out I went on this training scheme and I learned how to cook. Really got into it. Then I decided to go to France – someone I knew was working at this hotel in Paris and he got me a job in the kitchens. I worked my way up . . . learned the lingo. I was there ten years then I decided to take the risk and come back to open my own place over here. When I did, everything I touched seemed to turn to gold – I worked like stink, built up the reputation of my first place in Exeter then bought Le Petit Poisson.'

'What about the tattoo?'

'I lost it, didn't I? I found a surgeon in France who did it for me along with a nose job. The tattoo didn't really go with my new self.'

'Why did you decide to come back to England?' Gerry Heffernan sounded genuinely curious.

Darren Collins gave him a rueful smile. 'Got a bit homesick, didn't I? I spoke the lingo pretty well but it's not the same, is it?'

'Does Jean-Claude know about this?'

Darren nodded. 'He was working at the hotel in Paris at the same time I was. We became mates. When I wanted to set up a restaurant over here, he was the first bloke I thought of. You need a good sommelier, don't you? And a good head waiter. Jean-Claude can do both. Look, when I got out of jail, I started a new life . . . I mean that. There was no way I was going back to that place and I found something I was really good at . . . food. Darren Collins was another person – someone I'm not proud of and someone I didn't particularly like.'

Wesley leaned forward. 'Your fingerprints were found in Charlie Marrick's bedroom.'

There was a long silence. 'Okay. I suppose it's confession time,' the chef said with a sigh. 'If I don't tell you, you're going to find out sooner or later if you're doing your job properly. I was screwing Annette. It wasn't a regular thing but we scratched an itch from time to time if you see what I mean. That's why my dabs were in the bedroom. That's where we . . . er . . .'

'When was the last time you, er . . . ?'

'A few days before Charlie died. Look, it was nothing serious. Just a bit of fun.'

'Did Annette know you weren't French?'

Darren gave a bitter laugh. 'Do me a favour. She wanted a French celebrity chef, not a failed armed robber. I've got so used to playing the part now that it's become second nature. I probably even dream in French these days.'

'Does, er . . . Marie know about your change of identity?' Wesley was genuinely curious about how a man can change his whole identity and leave no trace of the old self behind.

Darren shook his head. 'She failed her French GCSE so there's no chance of her sussing that my French isn't exactly as the natives speak it. Look, I don't want her told. As far as she's concerned I'm Fabrice. I was born in Rouen and all my family are dead – killed in a house fire. There was a Fabrice Colbert from Rouen, by the way . . . he died when he was five. I sort of acquired his identity. Made the paperwork easier.'

Wesley raised his eyebrows. Technically, Darren had committed a crime. But he wasn't convinced that reporting it to the French authorities would do anybody any good. Besides, if Darren's story was true – if he'd managed to transform himself from an unsuccessful criminal to a successful chef – Wesley couldn't help feeling a sneaking admiration for his achievements.

'What about your real family?' Wesley asked with barely concealed curiosity.

Darren turned his head away. 'Dead. Like I said, they were killed in a house fire. I was brought up in a children's home. No relatives.'

Wesley stood up. 'I'm sorry.'

'Don't be. Darren Collins was a loser. Fabrice Colbert is a success.'

'And if Charlie Marrick threatened to tell the world that Colbert was really Collins?'

Gerry Heffernan let the question hang in the air. But Darren didn't rise to the bait. He merely shook his head, a sad smile on his face. 'I know what you're thinking but there's no way Charlie could have known my secret. How could he? It was a long time ago.'

'You realise we'll have to speak to Annette Marrick. She'll have to confirm your version of how your prints got into the bedroom at Foxglove House.'

'Fair enough. But don't say anything about . . .'

'I don't see any reason to share your secret with anyone . . . at the moment,' said Wesley. 'Unless our enquiries throw up something . . .'

'They won't. I'm innocent. I rowed with Marrick but I never hurt him.'

Heffernan stood up and the two men began to walk towards the office door. Then Wesley twisted round, Columbo style, to face the chef whose face was already relaxing into an expression of relief that the interview was over.

'Just one more thing, Mr . . . er . . . Colbert. Do you know a vet called Simon Tench?'

'Tench? I don't think so.' He raised a finger in the air. 'Hang on. Marie took the cat to the vet's in Tradmouth . . . something wrong with its eye. I think she saw a guy called Tench. Why?'

'It's just that Mr Tench has been murdered. And it looks similar to Charles Marrick's murder.'

Darren slumped back into his seat. Then his eyes lit up

with new hope. 'In that case, I'm in the clear. Why would I kill this vet? You tell me that?'

Wesley said nothing. He thanked Darren for his time and the two men left, passing through the restaurant. The only diners were a party of four at a table near the window, talking loudly, oblivious to the time and the fact that the staff were hovering, eager to clear the place so they could prepare for the evening.

'What do you think?' Heffernan asked as they climbed into the car.

'I believe him. But I think we should double-check his alibi . . . and see if he has any connection with Tench other than a few eye-drops for the cat.' He hesitated. 'In fact I found myself admiring him back there. He was in a children's home . . . started on a career of armed robbery then he pulled himself around and became a successful chef. You've got to hand it to him, Gerry . . .'

'But don't forget, Wes. Old habits die hard.'

With those words of wisdom ringing in his ears, Wesley turned the car around and headed back to the police station.

CHAPTER 6

Blood-letting was used to remove corrupt matter from the body. But how was corrupt matter removed from the monastic community itself? Brother William faced this question and eventually he discovered the solution. Are you intrigued, Neil? Have I whetted your curiosity? Shall I make my move in our blood game and tell you more?

Brother William was admitted to the Cistercian Abbey of Veland in Devon at the age of twelve. He was an orphan, taken in and educated by the brothers and taught their ways. At the age of sixteen he became a novice and around a year later he took his vows of poverty, obedience and chastity. This he did willingly, committing himself to God, for he was an innocent soul, more concerned with the spirit than the body. If he had known of the evil that he would face in that place that ought to have been a holy refuge from the sins of the world, then perhaps he wouldn't have vowed his freedom away with such willing joy. You see, Neil, Satan dwelled with the monks in that magnificent Abbey of Veland – the Satan that is within us all.

The writer re-read the words on the screen. It was almost ready to send to Neil Watson. He should know the truth about what happened to Brother William. But as to the other matter . . . Perhaps it would soon be time to make confession. Or to pay the ultimate price.

★

At least Wesley had managed to salvage a couple of hours of his Sunday afternoon. After their visit to Le Petit Poisson, Gerry Heffernan had decided that they needed a break if they were going to be fit for the rigours of Monday morning. Gerry had taken the *Rosie May* out for a sail around the headland to, as he put it, blow out the cobwebs.

Wesley arrived home to find a note – Pam had gone to Belsham vicarage. Maritia had phoned that lunchtime to offer her anniversary congratulations and when she'd learned that Della had let them down, she'd invited Pam and the children round to the vicarage for the afternoon. Wesley joined her just in time for a decent cup of tea. He joked to his sister that there was no sign of cucumber sandwiches – but then Maritia had never really been the cucumber sandwich type.

As he sat there in the freshly painted living room of the vicarage, listening to his sister's stream of chat and family news, Wesley's mind kept wandering back to the two recent murders. But one glance at Pam, cuddling Amelia on her knee while Michael played outside, attempting a spot of rudimentary tree climbing in the large vicarage garden, told him that she was tired.

Wesley caught her eye and then began to make farewell noises, saying that they'd better make a move as they had to get the children organised and prepare themselves for a hard week ahead.

Maritia smiled sympathetically. Like their mother, she was a busy GP with patients, paperwork and a new computer system to wrestle with each day, as well as her unpaid role as Vicar's Wife with responsibility for the flower rota and a week night Bible study. Maritia seemed to possess boundless energy – but then, Wesley thought, she had no children. Children were a great leveller when it came to sheer exhaustion.

It was as Pam was gathering their things together that

Maritia dropped her quiet bombshell. Not that anybody but Pam had any idea that what she said was even mildly explosive.

'Jonathan's coming up to stay for a few days next week,' she announced. 'We haven't seen him since before the wedding, have we, Mark?' She looked at Pam and smiled. 'You remember Jonathan, don't you, Pam?'

If this had come from anyone else, Pam would have interpreted it as a snide remark at her expense. But she knew that Maritia was quite unaware of what had passed between her and Mark's old school friend, Jonathan, just before the couple's wedding the previous year. For one thing she'd been far too busy to notice.

'Mmm.' She glanced at Wesley, glad for once that he was too preoccupied with work to hear the giveaway nervousness in her voice.

'Why don't you come round for dinner next Sunday?' Maritia put her arm around her husband's waist. 'It'll be nice to have a get-together.'

Mark kissed the top of his wife's head and Pam looked away, feeling a sudden urge to blurt out the truth, to shock these smug innocents. But she forced herself to smile.

'Yeah . . . great,' she heard herself saying, even though she had every intention of avoiding Jonathan at all costs. Jonathan was dangerous. Jonathan had threatened her marriage once and she wasn't going to let it happen again.

Wesley was quiet as they drove back home, deep in thought.

'Everything okay?' she asked, glancing round at the children. Amelia had fallen asleep in her car seat and Michael was looking out of the window entranced at the passing scenery of rolling fields and grazing animals.

'Yes,' Wesley replied. 'Apart from the fact that I've got two corpses on my hands – identical MO but no apparent connection between them. And on top of that some kids found a skeleton in the woods near Sunacres Holiday Park yesterday.'

Pam looked at him, shocked. 'That's not been on the news.'

'Early days. I had a missed call on my mobile earlier – Neil. Why don't you try and get him now?' Wesley wanted to distract Pam from his work commitments – Neil had his uses.

She took Wesley's mobile and tapped in Neil's number. But there was no answer. She tried his mobile but it was switched off. This wasn't like Neil. Maybe something had happened. Or maybe he was up to something and he didn't want to be contacted.

Pam, slightly uneasy, promised herself she'd try again later.

They made an early start on Monday morning. Carl Pinney was in the interview room with that indispensable accessory to life on the wrong side of the law – his brief. Carl regarded his solicitor as an infallible lucky charm that could get him out of all manner of trouble. Gerry Heffernan had nailed a lucky horseshoe to his back door once. It had fallen off and hit him on the head. He just hoped that the protection provided by Carl's brief would prove equally ineffective.

Wesley entered the interview room just behind his boss. He hadn't been able to contact Neil the previous evening and there was a small nag of worry in the back of his mind. After all, Neil had been receiving those anonymous letters . . . the ones that spoke of blood and death. Wesley would call him later – just to make sure he was okay.

They sat down opposite Carl Pinney and his solicitor, a bored-looking man in his mid-forties with a shiny suit and thinning ginger hair who kept glancing at his watch as though he'd rather be elsewhere. He didn't look lucky and he didn't look charming. But Pinney was relying on him.

Wesley gave Pinney a friendly smile. 'I expect you go out on Saturday nights, Carl.'

Pinney rewarded him with a look of utter contempt.

'Where did you go on Saturday . . . and who were you with?'

'What's it to you?'

'You know why you've been brought in, don't you?'

'Haven't a clue.'

'The knife you used in the attack on DC Carstairs is the same one that killed Charles Marrick.'

'I told you before. I found it.' He looked at his solicitor who avoided his eyes.

'There's been a development since then, Carl. There's been another murder. Exactly the same as Marrick's. Where were you on Saturday night?'

Pinney's eyes darted to and fro in panic. 'I weren't feeling well. I didn't go out. I got beaten up, you know. That bastard mate of yours put me in hospital. I've still got the bruises and they still bloody hurt. Takes a long time to get over something like that,' he added self-righteously. 'I think I've got post traumatic stress disorder.'

Wesley ignored this last remark. 'Is there anyone who can back up your story?'

'Our Chelsea.'

'Our Chelsea? Who's that?' asked Heffernan.

'Me sister. Me mam was out so we sent out for pizzas.'

'What time was this?'

Pinney shrugged. 'About six . . . seven. Dunno really. We ain't got a clock.'

'Where did you order the pizza from?' Wesley asked.

Pinney said a name which meant nothing to Wesley or Heffernan – one of the many small pizza delivery joints that plied their trade in the large seaside resort of Morbay. It would be checked out, of course, but even if the delivery driver saw Carl Pinney, it didn't mean he didn't nip out soon after the pizzas were dropped off and murder Simon Tench. To do that he'd need access to a car, of course. But Wesley would put money on his ability to hotwire and pinch any car that lacked adequate security and he would have honed his driving skills on the unofficial skidpans of the Winterham

Estate, terrifying the older residents with the noise of squealing tyres as the vehicles careered recklessly around the litter strewn streets.

Wesley made a mental note to ask someone to check on stolen cars at the relevant times. It was the only possibility: buses in the area were like rare protected beasts reported on in hushed tones by David Attenborough on BBC natural history programmes – infrequent and unreliable. And Pinney was hardly the type who'd walk miles on the off chance of finding a likely victim.

But the more Wesley thought about it, the less likely it seemed that Pinney was their murderer. The impulse attack – the knife in the alley or the snatched handbag – was his style. Not the calculated piercing of arteries. But they still had to be thorough and check out his story.

'Have you any pets, Carl?'

Pinney looked at Wesley as though he was mad. 'We had a dog once but that was years ago. Why?'

'Did you ever take it to a vet called Simon Tench?'

Pinney looked puzzled and shook his head. 'Never took it to no vet. It got run over in the end . . . killed. We never had to take it to no vet.'

Wesley and Heffernan caught each other's eye. Carl Pinney was no advert for responsible pet ownership.

'Have you ever heard of or met Simon Tench? He worked in Tradmouth. The Cornvale Veterinary Clinic.'

Pinney shook his head vigorously but Wesley could tell he was uneasy. He had recognised Tench's name – or that of the clinic.

The solicitor made a show of studying his watch. 'I think it's time my client had a break.'

Gerry Heffernan stood up. 'Break? We've not even started yet.'

Wesley put a hand on his arm. 'Quite right. We'll continue this later on. We've got to attend the postmortem of the latest victim.' He watched Pinney's face for a reaction but saw none.

And he had an uncomfortable feeling that they were wasting their valuable time.

DC Trish Walton was getting sick of keeping an eye on Annette Marrick at Foxglove House. She didn't like the woman but she did her best to hide the fact, to stay professional.

Annette had started to regard the policewomen assigned to provide her with support and protection as unpaid servants who made the tea, fielded phone calls and visitors and packed the dishwasher and washing machine. She had asked Trish to fix up a cleaning company to remove all trace of the murder and this was one thing Trish could sympathise with. Living with the reminders of violent death would be a nightmare for anyone.

Petronella Blackwell seemed to have made the decision to stay for the duration. Trish Walton had heard the story of her birth and adoption and was rather surprised that the young woman felt such loyalty to the mother who had abandoned her. But she sensed there was something else there too . . . some unknown factor. Some secret in the house that hadn't yet come out into the open.

Her task for that morning was to break the news of Simon Tench's murder and point out the similarities to the death of Charles Marrick. DCI Heffernan had told her to observe Annette's reaction and try and discover her whereabouts at the time of Tench's death. And, most importantly, she was to find out whether there was any connection, however slight, between Charles Marrick and Simon Tench.

She made a pot of tea and sat down with the two women. Three friends having a chat over a cuppa. Or at least that was the image Trish wanted to create to encourage confidences.

Annette was looking bored rather than grief stricken. She stared into her steaming mug absentmindedly. Petronella looked at Trish and gave her a shy smile.

'How did you sleep?' Trish asked, breaking the morning ice.

Annette looked at her. Trish saw a flash of contempt in her eyes. 'If you must know, I took something. Knocked me out for the night.'

Trish cleared her throat. It was time to ask the embarrassing question DI Peterson had instructed her to ask. She felt her cheeks reddening as she took a deep breath. 'Can I have a word with you alone, Annette?'

Annette touched Petronella's arm and Trish saw the young woman flinch before slowly edging away. 'I've got no secrets from my daughter. You can say anything you like and it won't bother her, isn't that right, Pet?'

Petronella didn't answer.

'Okay then. Were you having a sexual relationship with Fabrice Colbert . . . the chef?'

Annette smirked. 'What if I was? Not a crime is it? Fabrice and I had a bit of a fling . . . and it's true what they say about Frenchmen. Fabrice was as good in a bed as he is in a kitchen, I can assure you,' she added by way of explanation.

Trish felt herself blushing at the woman's candour. Petronella, sitting beside her, looked as if she wanted to shrivel up with embarrassment, shifting in her seat to put some distance between herself and her mother.

'Where did you meet?'

'Here. We couldn't go to his place because of his girlfriend.'

'Whereabouts in the house did you . . . er . . . ?'

'The bedroom. Where do you think? Swinging from the bloody chandeliers? And before you ask, it's all over now. It finished a couple of days before Charlie died – when he pulled that wine stunt. It was nice while it lasted but I can assure you it was purely physical on both sides. Nothing to commit murder over.'

Somehow the words had the ring of truth. Trish found herself believing her. And at least she could report back to Wesley Peterson that Annette Marrick had corroborated Colbert's explanation as to why his prints had been found at the murder scene without any prompting. All she had to do now was to break the news about the second murder . . . the one that seemed to be identical to Marrick's. She took a deep breath. 'Did you or Charlie ever know a vet called Simon Tench?'

'No. Why?'

'He was found dead yesterday morning . . . and it looks as if he was killed in the same way as Charlie was. We're trying to establish some sort of connection.'

Annette stood up and walked over to the window. 'Well, I don't know of any. And I knew all of Charlie's friends.'

'So you've never heard of Simon Tench?'

Annette shook her head. 'Never.'

'You've never had any animals . . . any pets you might have taken to . . . ?'

'Can't stand bloody animals,' was the reply. 'Neither could Charlie before you ask. His ex had a dog but he had it put down 'cause he couldn't stay in the same house with it.'

This caught Trish's interest. 'Where can we find this ex-girlfriend?'

'Search me.'

'Do you know the name of the vet who put it down?'

Another look of contempt. 'How the hell should I know? It was a long time ago . . . before I met him.'

This wasn't going anywhere. But Trish was getting a clearer picture of Charlie Marrick. He'd have his girlfriend's dog destroyed just because its existence didn't suit him. Trish, an animal lover, felt she would have disliked Marrick if she'd met him in life . . . even more than she disliked his wife.

'I'm going out. I need to do some shopping in Tradmouth. Is that okay with you?' she said to Trish sarcastically before sweeping out of the room.

Petronella, on the sofa, watched her go, looking rather embarrassed. 'Look, I'm sorry she's so rude.'

Trish smiled reassuringly. 'She's been under a lot of strain. Grief can affect people . . .'

'Grief? Is that what you think it is?'

'What else?'

'Relief,' she said with a vehemence that made Trish look at her intently. And when she looked she saw that tears were forming in Petronella's eyes. 'He . . .'

It occurred to Trish that this was the first time she'd actually been alone with Petronella. Up to now she had been concentrating on Annette, assuming the abandoned daughter who now lived in Bath couldn't be involved in any way. But perhaps she'd been wrong. 'Go on,' she prompted.

Petronella stood up, fists clenched, eyes full of tears and fury. 'If you want the truth, Charlie was a complete bastard. Whoever killed him deserves a medal and I hope you never find him because he's done the world a favour.'

Trish said nothing. She waited for Petronella to carry on, to get whatever grievance she had against the dead man off her chest.

But Petronella didn't elaborate on her statement. Instead she slumped down on the sofa and buried her head in her hands.

Trish decided a bit of gentle probing was in order. 'What do you mean, Petronella? What did Charlie do to make you hate him so much?'

Petronella looked up at her, her eyes red with unshed tears. 'Okay, if you want to know, I'll tell you. When I came here a couple of years ago to find my mum I was naive, trusting. Some would say stupid. Charlie put on a good act at first . . . all sympathy and pretending he was glad I'd found Annette and all that. He said I could stay as long as I liked . . . he seemed keener on the idea than Annette was. It wasn't till I'd been here a couple of weeks that I found out why.'

'What do you mean?'

Petronella looked her in the eye. 'Annette went out to the hairdresser's one day and I was left alone with Charlie. He . . . He was in his bedroom and he called downstairs to me to bring his mobile phone up. I didn't think anything of it but when I got there he was behind the door.'

'Go on.' Trish guessed what was coming but she hoped she was wrong.

She began to speak again, almost in a whisper. Her hands were shaking. 'I went inside, calling his name, saying I'd found the phone. But I didn't realise he was behind me. He slammed the door shut and locked it. He was laughing . . . saying he had something for me . . . a treat. Then he . . . he pushed me down on the bed and started pushing my skirt up. He was stronger than me. I tried to push his hands away but he was stronger than me. He was rough . . . he hurt me and when he'd finished he said something like "You enjoyed that, didn't you," even though I must have been crying. He . . .'

Trish sat down beside her and took her in her arms. 'It's okay. He can't hurt you now,' she cooed in her ear, aware that the cliché she had just uttered – the first thing that had popped into her head – was a lie. Charlie Marrick could still hurt her, even from beyond the grave. The memory of him would always be with her . . . polluting her life.

'I was so ashamed,' she sobbed into Trish's shoulder. 'After it happened I left right away.' She broke away from Trish's embrace, took a tissue from her pocket and blew her nose. Then she looked Trish in the eye. 'I was so ashamed that I let it happen.'

Trish, lost for words, held her close as she began to sob her heart out.

CHAPTER 7

Would Neil Watson have received the last letter yet? Possibly not. Post was usually late these days. The writer sat staring at the blank computer screen. There was so much more to say. Information to be fed out little by little – moves in the blood game. Neil Watson was losing the game at the moment. He still had no idea what he was dealing with.

The writer glanced at the clock on the mantelpiece. It was almost time to go. But not before the next letter was started.

The Abbey of Veland owned much of the land round about but most of it was rented out to tenants who farmed it and paid the abbey a generous rent. The abbey held great wealth and the abbot lived in some style while the brothers in their habits of rough, white, undyed wool, prayed eight times each day in addition to their strict regime of work and study. They rose at 2 am for the office of Nocturns, then Matins at 4 am, then Prime at 6 am, and so on until the day ended with Compline at 8 pm followed by a light supper. It must have been an arduous life. No wonder they looked forward so much to their time at the seyney house.

The writer switched off the computer. The letter would be continued tonight when there was more time.

The newspaper lay neatly folded and unread, on the breakfast table. The writer picked it up and began to scan the front page. *Police treating vet's death as murder* was the headline. Then there was the smaller headline at the bottom of the page. *Skeleton in woodland still unidentified.*

The writer's hands shook but it was important to stay calm. Nobody should know what really happened.

Even though it was so hard not to tell.

Colin Bowman seemed subdued that morning. However, Colin being Colin, he still gave Gerry Heffernan and Wesley Peterson a friendly greeting and offered them his customary refreshment before they made for the postmortem room. And it was over tea and biscuits that the pathologist confessed that he was dreading what was to come.

'I can't say I knew Simon well but he seemed a really nice chap,' he explained. 'It's one thing cutting up a complete stranger but it's quite another with someone you've met socially. I tried to get Roper from Morbay Hospital to do it but he's busy with a pile up on the by-pass.' Colin sighed. This was the first time Wesley had seen him like this. Even pathologists who are quite accustomed to death, he thought, have their limits.

'Our Sam says everyone at the surgery's really upset,' Heffernan chipped in. 'No one can believe that anyone would want to hurt Simon. According to our Sam, he got on with everyone and there's no way he had any enemies.'

'He had one,' Wesley said, then immediately regretted his flippancy.

Colin went on to ask how Emma was and Heffernan told him that her parents were on their way down to stay with her. Wesley felt a great wave of sadness engulfing him as he followed Colin and Gerry into the white postmortem room and saw the shell of what used to be Simon Tench lying on the stainless steel table.

As he went about his work, Colin was uncharacteristically silent and as soon as he'd finished, he nodded to his assistant who began to sew up the incisions Colin had made with quiet efficiency. Then Colin removed his green gown and signalled to the two detectives to follow him to his office. When he asked if they'd like another cup of tea they could tell that the question wasn't just asked out of politeness – he needed the tea to revive him, to calm his nerves. For some men it would have been a glass of whisky but for Colin Bowman it was a cup of strong Earl Grey.

'Well?' said Gerry Heffernan as the tea was poured from Colin's bone-china pot – a venerable antique.

'It looks exactly like the other one. Of course I won't know if the body contains hemlock until we have the toxicology report but the lack of defensive wounds certainly suggests he was incapacitated somehow when he was stabbed. There's no sign that he was restrained in any way.'

'And hemlock causes paralysis?'

'Oh sure. As I said in my report, its effects are not dissimilar to curare and that's used to paralyse patients during operations. It's a little slower acting of course, but quite effective. The muscles are paralysed but the mind remains clear until death. Nasty. There was no sign of quail in the stomach contents this time by the way. In fact he hadn't eaten for a while, although he'd had a wee dram shortly before his death.'

'Whisky?'

'That's right.' He paused for a few moments. 'There was something I noticed – some very faint scarring to the left forearm almost identical to the marks I noticed on Charles Marrick. It's very old scarring so it's probably got nothing to do with . . .'

'It's strange all the same,' said Wesley. 'What about a time of death?'

Colin shrugged. 'Any time between seven o'clock to ten

o'clock on the evening before he was found. Sorry I can't be more specific.' He drained his teacup and reached for the pot. This was a two-cup situation. 'I'll let you have all the lab reports as soon as they come in. I really hope you catch whoever did this. Simon never did anyone any harm . . . he didn't deserve . . .'

Simon Tench's death had driven all thoughts of the skeleton in the woods out of Wesley's mind. But he suddenly remembered there was something else he needed to ask. 'By the way, Colin, have you had a chance to examine those bones that were brought in . . . the ones that were found in the woods near Sunacres Holiday Park?'

Colin shook his head. 'Not yet, I'm afraid, but I'll make a thorough examination this afternoon. I trust you're going through your missing persons records.'

'I've got someone on it. But with Charles Marrick's murder and now this . . .' He left the sentence unfinished. Colin didn't need it spelling out.

As Wesley and Heffernan took their leave, Colin raised a hand in farewell.

'Any thoughts, Wes?' the DCI asked as they walked along the embankment by the river to a fanfare of shrieking sea gulls.

'Only that our two victims have nothing in common. One was a right bastard who'd nick his own granny's walking stick given half the chance and the other was said by everyone who knew him, including your son, to be some sort of saint. However, they're both male and around the same age.' He hesitated. 'What about Neil's letters? Could they have something to do with these murders?'

Heffernan frowned. 'No idea. But there's something we're missing here, Wes.'

The only thing they had to do was to find out what that something was.

★

Carl Pinney was still being held for questioning. His story about eating pizza with his sister, Chelsea, at the time Simon Tench was killed was flimsy to say the least . . . and it certainly didn't convince Gerry or Wesley who suspected that Chelsea would back up her brother against the police any day. With this uncertainty in mind, Pinney's clothing had been collected from his home by a couple of uniformed constables who had had to endure Carl's mother's swearing and abuse and young Chelsea's spittle in their faces.

The custody sergeant, Dan Zachary, had finished his shift. Another day closer to his eagerly anticipated retirement. He normally shook the dust of Tradmouth police station off his feet as soon as work was over and headed straight for home where he would cook a meal for his wife who worked in a care home. With no children to upset the equilibrium, theirs was a marriage of equals before it became fashionable.

But today Dan broke with routine and climbed the stairs to the CID office because something was worrying him . . . something he wanted to talk over with Gerry Heffernan. Dan had known Gerry for years, ever since he'd been transferred to Tradmouth from Morbay nick as a young detective constable. Gerry had risen in the ranks of CID to become chief investigating officer dealing with any serious crime that occurred in the Tradmouth area, but Dan had been content to stay in uniform, eventually carving out a niche for himself in the custody suite.

The CID office was buzzing like a beehive as Dan walked in. Computers were flickering and phones were ringing but Dan's eyes were drawn irresistibly to the crime scene photographs pinned up on the far wall.

He averted his gaze from the gruesome images and made his way to Gerry Heffernan's office, where the man himself was sitting back with his feet up on his cluttered desk, a picture of relaxation amidst the frantic activity. Sitting at the other side of Gerry's desk was a smartly dressed black man aged around thirty with delicate features and intelligent eyes. Dan recognised DI Wesley Peterson – his arrival in Tradmouth had caused a lot of talk, in spite of all the chief constable's diversity initiatives. But Wesley Peterson was an unassuming man who'd fitted into the team easily. He was popular with most – especially with Rachel Tracey if canteen gossip was to be believed. But Dan only listened to gossip in the course of duty. You could sometimes learn a lot from gossip.

In fact it was gossip that had brought him here. He had overheard someone talking in the canteen about Steve Carstairs' alleged attack on Carl Pinney, who was currently enjoying Dan's lavish hospitality in what he called 'The Pentonville Suite' – he liked to call all his cells after Her Majesty's more famous hotels. Dan had listened carefully to what was being said before returning to his desk to do a bit of checking. It was then he'd made an interesting discovery. A discovery that he thought he ought to share with DCI Heffernan.

He rapped on the glass door and Heffernan looked up, signalling him in with a welcoming grin. Dan let himself into the office and sat down on the spare visitors' chair beside DI Peterson.

'I've been looking through the records, Gerry. Comings and going down in the custody suite and all that. I've found a discrepancy.'

The two detectives watched him, all ears.

'You know your DC Carstairs . . . Steve. There's no record of him visiting the custody suite at the time Pinney claims he was beaten up.'

It was Wesley who asked the obvious question. 'Why wasn't this picked up before?'

'Pinney did have injuries – there's no question of that. He howled for his brief and made the accusation and because Carstairs had been down to see him before. Andy – the lad who was on duty – is new and I reckon he got mixed up.

Wesley looked at his boss. This seemed unlikely.

'He said Carstairs had been to see the prisoner and been on his own with him which I wouldn't have allowed if I'd been there. So when Pinney was found about half an hour later with injuries, it was assumed . . . But according to the log, the prisoner was taken his dinner after Carstairs left.'

Wesley sat forward. 'So Pinney was unhurt after Steve had left.'

'Looks like it.'

'So how did he come by the injuries?'

'Now that's where I did a bit of detective work.' He chuckled. 'Don't worry . . . I'm not going to apply to join CID at my time of life.'

'Go on,' Wesley prompted. Dan was an amiable man, one of the old school, and his retirement do – when Chief Superintendent Nutter would present him with the requisite clock/garden tools/television set – was booked for later in the year. He and Heffernan knew from experience that Dan preferred pleasant chit-chat to stating the bare facts. He wasn't a man to be rushed.

'Well, it turns out that I overheard a mate of Andy's saying that Pinney had dropped some food – or threw it more like – and Andy had to mop it up. Do you get my meaning?' He almost winked. 'Mop. Water. Slippy floor.'

Gerry Heffernan's smile started small at first then widened to a Cheshire cat grin. 'Pinney fell on the slippy floor and thought the chance of getting one up on Steve was too good to miss.'

'And nobody thought to check the sequence of events till now.' Wesley tried to keep the reproach out of his voice. Maybe if the victim hadn't been Steve who wasn't exactly popular in some quarters, the enquiries would have been more assiduous.

'We've been rather busy,' Dan said righteously. 'There's a lot of villainy about, you know. Now summer's coming and there're more yachts to nick from and tourists' cars to break into. All the records were there ready if there was an official investigation. I'd not had time to examine them, that's all.'

'I know, Dan. I'm not blaming you,' Wesley said quickly. 'It's just a pity Andy never thought to put two and two together.'

Gerry Heffernan thanked Dan profusely as he left and when they were alone he scratched his head. 'I suppose we'd better let the nutter know. At least we'll have another body to help with the investigation.'

'Who's going to confront Pinney? I think he'll tell the truth once he knows he's been rumbled.'

Wesley's mobile began to ring. He answered it and, after a short, monosyllabic conversation, he ended the call and frowned.

'Trish wants to meet me. She says she's got some new information about Charles Marrick – something she doesn't want to discuss over the phone.'

Heffernan raised his eyebrows. 'You get going then, Wes. And while you're out I'll have a word with our Mr Pinney . . . and this time his brief'll be miles away.' He thought for a moment. 'No. On second thoughts, I want his brief there. I want him to realise what a slippery little liar his illustrious client really is.'

Wesley left him to it and drove out to Rhode, wondering what Trish Walton's new information could be.

Neil Watson needed help. He'd called Annabel at the County Archives first thing that morning to ask her if she could dig out any more about Veland Abbey – something that would prove once and for all in writing that Stow Barton was the place where the monks had been sent to be bled and enjoy a spot of rest and relaxation. Annabel said she'd do her best and he knew she'd be true to her word.

He had allocated trenches to the more experienced diggers first thing that morning before giving the four students starting the dig that week their introductory talk and health and safety briefing. The diggers' staggered breaks would start soon and the site office would be used for refreshments, but until then, Neil had a few minutes to catch up on his paperwork. He sat down at the makeshift desk – a plank supported by two milk crates – and began to sort through some geophysics printouts and aerial photographs of the site that showed quite clearly where the manor house walls had once stood.

The trenches they'd opened were yielding good finds – mostly high-status medieval stuff with a smattering of Tudor green pottery which dated from the time Veland Abbey was dissolved by Henry VIII. Normally he'd have been pleased as a pig in muck if a dig was going this well but he felt uneasy. Perhaps it was the letters. Or perhaps it was the pit filled with the dark deposit that might be blood – probably was blood if it was a seyney house. And if it was the seyney house, his letter writer had got it spot on. And this thought unsettled him.

He looked up and saw Lenny standing in the doorway. He was wearing his Indiana Jones hat as usual and he was staring at Neil as though he was in some sort of trance.

Neil forced himself to smile. 'Hi, Lenny. What can I do for you?' he asked with as much bonhomie as he could muster . . . which wasn't much.

Lenny took a step into the room, the sound of his muddy boots thudding on the hard packed floor. 'Have the tests come back yet?'

'What tests?' Neil knew very well what he meant but he wasn't going to make it easy for him.

'That pit. It's blood. I told you it was a ritual site.'

'As soon as I hear anything from the lab, I'll let you know,' Neil said smoothly. 'Found anything in your trench so far this morning?'

'Only more oyster shells. I think we should dig through all this medieval stuff and get back to the . . .'

Neil stood up, raising himself to his full height. 'While I'm in charge, Lenny, we dig this site properly – scientific-ally – or not at all. If there's an earlier settlement, we'll find it sooner or later.'

'But I'm only booked in for another couple of weeks. What if . . . ?'

Neil took a deep breath. 'The site diary will be on our website so you can keep up to date with any developments.' He spotted Diane in the doorway. 'Diane, come in,' he said eagerly. 'Lenny was just going back to his trench, weren't you, Lenny?'

Lenny took the hint and left slowly, reluctantly.

'Having problems?' Diane asked when he was out of earshot.

'Our Lenny's got his own agenda and monastic manor houses don't feature in it, I'm afraid. To him it's a bronze age ritual site . . . probably a place of human sacrifice . . . and he won't be told any different.'

A shadow passed across Diane's face. 'Is it possible that he's right – that the monastic complex was built on an earlier site?'

'The landscape work we've done doesn't suggest it. I reckon Lenny's just got a fixation.' He paused. 'With blood and sacrifice.'

Diane said nothing. She turned to go.

'It was good of you to drop by yesterday. I was at a bit of a loose end and . . .' He was aware his words were clumsy but she turned round and gave him a shy smile.

'No trouble,' she said.

He had a sudden urge to confide in her but something stopped him. Perhaps he'd wait and see what happened. Maybe if he just played it cool the problem would go away. And Wesley had the letters – the police were involved. Perhaps if the writer got to know that, it'd scare him off.

'I'd better get back,' Diane said, almost as though she wanted Neil to stop her . . . to ask her to stay with him. But then he had the dig to think about.

'Okay,' he said. 'I promised Norman he could do some surveying. Will you . . . ?'

She nodded and hurried away, Neil staring at her disappearing back.

Wesley had left DC Lee Parsons to go through the missing persons records: they needed a name for their skeleton in the woods. Male, probably aged between thirty and forty with a watch, trouser zip, an assortment of buttons and a few fillings. He'd also told Lee to check out whether any of the guests at Sunacres Holiday Park had gone missing but he'd drawn a blank on that one. The park's owners had only been there five years and they claimed that nothing untoward had happened in that time. The previous owners were being traced but these things could take time.

Wesley enjoyed the drive out to Rhode, on the high winding road with the wide expanse of hazy sea down to his left. Charles Marrick probably hadn't appreciated all this beauty, Wesley thought to himself. By the sound of it, he'd been a greedy, self-centred man. Not the sort to count his blessings.

Trish Walton was waiting for him on the doorstep of Foxglove House. She was hopping from foot to foot like an excited child and her expression told him that she had some momentous information to share. As he opened the car door, she rushed towards him. 'Sorry I couldn't tell you over the phone but it's rather delicate.'

Trish led the way, walking down the drive, away from the house. Whatever she had to tell him, it would be something that shouldn't be overheard. He fell in by her side and they walked until they were out of sight of the upstairs windows, sheltered by the glowering rhododendrons,

'Well?' he said.

'Charlie Marrick was a rapist, sir. He raped his step-daughter, Petronella.'

'You're sure about this?'

Trish looked annoyed. 'She wasn't lying. No way.'

Wesley made conciliatory noises. 'Sorry, Trish. I had to ask.'

Trish looked embarrassed, suspecting she'd overreacted. But then she'd been with Petronella for the last few hours, in an atmosphere of heightened emotions, so it was hardly surprising. 'I'm sorry, sir. It's just that I've got to know her . . . and I'm feeling angry that he could get away with . . .'

'Well he didn't get away with it, did he? He's dead.' He paused, knowing he was about to say something that Trish wouldn't like. 'You realise this makes Petronella a suspect, don't you?'

'She was up in Bath at the time. She can't have had anything to do with it.'

'Has her alibi been checked?'

'She hasn't really got one. She said she was alone all day – off work doing some Open University essay but . . .'

'She had a good reason for wanting Marrick dead.' He sighed. 'In common with a lot of people, I should imagine. What about the other thing . . . Annette Marrick's relationship with Fabrice Colbert? Has Annette said anything?'

'She told me she'd had an affair with him – quite boastful she was. They used to meet here when Charlie was at work. They used the bedroom.'

Wesley smiled. 'By the way, he's not French you know. He used to be a minor villain called Darren Collins in a former life. Did a cookery course in the nick, went to Paris, had some cosmetic surgery, learned his trade in a top restaurant, changed his identity and the rest is history.'

Trish shook her head in disbelief. 'I've seen him on telly. I can't believe he's not French.'

'Oh he's got the act off pat now. But the one thing he

couldn't change was his fingerprints. If it wasn't for the fact that he left them all over Annette's bedroom.' He smiled. 'And probably all over Annette herself, we'd have been none the wiser.'

'Anyway, according to Annette it's all over now. It finished when Colbert found out about the wine scam.'

There had been times when he'd underestimated Trish but she had done well. 'Can you check exactly where Petronella was at the time of Simon Tench's murder?'

Trish nodded. 'I was here on Saturday night around that time and she did go out for a while. She said she was going into Neston to the supermarket. They're open till ten on a Saturday. She came back with some shopping . . . just bits and pieces. I assumed she just wanted to get out of the house. Annette isn't the easiest person to live with.'

Wesley thought for a few moments. 'As well as double-checking her story, maybe you can get her to talk about the people she knows . . . see if there's any way she could have met Simon Tench.'

Trish gave him a martyred smile. 'I'll have a go.'

'You're doing well, Trish. They trust you now,' he said. A word of encouragement never went amiss.

To DC Lee Parsons the world of CID had seemed a far more glamorous prospect than dealing with messy traffic incidents and shepherding drunks on a Friday night. But the reality hadn't really lived up to his expectations. Ninety-nine per cent of CID work, he'd discovered, was dull routine: taking statements, checking facts, writing up reports and making mundane phone calls . . . all in the hope that somehow, somewhere a connection would be made and the pieces of some complex jigsaw would fit into place.

He kept telling himself that, as the new boy, he got all the crap jobs. But even so, it was better than being in uniform. And at least he could tell any girls he met that he was a detective which sounded more impressive than a plain police constable – a wooden top. And there was one girl in particular – Sarah – who seemed rather impressed by his inside knowledge. He was definitely on a promise.

However, one piece of news that day had rather taken the spring out of Lee's step. It was all round the office that DC Steve Carstairs was coming back. Word had it that the accusations against him had been dropped. Lee didn't actively dislike Steve but he'd noticed that the office was certainly a more relaxed place when he wasn't there. He'd met the likes of Steve before. Jack the Lad with a fast car, sharp clothes and a swagger that told the world he was God's gift to policing. When Steve returned, Lee would keep his distance.

Lee turned his attention to his computer. Missing persons. Males in early middle age. From a few phone calls to watch manufacturers, he had discovered that the watch found near the body was a mid-range model available throughout the country around twenty years ago and discontinued in 1987.

Then there was the dental work. He'd sent the details to all the dentists in the area but nothing had come in as yet. However, Devon was the sort of place that attracted outsiders so he might have to search further afield. And there was always DNA of course. Samples had been taken but that sort of thing took time.

As he trawled the missing persons database for likely candidates, the plastic bag containing a gold signet ring caught his eye. It had been caked in the soil around a skeletal middle finger, barely visible until the bones were lifted from their resting place and cleaned up a little. Strange, Lee thought, that if it was a case of murder, nobody had attempted to bury the body. It must have been there for years lying in the undergrowth in a tangled spot of woodland where only wild animals prowled.

After an hour of searching, Lee concluded that no man of that age and height who had gone missing in the South

Hams area around the relevant time remained unaccounted for. Whoever it was hadn't been missed. Nobody had reported his disappearance. Either that or he'd come to Devon for some reason after being reported missing elsewhere.

Perhaps the man had travelled miles and had died alone, either from natural causes, accident or by his own hand, in that strange, isolated place. The thought made Lee Parsons feel rather sad.

DI Peterson's arrival in the office interrupted his thoughts. He looked across at Lee and smiled encouragingly. Lee hadn't known many people from ethnic minorities before but Peterson was okay. He didn't make you feel stupid . . . not like some.

'How's it going, Lee?' Peterson said, approaching his desk. 'Got a name yet?'

Lee shook his head. 'I don't think he came from round here, sir. Nobody answering the description was reported missing in Devon during that period of time.' He blushed. 'Well, there were three but they've all been accounted for. No luck with the dental records either. I think I'm going to have to try further afield. Maybe we'll have some luck with the DNA.'

'Let's hope so.' Wesley picked up the plastic bag containing the ring.

'I was just going to have a look at that, sir. There might be some initials or . . .'

Wesley couldn't help smiling at the young man's puppyish enthusiasm. 'I'll leave it with you then,' he said before making for Gerry Heffernan's office.

Ten minutes later Lee Parsons had discovered that the signet ring bore the initials BI. And as he rushed to the DCI's office to report his findings, he felt rather pleased with himself.

Rachel Tracey was relieved when the doorbell rang. Emma Tench's parents were expected but they seemed to have been a long time coming. Various domestic and work arrangements and a bad traffic jam on the M5 caused by an overturned lorry, had conspired to keep them from their daughter's side but now they were here.

Rachel tactfully stood back and tried to be unobtrusive during the tears and embraces. Emma had seemed too stunned for coherent thought and she hadn't been able to provide much information. But Rachel sensed that she was glad of her presence . . . of not being left alone with her pain. She'd sat for hours watching the DVD of the programme she and Simon had made together. *House Hunters*. She and Simon had been guided from property to property – all cottages in the Tradmouth area similar to the one they were renting – by a hyperactive blonde presenter. As Rachel watched the episode with her, time and time again until she knew everything they were going to say before they said it, she thought they seemed a nice couple. Intelligent but uncomplicated. The sort of people who just want to get on with their jobs and their lives. Not the sort of people who get murdered unless they are in the wrong place at the wrong time and the killing is motiveless. The more Rachel watched Simon Tench being led, good humouredly, from room to room, the more puzzled she felt.

Now that the victim's widow was in the care of her parents – who seemed, in Rachel's opinion, a nice sensible couple – further questioning seemed inappropriate. Besides, Rachel was sure she'd learned all she was going to learn from Emma Tench. The next thing on her list was a visit to Simon's work colleagues.

She drove to the veterinary practice on the road out of Tradmouth and parked in the car park. A car drew up beside her and disgorged a large woman with two equally large dogs – Irish wolfhounds, Rachel thought. Beautiful creatures. At the surgery entrance they met a woman carrying a basket containing a black cat with large, frightened eyes. One of the dogs gave a half-hearted bark for honour's sake but fell silent when its mistress gave a yank on the lead.

At reception she flashed her warrant card discreetly at a

young woman in a nurse's uniform. She needed to have a word with Mr Tench's colleagues. The young woman's eyes immediately filled with tears as if she'd been suppressing her emotions all day and now the dam was about to burst.

'He was a lovely man,' she began to sob. 'And so nice with everyone. It's awful, it really is. Was it a burglary? I heard it was a burglary.'

Rachel wondered how this story had got about. Someone had speculated and the theory had been taken as gospel, she supposed. It usually happened that way.

Fortunately she didn't have to wait very long amongst the dogs, cats, rabbits and assorted rodents. It amazed her how quiet and well behaved they all were. It was as though the creatures had agreed a temporary truce for the duration of their visit. Dogs wouldn't bark at cats, cats wouldn't chase rodents and so on. Or perhaps it was the atmosphere of the place that cowed them. They knew exactly why they were there.

While she was waiting, Sam Heffernan came out of one of the rooms off the reception area to call in a patient – a dopey-looking spaniel. He spotted Rachel and smiled. She smiled back. Keep on the right side of the boss's relatives. After a while a middle-aged man in a white coat, who bore a passing resemblance to a friendly Labrador, emerged from another room, walked over to her and shook her hand.

'I'm afraid I have to ask you and your colleagues some questions about Simon Tench, Mr Wicks.'

'Terrible business,' Peter Wicks, senior partner in the practice, muttered as he led her into his surgery. He looked at Rachel and frowned as if he'd forgotten something. 'I know you, don't I? Isn't it Rachel? Rachel Tracey? Little Barton Farm. You're Harry and Stella's daughter.'

Rachel smiled. Peter Wicks had been looking after the beasts at Little Barton for years now. Not that Rachel had had anything to do with that side of the farming business. She'd left all that to her father and brothers while she and her mother – along with her sister-in-law – looked after the holiday lets that were so essential to make ends meet.

'I trust all is well,' the vet said with professional politeness, making conversation. Maybe to get away from the unpleasant subject of murder.

'Fine as far as I know. I moved into a place of my own a few months ago.'

Wicks nodded earnestly. 'Of course. I was there for a complicated calving back in March and Stella mentioned something about it.'

Rachel said nothing, mildly annoyed with her mother for discussing her private living arrangements. But then the farming community was close knit: people took an interest in each other's business so it was hardly surprising.

'So what would you like to know about Simon? I can tell you now that he didn't have any enemies. He was popular with everyone – a good man and a good vet. He'll be sorely missed.'

Rachel had heard eulogies like this before about the recently dead. But this time, she knew it was meant sincerely. Simon Tench had been liked. Loved even. And his murder seemed to make no sense.

'It was a random attack surely. A robbery gone wrong.'

'I'm afraid it doesn't look that way, Mr Wicks. We think Simon was deliberately targeted. There was no sign of anything missing.'

Wicks shook his head. 'I find that so hard to believe. Who'd want to . . . ?'

'That's what we're trying to find out.'

The vet gave Rachel a weak smile. 'Of course you are. How's Emma bearing up? I was thinking of going round to see her . . .' He sounded uncertain of his reception. But then most people are lost for words in the presence of the bereaved at the best of times.

'I'm sure she'd appreciate that, Mr Wicks.'

The man nodded. 'Is there anything I can do to help?' he said. 'I've been wondering if we should offer a reward or something . . .'

Rachel smiled. 'Perhaps it might be worth discussing it with DCI Heffernan – he's in charge of the case. His son works here – Sam Heffernan.'

'Ah, Sam . . . nice lad. He mentioned something about his father being in charge of the investigation.'

'I know this might seem ridiculous but you said Simon Tench didn't have any enemies. Are you absolutely sure about that? Could there be someone he'd annoyed . . . someone who'd threatened him?'

The vet shook his head. 'There are times in our profession when farmers lose valuable animals and put the blame on us.'

Rachel nodded. As a farmer's daughter she knew that sort of thing happened on occasions when livelihoods were threatened and emotions ran high.

'But I'm not aware of Simon being involved in anything like that.'

'I understand he lost a valuable foal on the day he died.'

'Yes. I'm afraid these things happen. It's a cause of great regret of course but . . .' He shrugged. 'In this case I believe the owner took it philosophically – realised there's nothing Simon could have done.'

Rachel had heard this story before. The consensus of opinion seemed to be that the unhappy horse owner had nothing to do with Tench's death. But it would still have to be checked out. If the owner turned out to have borne a grudge against Charles Marrick as well for some reason, he or she would move rapidly up the list of suspects. But something told Rachel that things wouldn't be quite that simple.

'There was the burglary, of course. Simon was out on a night call and he came back here to the surgery for some supplies. He disturbed some little thug in a hoodie breaking in to nick ketamine – we use it as a tranquilliser for larger animals. Simon saw the light was on and came to investigate – kid pushed past him. Got away with the ketamine. That's all there was to it really. We did report it of course.'

Rachel's heart began to beat a little faster. There was a possibility – albeit a small one – that the kid in the hoodie was Carl Pinney. And if he was back in the frame, the DCI would be delighted.

She was about to thank the vet and leave when Wicks suddenly raised his hand as though he had remembered something. 'There was one incident not long ago. I almost forgot because the person involved doesn't use our practice any more. There's a smallholder near Neston ... city boy trying to play at farmers. You know the type.'

Rachel nodded. 'What happened?'

We had a call from this man. Barty Carter his name is. He made his pile in London – something in the city – and decided he'd try the country life. He thought it was all Barbours, green wellies and Range Rovers ... had no idea about real farming. He planned to keep pigs and develop his own range of designer sausages and luxury black puddings – well that's how he described them.'

'And?'

'When one of the pigs took ill he called Simon out. And Simon told him in no uncertain terms that he wasn't looking after his stock properly – basically because he hadn't a clue how to deal with animals rather than malice aforethought. Simon gave him a good telling off and threatened to report him to the authorities if he didn't get his act together. Carter wasn't pleased. Ordered Simon off his smallholding with a shotgun and never used this practice again.' He suddenly looked worried. 'I've been a bit concerned about those pigs actually. I was wondering if I should go up there ... if it's an animal welfare issue.'

'I could pop up there to have a word,' said Rachel. 'Call you in if necessary.'

After promising to arrange the visit, Rachel interviewed Simon's remaining colleagues. They all sang the same tune. Simon Tench was wonderful. Nobody would want to harm him.

But on the way out to the car, she called the police station on her mobile requesting a check on Barty Carter. And somehow she wasn't surprised when the reply came back and she discovered that Carter had form.

Trish Walton was only too glad to get away from Foxglove House and Annette Marrick's self-pitying complaints. On her return to the police station, she couldn't stop thinking about Petronella's revelation. Marrick's stepdaughter hadn't really been considered as a serious suspect and, as far as she knew, she had no connection with Simon Tench. But, on the other hand, her alibis for both murders were shaky and if you opened enough cupboards, all kinds of skeletons were likely to tumble out. And Charlie Marrick had raped her, which was motive enough in Trish's book for that particular murder.

Steve's vindication was the talk of the CID office. The consensus of opinion was that it was a triumph for common sense against the sort of villain who can mete out brutality to his victims but can't take even the lightest tap when he's on the receiving end. Police one, villains and their briefs nil. An honourable win.

DCI Heffernan promised to break the happy news to Steve and tell him that he was to report for work first thing tomorrow. They needed all the manpower they could get.

Heffernan seemed to be in an unexpectedly good mood, considering he had two unsolved murders and an unidentified skeleton on his hands. He told Trish to knock off early at half four. She'd had a tough few days nursemaiding the Marrick ménage, he said before telling her to go off and enjoy herself. Trish hadn't turned down his offer. She was glad to get away from the pressure of the incident room. And besides, she'd seen a pair of particularly desirable shoes in a Morbay shop a week or so ago and she was wondering whether they were still there.

She drove out to Morbay and, when she'd visited the shoe shop and decided that the shoes were too uncomfortable and far too expensive, she returned to her car and sat there for a while, thinking. She was within walking distance of Steve's flat. He would be returning to work first thing the next morning so maybe she should pay him a call and bring him up to speed on the case. After all they had been close once and, even though Rachel Tracey, her housemate, kept telling her she was well rid of him, there was still a slight pull there, a faint attraction normally suppressed, which floated to the surface and bobbed there occasionally.

Trish climbed out of her car and walked down the busy streets to Steve's flat. But as she arrived at the front door, she experienced a sudden flurry of panic. What if he wasn't in? What if he took her visit the wrong way? Interpreted it as a come-on?

She stood on the doorstep, shifting from foot to foot, in two minds whether to leave there and then and forget the whole thing. She was only there on impulse after all. But then Steve was a fellow officer and he had been falsely accused. She was giving him the support of a colleague and making certain he had the necessary information to do his job properly. Nothing more.

When Steve answered the door, he looked dishevelled and rather sheepish. He grinned at her nervously, almost as if he had something to hide. After a few seconds he stood aside to let her in and, as she entered, Joanne emerged from the kitchen and gave her a shy smile. Trish tried to smile back but she suspected the result was more of a snarl. It looked as if Steve had found plenty to do in his period of enforced idleness, Trish thought, her inner bitch rising to the surface for a split second.

Trish cleared her throat. It was probably best to stick to the subject of work. 'I presume the boss has been in touch about you coming back tomorrow?'

Steve looked puzzled and shook his head.

'He said he was going to call you tonight. I'm surprised he hasn't done it already . . . God knows we could do with an extra pair of hands. It's good news. You're in the clear. Pinney threw his dinner round his cell and slipped on the wet floor after the mess had been cleaned up. His story's been shot to pieces.' She tried to inject some excitement into her voice but Steve wasn't looking impressed.

He put his arm round Joanne, who stood rather stiffly beside him. 'I'd feel better if they'd believed my version in the first place over that little toe-rag's lies. Why is it they always have to believe these . . . ?'

'That's just the way it is, Steve – you know that as well as I do. They've got to investigate any complaints against the police. Sometimes it's not fair but . . .'

'It stinks,' Joanne piped up, folding her arms defensively.

Trish looked at her. 'Yeah. You're right. It does stink.' She turned back to Steve. 'I don't know if you want me to bring you up to date on the case.'

Joanne squeezed his arm, whispered something in his ear, then disappeared back into the kitchen. Trish waited until she was out of sight before she continued. 'A lot's happened since you . . . You know this vet's been murdered – same MO. But, unlike Charles Marrick, he didn't have an enemy in the world.'

'Random attacks then?'

Trish shrugged. 'The boss doesn't think so. Charles Marrick was a nasty piece of work. He raped Petronella Blackwell . . . his wife's daughter. And he swindled that chef, Fabrice Colbert . . . who's not French but that's another story. There must have been people queuing up to put the knife in. But this vet, Simon Tench, was just the opposite – everyone liked him.'

Joanne appeared again and resumed her place at Steve's side.

'Maybe he was leading a double life. Maybe he had a grubby little secret,' Steve said with a confident swagger, probably calculated to impress the new girlfriend. 'The boss wants me back tomorrow then?'

'That's what he said. I expect he'll be in touch.' Trish glanced at Joanne who appeared to be listening intently. 'By the way, how's your dad?'

Steve's expression gave nothing away. 'He's okay.'

She hesitated before saying, 'Probably see you tomorrow then,' and turning to go, uncomfortably aware that she'd said too much when Joanne was within earshot. But it was done now.

'Probably,' was Steve's cool reply just as the phone on the wall began to ring.

'That might be the boss now,' she said.

Steve, looking unimpressed, moved to pick up the receiver.

Gerry Heffernan had just telephoned Steve Carstairs, to tell him to be at his desk first thing the next morning. He'd delayed making the call, saying he wanted to make Steve sweat for as long as possible. Wesley, however, doubted if this tactic would do any good. Steve, as far as he could tell, was as thick skinned as your average elephant and any attempt at subtlety would be wasted on him.

As he finished his call, Gerry sensed that the news hadn't come as a surprise to Steve. But then he'd always been cocky and over-confident. Perhaps that's why Gerry always had to fight the urge to slap him down.

When Wesley wandered into his cluttered inner sanctum, he looked up and smiled. 'Come in, Wes, sit yourself down. Let's go over what we've got, shall we?'

Wesley said down with a sigh. They seemed to have a lot – especially about Charles Marrick – but, as yet, nothing seemed to make much sense.

'I really can't see any link between Simon Tench and Marrick,' Wesley began. 'Do you think Tench's could be a copycat killing? If one of our local nutters discovered the details of Marrick's death and . . .'

'We've not released the details. It's hardly public knowledge. And why target Tench?'

'Some people don't need a reason.'

'Tench must have let his killer in. Same with Marrick. It was someone they trusted.'

'Maybe.' Wesley shuffled his feet, at a loss for something else to say.

'We're just waiting for Tench's toxicology report from Colin. By the looks of it he didn't put up a fight, exactly the same as Marrick. If he was given hemlock to paralyse him it means that whoever's doing this has it all planned out carefully.'

But the DCI's thoughts were interrupted by a perfunctory knock on the door. When the door burst open DC Paul Johnson was standing there, his eyes bright with untold news. Paul was a tall, lanky young man, fond of athletics, and he almost bounded towards Heffernan's desk.

'Sir, I've just had a call from Cheshire police.'

Heffernan leaned forward. 'And?'

'I did a check like DI Peterson asked me, to see if there had been any similar deaths anywhere else in the country and there was a case in Chester a few weeks ago . . . bloke with neck wounds in a flat above a shop. Traces of hemlock found in the body. The coroner gave a verdict of suicide but . . .'

Wesley and Heffernan looked at each other.

'I called them and asked them to send the reports and photographs.'

'Good,' said Wesley. 'Are they still satisfied with the suicide verdict or . . . ?'

'They were but since they've been alerted to our two murders, they're looking at the case again. They're e-mailing me the details.'

Wesley thanked Paul. He'd done well. He looked at his watch. It was six thirty already but he didn't want to make for home until they'd seen what Cheshire were about to send. It might be nothing to do with their case, of course. Just a coincidence. But Wesley had an uncomfortable feeling that they were about to learn something important.

And half an hour later when Paul brought them the e-mail from Cheshire police headquarters in Chester, Wesley knew that their case had just become more complex.

It looked as though their killer had struck before.

CHAPTER 8

The writer rose early that morning and switched on the computer. It was time to continue the tale. It helped so much to put it all into words. That way, things made more sense.

There was corruption in the Abbey of Veland as there is in every place human beings gather together. What is it about our species that makes it fall prey to wickedness?

I think Brother William was a pure young man, an innocent. He didn't expect to encounter evil in the abbey that should have been his refuge from the world. The corruption must have begun in a small way. A touch here and a look there. But for some the lure of sin is too tempting to resist.

What happened to Brother William wasn't his fault. But all victims blame themselves. I should know that more than anyone.

Perhaps it would be wise to strike the last sentence out. It gave too much away. Another day or so and the letter would be finished. Another move in the blood game.

Gerry Heffernan had found it hard to get to sleep and when he did finally drop off, he'd been awoken by Sam leaving the house – an early morning call to a calving just outside Whiteley. Eventually he decided to cut his losses and get up, creeping around to avoid waking Rosie who'd rolled in late the night before.

For the past few days he'd been too busy to see Joyce and he was missing her company and her down-to-earth common sense. They'd been seeing each other for almost a year now but Rosie still didn't know of her existence and he saw no reason to upset the delicate balance of household relations by telling her. It was Gerry's secret and he told himself that he was just waiting for the right moment to reveal it – a moment which never seemed to arrive. Rosie had been close to her late mother, Kathy and he didn't want to risk upsetting her. Sam, however, knew all about his dad's lady friend and wished him luck. But then Sam had always been easy-going and pragmatic. A chip off the old block.

He arrived at the police station early to find the details of the Chester case waiting for him on his desk, in the small space in the centre that he left clear for anything he considered to be urgent. He'd glanced at them the previous night, just to get the gist of what was what, but now he intended to examine them in detail – to see if there was indeed a link to the two murders that had happened on his patch.

As soon as he picked up the papers, his office door opened and Wesley Peterson stepped into the room, looking annoyingly awake for first thing in the morning.

'You read it yet?' Wesley asked eagerly.

'Just about to, Wes. Come in, will you. Anything new?'

Wesley shook his head. Then he hesitated for a few moments. 'Steve's due back this morning,' he said, his expression giving nothing away.

Heffernan raised his eyebrows.

'At least it's another pair of hands. I've just heard through the office grapevine that Trish paid him a visit last night – gave him the good news.'

'Did she indeed? I wanted to prolong the agony so I didn't ring him till late. He never let on that Trish had already told him.' He rolled his eyes. 'I would have thought she'd have more sense.'

'Apparently he's got himself a new girlfriend – someone who works with his dad – so if Trish has any hopes in that direction . . .'

'You seem to know all the gossip, Wes.'

'We aim to please.' He sat down on the chair by the DCI's desk, collecting his thoughts. 'I had a quick read through the stuff from Cheshire before I went home last night.'

'And?'

'Sounds identical to our murders but the local force interpreted it as suicide. Victim tried to poison himself then, when that wasn't working fast enough, he stabbed himself a couple of times in the neck – struck lucky with the jugular vein. There was no sign of a break-in or a disturbance and the knife was on the floor as though the victim had dropped it.'

'Unlike our two cases. Wonder why the killer took the knives away when Marrick and Tench were killed.'

Wesley shrugged. 'The weapon that killed Simon Tench hasn't turned up yet. I've got uniform searching for it but it's a question of where to start. If Carl Pinney was telling the truth and the first one ended up in a carrier bag on the Winterham Estate, the second could be anywhere.' Wesley paused. 'Look, Gerry, I've been thinking. What do the victims have in common – Marrick, Tench and this new one up in Chester?'

'Dunno. What?'

'Well, they're all male. And they're all exactly the same age. Thirty-one.'

Gerry Heffernan scratched his head. Why hadn't he noticed something so obvious? But, as far as he knew, nobody had ever been murdered for being a certain age before. There must be more to it than that. 'What are you saying, Wes?'

'We need to know more about their backgrounds. Perhaps

we should visit Foxglove House and Tench's cottage and have a look through their things.'

'I was thinking of a trip to Chester, Wes. I'd like to talk to the team who dealt with the case.'

'And got it all wrong,' Wesley pointed out helpfully. 'If they put it down to suicide, they probably weren't paying much attention.'

'Well you can't blame them – it certainly looked that way. Anyway, I've got a cousin who's a DS at Chester police headquarters. I'm thinking of giving him a ring and arranging a visit. Nice place, Chester.'

Wesley looked at his boss. He was so transparent. He fancied a trip up north. He'd probably fit in a visit to Liverpool while he was at it for a family reunion. But on the other hand, they did need to have a closer look at the death of Christopher Grisham, the man whose bloody death in a Chester flat had been dismissed as suicide.

'Has your mate Neil had any more of those funny letters?'

'Not that I know of.'

'You don't think they can have anything to do with this?'

'It seems a bit strange that someone starts killing people by bleeding them to death then Neil starts getting letters about monks being bled. Coincidences happen but . . .'

'Anything from the lab?'

Wesley shook his head. 'I sent the second letter there but they didn't come up with anything useful.'

There was a knock on the door and Rachel bustled in, a sheet of paper in her hand. She waved it triumphantly at Gerry Heffernan. 'I talked to Peter Wicks at the vet's and he told me about a man who threatened Simon Tench. Smallholder called Barty Carter – city boy who fancies himself as a farmer.'

Wesley could hear the disapproval in her voice.

'This Carter didn't have a clue about looking after his livestock and when Tench pointed out the error of his ways, he was threatened with a shotgun. And Carter's got form.

Affray outside a London nightclub when he was eighteen. He's a violent man.'

Wesley caught Heffernan's eye.

'Okay, Rach,' the DCI said patiently. 'You check him out. But don't go alone, eh. You can take Steve . . . keep him out of mischief.'

Rachel disappeared back into the organised chaos of the CID office and Heffernan stood up. 'You wanted to have a look through Marrick's things . . . see if we can find any sort of link with Tench and this Grisham up in Chester.'

'Yes. And we can visit Tench's place as well. There must be some connection. Where are people of the same age thrown together. School? University?'

'Your guess is as good as mine,' Heffernan replied, reaching for his coat.

The post came unusually early that morning and Neil saw the letter, squatting on his doormat like some malevolent toad. He recognised the envelope – same as the others. This was all he needed first thing in the morning with the drive down to Stow Barton ahead of him.

It was about time Wesley did something, he thought to himself. What was the use of having an old friend in the CID if he couldn't do you a favour from time to time? But with these murders, Wesley had been rather preoccupied. No use whatsoever.

He rinsed a smear of marmalade off his fingers and donned the pair of heavy rubber gloves he kept for clearing out the sink when it blocked, as it had a habit of doing. Then he picked the letter up awkwardly. The gloves were too thick but at least this way there'd be no fingerprints except the sender's . . . and all the post office employees who had handled it as it made its journey to his door. He suddenly felt a little silly and took off the gloves.

He slit the envelope open and extracted the letter inside

using the corner of a tea towel, spreading it out on the top of the sideboard as the kitchen table was covered in crumbs as usual.

He read it through twice. The sender seemed to be telling the story of a Brother William and this new, personal slant rather intrigued him. The mention of evil – of Satan dwelling in the Abbey of Veland – seemed rather melodramatic. But then that was probably Lenny's style – if he was indeed the author of the letters. Neil told himself that he shouldn't jump to hasty conclusions.

The writer was treating it as a game. The blood game. But it takes two to play a game and Neil wasn't going to participate. Suddenly he felt less afraid. All he had to do was ignore his tormentor and he'd get sick of waiting for a response. The writer was a nutter. Nothing more.

He tried to forget about the letter as he drove to the dig. He wouldn't have to think about it again until it was time to go home, he told himself. He would put it from his mind and give it to Wesley like the others – get it off his hands.

Diane had arrived at the dig before him and he found her in the outbuilding that served as their site office. She greeted him with a shy smile and the news that the results had come back from the lab in Exeter. The soil taken from the pit contained traces of blood. However, further analysis was needed to tell whether that blood was human or animal. And the slim, corroded object had been x-rayed and found to be some sort of lancet. Another piece in the jigsaw of evidence that was now starting to form a clear picture.

He was about to make for the trenches when Diane touched his arm. 'Lenny wants a word.'

'That's all I need.'

'He's paid to come on this dig, Neil,' she said. 'He has as much right to your attention as anyone else. Mind you . . .'

Diane didn't have a chance to finish her sentence. There was a knock on the outbuilding door and a well-bred female voice called out a cheerful hello. Diane hurried back to her trench, passing Annabel on her way out.

Annabel bustled in, a folder under her arm and a smile on her face. She was usually closeted in the archives at Exeter during her working day and she was always glad of a trip out.

'News,' she announced. 'I've gone through all the old documents we've got concerning the Abbey of Veland and I've found a few new references to this site.' She placed the folder on Neil's makeshift desk and began to take out a sheaf of papers. 'There are two mentions of a grange at Stow Barton, latterly used as a seyney house – "an honest and convenient place for the letting of blood."'

Neil grinned, resisting the urge to punch the air in triumph. This confirmed it once and for all. But how had the author of his anonymous letters found out about the function of Stow Barton before he did. Someone must have been researching the site . . . doing their homework.

'Just one thing, Annabel. These documents you found . . . has anyone else been looking at them recently?'

Annabel shook her head. 'Not that I know of. But I can ask if you want. Why?'

'No, that's okay,' he answered lightly. 'Thanks a lot for your efforts. Fancy a guided tour round the site?'

Annabel looked keen. Anything to put off the drive back to Exeter.

'By the way, you haven't come across any reference to a Brother William in any of your documents, have you?'

'Not yet,' Annabel answered. 'But there's plenty of stuff I haven't had a chance to examine yet. And I want to dig out the Comperta – the reports made by Henry VIII's commissioners when they visited Veland Abbey prior to closing it down.'

'Any particular reason?'

'They were under orders to dig out any dirt there was about the monks' private lives.' She grinned. 'And the

Comperta often makes for interesting reading. You get all the stuff about pregnant nuns, monks indulging in sodomy and what they euphemistically called "solitary sin". And then there were the abbesses who were allegedly having it off with the abbot of a nearby house. All the scandal. Not that the commissioners were unbiased, of course. They were paid to find dirt so Henry could feel all self-righteous about destroying the corrupt monastic houses. Who can blame the commissioners if they made half of it up and laid it on with a trowel? It was what their political masters wanted to hear.'

They were outside now and Neil was leading the way to the pit. Or, in the light of the lab's findings, perhaps he should start thinking of it as the blood pit. He walked by Annabel's side, making for the trench that confirmed all her findings – something which, as an archaeologist, he found rather thrilling, physical and written evidence coming together in perfect harmony. Suddenly Annabel touched his arm. 'Who's that?' she whispered.

'One of the trainees. Name of Lenny. Why?'

'I'm sure I've seen him somewhere before.'

Neil ushered her onwards, out of Lenny's sight line. If Annabel had seen him before, it was possible he'd been at the archives. Finding out about monastic blood-letting. Just as his anonymous letter writer had done.

Annette Marrick didn't look at all pleased to see Wesley Peterson and Gerry Heffernan on her doorstep. She'd told the police everything she knew and it was about time she and Petronella were left alone.

Wesley was surprised that Petronella hadn't returned to Bath. She had a job there and, presumably, friends. And he'd sensed little empathy between Petronella and the biological mother who'd abandoned her at birth. But perhaps the fact that Charles Marrick had abused them both had created some kind of bond between them.

Annette led them past the closed living room door into the huge dining kitchen where Petronella was watching a property programme on the giant TV screen that almost dominated one wall of the room. The young woman looked up as they entered and gave Wesley a shy half smile. He thought she looked needy, vulnerable and thinner than she'd done when he'd first seen her.

'I'm having the decorators in to deal with the lounge,' Annette said unexpectedly. 'I just want to get everything straight. To get rid of . . .'

'Of course . . . I understand,' Wesley said quickly. He thought of the room next door as he'd last seen it, wondering whether the blood would begin to seep through the paint at any stage and keep returning like the famous bloodstain at Holyrood House in Edinburgh which marked the spot where David Rizzio died in the arms of Mary Queen of Scots. The thought made him shudder. But, he told himself, the decorators would be able to seal the stains in so that couldn't happen. Marrick's blood wouldn't return to haunt the living.

He caught Petronella's eye and she looked away. It was hard to judge what she was thinking.

Heffernan looked at Annette and came straight to the point. 'Look, love, sorry to bother you and all that, but we need to have a look through your husband's things. Okay?'

Annette could hardly say no. Instead she gave a vague wave of her right arm and told him to help himself.

'Where do we start?' asked Wesley as they made their way upstairs.

Gerry Heffernan didn't answer. He made straight for the smallest of Foxglove House's five bedrooms – the one that Charles Marrick had used as a study cum office. It had been searched already of course. But then the search had been for clues to a motive for Charles's murder. Now they were looking for his past. Something – anything – that would link him to Simon Tench and Christopher Grisham.

But if Charles Marrick had kept anything relating to his distant past, he hadn't kept it here. There was, however, a lot of material relating to his business that might be of some interest to the fraud squad. They left everything as they found it and shut the door behind them.

Annette was waiting for them in the hall when they came down the stairs. 'Find anything?' she said. She sounded casual but Wesley could detect a note of nervousness in her voice.

'Where would Charles have been likely to keep any mementoes of his school or university days?' Wesley asked.

'He wouldn't,' Annette said quickly. 'Charlie hadn't a sentimental bone in his body. He never talked about the past.'

'Did he go to school round here?'

'I think so but I couldn't tell you where. Like I said, he never talked about it.'

'University?'

'Do me a favour. Charlie was a businessman. Wheeler dealer. He wouldn't have wasted his time at university.'

Wesley – who had enjoyed three years studying archaeology at Exeter University and had emerged from the shades of academe with a first class honours degree – looked suitably chastened.

'Thanks, love. We'll be in touch,' said Gerry Heffernan, making it sound more of a threat than a promise.

'Where to now?' Heffernan asked as he climbed into the passenger seat of Wesley's car.

'I think we might have more luck at Simon Tench's place,' Wesley replied as he started the engine.

Rachel hadn't heard of Barty Carter through the farming community's normally efficient grapevine. He probably kept himself to himself, rather than co-operating with his farming neighbours as her parents did. He was a city boy, an outsider, which meant he'd have been treated with suspicion anyway.

She decided to do the driving. She'd never really trusted

Steve Carstairs behind the wheel – or anywhere else come to that. He drove like he lived – too fast and without much thought to the consequences of his actions.

'So where are we off to?' he asked as he sprawled in the passenger seat, taking up every available inch of space.

'Smallholding. Bloke called Barty Carter who's got form for affray. He had a row with our second victim, Simon Tench. About the only enemy Simon had in the world, that anyone knows of.'

Steve was silent for a few moments. Then he said 'Sometimes it's your friends you have to worry about more.'

Rachel glanced at him, surprised. 'That's very philosophical of you, Steve. What do you mean by that?'

Steve's face reddened. He wasn't sure what he'd meant. It had just sounded good.

'I hear there's a new woman in your life.'

There was a long silence. Then Steve cleared his throat. 'She's called Joanne – works with my dad. But it's early days.'

'How are you getting on with your dad?' she asked, taking advantage of this new openness.

'Okay.'

Rachel suspected that that was all the information she was going to get out of him for the moment so she concentrated on her driving. But when her mobile rang, she brought the car to a halt in a lay-by. She said hello then fell silent for a while before saying 'Who is that?' before the caller hung up.

'Well?' said Steve, sensing excitement.

Rachel turned to him. 'That was a woman – wouldn't give her name. She said if I wanted to know who Charlie Marrick was with on the day he died, I should ask Celia Dawn.'

'You want to do it now?'

'Better get this visit to Carter out of the way first.'

They found Barty Carter's smallholding down a narrow

lane off the main road to Neston. The metal gate was coming away from its hinges and a flaking sign gave the name of the property as Windy Edge and warned trespassers to keep out.

Even though Rachel had lived on a farm for most of her life, she had never smelled anything like the stench that greeted them as they got out of the car.

Rachel wrinkled her nose. 'There's no excuse for a smell like that – not if the stock's looked after properly.'

'I'll take your word for it,' Steve answered. He could hear the grunting coming from a rickety wooden shed to their left. Ahead of them stood the house. Filthy windows, flaking paintwork. No mod cons. The place was a dump.

'Wonder where he is.' Rachel began to walk towards the pig shed, her hand to her nose. The grunting of the animals sounded half-hearted and miserable, as though the effort was too much for them. She felt angry. And her anger increased as she pushed the shed door open.

The place was covered in slurry, as though it hadn't been mucked out for a few days. The creatures looked dispirited on their sparse, filthy straw. One thin animal, alone in a corner pen, lay on the ground, a hopeless look in its little eyes. It looked ill. Or perhaps it had just lost interest in life.

'We should call the RSPCA,' Rachel announced, her eyes alight with righteous fury. 'This isn't on.'

Steve said nothing. He had covered his face with his sleeve against the stench.

'Let's get out of here,' Rachel said.

Steve followed her out into what passed for fresh air. But as soon as they stepped outside, they saw a tall, slim figure standing in front of them, dressed in an ancient waxed jacket and tweed cap, legs slightly bent like a cowboy preparing for a shootout in front of the saloon. He was carrying a shotgun. And it was pointed straight at Steve Carstairs's head.

Rachel's heart missed a beat. But she took a deep breath

and held up her warrant card like a magic shield. 'Police. DS Tracey and DC Carstairs, Tradmouth CID. If I were you, I'd put that thing down.'

The man hesitated for a few moments, his eyes nervous, flicking from one to the other, assessing the opposition.

'You heard what I said,' Rachel said, trying to keep the terror she felt out of her voice. She lowered her left hand slowly and felt in her jacket pocket for her mobile phone. If she called out the Armed Response Unit they'd be there within fifteen minutes. But that would probably be too late.

It seemed like a long time before the shotgun was lowered slowly. 'What do you want?' the man called out. He was surprisingly well spoken, posh even. Somehow Rachel had expected a voice more fitting to his thuggish behaviour. But then thuggishness often didn't confine itself to the lower social classes.

'Are you Barty Carter?'

The answer was a curt nod.

'We'd like a word with you about Simon Tench. He was a vet. He treated your stock.'

'What about him?'

Rachel glanced at Steve who seemed to have frozen with fear. But then most people would if they found themselves on the wrong end of a shotgun barrel. 'Can we talk inside?'

Barty Carter hesitated again then he broke the shotgun barrel over his forearm, much to Rachel's relief. But she could see the pair of cartridges inside. The threat hadn't been an empty one. He began to walk towards the house and they followed him, Steve lagging behind, still shaken.

The house had seen better days. It was shabby and dirty and lacked a woman's touch. Old newspapers littered the floor and the scent of pig slurry hung in the air like a fog, probably brought indoors on the green wellingtons Carter was still wearing as he propped the shotgun up in the corner of the room before sitting down at a table, its surface invisible beneath layers of papers and empty lager tins.

Rachel picked up the shotgun, unloaded it expertly and put the cartridges in her pocket before looking around for somewhere to sit. But every available surface was covered in the detritus of Carter's existence so she decided to stand.

'Tell me about the row you had with Simon Tench.'

Carter stared at his hands. 'Nothing much to tell. It was a bad time for me. Wife had just left. She couldn't stand the country . . . wanted to get back to London. Me, stubborn bugger that I am, was determined to stick it out.'

Rachel suddenly saw that Barty Carter was out of his depth. He had had a dream of rural life – the unrealistic dream that lured so many in. And the dream had backfired, leaving him a pathetic shell of a man who lashed out at anyone or anything he perceived to be a threat. She almost felt sorry for him.

'My family have farmed for generations and it's a tough life even if you've grown up with it. Ever thought of cutting your losses and selling this place?'

He looked up at her, stunned. 'I don't know. I . . . Look what's this all about?'

'Simon Tench was found murdered on Sunday morning.'

Carter's mouth fell open. As far as Rachel could see, he was genuinely surprised. But some people were good actors.

'I'm surprised you haven't heard about it,' Steve had found his courage again now that the shotgun was out of Carter's reach. 'It's been on the TV news and the papers have been full of it,' he added with a hint of menace.

'I don't get the papers and the telly's broke,' Carter replied, a faraway look in his eyes. 'How was he murdered?' He glanced at the shotgun. 'Look, I never . . .'

'Tench was worried about your animals – he threatened to report you.'

Carter shifted in his seat, as though trying to summon up some anger. 'Bloody bureaucrats. Interfering . . .'

'He would have helped if you'd let him.'

'Look, I don't know anything about this murder. It's got nothing to do with me. You can take my gun . . . do tests. That'll prove it wasn't . . .'

'Where were you on Saturday night?'

'Saturday night I was in Neston. Went for a drink.'

'Just the one?' Steve said with heavy sarcasm.

Carter didn't reply.

'Which pub was it? And is there anyone who can confirm your story?' Rachel asked gently.

Carter shrugged his shoulders. 'I went to the Cat and Fiddle near the castle. Some of the regulars know me.'

Rachel knew the Cat and Fiddle – not Neston's most salubrious watering hole. If there were any questions to be asked in that particular establishment, she'd send someone else to do it.

'When did you last see Simon Tench?' she asked.

'Not since he came here that time.'

'And did he report you?'

'Some sort of inspector came round. I had to get rid of most of my stock. Just keep a few pigs now. I used to keep more . . . and hens. Used to make my own black puddings – sausages too.'

'But all that stopped.'

'Had to, didn't it? I just send the odd pig to the abattoir now. Nothing like it used to be.'

Rachel looked him in the eye. 'Black puddings. You need lots of blood for black puddings, don't you?'

'Yeah. But I'm not allowed to make anything here any more. Hygiene regulations. Bloody bureaucrats. My pigs are okay. Nothing wrong with them.'

'Good company, pigs. What is it they say? Dogs look up to you, cats look down on you but pigs are equal.'

For the first time Rachel saw Barty Carter smile. 'Look, I'm sorry that vet's dead. I admit I lost my temper with him but I can seen now that he was only doing his job.' He looked her in the eye. 'That's my trouble, Detective Sergeant. I lose my temper from time to time. It's just since my wife left. I . . .'

Rachel looked him in the eye. 'If you want my advice, I'd sell up. Cut your losses. In the meantime, muck out those pigs. Hose the whole shed down and give them fresh straw. There was one in there I was worried about so call the vet out if necessary – it's better than losing all your stock. And if you don't, I'll report you to the RSPCA. Okay?'

Carter nodded, resigned. 'I promise. I'll get 'em sorted. It's just that . . .'

'No excuses. Just do it. I'll be back to check. And I've got another bit of advice for you, when we come calling again – or anyone else come to that – leave your shotgun locked safely in its cabinet.'

'You were a bit soft of him,' said Steve as they got into the car.

Rachel sighed. 'I saw farming finish a lot of strong men in the foot and mouth outbreak – men who turned their shotguns on themselves. Carter thought he could play at it . . . but he was playing with fire and he got burned. I blame all these TV programmes. Start a new life in the country – run a farm or a restaurant or a hotel and get away from it all. Crap. It's tougher than the city life they leave behind. And more isolated. My parents have nothing but contempt for the likes of Carter but . . .'

'You feel sorry for him?' Steve allowed himself a sly grin. 'Never thought I'd see you turn soft, Sarge. But then he's not bad looking, is he?' he said before snuggling down in the passenger seat, enjoying the view of the rolling landscape as they sped back to Tradmouth.

★

Wesley Peterson wanted to make a search of Simon Tench's home, just to see if he'd kept any souvenirs of his school or university days. Any hint as to how he might have come into contact with Charles Marrick or Christopher Grisham. He'd studied their details and concluded that the three victims would all have been in the same academic year at whatever educational establishment or establishments they attended. Surely it couldn't be a coincidence.

If his instincts served him right, Simon Tench's academic career – unlike Charles Marrick's – would be an open book. And if they could find a link with Christopher Grisham as well, they would – in Wesley's opinion – be well on the way to catching their killer. He didn't put these optimistic thoughts into words of course. But he felt quietly confident.

He left his desk and walked to Gerry Heffernan's office, longing to share his thoughts. But as soon as he pushed the DCI's office door open, the telephone on the cluttered desk began to ring.

He stood there while Heffernan held a short conversation. From the greeting, he knew it was Colin Bowman on the other end of the line. This was news. As soon as Heffernan put the phone down, he signalled to Wesley to sit himself down.

'That was Colin. He's had the toxicology report on Simon Tench. It was hemlock again.'

Wesley flopped down in the visitor's chair. The news didn't surprise him. The scene of Tench's death was far too similar to that of Charles Marrick for the deaths to be unconnected. And the photographs of Christopher Grisham's corpse e-mailed down by Cheshire police, suggested that his murder too, had been committed by the same perpetrator. It seemed that the killer had struck in Chester and had then travelled down to Devon to continue his gruesome work. He said as much to Heffernan.

'Or our killer lives here and he popped up north for a couple of days,' the DCI replied, shooting Wesley's theory out of the water. But Wesley had to acknowledge that he could be right. The killer was more likely to be based in Devon and have made a special excursion to rid the world of Christopher Grisham.

'Did Colin mention our skeleton?' Wesley asked. Normally the discovery of an unidentified skeleton would have been a priority but the murders seem to have pushed it into the background. However, it still intrigued Wesley. It didn't belong to anyone who'd been reported missing in the appropriate period so perhaps it was some vagrant who'd fallen asleep in the copse of trees and never woken up. Perhaps they'd never know.

'He said there was nothing to indicate the cause of death but he was sending off some samples to see if they could extract some DNA. He was going on about all this scientific stuff but I couldn't make head nor tail of what he was saying.'

Wesley smiled. The boss rarely concerned himself with technical matters. 'I think it's time we had a search through Simon Tench's things.'

'Mmm. Apparently the wife's staying in a hotel with her parents.'

'That's good. Staying at the scene of the crime doesn't seem to bother Annette Marrick but Emma Tench . . .'

'Is a different kettle of fish. Nice girl. Shame. Must be awful for her.'

'So we're not treating her as a suspect?'

Heffernan looked up. 'Think we should?'

Wesley shook his head. 'No. Not really. And besides, she's a nurse. Nurses and doctors have more efficient ways of disposing of their enemies than hemlock and a knife.'

Heffernan frowned. 'It's almost as if it's some sort of ritual.'

'I was thinking that myself. But why? What's behind it?'

Heffernan didn't answer. He stood up and reached for his jacket. 'Let's go and have a look at Tench's cottage, shall we?'

Wesley followed him out, hanging behind as the boss did the rounds of the desks in the CID office, checking on how the troops were progressing. Wesley found himself staring at the huge notice board that covered the far wall. The crime scene photographs of the two Devon victims were up there in pride of place and they had just been joined by the e-mailed image of Christopher Grisham, the Chester victim. Wesley looked from one to the other. There was no way that Grisham was killed by a different person. The scene was too similar. The slumped body; the staring, horrified eyes; the blood pouring from the two neat wounds on the neck, almost like something from a vampire movie.

Half an hour later they arrived at Simon Tench's cottage and the constable on duty let them in. They entered gingerly, looking around. The bloodstains still stood out on the pale wood floor and most surfaces in the room had been dusted with fingerprint powder, giving the place a look of neglect.

'Where shall we start?' Wesley asked.

'Where do you keep all your old school photos?'

Wesley made for the sideboard under the window. He squatted down to open one of the three cupboards and when he found it full of crockery, he tried the next. This time he struck lucky. Beneath a tower of photograph albums was a pile of school photographs in cardboard frames. Half were Emma's but it was Simon's that interested Wesley. He pulled one out triumphantly and studied it. The name of the school had been printed thoughtfully in gold letters beneath the photograph of twenty-five adolescent boys – probably, Wesley guessed, in the sixth form – wearing striped ties and smart blazers.

'He went to St Peter's School in Morbay,' Wesley announced, turning the picture over. 'There are names on the back but I can't see Charles Marrick's or Christopher Grisham's.'

'Bang goes that theory then. They didn't know each other from school. Or university because Marrick didn't go.'

'Perhaps when we find out more about Christopher Grisham . . .'

'We'll be just as confused. Do you think this could be a psychopath, Wes? A random killer who just stalks his victims and . . . ?'

Wesley shook his head. 'No. The victims trust the killer enough to let him in. There's no sign of a break-in and, somehow, they're persuaded to take hemlock.' He looked at his watch. There was just time to have a quick look through Simon's things and get back to Tradmouth. Although their search would be more for inspiration than for any concrete clue.

An hour later they returned to the CID office in low spirits.

But the message waiting for them on Gerry Heffernan's desk, raised the mood a little.

The computer had just come up with a match for the DNA extracted from the bones found in the woods. There was no name but somebody with that particular DNA profile was responsible for the rape of a schoolgirl in Luton.

It was a cold case that had just become red hot.

CHAPTER 9

'Police appeal for information about skeleton found in woodland.'

The writer stared at the words until they were a swimming mass of grey then pushed the newspaper to one side and began to type.

Brother William had been put to work in the scriptorum copying holy words on to vellum. This was work he loved. Scratching away on the vellum, exact, precise. In the scriptorum his only fear was that he might make a mistake with his lettering. But out of the shelter of the scriptorum, Brother William knew he was in danger. Danger not only to his body but to his soul.

You might wonder, Neil, how I came by the information, but I assure you it is there for anyone to discover if they possess the wit and the tenacity. How puzzled you are by the game. Perhaps you are not as worthy an opponent as I had hoped.

The writer stood up. Enough had been written for now. The rest needed some thought.

'I don't believe this.' Gerry Heffernan waved the local paper in the air in a distinctly threatening manner.

Wesley sat in the visitor's chair in the DCI's office,

watching his boss, his expression impassive. 'What does it say exactly?'

'Read it for yourself.' He thrust the paper into Wesley's hand.

Wesley began to read. 'Police are hunting the killer they are calling "the Spider".' He looked at Heffernan, unable to keep a smile from his lips. 'The Spider? Where do they get that from?'

'Keep reading.' Heffernan had begun to pace up and down the office. Always a bad sign.

'They are calling him the Spider because he administers a drug that paralyses his victims before he kills them.' Wesley raised his eyebrows. 'Well, they've got that bit right. But how did they know? That's something we've been keeping quiet.'

Heffernan shook his head. 'I've no idea. Maybe Fabrice Colbert – or do we call him Darren Collins? – put two and two together when we were asking about the quail.'

'I can't see it myself. Not many people would know about quail and hemlock surely.'

'He's a chef. Perhaps he does.'

'It could be anyone. Some mortuary attendant who's seen the toxicology reports.' He paused. His next suggestion was bound to raise the boss's blood pressure. 'Or it could be someone here.'

'It'd better not be.' He marched to his desk and picked up his phone. 'I'm getting on to Ray Davenport at the *Tradmouth Echo*.'

'Journalists aren't supposed to reveal their sources, Gerry.'

'If he wants to be first in line for our press releases, he better had. This isn't supposed to be in the public domain.' He took a deep breath and put the receiver down again. 'Perhaps I should wait till I've calmed down a bit.'

'Good idea, Gerry. We don't want to fall out with Ray, do we? I think a little tact is needed here.'

The DCI didn't argue. But he looked as if he'd cheerfully

give the leaker of the information a public flogging with his own hands.

'They're expecting us at Chester police headquarters this afternoon, Wes. You ready?'

Wesley nodded, thinking of his workload. Neil had telephoned last night just as he'd arrived home from work. He'd had another letter and he'd read it out to Wesley who'd copied the words down carefully. The content alarmed him, just as it had alarmed Neil. There was a threat – 'I could even make you bleed' – which particularly disturbed him, as did the obsession with blood and Satan. Whoever sent these letters – whoever was playing the blood game – was seriously weird . . . maybe even dangerous. Wesley said he'd send an officer round to the dig to pick the letter up. And he warned Neil to take care – to watch his back and be careful who he opened his door to.

'Maybe you should ask him to stop with you,' Heffernan suggested when he brought him up to date with the latest development.

Wesley considered the suggestion. 'I'll ask Pam. Her mother's coming to stay with her tonight while we're in Chester.' He grimaced. 'If she turns up.'

'As long as she's gone when you get back, eh.' For the first time that morning, his mouth turned upwards in a wicked grin. He knew Wesley's mother-in-law, Della, of old. He looked at his watch. 'If we set off about ten, we should make it to Chester by the middle of the afternoon, traffic jams permitting. I'm looking forward to seeing our Howard again.'

'Howard?'

'My cousin. The one who works at Chester HQ.'

From the expression on his face, Wesley guessed that he was regarding the family reunion with eager anticipation. It struck him for the first time that he didn't know that much about the DCI's family up in the north-west. Perhaps he'd discover more when they were up there.

'I hear that our Rach was threatened with a shotgun yesterday.'

Wesley looked up, surprised at the change of subject — and that the boss could be speaking so casually about such a serious matter. 'A shotgun. What . . . ?'

'She and Steve went to see this Barty Carter. The one who had a row with Simon Tench. He greeted them by pointing a shotgun at them. And it was loaded.'

'Did Rachel tell you this?'

'No. It was Steve. He wants to call the Armed Response Unit in and organise a raid.'

'That figures,' said Wesley. Steve was known to favour the more dramatic aspect of policing.

'Apparently our Rach was a bit of a heroine. Talked Carter round and rescued an unspecified number of pigs from a squalid existence into the bargain.' He grinned. 'I've spoken to her and she doesn't think Carter's our man, by the way. She reckons he's more sad than bad. However, I've got someone having a look at his firearms licence. Can't have him going and pointing a dangerous weapon at all and sundry, can we?'

Wesley nodded. He trusted Rachel's judgement. But they'd keep a discreet eye on Barty Carter. Just in case.

'Rach had a funny phone call yesterday.'

'What kind of funny?' Wesley wished his boss would be more specific.

'Some woman telling her to talk to Celia Dawn — that's one of the women Annette Marrick was with when her husband . . .'

'And has she seen her?'

'Not yet. She's going to try her today.'

The main thing that had been on Wesley's mind since he'd left work the previous evening hadn't been mentioned yet. And, in his opinion, it was high time it was brought up. 'Anything else come in on that DNA match? The skeleton in the woods?'

'Not yet but I've asked for more information. Luton are sending us the file apparently.' He didn't look as if he quite believed it. 'Of course they didn't have all this DNA testing in those days but recently they've been going over evidence in some cold cases – putting samples they'd kept into computers or whatever it is they do. That's how they found a match with our skeleton.'

'Have they got a name for us?'

Heffernan shook his head.

'So the man in the woods was a rapist.'

'Of schoolgirls. He raped a schoolgirl. Aged thirteen.' Heffernan, the father of a daughter, looked quite upset about it. 'Still, it looks like the bastard got what he deserved.'

'We still don't know how he died. Could have been natural causes.'

'Could have been. Let's work on that assumption, shall we, Wes? Case closed.'

'Suits me. Especially when we've got "the Spider" to deal with.' He grinned.

Heffernan muttered something unrepeatable under his breath.

'I'm sending Trish to have a word with the headmaster at St Peter's School today. See if he can shed any light on Simon Tench's background. I understand his parents are dead.'

'That's right. The mother died when he was in his teens and the father had a stroke a couple of years ago. Sad.'

'Very. I still think the fact that all the victims are the same age is significant. Perhaps they went to the same primary school. Or perhaps they all went to St Peter's and the other two were just away on the day of the photograph for some reason.'

'What about Charles Marrick's parents? Surely they've been contacted.'

'I've thought of that, Wes. It seems they divorced years ago. The mother married again and emigrated to Australia and the father died in a car accident.'

'Not a close family then.'

'Doesn't look that way. I've been told that the mother's coming back for the funeral.'

'She might be able to provide some more background for us. If she'll talk.' Wesley looked at his watch. 'I'll have a word with Trish then we'd better make a move. It's a long way to Chester.'

'It certainly is. But it looks like our killer made the journey.'

As Wesley left the office, he was suddenly struck by a fear that the Spider could be lying in wait, ready to claim more victims, if they didn't catch up with him fast.

Neil Watson reckoned he deserved a lunch break like everyone else. But what you deserve and what you get are sometimes two completely different things.

He'd been rather surprised when a uniformed police officer turned up and took the latest letter away on the request of DI Peterson. He'd also given a formal statement in the not-so-formal surroundings of the cow shed cum site office. He said nothing to his colleagues about the purpose of the policeman's visit – as far as everyone on the site was concerned, he'd reported some petty pilfering of equipment on another site he'd worked at. Somehow he didn't want to share the truth with all and sundry.

He hadn't been able to sleep the night before for thinking about the letters. They were starting to scare him. Someone was watching him. They knew his movements and where he lived.

He'd read about 'the Spider' in the *Tradmouth Echo*. No wonder Wesley had been elusive, he thought. There was a serial killer on the loose in the Tradmouth area – a killer who paralysed his victims before letting them bleed to death. This modus operandi reminded him of the letter writer's obsession with blood and bleeding and the possibility of a link nagged in his mind. Last night Wesley had warned him to be careful and not to open his door to strangers and, for the first time in his life, Neil was really afraid.

He saw Lenny approaching and his heart began to beat a little faster. He straightened himself up, preparing for the encounter.

'Dr Watson. I've a theory about that pit – the one Diane said contained traces of blood. You see the Aztecs used to . . .'

'Yes, Lenny, I know what the Aztecs did. But we're a very long way from Mexico and there's documentary evidence that this was the place the monks from Veland Abbey used for blood-letting. They thought it was good for their health. They would have had to dispose of the blood somehow and it's very probable that they used that pit.'

Lenny looked disappointed. 'The trouble is with the archaeological establishment is that they won't open their minds,' he said.

Neil gave him a businesslike smile. 'We just go on the available facts. How are you enjoying the dig?' It was a bold question but the only thing Neil could think of to say on the spur of the moment.

But Lenny didn't answer the question. 'If you listened to me, you'd learn the truth about what happened here. I feel this is a site of great evil, Dr Watson. Great evil.'

The last letter had spoken of evil. As Neil took a deep breath he felt his hands sweating. 'Look, Lenny, I've been getting some strange letters. You don't know anything about them, do you?'

Lenny stared at him for a few seconds before stalking away, weaving his way past the open trenches. As he watched Lenny's receding back, Neil didn't hear Diane approaching. He felt a gentle pressure on his arm and swung round.

'Diane, you gave me a shock.'

'Sorry. Trouble with Lenny?'

'You could say that.'

'I . . . I was wondering if you fancied a trip to Veland

Abbey. It's open to the public and I thought we could take the trainees. It'd help to put this site in context.'

It was an excellent idea. And one that Neil hadn't thought of. 'Sure. Great,' he said, pulling himself together. 'We can arrange it over the next few days. Just don't put me in a car with Lenny.' He came to a sudden decision. 'I've been getting some weird letters and I think Lenny might have sent them.'

Diane suddenly looked wary. 'Lenny? Why should he . . . ?'

'I don't know. He seems like a bit of a nutter, that's all.'

'Maybe you're right,' she said quickly. 'Look, I'd better get back to the trench.'

Neil watched her as she hurried away. She was really quite attractive.

Celia Dawn's sullen daughter opened the door to the little pink house. As soon as she opened her mouth to say that her mother wasn't there – she was on the *Daisy Lady* again – Rachel knew that she had made the earlier call. However, when Rachel challenged her, the girl denied all knowledge. But she wasn't a good liar.

Rachel found Celia on the deck of *Daisy Lady*, sitting in the same place, almost as if she hadn't moved since Rachel's last visit. She looked nervous as she invited Rachel aboard – like a woman with something to hide.

There was no point wasting time. Rachel came straight to the point and told her about her daughter's phone call, asking her bluntly whether she'd been telling the truth about her whereabouts on the day of Charles Marrick's murder.

'The little bitch,' were the woman's first words. 'She never misses a chance to make trouble for me.' She thought for a few moments, choosing her words carefully. 'She's got the wrong end of the stick. It was all quite innocent.'

'What was?' Rachel could see that Celia's face had turned red beneath her make-up. She had been found out and she wasn't pleased. 'I think you'd better tell me what happened.'

'I didn't exactly lie to you . . .'

'Just left things out.'

'I can't see that it's important.'

Rachel said nothing. The tactic worked and the silence encouraged Celia to talk.

'Okay. Charlie came here to the boat around eleven thirty that morning. We . . . Just for old times' sake. It was all over but . . .'

'Obviously.' Rachel immediately regretted her sarcasm. She had to keep the woman on side.

'No, honestly, it was. But . . . Anyway, I told him I was meeting the girls at two and that he'd have to go.'

'The girls? I presume you mean Annette and Betina?'

She nodded.

'So you and Marrick went to bed and . . .'

'He was hungry. I keep some ready meals in my little freezer here – Winterlea's gourmet range. I put one in the microwave for him after we'd . . .'

Rachel suddenly remembered something. 'It wasn't quail and garlic potatoes by any chance, was it?'

Celia's eyes widened, as if Rachel had performed some remarkable mind-reading trick. 'How did you know?'

'The stomach contents at the postmortem,' she replied brutally and watched Celia wince. 'What time did Marrick leave?'

'Not long after one o'clock. He didn't want to bump into his wife, did he?'

'No, I don't suppose he did.' Rachel looked at the bruises on Celia's face, just visible beneath the blusher and eye shadow. 'What about those bruises? Did he do that?'

'No,' she said defensively. 'I walked into a cupboard door. That's the truth.'

Rachel didn't believe her but she let it go for now. 'Do you know a man called Simon Tench? He was a vet?'

Celia shook her head, avoiding Rachel's eyes.

'I'll have to ask you to make a statement.'

The woman nodded meekly. But Rachel suspected that this new version of events might prove to be as unreliable as Celia's original statement. In other words, a pack of lies.

The traffic on the M6 was dreadful – as it always was during the working day – and it was four o'clock by the time Wesley Peterson and Gerry Heffernan hit the Chester suburbs. Wesley had entered the address of Cheshire police headquarters into his sat nav and he was rather surprised when the disembodied female voice directed him to an ugly high-rise block, at odds with the city's historical image, not far from the Roodee racecourse and the elegant castle which housed the law courts.

They were expected, which was good. As was the tea they were offered in the office of the detective inspector who had conducted the initial investigation into the death of Christopher Grisham. The DI, whose name was John Heath, was on the defensive at first and Wesley sensed he was embarrassed about his swift conclusion that Grisham had died by his own hand. But then all the evidence had pointed that way and the coroner had seemed happy with the verdict. It was only the news of the similar deaths over two hundred miles away in Devon that had made DI John Heath reconsider his first assumption.

Some men would have become obstructive when their bubble of professional pride had been pricked but Heath seemed to take it philosophically. He was a big man, overweight, bald and nearing retirement. And he knew Gerry Heffernan's cousin, Howard, which endeared him at once to the DCI.

Heath said it would be easier to walk to Christopher Grisham's flat than to travel by car. He'd lived right in the centre, in one of the main streets given over to pedestrians. Wesley had never visited Chester before and he was glad to combine duty with a spot of sightseeing. He knew Chester was a walled city and that the walls were more intact than those of his old university city, Exeter: perhaps when the day's work was over, he could persuade Gerry Heffernan to indulge in some impromptu tourism.

John Heath led them through the streets, past the Grosvenor Museum and into wide thoroughfares thronging with shoppers. Wesley studied the buildings as they walked. Lofty, half-timbered shops rose up either side of the street – magpie black and white. Many had covered galleries on the first floor revealing a second tier of shops behind their balustrades. These were the famous Rows, unique to the city – a masterly method of medieval space-saving.

'So where did the victim live?' Wesley asked, wondering how much further they had to go.

'Right in the heart of things. Just coming up to our right. He had a flat in the Rows . . . top floor above an antique shop.'

Heath turned sharp right, weaving his way through a group of Japanese tourists, and led them up a narrow flight of steps to a wide walkway with a wooden balcony on one side and a row of small shops on the other. To the left of an expensive-looking antique shop was a door. Heath took a key from his pocket and placed it in the lock.

'The landlord's had a firm of cleaners in to get rid of the worst of it,' he said, wrinkling his nose. 'Grisham's stuff's still in here. His relatives haven't cleared it out yet. The rent was paid a couple of months in advance so the landlord's not in much of a hurry.'

'You wouldn't pay a few months' rent in advance if you planned to kill yourself,' Wesley observed.

'It might have been a spur of the moment decision.' There was a hint of resentment in Heath's reply, as though he thought that Wesley was being too clever by half.

Wesley had to concede that Heath was right. The fact that

the dead man paid his rent up front had been no reason to set alarm bells ringing. Unlike two virtually identical deaths in another part of the country.

They walked up a flight of carpeted stairs. The carpet was new and the paint was fresh. As they entered the flat Wesley saw that this was no cheap rented hell-hole – the walls in the wide hallway were pristine cream and the floor was solid oak. And the art work on the walls must have come from one of the exclusive galleries they'd passed on the way there.

Wesley pushed open the door to the living room. The sofa had been taken away and the carpet had been ripped up. 'This was where he was found?'

'That's right. Not a pretty sight. The constable who found him was sick.' Heath took a deep breath. 'The blood had seeped through and stained the ceiling of the shop below. They dialled nine nine nine when they saw it and a patrol car came round and the lads got the key off the landlord. There was no sign of anyone else being involved.'

'Have you spoken to Grisham's friends and family?'

'Yes. They said he never seemed the type. But then people surprise you, don't they?'

'He wasn't the type. He was murdered.'

Heath looked doubtful. Although he had alerted them to the similarities to the two Devon murders, Wesley felt that there was still a small sliver of doubt there. He wasn't one hundred per cent convinced that such an obvious suicide could possibly be murder.

'Didn't you think the use of hemlock was a bit strange?' Wesley asked. 'Wouldn't pills and booze be a more likely method of doing away with yourself?'

Heath looked smug as he strolled over to the bookshelves. 'See for yourself – lots of books of herbalism and the use of plants in medicine. Seemed to be his thing.' He picked out a book and passed it to Wesley. 'And there was this – life of Socrates. One of our DSs noticed it – he's a graduate . . .

classics. He said this Socrates bloke topped himself by drinking hemlock.'

Wesley nodded. He might have come to the same conclusion himself.

Gerry Heffernan had begun to snoop round, opening drawers and cupboards. He took a pile of photograph albums out of the top drawer of a sleek, birch sideboard and began to flick through it.

'Did Grisham have a girlfriend?' Wesley asked.

'Yes. But apparently it was cooling off before he died. Might have been why he killed himself. It all seemed to fit at the time.' It seemed that Heath was making excuses for his initial lack of suspicion. But Wesley had some sympathy for him. Hindsight was a wonderful thing.

'Where is she now?'

'Germany. She got a job there and went out shortly after we spoke to her. Forget what part she went to – could have been Munich . . . or was it Frankfurt? She got a job in some big hotel.'

'What was her name?'

'Jenny. Jenny Pringle. Nice girl. She hadn't been going out with Grisham that long but she was really shocked about what happened.'

'Did she live here with him?'

Heath shook his head. 'No, she worked in a hotel in the centre. Lived in.'

'You interviewed her yourself, I take it?' Heffernan spoke for the first time since they'd entered the flat.

'Yes. But as I said, she couldn't tell me anything much except that things between her and Grisham were cooling off. And she seemed to think Grisham might have been having some trouble at work.'

'We'd like to speak to her. Have you got an address?'

'I must have it back at the office but I don't honestly think she'll be able to tell you much. She hadn't seen him for a few days and when we called her to tell her he was dead she told us they'd rowed about her going off to Germany. She said her career was important to her. Her number was in his address book – that's how we got in touch with her.'

'So it all seemed straightforward? Man having troubles at work then his girlfriend announces she's going abroad.'

'You've got it in one. There's no way we suspected murder.'

'You checked the girlfriend's alibi?'

'What do you think we are? The Keystone Cops?'

Wesley could tell that his question had hit a sensitive spot. Which wasn't what he'd intended.

Before he could say anything Heffernan stepped in. 'Come on, John, we've got to ask.'

Heath took a deep breath. Maybe he had been too touchy. But on the other hand he had two detectives from another force there, questioning his professional competence. 'Of course we checked it. She was working at the hotel. They were busy and she was working an extra shift at the time the pathologist reckons he died.'

Wesley smiled. It was time good relations were re-established. 'Can you tell us about his working life?'

'He worked in an art gallery. The Potterton Gallery in Bridge Street. He was a partner in the business.'

'But there was trouble at work?'

'The gallery isn't doing well. The other partners said they should all chip in a bit of extra capital but Grisham said it was throwing good money after bad.'

'So his partners would have a motive for getting rid of him?'

'I suppose so. His life was insured and they benefit. It might even save the gallery. But both partners have cast-iron alibis. One was in the States and the other was at the hospital. His wife had their first baby the night Grisham died.'

Wesley and Heffernan looked at each other. It was time to move on. Heffernan produced photographs of some of

the Tradmouth *dramatis personae*: Fabrice Colbert, Annette
Marrick, Emma Tench, Carl Pinney, Barty Carter. Heath
looked at them blankly . . . except the picture of Fabrice
Colbert – or Darren Collins: he recognised him from the
television.

John Heath stood awkwardly near the door with his hands
in his pockets while the two Devon detectives made a search
of the flat. He wasn't sure what they were looking for and
he doubted if they'd find it. Someone had gone through
Grisham's things already and found no suicide note or any
other clue to his death.

But fifteen minutes later, Gerry Heffernan gave a shout
of triumph. 'Wes, come and look at this.'

Wesley, who had been examining Grisham's bank statements and finding nothing of much interest, hurried over
to the sideboard where the DCI had spread out a school
photograph. Around twenty boys, sitting neatly in rows in
garish striped blazers.

'Recognise anyone?'

Wesley stared for a few moments. One adolescent boy
looked much like another in his opinion. But when Heffernan
turned the photograph over all was revealed. The boys' names
were neatly printed on the back. And there they were.
Christopher Grisham, Simon Tench and Charles Marrick.

'Belsinger School. That's that posh boarding school near
Littlebury, isn't it?'

'You're dead right, Gerry,' Wesley said with a grin.

His mobile phone rang and after a short conversation he
turned to the DCI again, resisting the urge to punch the
air. John Heath probably thought he was cocky enough
already.

'That was Trish. She's just visited St Peter's School in Morbay.
They said Simon Tench only joined the school in the sixth
form. He'd been to a boarding school before that because his
mother was dead and his father was working away. When his

father returned to Devon, he sent Simon to a day school so they could be together. St Peter's didn't have the name of his former school to hand but they're going to dig through their records and let Trish know.'

'I think we've just saved them a job. It's Belsinger.' Heffernan chuckled.

'And Rachel's found out where Marrick ate his quail and garlic spuds. He had an intimate lunch with Celia Dawn on the day he died. Rachel's double-checking her alibi.'

'You two seem happy,' said John Heath, curious.

Heffernan caught Wesley's eye and grinned. 'Tell you what, John, we'll buy you a drink. We're celebrating.'

Neil Watson had rung Pam who'd told him that Wesley was away for the night. Chester. As a dedicated archaeologist, the fact that Chester was once the Roman settlement of Deva – home of Valeria Vitrix, the twentieth legion – immediately sprung into Neil's mind. There was a lot of good Roman stuff in the Grosvenor Museum. And there was a very interesting excavation of the city's Roman amphitheatre. He wouldn't mind a trip up there himself, he thought with a twinge of envy.

He was glad that relations with Pam were returning to normal. He'd missed their talks and their easy intimacy. The discovery of her fling with Jonathan had placed a wall of mistrust between them for a while and he resented this . . . as though Jonathan had deprived him deliberately of something precious. But his thoughts were interrupted by a tinny rendition of the Indiana Jones theme tune – his mobile phone was ringing.

He was surprised to hear Diane's voice on the other end of the line. She couldn't find her purse. She was certain she'd left it in the site office and Neil was the only person with the key. She was terribly sorry to bother him. She knew it was a nuisance.

He looked at his watch. It was coming up to eight o'clock and dusk was beginning to fall. 'Tell you what,' he said, 'I'll pick you up. You're in Neston aren't you?'

When Diane had recited her address and given him directions, he picked up the keys and locked up his flat carefully. He'd been far more cautious about his security arrangements since he'd started receiving the letters. You couldn't be too careful when there was a nutter playing games and making threats. A nutter who might also be a killer.

The roads were quiet when he picked Diane up at her flat and by the time they reached the dig the daylight had vanished. He hated driving on the narrow Devon lanes in the dark. At night they took on a sinister dimension as the hedges towered either side of the winding, single track road like magic thickets in a fairy tale and the headlights caught ghostly moths and scurrying creatures in their beam. As Neil drove, his hands stiff on the wheel, he felt as if he was on a theme park ride – a cross between the roller-coaster and the ghost train.

When he brought the car to a halt at the farm gate which gave the only access to the site, Diane leaped out to open the gate but Neil produced a torch from the glove box and said they'd leave the car there and walk down the rough track to the site office.

'Look, Neil, this is very good of you,' said Diane as they walked in the darkness. 'I'm so sorry to drag you out like this. I know I'm a nuisance . . .'

'Not at all. I hadn't anything planned.' He glanced at Diane and realised that he was glad of the distraction. He didn't want to be alone. 'Look, it's early. Fancy coming for a drink when you've . . . ?'

She smiled, almost as though this was what she'd been hoping for all along. A more cynical man might have wondered whether the lost purse was a ruse but Neil's mind wasn't that devious. He saw it as serendipity.

'That'd be nice,' she said.

Neil unlocked the heavy duty padlock that secured the site office door and entered, switching on the bare bulb dangling from the ceiling. A brown leather purse lay on the filing cabinet in the corner. Neil took it to Diane who was hovering in the doorway and she thanked him profusely. If it hadn't been there – if she'd lost it somewhere else – she didn't know what she would have done. All her credit cards were in there – her whole financial life – not that there was much finance involved as she was an archaeologist.

Neil let the wave of thanks wash over him. It wasn't often he was treated as a hero and he knew he should really make the most of it. As he locked up, his mind was on the question of where was the best place to go for a drink. Somewhere in Neston would be best, he thought, so he could drop Diane off and get home at a reasonable time.

They'd begun to make their way back to the car when Diane froze. 'What was that?'

They both stood quite still as their ears became attuned to the noises of the night. One faint sound was out of place and unmistakable. A voice, chanting on one note softly, hypnotically.

The excavation itself was some way away behind the site office and Neil hadn't really thought it necessary to look there and check that everything was as it should be. But now he changed his mind. There was somebody there. Somebody intruding on his excavation. His first thought was night hawks – treasure hunters. He'd had trouble with them before. But, in his experience, night hawks didn't usually chant.

He put an arm out to Diane, telling her to stay where she was. If she regarded him as a hero, he might as well live up to her expectations. He switched off the torch and crept round the side of the building. The moon was full and the scarred, pitted ground was bathed in a silvery light that enabled him to avoid the trenches.

The one thing he hadn't expected to see on the site was a cloaked figure standing within a circle of dancing candle flames, its arms raised, chanting to the moon. Neil froze and watched for a few moments as the figure began to move. It was at the edge of the circle now, bowing to the points of the compass, moving and muttering. And at the centre of the circle was the blood pit.

Neil began to creep forward when his foot caught on one of the small test pits he'd ordered to be dug on the un-excavated section of the site and he stumbled, swearing softly under his breath.

The figure in the circle of light froze, silhouetted against the candle glow and the moonlight. Neil's heart beat fast as he straightened himself up and looked around for Diane. He saw that she had flattened herself against an ancient wall that had once formed part of the monastic manor house and her presence gave him new courage. He wasn't on his own.

'What the hell's going on?' he called, flicking his torch on and trying to sound authoritative.

The figure hesitated for a second then took off at great speed before Neil could focus the torch beam, disappearing into the trees surrounding the field with its cloak billowing behind. Neil was only too aware of the trenches and pits that lay between him and the fugitive and that this sort of terrain could be treacherous in bad light. He knew that pursuit was useless.

'Did you see who it was?' asked Diane as she picked her way cautiously over the uneven ground.

Neil turned round. 'I can't be sure but I think our friend was trying to recreate a Bronze Age Aztec ritual.'

Diane allowed herself a snort of derision. 'You mean Lenny?'

Neil gave her a nervous smile. 'We'd better clock in early tomorrow – get rid of those candles before anyone sees them and starts asking questions. I only hope he wasn't sacrificing anything,' he said as an afterthought.

Diane linked her arm through his as they walked back to the car. And the watcher in the trees didn't emerge until they had driven off.

Wesley Peterson and Gerry Heffernan set out early the next morning. Six thirty – a very uncivilised hour in Heffernan's opinion. The previous evening they had met up with Gerry's cousin, Howard, at the small hotel on the outskirts of Chester, selected for them by DI Heath. They stayed in the bar till nine thirty when Howard had promised to return to his wife who hadn't been well. After Howard's departure, neither man had been in the mood to paint Chester red so they had an early night.

Howard was a cheerful, plodding sort of man and Wesley could see a distinct family resemblance to Gerry. The same nose. The same eyes. The same portly figure. Howard was quite happy to remain a sergeant and it seemed that he regarded Gerry as the thrusting, ambitious member of the Heffernan clan. But then he had never served in the Met as Wesley had. These things are all relative.

They arrived back in Tradmouth around lunchtime and Wesley knew it wasn't worth going home as Pam would be at work and the house would be empty. He was glad when Gerry suggested lunch at his place – a chance to catch their breath before returning to the hurly-burly of the incident room.

Trish Walton had phoned the DCI's mobile during their journey. St Peter's school had been through their records and found that Simon Tench had come to them in the sixth form from Belsinger School where he'd been a boarder. It was the link – it had to be – and now they needed to visit Belsinger to discover why three former pupils had been done to death in such a bizarre manner.

A tea-stained copy of yesterday's local paper was lying on Gerry Heffernan's coffee table and Wesley read the headline

– 'Police Hunt for Spider Continues'. Heffernan picked it up and grunted with disgust. He really did need to have a word with Ray Davenport – put an end to this sensationalist nonsense once and for all. Wesley was about to reply that, in his opinion, the story seemed quite accurate but he thought better of it. Discovering the identity of their mole in the CID office could wait. They had more important things to do.

Gerry Heffernan seemed reluctant to return to work and Wesley didn't really blame him. But some things couldn't be put off so they set out to walk through Tradmouth's narrow streets beneath a battleship grey sky. When they arrived at the police station, the CID office was busy, which was what the DCI liked to see and, as they entered, Trish Walton bounded up to them, an eager to please expression on her face.

'Do you remember that break-in at the veterinary clinic where Simon Tench worked?' she began. 'Well the intruder left a fingerprint and we've found it belongs to Carl Pinney. Some drugs were taken. Ketamine mainly. Horse tranquilliser.'

Heffernan looked at Wesley. 'So we've found our link between Tench and Pinney. Steve'll be delighted.'

'We've still not established any connection between Pinney and our other two victims. But if we find he's taken a trip to Chester . . .'

Trish looked at him in alarm. 'So it's definite then? The Chester killing's identical?'

Wesley had almost forgotten that the rest of the team hadn't yet been brought up to date on the Chester development. It was high time they were. He asked Trish to muster the troops – or what troops were still in the office and not out making door-to-door enquiries or interviewing potential witnesses – and Gerry Heffernan prepared to deliver his commanding officer's speech. He had brought photographs of the Chester victim and the crime scene with him and he gave them to Wesley to pin on the notice board.

Once the briefing was over, the DCI beckoned the new boy, Lee Parsons, over. The young policeman looked positively scared. Maybe he hadn't yet learned that Gerry Heffernan's growl was a lot worse than his bite.

'Lee. I want you to go and pick up Carl Pinney. He's due to appear before Morbay magistrates today – for mugging our own dear DC Carstairs. He'll get community service because, allegedly, it's a first offence – which only means he hasn't been caught at it before. He'll be thinking it's his lucky day but I want you to spoil it for him. We've matched his prints to a burglary at the vet's surgery where Simon Tench worked so I want him brought in again. Take DC Johnson with you – he'll show you what's what.'

Lee's apprehension had vanished. 'Right you are, sir.' He scurried off to find Paul Johnson. 'It'll be good experience for him,' Heffernan said softly.

Wesley couldn't argue with that. However, he was impatient to follow up their new lead about the victims' school days. If all three had attended the same boarding school, the answer might well lie there. They needed to visit Belsinger School as soon as possible.

An hour and a few phone calls later, they were on the road to the village of Littlebury – which lay on the coast just beyond Millicombe – and Belsinger School.

Steve Carstairs had been making routine enquiries – the only kind he seemed to get nowadays. He had been manning a road block with a couple of uniforms near Simon Tench's house – or a lane block to be more accurate – asking any passing motorists if they'd been in the area around the time Tench had been murdered and, if they had, had they seen anything suspicious.

It was all a waste of time in Steve's opinion. The killer

would hardly have been dancing in front of the traffic waving a blood-stained knife at passers-by. He would have been covered in blood and taking great care not to be seen if he had any sense. And there was no reason to doubt this killer's intelligence. He was running rings round them so far.

Steve was due to report back to the incident room at two and a middle-aged DC from Neston had just arrived to relieve him. He exchanged a few pleasantries with the man and passed on DCI Heffernan's instructions, anxious to get back to what passed for civilisation in Tradmouth. He was sick of being sent on all the crap jobs. It was as if the boss didn't trust him . . . which he probably didn't.

Steve drove back to Tradmouth, hunger gnawing at his stomach. He'd get something to eat at his dad's shop. Joanne would be there which was reason enough to call in. He hadn't seen her since Saturday night and now he was eager to see her again, which he found rather surprising. Perhaps it was true about the ones who played hard to get being the most desirable.

As he parked in the police station car park he looked out for Wesley Peterson's car but he couldn't see it. The boss and DI Peterson had been on some trip up north – probably living it up on expenses – and if they weren't back yet, it wouldn't matter if he was a few minutes late, he thought. Although since his little bit of trouble with Carl Pinney, he'd been more careful than usual about bending the rules. In the current climate, you had to watch your back. Instinctively, he turned to look up at the CID office windows as he scurried out of the car park. There were always those ready to stick the knife in.

He walked past the Boat Float where small craft bobbed up and down on the high tide, and hurried down the High Street towards Burton's Butties. The lunchtime rush was over so there weren't many sandwiches left in the refrigerated display just inside the shop doorway. He picked out a lonely ham baguette, sitting on its own on the top shelf and carried it over to the counter where Joanne greeted him with a shy smile.

'Hi,' she said, looking at him through her eyelashes like a coy teenager.

'Hi,' he said, holding out the baguette like a lethal weapon. 'You free tonight?'

She smiled shyly. 'I don't know,' she said. 'I'll have to check my diary.'

'How are things?'

'Okay. I've been busy looking for office jobs – something to use my computer skills – but I've not found anything. What have you been up to? Caught this Spider yet?'

But before Steve could answer, his father emerged from the back of the shop. 'Hello, son,' he said, a smirk on his lips. Steve hated it when he called him that. 'Fancy a drink after work?'

Steve looked at Robbie and saw the over-eager expression on his face. He was trying too hard. Suddenly Steve felt powerful, in control. At last after all these years it seemed he held some sway over the man who had blighted his childhood and his mother's life. He smiled at him but there was no affection in his eyes. Only contempt. 'Not today. I'll be busy.' He looked at Joanne and winked. 'I'll pick you up at eight. Okay?'

Joanne glanced at Robbie and felt herself blushing as Steve strutted out of the shop with his baguette.

'You want to watch him, you know, love,' Robbie whispered in Joanne's ear. 'I know he's my son but . . .'

But Joanne ignored her boss and began to clean the counter furiously.

Some people just wouldn't be told.

The village of Littlebury on the coast between Tradmouth and Plymouth was a magnet for tourists in the summer months, its main attractions being its fine beaches and Monks Island with its famous Art Deco hotel joined to the mainland by a strip of sand when the tide went out. Littlebury itself had spread over the years and bungalows had sprouted like mushrooms around its fringes. Belsinger School stood a mile to the east of the village at the end of a long, winding drive and, as he drove there, Wesley felt a thrill of excitement – the anticipation of the hunter who knew he was on the right trail. For three former pupils of the same exclusive boarding school to be killed by the same murderer could hardly be a coincidence. The school had to be the link. The three men had become involved with the killer because of their school connection. The old school tie had become a noose.

Gerry Heffernan gave a low whistle as Wesley turned the car into the drive leading to the school. The sign set beside the elegant Georgian lodge was written in gold letters on a black background and it informed them that they had arrived at Belsinger School, established 1854. Headmaster Dr Oliver Wynn.

They had telephoned ahead and Dr Wynn was expecting them. But they'd given no hint as to why they wanted to see him so, hopefully, he'd be quite unprepared. Which is exactly how Gerry Heffernan liked his witnesses to be.

The boys at Belsinger wore striped blazers and, it being summer term, straw boaters seemed to be *de rigueur*. Masters wore gowns and, as Wesley and Heffernan got out of their car, a gaggle of boys doffed their boaters to a passing teacher.

'Like stepping back in time, isn't it?' Heffernan whispered loudly.

Wesley didn't answer. Gerry was right. They could have been back in the days when establishments such as Belsinger trained up Queen Victoria's ruling classes to organise the British Empire with effortless efficiency.

He stood for a few moments studying the school itself.

The lodge at the gates had led him to expect a monument to Georgian classicism but Belsinger School was housed in a much older building. The Elizabethan entrance was rather magnificent; built with all the confidence and swagger of the Renaissance nouveau riche on the make. The wing to the left looked older and more ecclesiastical, its arched windows filled with delicate tracery which Wesley knew was of a much earlier date. This had been an important building in medieval times and Wesley was curious about its history. No doubt Dr Wynn would be able to enlighten him. It would be a good topic to introduce if the conversation showed any sign of flagging – they might get more out of the man if they put him at his ease.

Heffernan was glad of Wesley's presence. At least, as an old boy of a famous private school in Dulwich, he knew how to behave in such establishments. He said a polite 'excuse me' to a passing boy and asked to be directed to the headmaster's study. The boy duly obliged and ten minutes later they were waiting outside the head's study like a pair of recalcitrant schoolboys. Dr Wynn was keeping them waiting. And Gerry Heffernan didn't like to be kept waiting.

But just as he was about to approach the severe looking secretary in half-moon glasses who acted as guardian of Dr Wynn's gate, the intercom on her desk buzzed. She looked at the two policemen disapprovingly and told them they could go in. The headmaster would see them now.

Wesley put a warning hand on his boss's sleeve. No wisecracks. No ruffling of feathers. Dr Wynn would need to be treated with the respect he was accustomed to if they were to get the most out of him. Heffernan understood. He'd leave this one to Wesley who seemed to be at home in this sort of atmosphere.

Dr Wynn was a tall, thin man with a beak of a nose – a Ronald Searle headmaster from central casting. He stood up to shake their hands politely and invited them to sit.

Heffernan, who looked as though he'd been expecting six of the best, obeyed without a word.

'I understand from my secretary that you want to talk to me regarding a murder enquiry. Is that right?' He instinctively looked at Wesley for the answer to his question.

'Yes. We're actually investigating two murders – possibly three. All identical. You'll have heard about the murders of Charles Marrick and Simon Tench in the Tradmouth area?' He wasn't sure whether Wynn would follow news of gruesome murders. He looked the sort who was still coming to terms with reports from the Punic Wars.

But Wynn leaned forward, a gleam in his eye. 'The Spider, you mean. What's that got to do with me?'

'We have reason to believe the victims were old boys of this school.'

Wynn slumped back in his chair. He looked genuinely shocked. 'Good Lord. Of course I only took up this post three years ago so I wouldn't know the boys involved. Are you quite sure about this?'

'We'd be grateful if we could take a look at your records. And we'd like to talk to any teachers who might have known the victims if we may.'

'But surely this can't have anything to do with Belsinger . . .'

'It's the only link we've found between the victims. Charles Marrick and Simon Tench both attended this school.' He paused, watching the headmaster's face. 'And so did a third victim. Christopher Grisham. He was murdered up in Chester a few weeks ago. Identical MO.'

The headmaster fell silent for a while, lost for words for once. Then he looked up at Wesley, his lips pressed together in a stubborn line. 'I really fail to see what this can have to do with the school, Inspector. If these three former pupils remained in contact after they'd left Belsinger and became involved in something unsavoury, the school can hardly be held to blame.'

Wesley and Heffernan looked at each other. The headmaster

certainly had a point. Only there was no reason whatsoever to suppose the three victims had remained in contact. Charles Marrick and Simon Tench seemed to have very little in common. And there was no indication that Marrick and Grisham had been in touch recently, if ever.

'Are there any teachers here who would have known the victims? They probably would have been pupils here between 1989 and 1994.'

Dr Wynn thought for a few moments. 'There's Mr Foley – Physics. And Mr Vaughan – Music. Mr Hedge would have taught them history, no doubt. He retired recently but he still does some supply work for us – filling in for absent staff. I believe he's on some archaeological dig at the moment out at Stow Barton.'

Wesley looked at Heffernan who was sitting silently beside him. This was Neil's training excavation. He thought of the anonymous letters his friend had received and felt a thrill of excitement. He wanted to speak to Mr Hedge, sooner rather than later.

He gave the headmaster a businesslike smile. 'This is a boarding school. Presumably there are housemasters and . . .'

'Of course.'

'Would you mind looking at your records to see if these boys were in the same house? And if so, which one.'

Wynn gave Wesley a curious look. He had hardly expected this young black policeman to be so *au fait* with the life of a public school. But then he was well spoken and he exuded a certain air of quiet confidence so perhaps he had gone through the system himself. Although he rather baulked at the idea of any old Belsingians entering the police force at any rank below that of chief constable. 'Of course. I'll ask my secretary to look at our records.'

He lifted the telephone receiver and made the request. As they had time to fill, Wesley asked the question that had been on his mind since he'd first seen the school.

'How old is the building?'

Wynn looked rather gratified that he'd noticed the architectural gem that had become his fiefdom. 'The earliest parts date back to the thirteen century,' he began proudly. 'It was an abbey prior to the Dissolution. A house of Augustinian Canons. Monks Island was a part of the abbey property. Henry VIII sold the land and buildings off to one of his cronies, of course, after which it became a private house. When the family in question died out it became a school in the nineteenth century.'

Heffernan sat there in silence, listening to all this. As Wesley seemed to have established a rapport with the man, he was quite happy to leave all the talking to him. In fact he was rather glad of the break.

After ten minutes of historical chat, Dr Wynn's secretary produced the records for each victim with remarkable efficiency, along with tea in bone china cups.

Simon Tench and Christopher Grisham had been model pupils. Grisham was a talented artist while Tench was academically bright, especially at science and mathematics. Only Marrick had let the side down. Reading between the lines, he'd held the post of School Bully. Always in trouble with masters. Always at the headmaster's door for something or other. Like Tench he hadn't stayed on in the sixth form. But, unlike Tench, he hadn't gone to take his A Levels elsewhere and then on to university – he'd joined the vulgar world of commerce and made his fortune. Something Belsinger probably wouldn't choose to record in gold letters on their venerable oak honours boards.

But Wesley noted one thing with great interest. Charles Marrick, Simon Tench and Christopher Grisham had all been in Tavistock House under the guardianship of housemaster, Mr Dean. And, according to Dr Wynn, Mr Dean had retired three years ago to run a bookshop in Morbay.

As they took their leave of the headmaster, Wesley warned

him that they might need to visit the school again. But in the meantime he wanted to speak to Mr Dean. If he had been in *loco parentis* to the three victims for several years, it was likely he'd know their secrets. Or at least have his suspicions about what they were trying to hide.

Parents might not know everything their offspring get up to. But a housemaster used to dealing with adolescent boys was bound to know all the tricks. Or at least that's what Wesley was pinning his hopes on as they drove away from the school.

Carl Pinney had received the sentence of a hundred hours' community service for mugging DC Steve Carstairs. But, just as he thought it was safe to return to the Winterham Estate, Lee Parsons and Paul Johnson ruined his day. They were waiting for him outside Morbay Magistrates' Court.

'This is police harassment,' Carl protested as he was led towards the patrol car. 'I want my brief.'

'All in good time,' said DC Johnson patiently. 'We've sent someone to search your house.'

Carl's eyes lit up. 'You got a warrant?'

When Paul Johnson nodded, Carl's face was a picture of disappointment. The thought of getting one over on the pigs again had momentarily lightened his life. He'd thought he'd hit the jackpot with that DC Carstairs but he'd been found out. Shame.

Half an hour later Carl Pinney was sitting in Interview Room Two at Tradmouth police station, his bored-looking solicitor installed by his side.

This time it was a female officer who did the honours. She was blonde and quite fit, Pinney noticed, and she introduced herself as Detective Sergeant Rachel Tracey. She informed him that his fingerprints had been found at the scene of a break-in – the surgery where the Spider's second victim had worked as a vet. She then proceeded to say that a quantity of ketamine had been found hidden in his bedroom – the same drug that had been taken in the break-in.

Pinney, of course, knew better than to comment. If you kept silent they couldn't do anything about it. And it annoyed them no end.

Then he was asked if he'd ever been to Chester. Stupid question. Carl hadn't been much further than Plymouth. Then DS Tracey asked him if he'd ever met the vet, Simon Tench. The answer was a decisive no.

He knew they had enough to charge him with the break-in and drugs theft and he wished they'd just get on with it so he could get home.

But, just as Pinney and his solicitor thought it was all over, an officer came in and whispered in DS Tracey's ear.

She looked straight at him, her face expressionless, and he wondered what was coming next.

'They've just found a blood-stained knife – it looks like the sort that killed Simon Tench,' she said. 'It had been put in a waste bin in Tradmouth. The bin men spotted it when they emptied it. It's being tested for fingerprints and the blood's being matched with the victim's.'

Carl Pinney looked up at her, suddenly worried. 'What's that got to do with me?' he said with a hint of defiance.

'Don't worry. If there's a connection, we'll find it,' she said, glancing at his solicitor who yawned ostentatiously, obviously wishing he was somewhere else.

'Piss off,' said Pinney as he rose from his seat, sending it flying to the floor with a loud crash. The solicitor looked embarrassed and told him to sit down. He wasn't doing himself any favours.

Rachel enjoyed reading out the charges. Sometimes job satisfaction was a wonderful thing.

When Wesley and Gerry heard the news about Pinney's arrest, the DCI observed that the little toe-rag deserved it.

But even with this new link to Simon Tench, somehow neither man could see him as the murderer – particularly with the new developments up in Chester. And they mustn't forget the hemlock. The administration of hemlock to paralyse the victims before they were bled to death showed forward planning and subtlety way beyond the likes of Pinney. The Spider was undoubtedly intelligent which made him all the more dangerous. And there was no sign of a break-in at any of the murder scenes which meant the victims probably admitted the killer.

'So what's our next move, Wes?' Heffernan asked as he lolled back in his black leather executive seat, his feet planted firmly on his desk.

'I want a word with this housemaster, Mr Dean . . . and Mr Hedge, the history teacher – the one who's working at Neil's dig.'

'You thinking of those funny letters?' Heffernan asked as though he'd read Wesley's mind.

'I'll give Neil a ring and see if Hedge is there. We don't want a wasted journey.'

He made the call but a few minutes later he replaced the receiver, a look of disappointment on his face. 'Hedge isn't there this afternoon – hospital appointment. He'll be there first thing tomorrow.'

'I suppose it can wait.'

'Morbooks,' Wesley said suddenly.

'You what?'

'Morbooks. Mr Dean's bookshop. Let's go and have a word with him.'

Gerry Heffernan nodded. For want of any better leads, Mr Dean looked like a good bet. He might be able to throw light on some event in the past that connected the three victims. 'Let's not warn him we're coming. I've come to favour the element of surprise. If there is something to hide, we don't want to give him time to concoct a story, do we?'

Wesley couldn't argue with that. The retired housemaster's initial reaction to their questions might tell them a lot more than the answers he gave.

They drove to Morbay via the car ferry that shuttled to and fro across the River Trad. It took a few miles off the journey and, as the main tourist season wasn't yet upon them, there wasn't much of a queue on either side of the river. The roads leading through Morbay's outer suburbs to the town centre were congested as usual and Gerry Heffernan muttered under his breath as he sat in the passenger seat. But when they eventually reached their destination, they found a free parking space just outside Morbooks which improved the DCI's temper no end.

The shop stood in one of Morbay's smarter suburbs – a leafy, hilly area of Victorian villas, near the entrance to Pent's Cavern – a labyrinth of prehistoric caves which became a bustling attraction in tourist season. Wesley could see a handful of people at the Cavern's ticket office, queuing for admission to the depths below the earth where their distant ancestors toiled with flint tools. The Cavern's proximity to Morbooks would, undoubtedly, be good for Mr Dean's trade.

As Wesley pushed the door open, a bell rang loudly in the bowels of the shop. Bookshops had always held a fascination for him and once he was inside one, it was very difficult, Pam had often found, to get him out. Near the front of the shop was a large display of books about Pent's Cavern and prehistory in general and Wesley couldn't resist picking up a couple of books and flicking through their pages. Gerry Heffernan, meanwhile had spotted the Ships and Sailing section and was on his way to investigate when an elderly man appeared. He was medium height, bald as an egg, and there was a permanent expression of benevolent surprise on his round face.

'Can I help you, gentlemen?' he asked. There was a hint of wariness in his voice, almost as though he'd guessed they were policemen. Wesley hadn't thought he was that obvious.

Wesley flashed his ID card and said they were looking for a Mr Dean. The man replied that he was Mortimer Dean and asked how he could help. He sounded almost eager, playing the good citizen to perfection.

'We'd like to talk to you about some of your former pupils at Belsinger School. We understand that you were in charge of Tavistock House.'

There was no mistaking it. The man looked worried. 'Yes, I was housemaster at Tavistock.'

'You'll have heard that two of your former pupils have been murdered recently.' It was a statement, not a question. He glanced at Gerry Heffernan who was watching the former teacher as a cat watches a mouse.

'Yes. Tragic. Such a waste.'

'You knew the victims well?'

Dean shuffled his feet and looked round, uncomfortable. A customer brought a book to the till and Dean served him eagerly, almost as though he was glad of the breathing space.

'Well,' he began as soon as the customer had left the shop, 'I knew Simon Tench – very bright lad – he moved on to St Peter's School for the sixth form, of course, due to family circumstances. He was a nice boy. Great shame about . . .' He hesitated for a few moments. 'The other one – Charles Marrick – wasn't an easy boy to communicate with. He left us after his GCSEs. Not an academic.'

'I had the impression there was more to it than that.'

Dean looked flustered. 'Oh dear. I never like to speak ill of former pupils . . .'

Wesley smiled to put the man at his ease. 'It would help us a lot if you did.' He paused. 'A man called Christopher Grisham was found dead up in Chester in very similar circumstances.'

The colour drained from Dean's face and he put out a

hand to steady himself. 'No. Not Chris. He was . . . He was a lovely boy . . . as was Simon. Who on earth would want to kill him . . . or Simon? They were . . .'

'I notice you're not including Charles Marrick in your eulogy,' Wesley said, glancing at the DCI who was listening intently.

Dean swallowed hard. He looked as though he were about to burst into tears. 'Marrick was a nasty piece of work,' he hissed. 'When I heard he owned a successful wine business and had a big house in Rhode, my only thought was that the Devil looks after his own. He was trouble from the moment he started at Belsinger. If I'd had my way, he would have been expelled but the headmaster – the last one, not the present one, of course – wouldn't hear of it for some reason. Maybe that's why Marrick thought he could get away with . . .' He stopped in mid-sentence.

'Get away with what?' Heffernan asked. This was getting interesting.

Another shake of the head. 'He got away with a lot of things, that's all.'

'Some of them criminal?' Wesley felt that if he kept pushing, he might just get at the truth.

But Dean had closed his lips in a stubborn line. He wasn't talking. Not yet at any rate.

Wesley leaned forward. 'I can't understand why you're shielding him, Mr Dean. He's dead and we're trying to catch his killer. And the killer of two other men who, according to you, were innocent of any wrongdoing. Or were they, Mr Dean?'

He paused to give the man a chance to reply but Dean remained silent.

'Were the three victims friendly at all? Did they ever hang round together?'

'Children's friendships can ebb and flow, Inspector. Today's bosom friend is tomorrow's casual acquaintance and vice versa. I really can't be sure whether this particular trio were friendly at any particular time.'

Wesley was sure he was lying. He knew all right. But for some reason he didn't want to say. And Wesley wondered why.

Gerry Heffernan was growing impatient. 'Look, we're trying to find out who killed your former pupils. What are you trying to hide? Are you shielding someone? Another of your ex-pupils maybe?'

Wesley watched the man's face but he was giving nothing away. However, he suspected Gerry had touched a nerve. There was no doubt Dean was hiding something. But what and why, he had no idea.

Then he had a sudden thought. 'The last headmaster — is he still alive?'

'No. He passed away shortly after he retired.'

'How did he die?'

This time Dean's face clouded. He swallowed hard. 'I'm afraid Mr Hadderson took his own life. He cut his throat.'

Gerry Heffernan caught Wesley's eye. 'Did he have any family?'

Dean shook his head. 'No. He never married.'

'Brothers, sisters, nephews, nieces?'

Another shake of the head. 'Not that I know of.'

It was Wesley who asked the next question. 'Any lovers, male or female? Any close friends?'

Dean's face reddened. 'I . . . Well there was Norman Hedge.'

'Lover or friend?'

'That really isn't for me to say,' Dean replied, coy as a maiden aunt.

'Dr Wynn mentioned a Mr Hedge who taught history. He said he was taking part in a local excavation.' He looked Dean in the eye. 'I presume this is the same Mr Hedge?'

'That'll be Norman. Yes.' He looked worried. 'If you think

he might be a suspect, you're mistaken. Norman wouldn't hurt a fly. He . . .'

'That's as may be, Mr Dean,' said Wesley smoothly. 'But we still need to speak to him.' He caught Gerry Heffernan's eye. They'd learned all they could for now and pressing Dean further might be counterproductive. They'd call back soon. Besides, Wesley wanted to look at the postmortem report on Belsinger's former headmaster, Stanley Hadderson. He was wondering if there might have been more to the apparent suicide than met the eye. If the wounds on his throat were the same as those on the recent victims, it would open up a whole new set of possibilities.

Wesley took his leave, saying they'd call again, but trying to make the words sound as unthreatening as possible. If they were to get the full story out of Mortimer Dean, they needed him in a co-operative frame of mind.

But as soon as they'd left the shop, Dean turned the sign hanging on the door round to 'closed' and rushed to the back office.

He took a deep breath before switching on his computer. Like the police, he needed to know the truth.

CHAPTER 10

When I discovered the truth about Brother William it just seemed right to link it to my own story. We're the same, Brother William and I.

Perhaps I'm growing tired of this blood game. But I can't tell you what it all means. You'll have to find that out for yourself, Neil. Think of it as a test.

It was time to go back . . . and to pick up the local evening paper on the way. The writer needed to find out how much the police knew. With DNA testing available, they could do wonders these days and it surely wouldn't be long before they discovered his identity.

But would they make the connection? Probably not. The only way they could find out the truth was if a confession was made.

Perhaps I shouldn't tell. Perhaps it would bring nothing but misery. But I know I can't keep it a secret much longer. I know I deserve punishment for what I did. Maybe I deserve death.

The urge to tell the truth was overwhelming. But why Neil Watson had been selected as Father Confessor, the writer wasn't sure. Perhaps he'd just looked as though he might understand.

*

Wesley arrived home at seven thirty and Pam rushed to greet him as soon as she heard his key in the door. She'd had a tough day at school. And besides, she hadn't seen her husband since he'd set off early the day before, bound for Chester and a night at some anonymous small hotel. Pam was surprised at how much she had missed him. She wanted to see him – almost as much as she had back in those heady days when they'd first met.

As soon as he walked in through the door, he kissed her and asked how the children were. They were fine, she said. No problems. They were both in bed. Michael was reading and Amelia had fallen asleep immediately, exhausted by her day at the nursery. As if on cue, Michael appeared at the top of the stairs, a book clutched in his hand. Could Daddy read some of it with him?

Wesley ignored his growling stomach and hurried upstairs to do his fatherly duty and when he came down half an hour later, he found Pam slumped in front of the television, watching a cookery programme, too tired to do anything but lift her head and tell him that his dinner was in the microwave and suggest that he bring it in on a tray so they could catch up.

With the TV chefs chattering in the background, Pam launched into an account of the hellish couple of days she'd had while he'd been away. Her mother had deigned to stay last night but she'd expected to be waited on hand and foot and hadn't seemed in the least bit repentant about letting them down on the night of their anniversary. At work the headmistress was being a bitch to one of the classroom assistants, one of the other teachers was on the point of a nervous breakdown, and to top this she was going to have to spend most of next weekend doing point-less paperwork. Wesley put his arm around her. He sympathised – the police force was exactly the same. Perhaps, he said whimsically, there'd be a revolution soon – towering bonfires of forms and paperwork on the corner of each street. Beacons of freedom.

Wesley's thoughts were suddenly interrupted by the sound of a familiar voice coming from the television. He'd been about to go to the kitchen to fetch his dinner but instead he shuffled forward in his seat and searched for the remote control to increase the volume.

Fabrice Colbert was setting fire to something rich and creamy in a frying pan after pouring brandy all over it. It was a theatrical performance that had little to do with the kind of cooking that goes on in ninety-nine per cent of homes. But that was what Colbert's diners paid good money for.

'Wish you could cook like that.' Pam reached across and gave her husband a playful push.

'Mmm.' Wesley listened for a few moments to Colbert's – or rather Collins's – mock French accent and gave a derisory snort. 'Do you know his real name's Darren Collins and he's as French as I am? Comes from London. It's all an act.'

Pam raised her eyebrows in disbelief then she started to laugh. 'You'd never guess. He's got it off pat, hasn't he?'

Wesley had seen more than enough of Darren Collins over the past week or so and he was about to turn down the volume when something on the screen caught his eye. Behind the chef there was a banner anonouncing 'The Best Food Show – fifteenth to the nineteenth of June. Chester Pavilion'. His heart started beating more rapidly. Christopher Grisham had died on the sixteenth of June. Collins had been in Chester when he died. In fact he hadn't a believable alibi for any of the Spider murders. And a chef of his ability would know all about hemlock – if only to recognise the leaves of the wild variety and know that it wasn't wise to add them to a salad.

'What's the matter?' Pam asked.

He stood up. 'I've got to ring Gerry.'

'Are you two joined at the hip or something? You see him all day.'

Wesley realised that this would have to be done tactfully. 'I won't be long and I promise I'll try to make it to Maritia's next Sunday for lunch. That friend of Mark's will be there, won't he . . . Jonathan?'

Pam recognised a repentant husband when she saw one but this wasn't what she wanted to hear.

'I'll have a lot of work to do for Monday,' Pam said quickly. 'I'm sure Maritia won't mind if we can't make it. She'll understand.'

Wesley shrugged. Pam had a point.

After he'd eaten his dinner and switched the dishwasher on, he sneaked into the hall to call Gerry Heffernan. Perhaps it was time they had another word with their favourite celebrity chef. And if they could find that he had some connection with Belsinger School, so much the better.

It had started to rain in Morbay. It often rained, giving the lie to those posters back in the 1930s that boasted of the resort's sand, sea, sun and smiling, swimsuited beauties.

The pavements near Morbooks glistened in the feeble yellow streetlights. It was dark now. Evening. And Mortimer Dean had finished his meal and cleared away. He lived over the shop. He liked it that way. He loved his books as he'd loved his charges back at Tavistock House. His books were his children now and they didn't answer back. Or make trouble like Charles Marrick had done. Books were perfect companions.

He'd laid out biscuits on a plate in the kitchen, ready for his visitor. Chocolate biscuits of course. The very best. He didn't entertain that often. He had taken four pairs of glasses from the cupboard – two sherry, two wine, two spirits and two beer. He really had no idea what his visitor would like to drink. He had also filled the kettle in case tea or coffee was required, covering all eventualities.

He looked at his watch and had a final tidy round, realising that he'd become so used to solitude that a simple visit now filled him with panic. Once he'd taken entertaining in his stride – in his years at Belsinger the senior boys in Tavistock House and his fellow masters would often drop in for tea and chatter. But those days were long gone – a distant memory. Dean examined his reflection in the large mirror hanging above a mahogany sideboard too big for the room. He was getting old. A step nearer death every day. But at least he had his books.

When the doorbell rang he adjusted his bow tie in the mirror, hurried down the stairs and fixed a smile to his face as he undid the lock.

Friday dawned bright and sunny. And the sun had brought out the weekend sailors on the River Trad, escaped from the confines of their city offices a day early to make the most of their precious leisure time in their Devon retreats.

Even though the killer everyone was calling the Spider was still at large and the skeleton in the woods remained unidentified, Wesley felt remarkably cheerful. Although one look at Gerry Heffernan's face told him that the DCI didn't share his good spirits.

'Something the matter?' He felt he knew Gerry Heffernan well enough by now to do a little prying.

Heffernan sat at his desk, turning a cheap plastic pen over and over in his fingers. 'Joyce's mum was rushed to hospital yesterday. Suspected stroke. Joyce rang me last night – she was in a bit of a state so I went round.' He looked up. 'It doesn't look good, Wes.'

Wesley was rather surprised at this sudden rush of concern for his lady friend's elderly mother. After all, she had been an impediment to his relationship with Joyce since they'd met almost a year ago. Suffering from Alzheimer's, Edna Barnes had caused problems for them at every turn.

'Joyce is really upset,' Heffernan said softly. 'I wanted to stay with her at the hospital but . . .' He waved his arm to indicate the pile of paperwork on his desk.

'She'll understand,' said Wesley unconvincingly.

'Does Pam?' the DCI replied quickly, looking Wesley in the eye – he'd know if he was lying.

Wesley gave his boss an enigmatic smile, giving nothing away. 'Did you tell Rosie where you'd gone last night?' he asked out of curiosity. In his opinion the fact that his boss went to desperate lengths to keep Joyce's existence a secret from his daughter, was ridiculous. Rosie wasn't stupid. She was bound to find out sooner or later.

'This job provides the perfect alibi, Wes. I told her there'd been a new lead in the case.'

Wesley sighed and shook his head. 'You're going to get found out one of these days. And talking of new leads, are we paying Darren Collins another visit this morning?'

'I suppose we should. If he was up in Chester at the time Christopher Grisham was killed . . .'

'And what about this Celia Dawn – the woman who gave Marrick his quail lunch?'

'Rachel's been checking that one out. Ms Dawn was telling the truth about where she got the quail – it's part of Winterlea's new gourmet range apparently.' He snorted with derision. He was more of a fish and chips man himself.

'And we need to have a word with this Norman Hedge. He'll be at Neil's dig so we can call there after we've seen Collins. Okay?'

'Anything new come in from Forensic on those letters Neil's been getting?'

Wesley shook his head. 'Nothing useful.'

'Think there's a chance our Spider could have written them?'

Wesley opened his mouth to say something but his train of thought was interrupted by the urgent ringing of the phone on Heffernan's desk. The DCI picked it up.

It's always hard to judge what's being said from hearing one side of a conversation and Heffernan's contribution seemed to be a series of affirmative grunts. But Wesley could tell by the expression on his face that the news was good . . . if not exciting.

When he'd put the receiver down, he looked up, a smile of smug satisfaction on his face. 'That was Luton police. I told them about the initials on that ring – BI – and they went through their records. We've got a possible identification for our skeleton in the woods. They've come up with a character called Barry Ickerman who hasn't been heard of since 1989. They assumed he'd just left the area – wife said he'd walked out and she didn't know where he'd gone. Turns out he was a suspect in that rape they mentioned – only they didn't have the DNA technology in those days.'

'But at least they kept the samples.'

'Too right.' He rubbed his hands together gleefully. 'It's great this. Run a few samples from unsolved cases through some machine at the lab and it comes up with a name. Just like magic isn't it.'

Wesley had to smile at the DCI's childlike enthusiasm.

'They're faxing us everything they'd got on Ickerman. His ex-wife's still living in Luton so at least we can hand the body over for burial.'

'So we're not treating it as suspicious?' Wesley said hopefully. Getting rid of the bones in the wood would be one thing less to worry about. And with the Spider about, they could do without distractions.

Heffernan shook his head. 'There'll be an inquest and my money's on an open verdict. End of story unless new evidence comes our way.'

That was it. They could forget about the bones in the wood and concentrate on more urgent matters.

Wesley was about to leave the office when he hesitated

at the door and turned round. 'Wonder what Ickerman was doing in Devon,' he said.

Heffernan gave a dramatic shrug. He didn't know. And he certainly didn't care. The man had been a pervert. Good riddance.

It was just routine. At least that's what Rachel Tracey and Paul Johnson told the headmaster of Belsinger School. At his morning briefing Gerry Heffernan had told them to go to the school and ask any teachers who had known Marrick, Tench and Grisham some pertinent questions.

Someone must know something, Rachel said to Paul as they drove out to Littlebury. The three victims must have something in common besides the fact that they were in the same house at the same school at the same time. Or perhaps they didn't. Perhaps the Spider, for some reason best known to himself, harboured a murderous hatred of all boys who had been in Tavistock House that particular year.

Bullying was the first thing that sprung to Rachel's mind. What if another boy had been bullied beyond endurance by Charles Marrick and his cronies and had resorted to the ultimate revenge? If this was the case, Paul Johnson pointed out, it meant that Tench and Grisham must have been Marrick's accomplices. Rachel had a good feeling about this theory. Bullying could blight lives. She felt a little uncomfortable as she recalled her own school days. She was only too aware that she had been bossy and intolerant of the weaknesses of others. But had she been a bully? Perhaps she'd been a borderline case. And that was something she wasn't exactly proud of.

They were expected, which relieved Rachel of the burden of awkward explanations. A fearsome secretary in half-moon glasses showed them into the headmaster's study. Somehow it was exactly as she'd imagined a headmaster's study in a public school to be – oak panelled and masculine with an array of gleaming silver sports trophies on display amidst the old school photographs. It was like something out of an old film, she thought. Hardly real. And quite unlike the comprehensive school she and her brothers had attended.

Dr Wynn was all co-operation. He'd already had a visit from a DCI Heffernan and a DI Peterson and was prepared to help in any way. He'd mentioned the enquiry to some of the longer-serving members of staff who'd been there at the time the victims had been pupils and they were happy to share their reminiscences, even though they doubted whether they could be of much help.

Dr Wynn announced that they could use the staff room to conduct their interviews. He spoke as though he was doing them a special favour and Rachel guessed she was supposed to sound duly grateful for the gracious concession. But she didn't. It was a murder investigation and she was calling the shots.

The staff room was like a larger, untidier, version of the headmaster's study. Dark oak panels and venerable leather armchairs gave it the feeling of a gentleman's club. Rachel felt like picking up one of the felt-tipped pens that lay on the table by the window and scrawling some obscene graffiti about the place. It was too smug by half.

There were four teachers in all who'd been serving at the chalk face when the three victims were schoolboys. Physically they were all quite different but Rachel thought they all looked similar somehow with their dusty black gowns flapping behind them. There was something semi-monastic about them, absorbed over the years by living in an atmosphere of male scholarship. It would do Belsinger good, Rachel thought, to go co-ed. Or better still, to be absorbed into the state sector. But that, she knew, would never happen.

She could sense these men weren't comfortable in the presence of a woman in authority. She had passed younger teachers in the corridor, of course – the new generation. But the men she was interviewing were as extinct as the dinosaurs, hanging on to their posts by their fingertips until retirement loomed. Which surely couldn't be far off for any of them.

They answered all the questions she put to them politely, of course. Yes, they had known the boys in question but not well – apart from Marrick who'd been a notorious trouble-maker. If anybody had known them well, it would have been their housemaster, Mr Dean. He'd have been aware of every-thing that went on. That was his job.

The four men seemed to be speaking from the same script, almost as if they'd concocted their story between them beforehand. When they had gone, Paul pointed out that there might be nothing sinister about the similarity of their state-ments – it might just be the truth. But this wasn't what Rachel wanted to hear. These men were hiding something. Closing ranks.

In the end it seemed there was nothing more they could do at Belsinger School. Rachel Tracey had to acknowledge that it was hardly worth getting a search warrant and tearing the place apart just to satisfy her prejudices. If there had ever been any evidence on the premises, it would have disappeared years ago. But there was one thing she wanted.

She asked the fearsome secretary as sweetly as she could, for a list of all the pupils who'd been at Belsinger at the same time as the victims. Fortunately in this at least, Belsinger seemed to have bowed to the twenty-first century and Rachel was presented with a computer printout. The secre-tary said proudly that she'd given herself the task of putting all the school records on her database and she'd got back as far as the 1950s. Rachel allowed her a grateful smile. The woman's single-minded industriousness had made her job much easier.

It wasn't until she returned to Tradmouth police station that Rachel bothered examining the list she'd been given. And when she read it, she noticed one name in particular in the year above Marrick and his contemporaries. Bartholomew Carter.

Barty Carter had never once mentioned that he'd known Simon Tench from his school days. And Rachel wondered why.

'I hope we get coffee. I had a look at the menu last time we were there – do you realise a small cup of coffee costs three quid?'

'So Darren Collins hasn't given up robbery after all,' Wesley grinned.

Gerry Heffernan stayed silent for the rest of the journey. Whether he was anticipating the coffee at Le Petit Poisson or planning what he was going to ask the Great Chef about his trip to Chester, Wesley wasn't sure.

Normally, Wesley would have suggested walking to the restaurant but there was drizzle in the air and time was tight. Besides, they were due at Neil's dig straight afterwards to speak to Norman Hedge, the victims' old history teacher.

The restaurant was shut but they rang the bell. Jean-Claude Montfort greeted them like old friends, which Wesley thought rather surprising as they'd brought nothing but trouble to Le Petit Poisson. Perhaps he was just doing his bit for Anglo-French relations.

The chef was in his kitchen. It was remarkable, Wesley thought, how he kept up the French accent, even under the severest pressure. But then the new identity had probably become second nature. As far as he was concerned Darren Collins no longer existed.

He ushered them into his office. Coffee wasn't offered.

'I thought you'd finished with me,' he said, rather peeved. 'I've told you everything I know. And I never knew that other bloke . . . the vet.'

'You were in Chester on the sixteenth of June,' Wesley said, watching his face.

'That's right. I was up there for The Best Food Show. Did a TV recording there. What's that got to do with . . . ?'

'Another man was murdered on that day.' He paused for effect. 'He was killed in exactly the same way as the others. And he lived in the centre of Chester.'

He let the implication sink in.

Darren Collins – better known as Fabrice Colbert – shook his head vigorously. 'I don't know anyone up there. And I was never on my own. It was bloody hard work. We stayed in a hotel near the venue – a couple of my chefs here and the TV crew. Ask them – they'll all tell you the same thing. When I went into the city centre I was with someone all the time. We were a team.' He sounded anxious, eager to be believed. But then anybody would if they were suspected of murder.

'Have you ever had any connections with a public school near Littlebury called Belsinger?'

Collins snorted. 'Public school. Do me a favour. I was a failing comp man.'

'Charles Marrick went there. And the other victims.'

'That figures. So who was murdered in Chester? I never read anything in the papers about a murder up there.'

'We're keeping it low key. We don't want to start a panic. You sure you've no connection to Belsinger School?'

'None whatsoever.'

'We'll check and double check,' Heffernan said, a slight threat in his voice.

'Check then. But you'll be wasting your time.'

Either Darren Collins was a remarkably good actor or he had nothing to hide. But Wesley couldn't help remembering how he'd fooled the entire country with his change of identity – he himself would never have realised Fabrice Colbert wasn't French unless he'd seen the evidence. Which meant Collins' acting ability was second to none.

'How's Annette?' Collins asked. He sounded genuinely concerned. But that might have been an act too.

'As far as we know she's okay. I was wondering if you'd decide to visit her . . . now she's on her own.'

Collins shook his head. 'I've gone back to the straight and narrow – Marie never knew about Annette, by the way, and I'd like it to stay like that. I don't think it'll take Annette long to get someone else to keep her warm at night. And whoever it is, he has to be an improvement on Charlie.'

Wesley sensed the man was in the mood to talk. And he might as well make the most of it. 'You've met Annette's daughter, Petronella Blackwell?'

'No. I never met her.'

'Did Annette talk about her?'

The chef shrugged. 'A bit. She said she had this thing about finding her real mother – about blood being thicker than water. And Annette said she was very clingy . . . needy, which seems a bit odd at her age. If you ask me, she sounded a bit unbalanced.'

'She claims Charles Marrick raped her,' he said, watching Collins's reaction carefully.

Collins swore under his breath. 'That's sick . . . his own stepdaughter.'

'I reckon Marrick and Petronella must be nearly the same age.'

'Even so. Look, Charlie was a devious, vicious bastard and a bully – and those were his good points. But I never imagined he'd do anything like that.' He looked Wesley in the eye. 'There won't be many tears at Charlie's funeral, I reckon.'

'As far as we know, the other victims didn't share Charlie's tastes. Simon Tench was happily married and well liked. And the victim up in Chester, Christopher Grisham, seemed an ordinary sort of man – no vices that we know of. The only thing they appeared to have in common was Belsinger School. They were all in the same house, in fact.'

Collins shrugged. 'Then if I were you, I'd take a closer look at the place.'

Gerry Heffernan stood up. He didn't like being told his job but his instinct told him that Darren Collins was probably right.

'You'll give us the details of the people you were with in Chester?'

Darren Collins obliged without a word of protest. Meek as a lamb.

Neil Watson stood beside trench three and watched as Norman and Muriel scraped away. From time to time Muriel would straighten herself up and place her hand in the small of her back. Digging was hard physical work – most beginners didn't realise that.

He looked down at the mobile phone in his hand. He'd just received a call from Annabel that puzzled him a little. She had just found some more material about Veland Abbey's seyney house in the cathedral archives – accounts for building alterations and various mentions of the place in contemporary records. But one promising book – a journal the last abbot had written before the abbey's closure – was missing. It was catalogued all right but it wasn't where it was supposed to be. Either it had been put elsewhere – which was possible but unlikely – or someone had taken it. Neil, sensing Annabel's frustration, had made sympathetic noises and told her to keep up the good work. But he couldn't get the journal out of his mind. He wanted to see it; to know what the abbot had written all those centuries ago . . . and whether he'd mentioned Brother William.

He stood there watching as Diane scraped away in trench one, a faraway look in her eyes. They had arrived at the site early that morning to remove any evidence of the strange ritual they had witnessed the previous night. But they'd been too late. There was no trace of any candles apart from a few splashes of wax. Lenny – they were still assuming it was Lenny – must have returned after they'd gone and taken the stuff away himself.

Lenny seemed subdued today, digging silently in trench four where they were uncovering a midden containing animal bones, broken pottery and oyster shells. The monks had eaten and drank well here at the Seyney House and they'd left the evidence behind.

The sound of Wesley's voice made Neil look round. His friend was striding towards him and Gerry Heffernan followed behind, watching the diggers with a bemused look on his face.

'Don't suppose you've had any more letters?' Wesley asked quietly once greetings had been exchanged.

Neil shook his head and when Wesley asked where they could find Norman Hedge, he pointed to trench three, rather surprised as the retired history teacher wasn't his idea of a man who could help the police with their enquiries. He said as much to Wesley who gave him a meaningful wink before whispering that it was always the quiet ones and approaching Norman Hedge, warrant card to the ready.

Neil was right. Norman Hedge hardly looked like public enemy number one – more like a retired schoolmaster who'd never had dealings with the police before . . . and certainly not on the wrong side of the law. He looked nervous and it fell to Wesley to put him at his ease and assure him that they needed his help, not his wrists in handcuffs.

Wesley suggested they visit a pub they'd passed on the main road for a coffee and a chat. This seemed to reassure Norman, as had Wesley's casual mention that he'd studied archaeology at university and that he was a friend of Dr Watson, the director of the dig. By the time Wesley had brought the car to a halt in the pub's car park, they were getting on like a house on fire and Gerry Heffernan was feeling a little left out.

As it was coming up to lunchtime they decided to have a sandwich and Norman joined them. While Heffernan was at the bar ordering their food and drinks, Wesley began the questioning – gently so that Norman had no idea that he was being interrogated.

'I expect you've heard about the recent murders of Charles Marrick and Simon Tench. And a man called Christopher Grisham was found dead up in Chester a few weeks ago.'

The man's mouth fell open for a second. 'I . . . I hadn't heard about Christopher. That's awful. I can't believe anyone would want to . . .'

'You knew all the victims?'

'Yes. I taught them all. They were at Belsinger School. All in Tavistock House. You don't think . . . ?'

'Think what?' It was Heffernan who spoke, impatient with Wesley's kid glove approach.

'That their deaths are connected with the school in some way. But I don't see how they could be. I mean . . .'

'We're keeping an open mind at the moment. However, Belsinger School appears to be the only thing the victims had in common. As far as we know they didn't remain friends after they'd left school. In fact they lived very different lives.'

Norman sighed. 'That's hardly surprising. They certainly had nothing in common at school. Simon Tench was a nice lad. Highly intelligent. Chris Grisham might not have been as bright as Simon but he was a pleasant, quiet boy – very good at art if I remember rightly. No trouble to anyone.'

'What about Charles Marrick?'

There was a long silence. Then Hedge looked Wesley in the eye.

'In my opinion, Inspector, Charles Marrick was evil. I suppose these psychiatrists would have a fancy name for it but I'm old fashioned. I taught a lot of boys during my time at Belsinger but I've only come across one who could be described as truly wicked and that was Marrick. He had no empathy for the feelings of others, you see. It wasn't that he didn't realise he was hurting people, he just didn't care if it gave him pleasure or advantage. He was completely amoral

– his only creed was if I want it, it's mine and damn the consequences. And he was manipulative. He used people, Inspector. And somehow he always ended up getting away with it. He could be very charming when he wanted something. But I saw through him even if others didn't.'

Wesley and Heffernan looked at each other. This time it looked as if they were getting somewhere.

'You're the second person to describe Marrick as evil, Mr Hedge,' Wesley said. 'We've spoken to the boys' housemaster, Mr Dean. He runs a bookshop in Morbay now.'

'Indeed.' His expression gave nothing away.

Wesley decided it was time to tackle the subject that was foremost in his mind. He took a deep breath. 'Mr Dean told us that you and the late headmaster of Belsinger, Mr Hadderson, were close friends.' He watched the man intently. His face was impassive but he sensed that he was hiding deep emotions – putting on a familiar mask to conceal his feelings. Just as he had done for so many years at Belsinger. He was used to the charade.

'Did he?' Hedge took a sip of coffee.

'I can assure you, Mr Hedge, that whatever you tell us will be treated in confidence. If we're to catch whoever killed your former pupils, we need to know everything.'

Hedge took another sip from his cup, something to do with his hands while he thought. Then suddenly he seemed to come to a decision. 'If you must know, Stanley and I were lovers,' he said suddenly, looking at the two policemen to see if their faces had registered shock. When he saw that they were both looking at him with polite interest he carried on. 'We came from a generation that treated our kind of relationship as a crime, Inspector. In fact you could go to prison for it. We had to be very discreet. We knew that if our relationship came to the ears of the pupils' parents . . .'

'They might not be as tolerant and understanding as . . .'

'Quite, quite. As you can imagine we went to great pains to hide our . . .'

'But Marrick found out?' It was a pure guess on Wesley's part. But it was worth a try to see if the question hit its target.

Hedge's face turned red. 'How did you know?'

'Did he blackmail you?'

'He was far more subtle than that. He goaded Stanley. He knew that he was in a position to ruin him. Nothing was ever said openly, of course. Just hints, insinuations. And he implied that he'd think nothing of making false allegations concerning our dealings with the boys in our care. It would have been complete rubbish of course but filth sticks, Inspector, as I'm sure you'll know. It would have finished Stanley's career and mine. Ruined the school. And the school was Stanley's life so he adopted a policy of appeasement which, in my opinion, is always a mistake. Poor Stanley thought it was his only option. I told him to call Marrick's bluff but . . .'

'You and Stanley must have been very relieved when Marrick left the school.'

Hedge nodded.

'I understand that Mr Hadderson took his own life,' Wesley said gently.

A shadow of pain passed across Hedge's face. 'Yes. But that had nothing to do with Marrick. He discovered he was ill. A brain tumour. He was a proud man. He couldn't face the indignity of a slow death . . . of losing his faculties and being dependent on . . .'

'I'm sorry,' said Wesley and Gerry Heffernan muttered something that sounded sympathetic a split second after like an echo.

'Did you, er . . .' Wesley searched for the right words. 'Did you ever suspect that his death might not have been suicide?'

Hedge looked shocked. 'No, not at all. But . . .'

'But what?' Heffernan leaped on the moment of doubt too eagerly in Wesley's opinion.

'No. Of course he killed himself.'

'He didn't leave a note?'

Hedge shook his head, still shocked.

Wesley decided to change the subject. The man obviously believed there'd been nothing suspicious about the death of his partner in life. But Mortimer Dean had spoken of a cut throat. Perhaps it was just a coincidence. Or perhaps it was worth investigating further.

'Can you tell us anything else about Charles Marrick? Anything at all.'

Hedge frowned. 'There was something shortly before he left. But Stanley never told me what it was, which was unusual. We didn't usually have secrets from each other.'

'You've no idea what it could have been?'

Hedge shook his head. 'Whatever it was was kept very hush hush. I suppose Marrick's housemaster might have known – Mortimer Dean.'

'When exactly was this?'

'I think it must have been towards the end of term – after the exams when things were a bit more relaxed than usual. I can't be sure, of course, but that was the week Marrick disappeared. Nothing was said, of course, but I sensed it. Things weren't right.'

'So Marrick disappeared before the end of the term?'

'Most of the teachers were glad to see the back of him if the truth were known. There was a strange atmosphere in the school during those couple of weeks till the summer term ended. I asked Stanley if something was wrong but he said he couldn't tell me. It was a confidential matter.'

'And he never mentioned it again?'

'Never. I had the impression it was something he'd rather forget.'

'And the other victims – Simon Tench and Christopher Grisham?'

'It was after they'd taken their GCSEs, Inspector. The boys

were demob happy, filling in time. Then Simon transferred
to a sixth form elsewhere and Chris didn't take history A
level so I had little to do with either of them from then on.'

Gerry Heffernan had had enough. He was growing impatient. Being a naturally inquisitive person himself, he found
it hard to believe that in the cloistered world of Belsinger
School, the entire staff wouldn't have known if something
serious had happened. He said as much to Hedge, rather too
brutally in Wesley's opinion.

Hedge looked hurt. 'I can assure you, Chief Inspector, that
I'm telling the truth. Whatever it was was hushed up –
suppressed very effectively. Only a handful of people knew
and they weren't telling. But I did overhear Stanley speaking
on the telephone once. He mentioned a girl. No name. He
just referred to "the girl in question". Please believe me, I've
told you all I know.'

When they took Hedge back to the dig Wesley didn't
stick around to say hello to Neil. It was high time they had
another word with Mortimer Dean.

Helen Spilling's part-time job at Morbooks was perfect.
Interesting and relatively undemanding, it fitted in perfectly
with the school run. Mr Dean – somehow she'd never felt
it appropriate to call him by his first name – was a bit of
an old woman but that wasn't a problem. She'd had far worse
bosses in her time.

When she arrived at the shop for her usual Friday afternoon shift, Helen was surprised to find the door locked. Mr
Dean must have shut up at lunchtime to visit the warehouse,
she thought, taking the keys from her handbag. But he was
bound to be back soon and in the meantime she'd make
herself a cup of tea in the kitchen at the back of the shop.

As she let herself in she noticed that the open sign was
lying on the mat, which was unusual: Mr Dean was so
pedantic about that sort of thing and he always turned the

sign to closed if he had to shut the shop for any reason, even if he slipped out for a few moments to buy a paper or a sandwich. Helen felt a little uneasy but she told herself she was being stupid. Everybody makes mistakes sometimes – even Mr Dean – and the sign had probably fallen off as he shut the door behind him.

When Helen slipped behind the counter, she noticed that the till was open and empty – just as Mr Dean left it when he shut up the shop last thing at night. But the shop would surely have been open that morning, she thought. If he was shutting for any reason, he would surely have let her know.

She stared at the till for a while. Mr Dean took the float upstairs every night – just to be on the safe side because there was so much crime about these days. If she was to open up the shop, she needed some change and the cash box was kept in the top right-hand drawer in the dresser. She was sure that Mr Dean wouldn't mind if she went up to the flat to get it. Besides, he might be ill and in need of help.

Helen turned the sign on the door to closed and flicked up the latch. If she was upstairs she didn't want anybody roaming around the shop unsupervised. Only the other week somebody had pinched an expensive book – a guide to the Bible strangely enough. The thief had obviously glossed over the Thou Shalt Not Steal part.

The door at the bottom of the stairs stood open. Mr Dean never left it open and Helen suddenly felt apprehensive. She'd never considered herself a nervous or imaginative sort of person but she felt something was wrong. She took a deep breath and began to climb the stairs leading up to Mortimer Dean's flat.

In the silence every sound seemed to be amplified, especially the buzzing of the bluebottle that dive-bombed her head and then flew round in circles, preparing for another attack. Helen's hand was shaking as she pushed open the flat door and called out Mr Dean's name. Feebly at first then a little louder. But there was no answer. Only silence and the relentless buzzing of the bluebottle, louder now as though the original insect had been joined by its friends. As she crossed the threshold, she saw Mortimer Dean lying slumped on the sofa. A glass had fallen on to the carpet by his feet. A whisky glass – Mr Dean's favourite tipple was a decent single malt.

She stared at the man in horror. There was no question about it. Mortimer Dean was dead.

Wesley Peterson and Gerry Heffernan – all dressed up in overalls and plastic gloves, just in case – stood together, staring at the body of Mortimer Dean.

'Natural causes?' Heffernan suggested hopefully. With their current workload, the last thing he wanted was another suspicious death on his hands.

'Who knows?' Wesley answered, studying Dean's face. The dead man looked rather surprised. His mouth was open and his eyes stared into space.

'Well it certainly isn't our Spider,' Heffernan said with what sounded like relief. 'Not a drop of blood to be seen.' He glanced round. 'Is someone taking a statement from the lass who found him?'

Wesley answered in the affirmative. Everything was being dealt with. They were just waiting for Colin Bowman to arrive. He'd been in the middle of a postmortem on a suicide victim when they'd called. He hadn't sounded his usual cheerful self..

He bent down and picked up the whisky glass that lay on the floor by Dean's feet. Wesley suspected that it had probably fallen out of his hand. He brought it up to his nose and sniffed it. Then he handed it to Gerry Heffernan.

'Does that smell a bit strange to you, Gerry?'

Heffernan sniffed at it and shrugged. 'Might be worth getting it tested, seeing as our friend here had connections with the three victims.'

Wesley dropped the glass into an evidence bag.

'I must say I can't see anything suspicious, Wes. He could have had a heart attack or . . .'

But Wesley wasn't listening. He was making his way to the small kitchen which lay through an arch off the living room. A few seconds later he emerged holding another glass in his gloved hand. 'This was on the draining board. Someone had washed it up. I wonder if Mr Dean was entertaining a visitor when he died.'

'It might just be a glass he used earlier and washed up.'

Wesley looked at the glass in his hand. Gerry Heffernan could be right. But he'd get it checked for prints just the same. You never know your luck. He suddenly remembered something he'd been meaning to tell the boss; something Dean's death had driven out of his head. 'By the way, Gerry, when we called in at the station Rachel spoke to me. She'd been to Belsinger and got a list of former pupils. And guess who was on it.'

'Surprise me.' Heffernan wasn't in the mood for guessing games.

'Barty Carter. He wasn't in Tavistock House and I think he was in the year above Marrick and co. but he was there all right. Funny he never mentioned that he'd known Simon Tench from school.'

'Perhaps he didn't. I remember at school we didn't really mix with people who weren't in our year.'

Wesley felt rather deflated. But he had to acknowledge the boss was right. Maybe Barty Carter hadn't even recognised Tench. 'I've told Rachel to check it out anyway.'

'Let's just hope the bugger's got rid of his shotgun,' Heffernan muttered under his breath.

Wesley suddenly felt uneasy. Carter was volatile, unpredictable. What if he'd put Rachel in danger by telling her to go there again? But he told himself that Rachel knew what she was doing. She'd be okay. 'If he was at Belsinger,

Carter might be able to throw some light on this girl Hedge was talking about.'

'Girl?'

'The girl who may – or may not – have been connected with the serious incident Hedge mentioned. The one Marrick might have been involved in.'

'It's all so vague, Wes. They'd obviously not discovered the joys of gossip at Belsinger.'

Wesley grinned. 'All male community. Positively monastic.'

'I thought they were usually the worst,' said Heffernan absentmindedly, picking up a pile of mail that lay on Dean's sideboard. The dead had no privacy.

Wesley wandered over to the computer desk that stood in the corner of the room. Dean's computer wasn't the latest model but it was sufficiently up to date to satisfy the technical needs of the average person. Wesley switched it on and, with a few clicks of the mouse, Mortimer Dean's e-mails appeared on the screen.

'He sent a rather interesting e-mail yesterday,' Wesley said, making himself comfortable by the computer.

Heffernan looked wary. He'd never managed to get along with a computer in his life. If he touched one either the screen turned blue or the whole thing blew up. 'How do you mean, interesting?'

Wesley began to read. 'Frankie, I really must see you. The police have been asking questions. I know it might be difficult for you but is there a way we can meet? I'm afraid things have got out of hand again. I know it seems strange that our roles are reversed now but I'm genuinely frightened for our friend and I don't know what to do about it. Yours ever, Mortimer Dean.'

There was a sharp intake of breath. Then the DCI asked the inevitable question. 'Who's Frankie and who's our friend?'

Wesley noted down the e-mail address. 'We can get this traced. But Frankie can't be far away if he wants them to meet.'

'Not necessarily. He says it might be difficult.'

Wesley had to acknowledge that Heffernan might be right. Frankie, whoever he – or was it she? – was, might be miles away.

They heard voices on the stairs interspersed with inappropriately hearty laughter. Colin Bowman had arrived.

And when he examined Mortimer Dean's body he announced that he couldn't say for certain how he died until he conducted the postmortem. But his first instincts were that he had ingested some sort of poison.

It was possible they might have another murder on their hands.

Rachel felt nervous as she drove out to see Barty Carter. She'd spoken to her mother the night before and received the farming community's verdict on the man, which wasn't good. But Rachel felt sorry for him, her pity mingled with just a hint of admiration for the way he'd stuck it out on the smallholding. He'd had problems but he hadn't given up.

However, she was reserving her judgement. He hadn't told them that he'd been at school with Simon Tench. Perhaps he had something to hide.

Gerry Heffernan and Wesley Peterson had no idea that she'd gone there alone but she'd thought it best. Carter would be more likely to confide in her if she didn't have someone like Steve Carstairs in tow, flashing evil looks, playing the hard man. Carter needed the gentle touch. A bit of tea and sympathy. But if he hadn't done anything about those pigs, she'd still give him a hard time.

When she arrived at the smallholding, she saw that Carter had taken her orders to heart: the pig shed had been thoroughly mucked out and the pigs were grunting happily in their fresh straw. As she stood watching the creatures one curious sow came to say hello and Rachel rewarded her with a vigorous scratch on the back of the neck sending the animal into an ecstasy of joyous rubbing and snuffling. Rachel had always had a way with pigs on her parents' farm. But it wasn't something she wanted generally known around the police station.

'Hello.'

Rachel swung round to see Barty Carter standing with his hands in the pockets of his jeans, watching her with a nervous half smile on his face.

'The pigs look a lot better.'

Carter stared at the ground, contrite. 'I thought I'd better get my act together.'

'You've done well,' Rachel said quickly.

After an awkward silence, Barty Carter smiled – a smile that transformed his face and made him, in Rachel's opinion, the right side of attractive. 'So you're not going to report me, Detective Sergeant?'

Rachel hesitated. It wouldn't do to seem too soft or to let him think he'd got away with his previous behaviour altogether. 'I'll be keeping an eye on the situation, Mr Carter. But from what I can see, you seem to be making progress.' She looked round. 'Is there somewhere we can talk?'

Carter led her into the house and she noticed that he'd made an effort here as well. The place looked a good deal cleaner and the paperwork that had been scattered over every available surface was stacked in neat piles.

'I'm trying to sort everything out,' he explained. 'When my wife left I went through a bad time but . . . I've decided to get my life on track again.' He looked at her, sheepishly. 'I poured all the booze down the sink the night after you came. I don't know, maybe it took a visit from the police to give me the kick up the backside I needed. I just hope I can bloody keep it up.'

Rachel smiled. 'Look, if you want any advice on farming or . . . I'm sure my dad or one of my brothers would be able to have a chat . . . pass on their experience.' The Traceys didn't have a high opinion of posh people from the city who had the same attitude to farming as Marie Antoinette had to shepherding – a pretty game. But Rachel could be very persuasive when she put her mind to it.

Barty Carter gave her a shy, grateful smile. 'Thanks. I can't go on calling you Detective Sergeant, can I? What's your first name?'

'Rachel.'

'Thanks, Rachel. Er . . . did you come to check on the pigs or is this just a social call?'

'Neither really.' She paused. It was time to slip back into the role of police officer. She'd have to put her sympathy on hold and watch out for lies and evasions. 'Last time I visited you didn't mention that you'd been to school with Simon Tench.'

'I didn't think it was relevant. He was in the year below me and I didn't really know him. In fact I didn't know him at all. We weren't in the same house so our paths never crossed.'

The explanation sounded perfectly plausible to Rachel. There were girls in the year below her at school she would walk past in the street and not recognise. But she had to continue with the questioning. There might be something – some snippet of apparently irrelevant information – that might be of some help. 'Did you know Charles Marrick or Christopher Grisham?'

Barty Carter shook his head. 'I don't recognise the second name but the first one rings a bell. I seem to remember someone nudging me in the corridor and whispering 'That's the famous Charlie Marrick.' But I didn't take much notice at the time. I had other things on my mind.' He grinned. 'I was in the lower sixth and we used to sneak out to the nearest pub. I think there were a couple of local girls who took my fancy. Consequently, I didn't take much notice of the famous Charlie Marrick.'

'Can you tell me anything about him?'

Carter shrugged. 'I think he was usually in trouble for

something and I heard a whisper there was an incident with a girl but . . . Sorry I can't be more help.'

'You never thought to tell us you knew Marrick?'

'I didn't know him.'

Rachel usually had a suspicious mind – it probably went with the job. But there was something in Carter's manner that made her think he was telling the truth.

'Is there anything else . . . anything at all? You might not think it's relevant but . . .'

'Sorry, that's all I know. But there is something I'd like to ask.'

'What's that?'

'Any chance of us going out for a drink one night?'

'Nice try,' Rachel muttered. Then, after a few moments' thought, she said, 'We'll see,' with a businesslike smile.

As Carter watched her drive off, her wheels churning up the mud produced by the leaking tap near the gate, he suddenly felt more optimistic than he had done for months.

Brother Francis sat by his computer and stared at Mortimer Dean's e-mail. Dean had kept in touch with him since he'd left Belsinger. There'd been a rapport between housemaster and pupil. Nothing sexual, more a recognition of a sympathetic soul. They'd exchanged letters at first then later, with the advent of technology in the ordered world of Shenton Abbey, they'd corresponded by e-mail. Nothing profound or spiritual – Dean had been a devout atheist – but pleasantries and news of old boys.

There had been no mention of Charlie Marrick, of course. By tacit agreement it was never spoken of. As if ignoring it would make it vanish as though it had never happened.

But Brother Francis knew it had happened. He'd been there. It was something he'd shared with his confessor before he took his vows; something for which he knew he'd received forgiveness. But even though he'd received his absolution, the very thought of that terrible time made him feel physically sick. It was an indelible stain on his life. Something he could never get rid of by reason and prayer. He still dreamed about it, even after fifteen years. It would be with him until he died.

Brother Francis hadn't concerned himself with Greek mythology since his school days at Belsinger. But he knew Nemesis was the goddess of retribution. And, in spite of his higher calling, he could sense that she was very near. Just biding her time.

CHAPTER 11

Ever since they found him, I've been longing to tell the truth but somehow I can't find the words. Perhaps if I write more about Brother William, you'll understand.

You'll wonder why I've chosen you, Neil. But the truth is, I don't know. Why are any of us chosen for anything?

Imagine those monks at the seyney house. How they must have been back then – warm and relaxed after their blood-letting. Brother William must have been at ease, unsuspecting, and I've been wondering about his relationship with Brother Silas before it happened. Those tragic events at the seyney house can't have come from nowhere. There must have been a preparation. Watching eyes, full of desire. There must have been some hint of sin. Perhaps Brother William had been too innocent to recognise the signs.

Sometimes I feel as if I'm about to go mad. As if all this putrid filth will burst from my body and I will die like I deserve to.

The writer's hand shook. The last letter had been posted and Neil would receive it next morning – Saturday. This latest one would be the final word before the truth was revealed. The time was almost near. But what was the worst that could happen? Only death.

*

Rachel seemed quiet when she returned to the CID office. Wesley asked her if anything was the matter but she shook her head and gave him an enigmatic smile that would have put the Mona Lisa to shame.

'Did Barty Carter have anything interesting to say for himself?' Wesley asked.

The smile was still playing on her lips as she replied. 'He claims he didn't know Tench and Grisham, even though they went to the same school. They were in different years and different houses and he says their paths didn't cross.'

'Think he's telling the truth?'

'Probably. However, he does remember Charlie Marrick having a bit of a reputation. And he remembers hearing rumours of some scandal involving a girl . . . but it was all hushed up. And before you ask, he's no idea what it was all about. Apparently he had other things on his mind at the time.'

Wesley thought for a few moments. 'Do you believe him?'

Rachel nodded. 'Yes. I do. I'm sure he's got nothing to do with this. It's just not his style. Anyway, what's his motive?'

'That's the sixty thousand dollar question, isn't it . . . the motive. From the picture I'm building up of Charles Marrick, I can see why he'd be a potential victim. But the others . . .'

'I know.' Rachel gave him an apologetic shrug. She was as puzzled as he was.

'Any progress with Celia Dawn's alibi?'

'I haven't been able to prove she wasn't where she said she was if that's what you mean. Think it's worth getting a search warrant? After all she did give him his last meal.'

'I don't think it's top of the boss's list of priorities.' Wesley sighed. He suddenly felt tired. 'Do you think Marrick beat her up?'

'She says not and, as far as I can see, she has no links with the other victims. But I'll keep digging,' she concluded wearily.

'What about Petronella Blackwell?'

'Her supermarket alibi for the time of Simon Tench's murder stands up. She used her credit card.'

'Doesn't mean she didn't make a detour on the way home.'

'Her alibi for Grisham's murder's been checked out too. She was off work for a couple of days at the time . . . claims she was doing Open University work.'

'But she could have nipped up to Chester.'

'No reason to think that.'

'Suppose not,' said Wesley wearily, aware that he was clutching at any available straw.

At that moment Gerry Heffernan appeared at his office door. 'Who's going to get me the postmortem report on the last headmaster of Belsinger – the one who committed suicide? Stanley Hadderson his name was,' he called out as a challenge to the minions at their desks. When Steve Carstairs signalled that he'd be the one to oblige, the boss returned to his lair.

Wesley followed him. He shut the door behind him and sat down.

'Anything new, Wes? Anyone been in to confess?' He sighed wistfully, imagining the scene.

''Fraid not, Gerry. Rachel's been to see Barty Carter.'

Heffernan looked up expectantly. 'And?'

'He didn't tell her much.' He hesitated, a grin spreading across his face. 'But she's got a bit of a spring in her step.'

Heffernan raised his eyebrows. 'I thought he was supposed to be a washed-out failure with a drink problem. Hardly our Rach's type.'

'Maybe she feels sorry for him,' Wesley said, hardly believing it himself. The Rachel he knew wasn't a sucker for lame ducks.

'That'll be a first,' Heffernan mumbled before picking up a handwritten list that was lying on his desk. 'I've been on to Colin. Asked him to do Mortimer Dean's PM as soon as possible. I asked for the toxicology report to be top priority.'

'You think Dean was poisoned?'

'Don't you?'

'Hemlock? The Socrates touch. He was a teacher who was ordered to drink it for supposedly corrupting the youth of Athens.'

'And Mortimer Dean corrupted the youth of Belsinger School? Come on, Wes, there was no hint of anything like that, was there? If anyone was a corrupting influence at Belsinger, it's my bet it was Charles Marrick. It really beats me why he wasn't expelled as soon as he started making trouble.'

'If Hedge is telling the truth, Marrick was blackmailing the headmaster, Stanley Hadderson, about their relationship. This was a few years ago now and having openly gay members of staff in a boys' boarding school would hardly have gone down well with the parents, however enlightened and liberal they liked to appear at their London dinner parties.

Heffernan sighed. 'You're probably right, Wes. That little bastard Marrick had Hadderson by the short and curlies. By 'eck, Wes, he must have been a nasty piece of work.'

'But he always kept one step ahead of the law.'

'He cheated Darren Collins. That was fraud. We could have had him for that.'

'And what's the betting he'd blame whoever supplied him with the dodgy wine. He'd make sure he came out of that one squeaky clean. That's what I hate about people like that.'

'Give us a good, honest villain any day, eh, Wes.'

Wesley smiled. 'And what about the other victims. There's nothing to suggest that they were anything other than blameless, upright citizens. And, according to their school records, they were model pupils.'

Heffernan looked up. 'Charlie Marrick was teflon coated because of what he had on Hadderson – that might have applied to his inner circle of mates as well.'

'But there's nothing to indicate that they were his mates, is there? Quite the reverse in fact.'

'Opposites attract, Wes. You know that as well as I do. How many kids from good homes become involved with undesirable friends? Doctors' and vicars' kids who go to the bad on booze and drugs. And policemen's kids of course: there was this DI in Neston – his son started hanging around with . . .'

'Okay, Gerry, I get the picture.' He found the thought an uncomfortable one. He was only too aware that he wasn't giving his own children enough paternal attention. If they went wrong, he'd only have himself to blame. 'But we've not heard any hint that Tench and Grisham were bad uns, have we?'

Heffernan sighed. 'Have you asked Tom in Forensic if he's traced that e-mail address? Frankie, whoever he or she is.'

'I thought you were doing it.'

Heffernan snorted. 'You know I never have anything to do with computers if I can help it. That Tom terrifies the life out of me.'

Wesley had to smile. Forensic's foremost computer expert was an amiable unassuming young man. But his virtuoso skill with the keyboard left Gerry Heffernan in awe, as if he was in the presence of great genius.

'Have you seen the evening paper yet?'

Wesley shook his head.

'Our mole's been at it again.' He reached over and picked a newspaper up off the floor by his desk It was the *Tradmouth Echo*. That day's edition. 'Here, look at the headline.'

He passed the paper to Wesley who scanned the front page, frowning. 'Police connect Morbay bookshop death to Spider enquiry.'

'Have you talked to Ray Davenport?'

'He's avoiding me, Wes. Every time I call him he's out – or his secretary says he is. I think we need to go round there. Have a word.'

Wesley looked at his watch. It was four thirty already and,

with the pressure of work, the leaking of inside information to the press was hardly on their list of priorities. Not when the Spider might be out there, waiting for his next victim.

'Can it wait till tomorrow, Gerry? Or we could ask the press officer to have a discreet word.'

Heffernan slumped in his seat. 'Suppose so. But the information must have come from someone here and I want to know who it is.'

'You could give the team one of your little pep talks,' Wesley suggested. He had known Heffernan's 'little talks' reduce new recruits to CID to quivering wrecks.

'I might just do that. You don't think it could be Steve Carstairs, do you? He's been unusually quiet since the Carl Pinney incident.'

'I've heard he's been doing a bit of bonding with his long-lost father. And Trish told Rachel that he's got a new woman. Maybe he's been transformed by the power of love.'

Heffernan snorted. 'Transformed by my boot up his backside more likely. Not like you to come over all romantic, Wes. What's up?'

'Nothing's up.' Wesley smiled, impatient to change the subject. 'I think it'll help us to go over everything we've got so far. Is that okay with you?'

Heffernan sighed. 'Until we get those postmortem results and Tom's verdict on that e-mail address, we might as well get things straight in our heads.'

Wesley took a sheet of blank paper and cleared a space on the desk before putting it down neatly in front of him and taking a pen from his inside pocket.

Heffernan looked at him expectantly. 'Right, where do we start? Charles Marrick's murder?'

Wesley wrote something down. 'Yes. Charles Marrick's found dead. Cause of death loss of blood through two puncture wounds in the neck and he had ingested an infusion of hemlock, possibly administered to paralyse him so that he couldn't summon help. Colin reckoned he would have been unable to move but aware of what was happening – knowing he was bleeding to death and not being able to do a thing about it.'

'Not a nice thought. So who are our suspects?'

'Carl Pinney. Nasty little thug and drug user of the parish of Winterham in the badlands of Morbay. He was in possession of the murder weapon and wasn't afraid to use it. Claimed he found it. Only trouble is, I can't see that hemlock's really his style. However, he did break into Simon Tench's surgery to nick drugs.' Wesley thought for a moment. 'The drug they took . . . ketamine; that's a tranquilliser. If you wanted to make sure someone couldn't fight back, you could use that rather than mess about with infusions of hemlock. Not that any of the victims would take anything Pinney gave them so I think that theory's a non-starter. And there's nothing to link him to the Chester case.'

Heffernan raised his hand. 'There's always our second suspect, Fabrice Colbert, alias Darren Collins. Reformed robber and celebrity chef. Marrick had just tried to defraud him by passing off cheap weasels' piss as expensive wine so Collins wasn't a happy bunny. And he was having it off with the victim's missus. Motives coming out of his ears, that one – and preparing hemlock'd be a doddle for a chef of his experience. And he's got a temper – you can see it on his TV programme every week.'

Wesley looked sceptical. He strongly suspected the chef's ranting and raving was an act, bordering on the theatrical. 'We've nothing to connect him with Tench or Grisham.'

'True. What about Annette Marrick?'

'She's hardly the grieving widow and Marrick did rape her daughter . . . allegedly. If you ask me, the woman's as hard as nails. But she does have an alibi.'

'A dodgy one, Rachel reckoned. And one backed up by another possible suspect – Marrick's ex-lover, Celia Dawn, who admits she had lunch with him the day he died.'

'What about Annette's daughter, Petronella Blackwell? Has she gone back to Bath yet?'

Wesley shook his head. 'No. She's still with her mother.'

'Odd relationship.'

'She is her mother. Her adoptive parents are both dead now so perhaps she's clinging to her only blood relative. Who knows? It must be an emotional thing, finding your mother after years without her.'

'She claims Marrick raped her. That gives her a damn good motive. And the same goes for Annette. They both had good reason to want him dead. None of Petronella's alibis for any of the murders are watertight. When Marrick died she said she drove down from Bath when Annette called her. However, Annette made the call to her mobile so she could have been anywhere – on her way back from Rhode for instance. She said she was off work alone in her flat earlier that day – no witnesses. And Annette herself could easily have nipped back home and done the deed. If we did more digging, I'm sure we could drive a coach and horses through their stories.'

'Did Petronella know Tench or Grisham?'

'Not that we're aware of.'

Wesley thought for a moment. 'We keep hearing that there was some girl involved with Marrick at school. Annette's much older than her husband but Petronella's nearer his age . . . maybe a couple of years younger. Any chance she could have known him back then? The others could have known about something she did and she killed them to shut them up.'

'We can check out where her adoptive parents lived but it seems too much of a coincidence if . . .'

Wesley sighed. 'You're probably right. What about Celia Dawn, Marrick's bit on the side who popped a Winterlea's gourmet meal into the microwave for him?'

'Yeah. If he was such a bastard, why was she feeding him? Maybe she had an ulterior motive.'

'Possibly. But we still have a big problem.'

'What's that, Wes?'

'We've got the world and his wife queuing up to murder Charles Marrick. But the same can hardly be said of Simon Tench and Christopher Grisham. Exactly the same MO and they were at school with Marrick. Same year, same house. That has to be the connection. But now their old house-master's dead . . .'

'He can't tell us what that connection is.'

'Too right.'

'Marrick was blackmailing the headmaster and the history teacher because they were gay. And Dean described him as evil. He was a crook, a blackmailer and a rapist and good-ness knows what else. I'm just surprised that he never came to our attention.'

'The really clever ones don't, Gerry. That's the trouble.' He thought for a while, absentmindedly sketching a dagger dripping with blood on his sheet of paper. 'Why were the others killed – Tench and Grisham? That's what I really can't understand.' He looked up. 'I've made a call to Cheshire police to ask if they can trace Grisham's girlfriend – Jenny Pringle. She went over to Germany to work in a hotel shortly after Grisham's death.'

'I don't see how that's going to help.'

Wesley shrugged his shoulders. 'Neither do I. But it might be worth talking to her. She might be able to tell us some-thing about Grisham's associates. If he knew anybody who's subsequently turned up down here . . .'

'It's a long shot,' Heffernan grinned. 'But we might be able to get a trip to Germany out of it. I fancy a cruise up the Rhine.'

Wesley smiled to himself. Their budget hardly ran to foreign travel but he'd let Gerry dream. 'What about Barty Carter?'

'What about him? Somehow I can't see him as our man, can you?'

After a few moments' thought, Wesley shook his head. 'Not really. If it was Carter, it'd be a shotgun in the face . . . not hemlock and a knife in the throat. There's something almost ritualistic about it, isn't there? Almost as though there's some significance in the manner of death.'

'Ruddy sadistic if you ask me, which brings me to those letters Neil's been getting. They're all about people bleeding to death. Reckon our killer wrote them?'

'I've no idea but I think Neil does. They've really put the wind up him.'

'You should tell him to watch out.'

'He doesn't need telling, he's nervous enough already. He says there's a weird character at the dig who might be his letter writer – name of Lenny – but he's no proof.'

'We could check him out.'

'Mmm. Another possibility is that the letters are from someone who saw him on the telly.'

'Tench was on telly in that property programme.'

'But Marrick and Grisham weren't. Let's face it, Wes, we're as much in the dark now as we were when Marrick was first found. More so. We thought it was a straightforward stabbing then and we had Pinney and half the low life of Devon in the frame. It's these others – Tench and Grisham – who've put a spanner in our works. And Grisham's death means the killer's been on the move.'

'Darren Collins was up in Chester at the time he died.'

'Yeah. Maybe we should bring him in again. Try a bit harder. He'd know how to cook up hemlock, wouldn't he?'

'He probably only serves it to restaurant critics who've given him a bad review.'

'Our Spider's never seen in blood-stained clothing and he's very careful to clear up after himself. He's methodical.'

'Like a chef.'

Wesley didn't reply. But he knew he and Heffernan were thinking the same thing. The more they considered the question, the more it looked as though Fabrice Colbert — alias Darren Collins — was an obvious suspect. They still had no idea why he should wish to kill Tench and Grisham. But, given time, they might come up with some plausible motive . . . if luck was on their side.

'Anything on the knife they found in Tradmouth?'

'Tench's blood was on it but no prints. It's the sort that can be bought anywhere . . . just like the one Pinney says he found.'

'Not an expensive chef's knife then?'

Wesley spotted a file on the boss's desk, nestled amidst all the other paperwork — some important, most not — jostling for a place in his overflowing in tray. 'Is that Colin's report on those bones in Sunacres Wood?'

Heffernan grunted. 'Could be. To tell you the truth, I've no idea what's on this desk any more. And the bones are hardly a priority now, are they? They belong to some sex offender who disappeared back in 1989. He probably crawled into the woods to die and good riddance. I don't think we need to trouble ourselves too much with this one, Wes. Colin can't even give us the cause of death. I reckon it was probably hypothermia or something like that. Natural causes.'

'The Forensic report said there were minute traces of blood on some of the stones and branches scattered around the bones and in soil samples taken from the surrounding area. Much of it must have been washed away but the shelter of the trees and undergrowth preserved some of the evidence over the years.'

'Okay, he had an accident — cut himself open on a branch and severed an artery or something. There's absolutely nothing to indicate that it was suspicious.'

'Apart from the fact that he was a sex offender.'

'And you think someone took exception to his nasty little habits and did him in? You sometimes think too much, Wes.

Let's forget about this one, eh. We've got enough on our plate at the moment.'

Wesley still felt uneasy about the possibility that Barry Ickerman might have bled to death – just like the Spider's victims. But he told himself that the boss was probably right – he thought too much. He made connections where there were none and made unnecessary work for himself when he should be getting home to Pam and the children.

'Get home, Wes,' Gerry Heffernan said as though he had read his mind. 'We'll make a fresh start tomorrow. Dean's PM's first thing and Tom should have that e-mail address for us by then.'

Wesley didn't need telling twice. He hurried to his desk and read through some notes he'd made for himself. Facts he wanted to remember. He'd walk home because he needed time to think. Rachel gave him a shy smile as he left the office but she didn't ask where he was going, which was unusual. Rachel usually liked to know everything. That's why she was good at her job.

When he was halfway home, climbing the steep, winding street that led up to his house overlooking the town, he began to wonder if there was something they were missing – something obvious. Perhaps everything would seem clearer after a good night's sleep, he thought.

Or perhaps tomorrow things would be as confusing as ever.

The letter arrived the next morning. Saturday. And Neil's first instinct had been to destroy it, to rip it into pieces. It sat there in his hand for some time, irresistible like some horror film watched from behind the sofa. When he eventually tore it open and read the letter inside, he sensed that the writer wanted to share some secret with him. Perhaps a secret that was too terrible to tell in the conventional way. What it all had to do with Brother William and the function of Veland Abbey's seyney house, he had no idea. But as he read it, he knew that he'd been wrong about Lenny being the author – it just wasn't his style at all.

He decided to take advantage of his day of leisure and drive to Tradmouth to see Wesley and Pam. Wesley hadn't been of much help so far but he'd want to see this new letter. And talking it over – sharing the burden – would make Neil feel better.

He arrived at the Petersons' house at ten fifteen and found Wesley dressed for work while Pam lounged in her towelling dressing gown playing with the kids and reading the paper at the same time – women, so he'd heard, were adept at multi-tasking. She greeted him with a shy smile and asked him how the dig was going. But as soon as he told her it was going well and that he was going to be on the local TV news again on Monday, their conversation was interrupted by Wesley who summoned him into the kitchen where he'd made coffee for both of them. He was due at work shortly, he said, and couldn't be long.

'I've had another letter,' Neil blurted out as he sat down and pushed the envelope across the kitchen table.

Wesley read it and looked up, his face serious. 'Have you any idea who this Brother William is? Or what happened to him?'

'Annabel's been looking in the archives for any reference to a Brother William in Veland Abbey but one of the books she wanted seems to be missing – the journal of some abbot of Veland who was around at the time of the Dissolution. Look, do you think the letters have got anything to do with these Spider murders?'

Wesley hesitated. He didn't want to frighten Neil but, on the other hand, he couldn't put his hand on his heart and swear that they weren't connected. He decided to opt for the honest answer. 'Sorry, we can't be sure. The other letters you've given us have been examined but we're still in the dark, I'm afraid.'

Neil leaned forward. 'The letters mention blood – people being bled. That's what this Spider does, isn't it – bleeds his victims to death? What if it's him who's writing them?'

Wesley felt helpless. Neil could well be right. But the letters had yielded no clue about their author.

'You suspected someone at your dig, didn't you? Lenny was it?'

'Yes but now I'm not so sure. He doesn't seem particularly interested in monks. Annabel was sure she recognised him so I thought he might have been snooping in the archives. However, she told me yesterday that she saw him once protesting at some hunt she went to.'

'Another dead end then. What about Norman Hedge?'

'What about him? He's a retired teacher. A nice, harmless man.'

'So you don't see him as your letter writer?'

Neil shook his head.

Wesley put a hand on Neil's arm. 'Look, there's absolutely no evidence that your letter writer is our killer. I know there's all this mention of blood but you're digging up the place where monks went to be bled so it's probably a coincidence.' He didn't know whether he believed what he was saying but he wanted to allay Neil's fears.

He looked at his watch. He had dallied at home long enough – mainly in an attempt to keep Pam onside. Gerry Heffernan reckoned that as they'd been working long hours all week, they needed a little rest and relaxation if they were to be of any use to the enquiry. Wesley had been ordered to take his time and meet the boss at the police station at eleven before going on to the hospital for Mortimer Dean's postmortem – something Wesley wasn't looking forward to.

After telling Neil to make himself another coffee and stay and keep Pam company, he kissed Pam goodbye and told her he'd try not to be late back. In fact if her mother had a guilty conscience about letting them down last weekend and was willing to babysit, they'd go out for a meal that evening. As Neil watched Wesley go, Pam asked him to entertain the kids while she got dressed. Neil fixed an awkward grin to his face – he'd have preferred minding a pool full of man-eating crocodiles than a couple of young children. But he wasn't going to let Pam know that.

Steve Carstairs held Joanne's hand. He knew it was the sort of thing teenagers did but he didn't really care. The previous night they'd been out for a drink but once again she'd made an excuse not to stay at his flat. She was still playing hard to get but Steve found he was quite enjoying the challenge.

That morning he'd picked her up at her small bed-sit in Bloxham, not far from the harbour, and given her a lift into Tradmouth, hoping that soon all his good behaviour would be rewarded. She was starting work at eleven and he was supposed to have been in the CID office an hour ago. But he had his story ready in case Gerry Heffernan made one of his wisecracks. He'd been to pick up the inquest report on the ex-headmaster of that posh school the Spider's victims went to. He'd picked it up first thing before he called on Joanne and he had it there in an envelope ready to present to the boss. That would shut him up.

When they reached Burton's Butties, Steve and Joanne stood facing each other as if neither wanted to be the first to make the parting move. 'See you tonight, then?' Steve said, trying to sound casual.

'I don't know. I'll ring you.'

Steve bent to kiss her. Then he stood back, his hands resting on her shoulders. 'You're gorgeous, you know that.'

Joanne gave him an enigmatic smile. 'So you keep saying.'

He looked into her eyes. What more did she want? He'd never known a female resist his undoubted charms for so long before and, somehow, her unattainability increased her allure. She was driving him crazy, playing with him. And now he wanted her more than he'd thought it possible to want any woman. He was surprised – and a little disturbed – by the depth of his feeling. It was usually a quick shag and farewell in the morning. But Joanne was different.

'You could stay at mine tonight,' he whispered. 'Or would you rather I stayed at yours?'

'We'll have to see,' she replied, her face inscrutable. 'Look, Steve, don't rush me, eh.' She stood on tiptoe and kissed his nose. 'Your dad's going to tell me off if I'm late so I'd better go.'

As she disappeared into Burton's Butties, Steve could see his father busy in the back of the shop. He toyed with the idea of going in and saying hello but he decided against it. The old bastard had ignored him for long enough. It was time he had a taste of his own medicine.

He turned towards the police station and spotted Wesley Peterson walking up the High Street. He wondered whether to slip down one of the side streets, to pretend he hadn't seen him. But it was too late. Peterson had raised a hand in unenthusiastic greeting. The feeling was mutual.

'I picked up the inquest report on Stanley Hadderson,' he said, falling into step beside the inspector. It was best to stick to work matters.

'Good. What does it say?'

'Suicide. He got into the bath and cut his throat with one of those old-fashioned razors. Took his own life while the balance of his mind was disturbed. He had a brain tumour – probably didn't have long to live anyway.'

'Any toxicology report?'

'Tests were done but nothing was found.'

'No hemlock then.'

Steve shook his head. They were approaching the Memorial Gardens and Tradmouth's handsome new library loomed to their right. Not far to go now. Wesley decided that he should make an attempt at conversation. Steve might have been a pain in the neck in the past, but they had to work together so they might as well be on reasonable terms. 'Was that your girlfriend? Been going out long?'

'Not long.'

'I recognise her. She works at the sandwich shop, doesn't she?'

'Yeah. She works with my dad. That's how we met.'

A long silence followed as they entered the police station and climbed the stairs to the CID office. Perhaps, Wesley thought, he shouldn't have ventured on to personal territory. You live and learn.

As soon as Gerry Heffernan spotted Wesley, he summoned him to his office. He had news to impart.

'I've caught our mole,' he said viciously. 'I went and had a quiet word with Ray Davenport last night and it seems he's getting his story through one of the girls who works for him. New and keen, she is – hopes to end up in Fleet Street.'

'So who's been feeding her the information?' Wesley wished he'd come to the point.

'Our mole. I want you here while I cut off his balls and put them in my trophy cabinet.'

Wesley opened his mouth to say something but he thought better of it. In the mood the DCI was in, it was better that he was allowed to let off some steam. He just felt a little sorry for the mole – whoever it was.

Wesley was surprised when DC Lee Parsons knocked on Heffernan's door. Wesley could see his youthful face through the glass. He looked terrified. Heffernan growled a 'come in' and the young man shuffled in and shut the door behind him. He looked more guilty than most villains he'd locked away in the cells – and a good deal more fearful. He wasn't invited to sit.

'You've got a new girlfriend, I believe,' Heffernan began innocently.

'That's right, sir.'

'Reporter on the *Echo*, isn't she?'

The young DC swallowed hard. He knew what was coming.

'Bit of inside information impresses the girls, doesn't it? They like to feel they're with someone who has his finger on the pulse.'

There was no answer but the young man's eyes widened in terror.

'The postmortem results for Marrick and Tench were confidential. We like to keep things like the fact they were poisoned with hemlock back from the hoi polloi because that way we can sort out the real killer from all the nutcases who crawl out of the woodwork making false confessions to brighten up their dull little lives.' He looked Parsons in the eye. 'But you had to go and impress your girlfriend with your inside knowledge, didn't you. Was it her who thought up "the Spider" or you? Her at a guess. You don't look the imaginative type.'

'Well?' said Wesley. 'Was it you who leaked the information?'

Parsons cleared his throat. 'Yes, sir,' he croaked. 'Sorry, sir. I realise now that it was a stupid thing to do but . . .'

'But what?' Heffernan hissed, standing up, looming over the unhappy constable like the Grim Reaper.

'Well, I didn't think it would do any harm telling Sarah. I mean . . .'

'You knew she worked for the *Echo*?' Wesley said with some incredulity. It was many years since he'd been that naive and he'd almost forgotten what it was like.

'When she talked about her job she said it was all reporting village fetes and the mayor's charity engagements. I never thought . . . She seemed really interested in these murders and . . .'

'So you gave her chapter and verse.'

Lee Parsons hung his head. 'I'm sorry, sir. It won't happen again.'

'Too right it won't.'

'Please, sir, I know I've screwed up but . . .'

Heffernan shook his head. 'Just get out of my sight.'

Parsons hurried out as if the Devil himself – or Gerry Heffernan which was probably worse – was in hot pursuit. When he was out of earshot Wesley spoke. 'What are you going to do, Gerry? Return him to uniform?'

'I'd like to but at the moment we're short handed.' He shrugged. Lee Parsons's place in CID was probably safe for now. Providing he'd learned his lesson.

'I don't suppose there's any serious harm been done.' Wesley smiled. 'And it might alert potential victims to the dangers of taking drinks laced with hemlock from strange men. By the way, Steve Carstairs picked up the inquest report on the ex-headmaster, Stanley Hadderson. It was suicide all right and there was nothing suspicious in the toxicology report. And Hedge was telling the truth – he did have a brain tumour. Inoperable.'

'No sign of hemlock?'

Wesley answered in the negative. Then he took Neil's letter out of his pocket. He'd already put it in an evidence bag ready to send to Forensic. He pushed it across the desk and Heffernan read it.

'Weird,' was the DCI's verdict. 'All this stuff about blood-letting. Do you reckon our killer wrote them?'

'If he did, I'd have expected something more specific . . . even boasting about what he'd done.' He hesitated. 'But there is a link with the victims. Norman Hedge is taking part in Neil's dig. And I've been thinking . . . perhaps the killer uses hemlock because he can't overpower the victims physically. Hedge is elderly – no match for the likes of Marrick and co. And if the victims take the hemlock, they must trust their killer. There's nobody more trustworthy than your old history master come to call.'

Before Heffernan could reply, there was a knock on the

door. This time it was Tom from Forensic. He had a sheet of paper in his hand and he looked pleased with himself.

'I've been on to the service provider.' He paused, as if he was about to impart some dramatic information. 'And you're not going to believe this,' he said with a gleam in his eye.

'Try us,' said Wesley, wishing Tom would come to the point.

'It's a monastery.'

This made Gerry Heffernan sit up and take notice. 'A monastery? You mean monks have computers?'

'Why not? It's a place called Shenton Abbey not far from Plymouth.'

'Thanks, Tom,' Wesley said, wondering about the significance of this new development. It was possible that the 'Frankie' Dean was corresponding with was a former member of Belsinger's staff, retired to a life of prayer or contemplation. Or perhaps an ex-pupil – someone who knew the victims.

He saw the list of former Belsinger pupils lying on top of a pile of witness statements on Heffernan's desk and picked it up. 'There's only one Francis listed here, Gerry. He was in the same year as the victims and he was in Tavistock House. Francis Duparc. It could be our Frankie. He might work at Shenton Abbey – he doesn't necessarily have to be a monk.'

'Whatever he is, we need to talk to him. If it is this Francis Duparc and our Spider is going round eliminating everyone who was in that year at Tavistock House, he could be in danger.'

'Only if the killer knows where to find him.' Wesley looked at his watch. 'We should be on our way to the hospital. Mortimer Dean's postmortem.'

Gerry Heffernan scratched his head. He'd almost forgotten about their appointment with Colin Bowman. Or perhaps he'd put it out of his mind because it was difficult to face a postmortem on a sunny Saturday.

But there were some things that couldn't be avoided. And duty was one of them.

Barty Carter hadn't ventured into Tradmouth for some time. But he needed to eat – bread and milk and some tins to keep him going. In days gone by his wife had seen to that sort of thing but since she left he'd had to make occasional forays into town, scurrying in then scurrying out again, keeping his head down, courting an anonymity that was hard to win with the odour of the farmyard clinging to his battered waxed jacket.

Today he parked the mud-splattered Land Rover he'd bought when he arrived in Devon to give him the appearance of a genuine son of the soil, in a side street and made his way to Winterlea's supermarket. He had made a mental list of his requirements which included nothing stronger than a few cans of Boddingtons. Since he'd met Rachel Tracey, he'd felt more hopeful about the future. Even the pigs seemed to sense it.

When he was in London he'd held down a high-powered job – dealt with contracts worth millions. The countryside had defeated him once but now he was going to get up and fight. It was Saturday – he'd ring Rachel and ask her out for a drink. He'd say he needed her advice on some agricultural matter. And if she refused, he'd try again. Never had the arms of the law – long or otherwise – looked so inviting.

He walked on, enjoying his pleasant daydreams, barely aware of the crowds of shoppers milling through the High Street. It wasn't until he almost collided with a woman emerging from a gift shop, that he was jolted from his reverie.

The face on the other side of the road looked familiar. But it was a while before Barty realised where he had seen it before. Back in his days at Belsinger he had seen that face most days . . . but it had hardly registered on his consciousness.

When he saw Rachel Tracey again he would mention it to her. Who knows? She might be impressed by his powers of observation. He took his mobile phone from his trouser pocket and began to search for the card she'd given him with her number printed on it.

CHAPTER 12

Extract from 'The History of Veland Abbey' available from all good local bookshops

Late in 1535 the methodical John Tregonwell, a Cornishman and a subordinate of Thomas Cromwell, was ordered to visit various religious houses in the South-West and report back to his master. Of all Henry VIII's commissioners he seems the most reliable and independent and he didn't mince his words.

On visiting Veland Abbey he reported that 'The house is well repaired but £300 in debt. I send you a shoe called Mary Magdalen's shoe and St Helena's comb and St Margaret's tooth. I send you also a book of the miracles of St Petroc which I found in the library. The Abbot of Veland is a virtuous man. But his monks are more corrupt than any others in vices with both sexes.'

Wesley Peterson and Gerry Heffernan strolled back to the police station. The postmortem was over, much to Wesley's relief.

Colin Bowman stuck to his opinion that Mortimer Dean had probably been poisoned and samples had been sent off to the lab. Although Colin, ever cautious, wanted to wait for the results before he committed himself to a formal report, he admitted – albeit cautiously – that hemlock was a possibility. The dead man had consumed whisky shortly before his death – just like the others. But Colin concluded that this might just be a coincidence – lots of people, including himself, enjoyed a drop of Scotch at the end of a busy day. Colin's tentative verdict was that Dean had taken his own life. But Wesley had seen that extra glass on the draining board, washed and wiped carefully of any tell-tale fingerprints. Someone had wanted it to look like suicide but he wasn't falling for it. He was certain that Mortimer Dean had known the identity of the Spider. And now Mortimer Dean was dead.

And there was someone else who might know what, if anything, had happened at Belsinger School all those years ago. Frankie – the recipient of Mortimer Dean's last e-mail. As soon as he was back in the office, Wesley looked up the phone number of Shenton Abbey and his call was answered by a Father Joseph who seemed rather excited at the prospect of a visit from the police. Wesley went to some pains to re-assure Father Joseph that he only wished to speak to a potential witness and that there was no question of anyone at the abbey being hauled off to the cells. After this reassurance, Father Joseph became almost gushingly co-operative and confirmed that Francis Duparc was indeed at the abbey and that he was now known as Brother Francis.

Brother Francis wouldn't be available to speak to him until Monday, during his recreation period. The words were said with a certainty that brooked no argument. Brother Francis answered to a far higher authority than the police – he was out doing God's work that afternoon and an interview on the Sabbath was out of the question. Wesley, using all his store of tact, asked whether he could spare half an hour that afternoon as the matter they were investigating was rather serious. Somehow he didn't like to mention the word murder to this man he imagined to live on a higher, more unworldly plain than most mortals. In the end Father Joseph relented and told him that Brother Francis was helping out a priest at an inner city parish in Plymouth that afternoon. The monks at Shenton Abbey weren't an enclosed order, he added – they involved themselves in the community and the life of the area. He told Wesley where he could be found and Wesley wrote down the address.

The fact that Brother Francis was helping at a Catholic church in the middle of a Plymouth council estate made Wesley uneasy. If he'd been a member of an order that had no dealings with the outside world, he would undoubtedly have been safe. But if he was out and about, anyone could get to him. And that included the killer.

But he told himself that Brother Francis would almost certainly be working with others and then he would return to the abbey where privacy would be a rare commodity – almost like the boarding school he had attended in his youth. He would eat in the abbey refectory with the other brothers. No risk of a hemlock nightcap. Unlike the other victims, he'd be perfectly safe.

As they didn't want a wasted journey, Wesley called the presbytery of St Giles' church to make sure Brother Francis was still there. A woman with a soft Irish accent, possibly the priest's housekeeper or a stalwart lady of the parish, said that Brother Francis would be there helping at the homeless drop-in centre till five. She sounded disapproving, as though she imagined the presence of the police would set the cat amongst the charitable pigeons. Perhaps she imagined that they were coming to harass the unfortunates who came to the church hall seeking shelter and a bowl of soup. But when Wesley told her that all they wanted was a chat with Brother Francis about something he might have witnessed, she softened a little and said she'd tell the brother to expect them.

When Wesley broke the news to Gerry Heffernan that they had an appointment with Francis Duparc, the DCI didn't seem as excited as Wesley had expected him to be.

'Before we see him, I want another word with that Norman Hedge,' he said. 'He knows more than he's telling if you ask me. With a little persuasion, he might be able to give us the low-down on Duparc. And, who knows, he might know who "our friend" is.'

Wesley looked puzzled.

'Mortimer Dean's e-mail to Frankie: I'm frightened for our friend. Who's he talking about? That's what I want to know. Mind you, it'd be just our luck if this Brother Francis has decided to take a vow of silence.'

'That's the Trappists, Gerry. He's a Benedictine.' He looked at his watch. 'Well I suppose Norman Hedge lives on our route so we can have a quick word if that's what you want.'

When they left the office Rachel was talking on the phone. She blushed when she caught Wesley's eye and he wondered why. Perhaps all would be make clear in due course.

Neil called in at the dig on Saturday afternoon, just to check that everything was okay. When he arrived he saw no sign of disturbance. Just an archaeological site with the foundations of a substantial, high-status building, clearly visible now and laid out before him like a plan in the rough brown earth.

He hadn't heard a word from Annabel since her despondent call the previous day when she'd reported that the last abbot's journal was missing. Someone had taken a contemporary account of life at Veland Abbey from the archives – either that or some wannabe librarian on work experience had put it in the wrong place. These things happened. But he was still curious. He wanted to know exactly what had gone on at the seyney house. And whether Brother William had ever actually existed.

He looked around. Everything was ready for an early start on Monday and there was nothing more to do. The powers that be had declared the training excavation a success, for which Neil was truly thankful. The archaeological unit's funding was always a headache and at least the payments from the trainees had helped to fill the coffers a little as well as spreading the word.

He was just about to leave the site, locking the gate behind him, when his phone rang. He heard Diane's voice on the other end of the line and his heart lifted a little. She was asking what he was doing. She was inviting him round. Things were looking up.

Half an hour later he was at Diane's door. She lived in a flat on the outskirts of Neston – a slightly rundown Victorian house with flaking green paint. Cheap and not particularly cheerful.

Diane led Neil to her flat on the first floor which turned out to be more spacious than he had imagined. Diane had tried to conceal its basic shabbiness, cheering it up with bright Indian throws and wall hangings which, as Neston was known for that sort of thing, had probably been bought locally.

'I've just been to the dig to check things over,' Neil said as he made himself comfortable in a sagging armchair.

'No sign of Lenny?'

Neil shook his head. 'I reckon we gave him the fright of his life when we turned up that night. He seemed remarkably quiet yesterday, didn't he?' He hesitated. 'I've had another letter.'

Diane began to finger the beads around her neck. 'What does it say?'

'It rambles about this monk who lived at Veland Abbey. Brother William. I've asked Annabel to go through the archives for any reference to him but . . .'

'But what?'

'I'm just scared the letters might have something to do with these Spider murders. My mate Wesley's working on the case – the victims were left to bleed to death and . . .'

The colour drained from Diane's face. 'But why should the killer write to you?'

'I was on telly, wasn't I? I stuck my head above the parapet.' He paused. 'Whoever wrote these letters is interested in history. He knows all about the abbey and the seyney house.' He thought for a moment. 'Norman Hedge was a history teacher and he's interested in the history of Veland Abbey. He was the first to put his name down for that trip to the abbey ruins next week.'

Diane considered this possibility for a few seconds. 'You think it could be him?'

'Probably not. He seems remarkably sane. Lenny's probably a better bet with all his bronze age ritual stuff. Or is it the Aztecs?' Neil said, earning himself a smile. 'Very big in Devon, the Aztecs.'

Diane sighed. 'Poor Lenny.'

'You're not sorry for him?'

'Aren't you? Just a little bit?' She sat on the arm of Neil's chair. He could smell her perfume – Patchouli oil, the scent that was the biggest seller in Neston's foremost New Age supermarket.

She bent towards him and he reached out to touch her face. Before he knew what was happening they were kissing, tentatively at first, then with more passion. Diane stood up and held out her hand. Neil took it, clasping her fingers tight, and allowed himself to be led towards the bedroom.

On the way to Plymouth, Wesley and Heffernan had stopped off at Norman Hedge's little modern bungalow on the outskirts of Millicombe. But even though his pale blue Ford Fiesta was parked in the drive, Hedge wasn't at home – or he wasn't answering his door.

They gave up and drove to Plymouth. St Giles' church was easy to find. It was stark and modern – built in the architectural nadir of the 1960s – as was the church hall

attached to it. Saturday was the day St Giles' church enter-
tained the homeless and there seemed to be rather a lot of
them, Wesley noted with a little sadness. A local doctor had
come along to give medical treatment and advice in one of
the small offices off the main hall and there was a long queue
for his services. Brother Francis was doling out bread and
steaming soup with the parish priest, exchanging a few words
with the men as they collected their food, asking how they
were and generally exuding sympathy.

Brother Francis looked the part. Tall and thin with the
long, sensitive pale face of the ascetic scholar, he wore a small
neat beard. He could have come from any century in his
dark monk's habit. But his surroundings were firmly rooted
in the present day.

Wesley felt awkward standing there watching the gaggle
of men – and a few women – who were lining up so patiently
for their humble meal. He knew that a good proportion of
them would have seen the inside of a prison at some time
in their life and he also knew that they'd probably consider
him as an enemy. A representative of the society that had
rejected them and kicked them in the teeth.

He waited patiently until the queue had dwindled, Gerry
Heffernan standing silently at his side. 'Poor sods,' was his
only comment. Unlike many in CID, Wesley had always
known that the boss had a marshmallow heart.

Brother Francis looked wary as they approached. If he
worked with the homeless, he was probably used to the
police coming to call. And ready to leap to the defence of
the underdog.

Wesley showed his ID discreetly, not wanting to cause
alarm. 'Brother Francis?'

The monk nodded.

Wesley smiled sweetly. 'We're sorry to bother you. Very
good work you're doing here.'

'Very necessary work, Inspector . . . unfortunately. How

can I help you?' There was still some wariness there, despite Wesley's best efforts to appear sympathetic and unthreatening.

'I believe you received an e-mail recently from a gentleman called Mortimer Dean.' It was a statement not a question.

Brother Francis nodded. 'That's right. Mortimer was my teacher. My housemaster in fact. We've kept in touch over the years and . . .'

'I'm afraid I've got some bad news. Mr Dean was found dead yesterday morning. I'm very sorry.' Wesley bowed his head – he thought it was appropriate – while Gerry Heffernan looked on, solemn as an undertaker.

Brother Francis made the sign of the cross and mumbled a prayer. When he'd finished he looked up. 'How did he die? Was it a heart attack? A stroke?'

Wesley glanced at his boss and knew that it was up to him to do the talking. 'At first we thought he might have taken his own life . . .'

Brother Francis looked horrified. 'I can't believe that. Mortimer had no reason to kill himself.'

'But now we think there's a possibility he might have been murdered.' Wesley watched the monk's face. There was a flicker of horror there, swiftly suppressed.

'Nobody would want to kill Mortimer. He had no enemies. He was a retired schoolmaster who ran a bookshop – an inoffensive man. Well liked.'

'You don't know how he died yet,' Heffernan observed, neglecting to add that they didn't either. All they had was guesswork until Colin Bowman received the toxicology report he was waiting for. 'For all you know he could have just been in the wrong place at the wrong time – a stranger could have killed him in the course of a robbery – nothing to do with his personality at all.'

Brother Francis swallowed hard. 'How did he die then?'

'We think he was poisoned.'

Brother Francis looked stunned. 'I can't believe it. He must have taken something by accident. Nobody would want to harm Mortimer,' he reiterated. But he looked a little less sure of himself now.

'He mentioned someone in his e-mail – our friend. Who was he talking about?'

The monk turned pale and his eyes widened in alarm. 'I . . . I . . .'

Wesley could almost see his brain working, trying to get out of answering the question without actually committing the sin of lying. 'Well?' he prompted.

'It was just someone Mortimer helped once a long time ago, that's all. It can't possibly have anything to do with his death.' He pressed his lips together. That was all he was prepared to say on the subject.

Wesley tried a fresh approach. 'Did you know Charles Marrick?'

The monk looked wary. 'Yes. We were at Belsinger together.'

'What about Simon Tench and Christopher Grisham?'

'Likewise. We were all in Tavistock House.'

'You'll know they're all dead. Murdered by the same person. The papers are calling the killer the Spider.'

'I had heard, yes.' He shook his head, a look of genuine sadness on his face. 'Terrible.'

'The only thing the victims seemed to have in common was Belsinger School . . . and Tavistock House in particular. Unless you can think of anything else . . .' Wesley looked at him expectantly but the only reply was a shake of the head.

'Can you think of anyone who'd want these men dead?' Heffernan asked bluntly. 'Anyone who had a grudge against them? Anything they'd done during their time at school or after they left?'

'I know I shouldn't speak ill of the dead, Chief Inspector . . . or pass judgement on my fellow man, but Charles Marrick wasn't – how shall I put it – a good influence.'

Wesley picked up on the carefully phrased reply. 'But he was an influence? He was the sort of boy others followed?'

'Ever read *Lord of the Flies*, Inspector?'

Wesley nodded. He'd read William Golding's novel about the primitive nature of boys left to their own devices pretty early on in his school career.

'It's often the strongest who become the natural leaders, not the most virtuous. The Devil works very efficiently in the hearts of men, Inspector. Boys admired Marrick. They looked up to him.'

'And you?'

'I discovered the nature of the beast pretty early on. In spite of my calling, I've rarely encounter real evil. But there were times I thought I saw it in Marrick.'

'So you can understand why someone would want to kill him?'

'He must have hurt a lot of people in the course of his life. Perhaps he pushed someone too far. But we have to understand what made him like that. His parents divorced when he was young and he was rejected by . . .'

Gerry Heffernan rolled his eyes. He was a churchgoer himself but sometimes he found conspicuous virtue rather irritating. 'Oh please. Don't make excuses for him. What about the other two – Tench and Grisham? What were they like?'

'Just ordinary boys . . . like myself I suppose.'

'So who'd want them dead?'

Brother Francis said nothing for a few moments. Then he shook his head. But something in his eyes told Wesley that he knew more than he was admitting. A gaggle of scruffily dressed men had just entered the hall and were making their way towards the soup like lions approaching a water hole.

'I'm sorry, gentlemen. I've told you all I can,' Brother Francis said as he stirred the blood-red tomato soup, ready to ladle it into the bowls that stood stacked at his side.

Wesley and Heffernan knew they weren't going to learn any more so they thanked him and left. At least they knew where to find him.

As they walked to the car, Wesley had the feeling that something Brother Francis had told them was very relevant to the case. Maybe it was just something small he'd said, a passing comment. When Gerry Heffernan asked him what was on his mind, he didn't answer. He was trying to think.

Neil Watson had never been able to sleep during the day. And even if he'd had that happy ability, he rarely had the opportunity. So after he and Diane had made love, he lay awake, watching her sleep, listening to the soft sound of her breathing and wondering what had brought about his sudden rush of good fortune.

He didn't really know much about Diane, apart from the fact she had studied archaeology at Reading University. But it was early days. They had all the time in the world. If they felt so inclined.

As he lay there restless, perhaps even a little bored, he began to think of all the things he should be catching up with on a Saturday: shopping for the bare essentials; tidying up his flat so that it was fit for human habitation. He remembered the remains of last night's takeaway were still lying strewn on his coffee table but he supposed they could stay there another day.

Careful not to disturb Diane, he slid out of bed and crept across the bedroom on tiptoe, towards the chair where his clothes lay in an untidy heap. As he dressed, it struck him for the first time that perhaps his afternoon liaison had been a little unwise. He and Diane were colleagues – they were contracted to work together on the training dig all summer and if it didn't work out between them, things might be embarrassing at best and distinctly unpleasant at worst. He had always thought it a mistake to mix business with pleasure but there had been a few occasions when he'd broken his own rules – usually with disastrous consequences.

He let himself out of the room. He needed coffee – something to clear his head – and once he'd put the kettle on, he flopped down on the sofa and picked up that day's newspaper. He didn't often have a chance to catch up with the news so he settled down to indulge himself until Diane woke up and joined him.

He glanced at the door, a sudden feeling of panic rising in his stomach. What if Diane expected more from the relationship than he was willing to give? But he tried to put the thought from his mind and flicked through the paper, his mind only half on what he read.

After a while, bored with the news, he stood up and wandered over to the tall bookcase in the corner of the room. You can tell a lot about people from the books they keep, he thought. He'd said that to Pam Peterson – or Stannard as she'd been back then – when they'd first met. But, being a student of English, Pam's selection of reading matter had been spot on. It was just a pity he'd been too lazy at the time to pursue the relationship and allowed his housemate, Wesley, to get there first. There had been times when Neil lay awake in the small hours, wondering how things would have worked out if he'd been more assertive. But then living with an archaeologist was probably as bad as living with a policeman as far as dedication to work was concerned, so Pam wouldn't necessarily have been any better off.

Diane's reading taste ran from historical mysteries, through archaeological textbooks to general history, especially the Tudor period, interspersed with a smattering of cookery and self-help books. But one book looked out of place: a dirty, decaying volume of great antiquity, encased in a clear plastic bag, which lay flat on the top shelf next to a book about the dissolution of the monasteries. Neil reached out and touched it. He couldn't help himself. Besides, Diane was asleep so she'd never know that her privacy was being invaded.

As he lifted the book, he realised there was something underneath. Bits of flimsy paper. Newsprint. Cuttings. Curious, Neil carried them over to the coffee table and began to read.

Diane must have cut the articles from the local paper. He read the headlines. 'Boys' grim discovery.' 'Bones found in wood.' 'Police appeal for information about skeleton.' 'Can you give a name to mystery skeleton?' 'Who is B I?' 'Bones belong to sex offender.'

When the bedroom door opened he looked up guiltily. Diane was standing there dressed in a black silk kimono, staring at the newspaper cuttings in Neil's hands. He could see that her face had turned ash pale.

'What are you doing with those?'

'I found them on the shelf. Why? What's the matter?'

She marched over and snatched them from his hand, ripping them, leaving Neil clutching the remnants.

Neil stood up. 'What's the problem? Do you know something about this skeleton business? If you do, you should ... '

There were tears in her eyes as she rushed over to the bookshelves. She picked up the book in the plastic bag and carried it over to the chest of drawers where her computer stood, still switched on, a screensaver of a firework display going through its silent routine. She hugged it to her for a few seconds then she thrust it into the top drawer.

'What's the book? It looks old. Is it ... ?'

'Just mind your own business. Leave me alone,' she snapped.

He walked over to her and put his arm round her shoulder. She was sobbing now. Shaking. In her agitation she had brushed against the computer mouse and the screensaver was replaced by a page of familiar-looking text. Neil stared at the words for a few moments, the truth dawning slowly.

He took hold of her shoulders and swung her round to face him. 'It was you. You wrote the letters.' He'd thought that when he came face to face with the author of his letters, he'd feel angry. But instead he felt stunned . . . and confused.

She let out a shuddering sob and slumped in his arms, tears and mucus streaming down her face. Neil put his arms around her and held her close, stroking her hair, comforting her like a frightened animal.

'I didn't mean to kill him. It was an accident. I didn't mean . . .' Her voice was muffled by sobs.

Suddenly he felt a thrill of fear. He was alone with a killer. A couple of hours before they had become lovers but now she was a different person. And the change terrified him. Wesley had suspected the letters might be linked to the Spider murders and, if he was right, he could be in real trouble.

'Why don't you tell me what happened?' he whispered in her ear, playing for time, feeling in the pocket of his jeans to make sure his mobile phone was still there. .

'I tried to tell you in the letters. But I just ended up writing rubbish . . . playing games so I didn't have to face the truth. I wanted to tell you . . . I did my best.'

'And what is the truth?'

She shook her head and said nothing.

'What's all this stuff about Brother William?'

She turned away and shuffled over to the chest of drawers slowly, like an old arthritic woman. She opened the drawer, took out the book she had just hidden and placed it into Neil's hand. 'I went to the archives,' she said almost in a whisper. 'I was looking for stuff about Veland Abbey and I found this. It's my own story . . . what happened to me. I know it was wrong but I took it. I had to have it.' She looked at him and he saw that her eyes were brimming with tears. 'I killed a man, Neil. I'm a murderer. I wanted to confess but I couldn't . . .' She shook her head and began to sob again, her whole body shaking.

Neil took a step back. 'I'll take the book back for you,'

he said quickly. 'I'll say it was taken out by accident with a pile of other books. Or, better still, I'll just put it back on a shelf and they'll think it's just been put in the wrong place.' He knew he sounded too eager. He was appeasing a mad woman. And madness frightened him. Scared him stiff.

He wished he was somewhere else. Anywhere. The woman standing there was a stranger to him. He felt the mobile phone in his pocket again. He needed to speak to Wesley. But he didn't dare make the call for fear of upsetting her.

'The kettle's boiled. I'll make some coffee, shall I?' He moved slowly, like someone backing away from an unpredictable animal and as he poured the coffee, he knew she was watching him.

Early Saturday evening on neutral ground. That was the arrangement Rachel Tracey had made. Just a drink. Casual. Nothing heavy. She had told her housemate, Trish Walton, where she was going – she felt someone should know, just in case – and Trish had said she was mad. He'd threatened her with a shotgun after all.

But Rachel's instincts told her she'd be safe. Barty Carter was a man who'd been driven to the edge by circumstances and his ex-wife. As Saturday afternoon had worn on, she'd experienced a few small doubts, of course. She'd made a mistake once – a bad mistake that had almost cost her her life. But she kept telling herself that this time things were different. This time she could trust her judgement. Anyway, it was only a drink and she'd said she could only spare an hour or so because of the demands of work.

She'd arranged to meet him at the Tradmouth Arms at seven – she thought it best that he didn't pick her up at the rented cottage that she shared with Trish just outside Tradmouth, even though it would be on his route. And Gerry Heffernan lived next door to the Tradmouth Arms so she'd feel that there was somebody there in the unlikely event of an emergency. Her mother would have laughed at her if she'd known about the precautions she was taking. She would have said that if she was that uneasy about going for a drink with someone, she shouldn't be seeing them in the first place. Mothers were always right, of course. But sometimes daughters felt the risk might be worth it.

She wore jeans and a white T-shirt – high necked because she didn't wish to give the wrong impression – and parked her small car by the waterfront. She'd timed it so she would arrive five minutes late. The last thing she wanted was to be waiting in the pub on her own. She might pride herself on being a woman with modern attitudes but there were still some things a girl just didn't do.

He was waiting for her at a table near the door. He'd reserved a chair for her and stood up as she approached.

'Rachel. Nice to see you.' Barty Carter sounded nervous, which she found rather gratifying. He'd abandoned his worn, stained clothes and his disreputable Barbour for clean jeans and a blue linen shirt. They were well cut – probably expensive: leftovers from his days of city prosperity perhaps. He looked good. Scrubbed up well, as her mother would say. 'What are you having to drink?' he asked eagerly.

She pondered the question for a few moments then opted for an orange juice. She was driving. And, besides, she wanted to keep a clear head.

When he returned with the drinks Rachel asked him how his animals were. The pigs, he said, were well. And he was keeping the sty clean. He'd started doing jobs round the smallholding – all the things he'd been putting off doing since his wife left. It had taken Rachel and Steve's visit and the incident with the shotgun to shock him out of his downward spiral. He'd reached the bottom and now the only way was upwards. He had Rachel to thank for bringing him to his senses – for stopping him feeling sorry for himself, he said, looking at her like an adoring puppy.

He was taking stock of his life. Seeing where he should go from here.

Rachel made encouraging noises. It wasn't often she was credited with saving someone's sanity. But the burden of his gratitude lay heavy on her shoulders and she found that she wasn't altogether comfortable with the role of rescuer.

Their hour was soon up and Rachel began to regret her self-imposed time limit. To her surprise she found herself enjoying Barty Carter's company. He mentioned his ex-wife from time to time but he didn't harp on about his troubles, for which she was exceedingly grateful. Self-pity makes for a long evening.

When she told him she'd have to be off soon, he asked her how the case was going. Were they any nearer cracking the Belsinger connection? Rachel gave the usual noncommittal reply – the enquiries were still ongoing.

'It's funny,' he said, frowning. 'I saw someone I knew from Belsinger in Tradmouth today. Well I didn't really know them – more knew of them. Saw them around all the time. I'm sure it was the same person. I'm good on faces.'

Rachel was suddenly alert, like a hound that had caught the scent of its quarry on the breeze. 'Who are you talking about?'

Barty Carter proceeded to tell her, chatting away oblivious to the fact that he might just have become a key witness in a murder enquiry.

The killer flicked through the pages of Saturday's paper. They were using that name again. The Spider. It was a name to frighten children. Tabloid shorthand for a monster. It was mocking the killer's purpose. Mocking all that suffering.

The killer put down the paper, picked up a small address book and began to turn the pages. There he was. Francis Duparc. The killer recalled his face. Serious, dark, eyes wide with fear. And something else – fascination.

The clock in the corner told the killer it was nine o'clock. It was time to return to life. To put on the mask of normality.

Pam Peterson was having a dream, not a pleasant one. She was being chased up a hill by somebody or something she couldn't see and her legs would only move in slow motion. Her pursuer was catching up fast. And when she turned round she saw that it was Jonathan. She woke up sweating and breathless, her heart pounding, and looked at Wesley who appeared to be fast asleep beside her.

Della had turned up to babysit the previous evening, still unrepentant about letting them down the week before, talking as if she was doing them a huge favour. They'd had a pleasant meal at the Angel but Pam's mind had been on the Sunday lunch she was due to have with Maritia and Mark later that day. Jonathan would be there and the thought made her feel slightly sick. She'd feel safer if Wesley could have been with her. But, on the other hand, if Jonathan decided to make life awkward for her and drop hints about what had happened . . . Wesley was a detective, after all. He would be bound to pick up the undercurrents.

She glanced at the alarm clock – it was seven forty-five. Wesley would probably have to call into the police station that morning but first he'd promised to go down and make her breakfast. She turned back to him and kissed him gently on the forehead.

He stirred, a small smile playing on his lips, and was about to reach out to her when the phone beside the bed began to ring. Wesley muttered something softly under his breath and opened his eyes. It had to be for him. Nobody but the police station would call at that time on a Sunday morning.

He rubbed his eyes and sat up before picking up the receiver. It turned out that he was half right. It was Rachel Tracey but she wasn't yet at work. However, she did have some news.

Wesley put the phone down and turned to Pam. 'Sorry. I've got to go into work right away.' He smiled. 'Well as soon as I've made your breakfast.' He grabbed his towelling bathrobe from the end of the bed. 'Rachel had a date last night and discovered something rather interesting.'

Pam was about to say something risqué but decided against it. 'About this Spider?' she asked.

'Possibly. And if she's right it rather turns everything on its head.' He hesitated. 'I'll try and make it to Maritia's for lunch . . . promise. I'll tell Gerry I . . .'

'Don't worry. Maritia'll understand,' Pam said quickly.

'I know. But I want to have Sunday lunch with you and the kids,' he said before darting off downstairs to make the breakfast.

An hour later he was at the police station, perched on the edge of Rachel Tracey's desk, listening to a word for word account of Barty Carter's revelations.

'Do you think it's important?' she asked, thinking that perhaps, in her enthusiasm, she was making too much of it.

Wesley thought for a few moments. 'I don't know. Is Carter willing to make a statement?'

'I should think so.'

He hesitated. 'What if . . . ?' He stopped himself. 'Look, I'm going to call Cheshire police. There's something I want them to chase up.' He looked across at Gerry Heffernan's glass-fronted office. It was empty. The boss was probably having alarm clock malfunction problems – they happened to him regularly. 'When the boss gets in, tell him I need to have a word with him. Tell him it's urgent.'

'Right you are,' answered Rachel, wondering whether she should volunteer to be the one to take Barty Carter's statement.

Diane had confessed to killing a man and Neil wasn't sure what to do about it . . . or whether to believe her. When she was a child she'd killed him in the woods and left him to rot there. She'd nursed her terrible secret for years and at times she'd almost forgotten it, shoved it away into the dark recesses of her mind. Until she'd come across the story of Brother William, a story that had seemed to mirror her own.

When the two boys discovered the bones, Barry Ickerman had sprung back to life — a grim Lazarus who nobody welcomed back from the dead. Least of all Diane. Neil hadn't stayed the night at her flat. It hadn't seemed appropriate somehow. After the first shock of discovery he'd decided not to call Wesley for the time being. Diane had seemed too fragile to face police interrogation. And he'd needed time to think.

She had seemed calm enough when he'd left her but he hadn't taken the book — the journal of the last abbot of Veland — home with him as he didn't want to push things. There would be plenty of time to return it to archives.

As he sat there sipping coffee alone in his Exeter flat, he considered his next move. Diane had only been a child when it had happened so surely there was no chance of her being prosecuted. He had told her this when he suggested that she should contact Wesley herself and speak to him but she'd said she couldn't face it and begged him not to betray her secret. He'd agreed — after all, it had happened a long time ago and a few more days wouldn't make much difference.

The story she had told him kept running through his head. The isolated woodland, the man, the terrified child. The penknife that had been her only form of defence against his strength. The shock of metal meeting flesh as he lunged at her. The horrible gurgling sound as he collapsed in the undergrowth, his hands grabbing at her clothes, blood gushing from his wound.

She'd left him there, bleeding to death, fighting for life and for years she'd pretended that it had never happened. But the event had haunted her. She'd seen the man in her night-mares. She'd seen him in dark corners, watching her. Reaching for her out of the shadows beneath her bed; from the recesses of her wardrobe; from every doorway of a darkened street.

The torment had eased over the years and often she went for weeks without thinking of it. And when something did trigger the memory, she found she could pretend it never happened – that it was only a bad dream that had no substance. After all, no body had ever been discovered so perhaps she had imagined it all.

But when she'd visited the archives to discover what she could about the Stow Barton site, she'd found the book and Brother William's story had hit her immediately like a hammer on the skull. She had known exactly what the man wanted, even back then. And she had watched his blood spill out on to the earth.

She understood Brother William. She almost felt they were one. Brother William would have known exactly what she went through.

Neil had listened as she'd poured out her story and now he wondered what his next move should be. What if she wasn't willing to confide in Wesley? Should he tell him himself or should he keep his new knowledge to himself?

The police were looking for whoever killed Barry Ickerman, the man in the woods. And he'd told Wesley about the letters so he could hardly fail to mention the fact that he now knew the identity of their sender. On the other hand, if he said nothing and the letters stopped, the whole thing would just remain a mystery. Another unsolved puzzle.

It was something that needed a lot of thought.

Vespers was almost over and the chanted prayers made Brother Francis feel a little calmer. He had wrestled in prayer for most of the day, pleading with God for guidance. And now he knew what he had to do. He had to seek Father Joseph's advice.

As he knelt, the images flooded unbidden into his head. The beach. The laughter. They had used a sheath knife, specially sharpened for the purpose. They had all submitted to the ritual, holding out their forearms for the cold touch of the knife. There had been no worry about infection in those days. And even if there had been, the fear of Charlie's displeasure would have trumped any misgivings about bacteria. Charlie had decreed it, therefore it was law. And shy boys like Frankie Duparc, anxious to be accepted into the chosen pack, would have walked barefoot over hot coals if Charlie Marrick had told them to.

Charlie was pack leader. His word was law. And he liked to surround himself with boys who were weaker than himself. Simon – the Swot – Tench. The sensitive, artistic Chris Grisham. And of course there'd been Frankie. Frankie – the weedy child with the slight stutter – who'd spent his life in penance for what had happened back then.

Vespers was over. He stood up for Father Joseph's final benediction. Soon he would have to decide whether to reveal everything to the police. Or to stay silent.

Monday morning dawned bright and sunny. Perhaps, Wesley thought optimistically, they would soon make a break-through. Barty Carter had already given Rachel a detailed description of the person he'd seen in Tradmouth but Wesley wasn't sure how useful it was. The fact that somebody might have had associations with Belsinger School at one time hardly made them a murderer, and it was always possible that Carter was mistaken. But at least it was another line of enquiry.

Wesley felt refreshed after the weekend, even though he had spent a good deal of it at work. He had made it to lunch at Maritia's, unlike Mark's friend, Jonathan, who had

had to return to London late on Saturday for some unspecified reason. Wesley had been rather relieved. He hadn't really
taken to Jonathan – he was far too shallow and materialistic
for his taste and he was rather surprised that he and Mark
had remained close. Wesley's brother-in-law, the Vicar of
Belsham, hardly seemed Jonathan's type. But then they had
known each other since their school days so there was probably some deep bond there that Wesley knew nothing about.
He sensed that Maritia wasn't that keen on her husband's
friend either. But she had never said anything. Maritia had
always been one to keep the peace, even when they were
small.

Pam had enjoyed the lunch, he could tell. But perhaps
her good mood was due to the fact that the summer term
would soon be at an end and she was anticipating six weeks
of freedom. Wesley had secretly been looking at holiday
brochures – weighing up the options. He fancied France this
year. Pam loved France and a slice of sunshine and history
would do them all the world of good.

His dreams of pepper pot towers, mellow medieval squares,
good food and abundant wine were interrupted by Lee
Parsons. He had been quiet since disgracing himself with the
lady of the press. If Gerry Heffernan had his way he'd make
a rapid return to uniform as soon as the Spider case was
resolved. But in the meantime they needed the manpower.

'Sir, there's been a call from a DI Heath – Cheshire police
headquarters in Chester. He wants you to ring him back.
I've left his number on your desk, sir.'

Wesley thanked the young constable who, these days, was
the picture of contrition – the sinner repentant. Perhaps he'd
have a word with Gerry and recommend mercy. After all,
he was in rather a good mood.

He dialled John Heath's number, hoping he had something juicy to report, not just a sorry tale of how he'd come
up against a brick wall.

Heath sounded cheerful – almost too cheerful for a Monday morning. Someone had been round to the hotel where Grisham's girlfriend, Jenny, worked and had a word with one of her friends – a girl who'd been on holiday when Jenny was interviewed following Grisham's death.

The friend – a pretty Polish girl called Magda who seemed to have made quite an impression on the interviewing officer – had said that Jenny was a quiet girl who never talked about her background. Magda, who spent a lot of time in a local cyber café, had received an e-mail from Jenny just the other day saying that she was enjoying Germany. As far as Chris Grisham was concerned, Jenny hadn't talked about him much and she'd applied for the job in Germany before he died which made Magda conclude that theirs wasn't exactly the romance of the century.

Wesley thanked John Heath. He didn't know whether all this information was relevant. Jenny Pringle up in Chester had gone out with Christopher Grisham. Grisham had died – supposedly by his own hand – and then she'd taken a job in a hotel abroad. End of story.

He was about to end the call when Heath spoke again. 'We didn't find any pictures of this Jenny at Grisham's flat but Magda's got a photograph of some of the hotel staff and Jenny's on it. Shall I e-mail it to you?'

Wesley hesitated, wondering if it would be a waste of time and effort. But then he decided that it would do no harm and thanked John Heath again. They might as well cover all possibilities.

As soon as he put the phone down, it rang and when he picked it up, he heard Neil's voice on the other end of the line.

'Wes, can we talk? I'm at the dig. Can you come out here?'

'Have you had another letter?'

'No, but I need to speak to you . . . in confidence.'

'Look, I'll come out as soon as I get the chance.' He looked up and saw Gerry Heffernan approaching his desk. 'Sorry, Neil, I've got to go.'

He put the phone down. Neil would have to wait.

CHAPTER 13

From the report of John Tregonwell, King's Commissioner, November 1535

'The monks spend much time at the seyney house in Stow Barton which is a goodly house and the rule is there relaxed, encouraging much worldliness amongst the brothers. The brothers there delight much in playing at dice and cards and therein spend much money. It was confessed and proved that there was a frequence of women coming to this Stow Barton and I heard of one event so terrible that the brothers and the servants would not speak of it. But I may yet discover the truth.'

Brother Francis sat in the chair opposite Father Joseph, head bowed in silent prayer.

'What was it you did, my son?'

'Something terrible.' The answer came out in a whisper.

'Tell me.' Father Joseph leaned forward, his sad brown eyes full of concern.

Brother Francis slowly rolled back the left sleeve of his habit. There was a faint scar just above the wrist. Father Joseph looked at him, shocked. 'You tried to take your own life? Is that what you're trying to tell me?'

Brother Francis bowed his head. 'I was sixteen. Little more than a child. There was this other boy. He . . .'

'What did he do, my son?'

'He chose us. It was like a madness. I can't explain.'

'Go on,' Father Joseph prompted gently.

'He cut us. We had to drink each other's blood. It was a ritual he thought up – to prove our loyalty to the group.'

Father Peter smiled. 'Becoming blood brothers? It's not unknown in certain tribes, I believe. A rite of passage. Is that all you have to tell me?'

There was a long silence. But Father Joseph was a patient man and he knew there was more to come.

'One day it all went too far and the bleeding wouldn't stop. We ran away. Something terrible happened and we did nothing. We ran away.'

Father Joseph could see there were tears in the brother's eyes. He touched him gently on the shoulder, a gesture of reassurance. 'What was this terrible thing that happened, my son?'

A tear trickled down Brother Francis's face and glistened on his chin.

Trish Walton watched as Steve Carstairs preened himself in the small mirror he kept in his desk drawer, well away from Gerry Heffernan's gaze. If the boss had seen him, he wouldn't have heard the end of it.

'Going somewhere nice this lunchtime?' Trish said, trying to make the question sound innocent.

'No.' Steve sounded defensive. He looked at his watch. It was coming up to one o'clock. 'Just to the sandwich shop – meeting my dad.'

'Your dad gives you a discount, does he?'

'Something like that,' he replied quickly. He didn't mention that the real attraction at Burton's Butties was Joanne. But Trish could see right through him.

'How is she, then?'

'Who?'

'Joanne. The one who works with your dad in the butty shop.'

'She's fine. And for your information the shop job's just temporary. She's after a career in marketing.'

'Selling sandwiches, you mean?' she said with a grin.

Steve turned away. He wasn't having his ex-girlfriend belittling his latest. But there was always the possibility that Trish was a bit jealous and he found this thought rather gratifying.

He hurried out of the office. 'Enjoy yourself,' Trish called to his disappearing back. But he ignored her. Or perhaps he was just too preoccupied to hear.

'Trish, have you got those statements from Simon Tench's colleagues?' Trish looked round. Wesley Peterson was coming towards her, a frown of concentration on his face. 'I'd like to speak to them again – and his widow. Can you see to that first thing this afternoon, please? And Chester police are going to e-mail a photograph but they're having problems with their computers. See if it's come in, will you? When it does I want Rachel to take it over to Barty Carter's as soon as possible.'

Trish smiled sweetly. More work. As Wesley walked away, she checked the computer. Chester's e-mail was coming in and she clicked on the attachment. A smiling group of young people suddenly appeared on the screen, probably in a pub on a night out. Trish stared for a while. Then she rushed after Wesley, a worried look on her face.

'The picture's come in.' She took a deep breath. 'I recognise one of the people on it. But it can't be. It doesn't make sense.'

Wesley looked her in the eye. 'Well, aren't you going to let us into the secret? Who is it?'

Wesley had been hoping to get home at a reasonable time but with Trish's revelation, everything had changed.

Gerry Heffernan had sent Rachel along to Barty Carter's smallholding with a copy of the photograph. Carter had told

Rachel that he'd seen someone he recognised from his school-days in Tradmouth. According to Rachel, he'd been quite certain – but Wesley, who had never been very good with faces, had his doubts. However, if Carter confirmed that the face on the photograph belonged to the person from his distant past, everything might begin to make sense. Or not as the case may be.

Steve was still out and Wesley was just about to try his mobile number when the phone on his desk rang. It was Neil again. 'Look, Neil, can it keep till later? All hell's broken loose here and . . .'

'Wes, I need to see you . . . it's about that skeleton in the woods.'

Wesley tried to keep the impatience he felt out of his voice. There were times when Neil let his imagination run away with him. 'Can it keep, Neil? I'm just in the middle of . . . I could send someone from uniform round to take a statement. Is that okay?'

'No,' Neil said quickly. 'I don't want some plod coming round with a notebook and a blunt pencil. I need to talk to you.'

Wesley hesitated for a moment. If Neil was willing to wait, his information couldn't be that urgent. 'Sorry. I'll call you as soon as I can. Okay?'

'She's not turned up for work.'

'Who hasn't?' Wesley asked, puzzled by Neil's sudden change of subject.

'Diane.'

'Have you called her?'

'Not yet but . . .'

'Why don't you call her if you're worried? Look, Neil, I really have to go. I'll talk to you later.'

At that moment Gerry Heffernan came stomping out of his office. 'Where's Steve? Try and raise him on his mobile, will you someone?'

'I've already tried. There's no answer,' said Wesley.

'Keep trying.'

The phone on Wesley's desk rang again. This time it was Rachel. Barty Carter had confirmed that the person in the Chester photograph was the same person he saw in Tradmouth. The face from the past – from Belsinger School. Gerry Heffernan gathered what troops were there and stood in front of the notice board with its gruesome photographs of the Spider's victims.

But just as he was about to begin his briefing, Wesley's phone began to ring again. He answered it and signalled to Gerry Heffernan. This was something important.

Heffernan was standing beside him, waiting for the call to end. 'Well?' he said as soon as the receiver was put down.

'That was Father Joseph. Brother Francis has disappeared. He's not told anyone where he's gone.'

'A disappearing monk,' said Gerry Heffernan, rolling his eyes to heaven. 'That's all we flaming well need.'

Brother Francis had taken the call. He had told the brother with him that it was someone from St Giles' calling about the arrangements for the next open day for the homeless. But he had lied – a sin that would have to be atoned for like all the rest. He could hardly have told the truth. That it was his past – his very own Nemesis – come to settle the score at last.

He knew it was wrong to take the abbey's old Fiat that was used by any brother who needed it to travel on the Lord's business. This was nothing to do with doing good or helping the community. This was Francis's business and his alone.

He crept into the courtyard where the trio of aging cars was kept, serviced and cared for by Brother James who'd been a mechanic in his former, worldly life. The keys to the Fiat were in the ignition – the brothers worked on trust –

and Francis looked round to make sure nobody was watching before he started the engine. He didn't want to have to explain what he was doing or where he was going. He had to face this alone.

The meeting was to take place not far from where it happened. Appropriate really that things should turn full circle. That he should make his final atonement in that place where his life had been cursed for ever.

He was a cautious driver who always stuck to the speed limit and he'd calculated that it would take him half an hour to get there. He took the A roads until he saw the sign to Littlebury and, when he turned off, the lanes became narrow and winding, single track in places with tall hedgerows towering either side. He prayed as he drove, for protection, for forgiveness.

It had begun to rain, a light drizzle which cast a fine veil over the green, rolling countryside and, as he passed the gates of Belsinger School, his heart sank. It had been an awful place. Cruel. Brutal. Charlie Marrick had just been the personification of that cruelty. The bully whose activities had been tolerated by the powers that be. Until it had all gone too far.

He turned the car into the narrow and overgrown lane – little more than a track – that led to the place. To his own private hell.

As he parked the Fiat he saw another car pulled up on the verge by the path leading to Belsinger's patch of woodland. Nemesis was there already. Waiting for him.

There was no reply from Steve's phone and when Paul Johnson called round at his flat he found that there was nobody in.

However, Gerry Heffernan didn't seem particularly worried. It was just like Steve to go AWOL when he was needed.

It seemed that a car belonging to Shenton Abbey was missing, presumably taken by Brother Francis, and all patrols had been alerted to be on the look-out for the small red Fiat. Wesley had a foreboding that Francis was in danger. And he felt helpless.

Heffernan's mobile phone began to ring and, when he answered it, Wesley watched as his face turned an unhealthy shade of red.

'Where the hell have you been? We've had everyone out looking for you.' He turned to Wesley. 'It's Steve. Bloody idiot says he's only just heard I was after him.' He barked into the phone again. 'Get back to the station now.'

'Well?' said Wesley when the call was ended.

'Steve says he's been to the supermarket. He doesn't half sail close to the wind that one.'

'What about . . . ?'

Gerry Heffernan shook his head. 'It'll wait.'

Wesley hurried from the room. There were things to do. He just hoped they wouldn't be too late.

At five o'clock Neil and his helpers packed up. People had been asking where Diane was all day and Neil had used the tried and trusted story that she was ill. Nobody questioned illness – apart from Lenny. When he had asked what was wrong with Diane, Neil had mouthed the words 'women's troubles' and Lenny had fallen uncharacteristically silent.

Neil had put a brave face on it all day but as the day wore on and Diane still wasn't answering her phone, his anxiety had increased to the point where he could think of little else and he almost forgot that Wesley hadn't called him as he'd promised. He was quite relieved when it was time for all the equipment to be put away so that the diggers could go home. He helped the students lock everything away in the site office and put tarpaulins over the trenches because rain was forecast that night. Then, when everyone had gone, he drove off, after locking the gate to the excavation field carefully behind him.

He was aware that he was driving too fast down the country lanes but he needed to reassure himself that Diane was okay. When he reached the A road he put his foot down and the old yellow Mini protested with a judder. It seemed an age before he arrived at Diane's flat but the drive had only taken half an hour.

As he emerged from the car, he had a feeling that things weren't right. Diane's curtains were closed for a start. He opened the wooden gate and the hinges creaked, breaking the expectant silence, and when he pressed her doorbell he could hear it ringing in the distance but there was no sign of movement; no twitch of a curtain or faint rumble of foot-steps on the bare floorboards.

Neil stood for a while, wondering whether he should try Wesley's number again and ask for his advice but then Wesley had made it quite clear that his mind was on other things. Neil was on his own.

Except in matters archaeological, Neil Watson often found it hard to trust his own judgement. And as he stood there, shifting from foot to foot at Diane's front door, he was torn between driving back to Exeter and taking some decisive action. He struggled with the conflicting options for a while before pressing one of the other doorbells. Maybe one of Diane's neighbours would know where she was.

There was no answer from the first but the second bell produced a tired-looking young Chinese woman who listened politely to his concerns and let him into the hallway. She was a nurse, she explained, and she'd been on night duty so she'd been asleep most of the day. She hadn't seen Diane but, she admitted, it wasn't like her to leave her curtains like that. By the time they'd stood there in the hall for a few minutes wondering what to do, the young woman, who introduced herself as Eliza, looked as worried as Neil felt.

The landlord, Eliza said, had a key. But, failing that, she added shyly, a credit card sometimes worked – she'd resorted to that solution several times when she'd forgotten her own key. Neil took the hint and, with the help of Eliza who proved to be far more experienced at breaking and entering than he was, they managed to open the door to Diane's flat without much trouble.

Eliza's hearing must have been more acute than Neil's because he was still looking around, trying to get his bearings while she was making a bee-line for the bathroom. He was about to follow her when he heard a low moan. Then he broke into a run.

'Don't come in,' Eliza called as he hovered in the bathroom doorway. 'Just ring for an ambulance. Quick.' He knew it was Diane in there but he asked no questions. He pulled his mobile from his pocket and made the call. Then he phoned Wesley. He'd need to know about this.

Eliza was talking, mumbling reassuring words and she worked on Diane's prone body with quiet efficiency. Then he heard a groan.

Diane was alive. Just.

Brother Francis knelt on the earth, oblivious to the scent of wet vegetation and the damp that penetrated the thick cloth of his habit. Tears trickled down his cheek and he cursed himself again for his weakness.

'I'm so sorry,' he sobbed.'

The figure started to walk round the kneeling monk, slowly, like a scientist studying a particularly interesting specimen.

Francis knew it was no use arguing that he, along with Chris Grisham and Simon Tench had been innocents in those far-off days. Boys caught up in wild games. Hypnotised by the will and whims of a much stronger personality . . . the personality of Charles Marrick who had been as persuasive in those days as Satan himself. Francis said nothing in his defence and he bowed his head in the heavy, threatening silence. The birds seemed to stop singing: nature held its breath as though death was near. The death Francis was expecting and which he knew he deserved.

Their eyes met in a split second of sympathy. Then the knife began to descend, slowly, almost ceremoniously. But its journey was suddenly interrupted by the ringing of a mobile phone.

CHAPTER 14

From the journal of Abbot Thomas Standing – 15 November 1535
I write as an unworldly man yet the world and all its evils are ever around us. John Tregonwell left soon after the hour of Terce for his native Cornwall. I fear he desires to put an end to our house at Veland and has reported much to his masters. And yet he knows nothing of the matter concerning Brother William. If he did, I fear the lad would be hanged as a common criminal and that I cannot allow for I know he was driven to his crime.

Another call from Neil. Wesley felt a little guilty as he answered the phone. It was the third time Neil had tried to get hold of him which suggested that he had something important to say. However, because of the new developments in the Spider case, he hadn't had a chance to call him back.

'She's been taken to hospital,' Neil said as soon as he answered the phone. 'She tried to kill herself.'

'Who?' Sometimes Neil tried his patience.

'Diane. She killed Barry Ickerman. The skeleton in the woods. That's what I've been trying to . . .'

Wesley listened carefully as Neil outlined what he knew. If it weren't for the current emergency, this would be his top priority. But as it was, there were lives at stake. 'Where are you now?'

'Tradmouth Hospital. How soon can you get here?'

Wesley took a deep breath and looked at his watch. 'Sorry, we've got an emergency here. I'll see you as soon as I can . . . I promise.'

There was a long silence. Then, 'I've found out all about Brother William.'

'Good,' said Wesley. Even in a dire situation, Neil's mind was still on archaeology.

'Look, Neil, I've got to go. I'm sorry. I'll get back to you soon. Promise.'

He felt bad but it was all he could do for now. They had to find Francis Duparc – and he only hoped they wouldn't be too late.

'They've tracked down the mobile phone signal. It's in the vicinity of Belsinger School. And the helicopter's spotted a red car parked in the lane just by the woodland at the edge of the school grounds. According to Father Joseph at Shenton Abbey, their missing car's a red Fiat.'

'It looks like they're together,' said Gerry Heffernan quietly. 'Let's hope we're not too late.'

'So what's happening, sir?' Steve Carstairs stood there with his mouth open. He looked confused. And a little lost.

Wesley gave him a sympathetic glance as the phone on Gerry Heffernan's desk rang. The DCI picked it up and barked a 'hello'. After a few seconds he looked up at Wesley. 'They've found Francis. He's been taken to Tradmouth Hospital. But the killer's got away . . . disappeared. We've got the registration number. All patrols are on the look-out for the car.'

Wesley thought for a moment. 'Let's go and have a word with Brother Francis. I want to know once and for all what all this is about.'

'You and me both.' Heffernan turned to Steve. 'You stop here. If anything comes in let us know right away if not sooner.'

'What's going on, sir?'

Wesley had rarely seen Steve worried before. But there's a first time for everything.

They had to talk to Francis Duparc urgently and twenty minutes later they were sitting at his bedside. Heffernan gave Wesley a nudge: he'd let him do the talking.

There was no time for pleasantries, however brief. 'We need to know what's going on.'

The monk raised his right hand weakly. The blood was beginning to seep through the dressings on his upper body. The killer hadn't been controlled and methodical this time: it had been an unfocused, half-hearted attack and he'd had a lucky escape. Perhaps someone up there had been looking after His own, Wesley thought fleetingly.

'Have you found . . . ?' His voice was stronger than Wesley had expected.

'Not yet. But all patrols are out looking. We need to know the whole story. Why don't you start at the beginning?'

Francis considered the question for a few moments. 'Very well,' he said before pausing to gather his thoughts. 'I'd never encountered real wickedness until I met Charles Marrick at Belsinger,' he began, a tremor in his voice. 'I'm not talking about naughtiness or what they call nowadays challenging behaviour. Charles wasn't necessarily naughty at school – he was too clever for that – too sly to want to draw attention to himself by getting into trouble. But he – how shall I put it? – lacked basic human feeling. He considered himself the centre of the universe and thought the rules of morality didn't apply to him – not that we realised that at the time, of course. He used people for his own ends. And he gathered a little clique of weaker boys – including myself – around him. You have to understand, he was very charismatic, Inspector. If he hadn't . . . if he hadn't been the way he was, he might have been a natural leader. He had a terrific influence over us. And he manipulated us so that we'd do anything he suggested.' He hesitated.

'Go on,' Wesley prompted.

'He devised rituals. Mind games. I find it hard to believe he had such power over us, Inspector, but I assure you that power was real.'

'What were the rituals?'

Francis rolled up the left sleeve of his hospital pyjamas. 'Blood. He used to cut us with a sharpened penknife and make us drink each other's blood. The idea's preposterous now but for impressionable adolescents at midnight on an isolated beach by the light of a fire . . . As I said, he knew exactly how to manipulate us and keep us in his power.'

He held out his arm to Wesley. The faint scar was visible even after all these years. Wesley had seen such scars before – on the dead flesh of Charles Marrick and Simon Trench.

'Tell me about the girl. A former Belsinger pupil called Barty Carter said he saw her in Tradmouth. She was the caretaker's daughter, I believe.'

Francis swallowed hard and tears began to fill his eyes. 'Her name was Janet. Janet Blincoe. I've never forgiven myself for what happened. Not that we realised what Charlie intended to do. He was more grown up than we were. It almost seemed as if he was born that way. We hardly knew anything about sex – not like Charlie who claimed to have had half a dozen girls before he was sixteen.'

'Lads like to boast,' Heffernan chipped in. 'Doesn't necessarily mean it's true. Could all have been fantasy . . . wishful thinking.'

Francis looked at him. 'In general I'd say that you're probably right, Chief Inspector. But in Charlie's case I wouldn't have been surprised if it had been true. As I said, he wasn't like the rest of us.'

'So what happened?'

'Janet had been hanging around us. I think she must have had some sort of crush on Charlie.'

'And he took advantage of the fact?' Wesley said.

'You could say that.' He thought for a few moments, considering the best way to begin his narrative. 'Mortimer Dean, the housemaster, wasn't very observant – Charlie could run rings around him. It was easy for us to sneak out of Tavistock House because there was a broken catch on one of the ground floor windows. It was summer, really warm – and one night we let ourselves out after midnight. We didn't realise Charlie had told her to come with us. She met us in the school grounds – by the cricket pavilion – and we went down to the beach. Charlie was very quiet. She was chatting a lot, trying to make him notice her. She was only fourteen – a couple of years younger than us – and we thought she was just a silly kid. We didn't know why Charlie had said she could come.'

Wesley pictured the scene. It was easy to envisage the boys following their pack leader – doing things they wouldn't normally dream of doing as they returned to a feral state under the influence of a more powerful personality. He waited for Francis to continue.

'When we got down to the beach, Charlie made an announcement,' he said after a few moments. 'He said she was to undergo the blood ritual – to be one of us. None of us liked the idea but, as I said, Charlie's word was law. We didn't argue.'

'So what happened?' Gerry Heffernan leaned forward, anxious to hear the rest of the story.

'Things went too far.'

'What do you mean?'

Francis opened his mouth but no sound came out, as if he couldn't bring himself to put what had happened into words and give the truth the power of being released into the open. Wesley let him take his time and eventually his patience was rewarded.

'Charlie raped her, there in front of us,' Francis whispered. 'Then he told us to . . . It was as if we'd been taken over by something evil.' He shook his head as the tears began to flow down his cheeks. 'It was madness. She was screaming and crying but . . .'

'So you all raped her?' Gerry Heffernan couldn't keep the horror out of his voice.

'I've been paying for it all my life.' He buried his head in his hands. 'Charlie kept egging us on and . . .'

'And you never thought to say no? You never thought to stop it?' Heffernan's voice was getting louder and Wesley put a restraining hand on his arm.

'None of us did. It was like . . . like a collective madness. A frenzy. I know I can't make excuses for what we did. There is no excuse.'

'So you all joined in? Even Simon Tench?'

Francis nodded. 'You're wondering how someone like Simon could carry on with his normal, respectable life after doing that. Well the human mind can fool itself that an event that's too painful to live with never even happened — a defence mechanism, I suppose. I think Simon and Chris blotted it out completely. And if you'd asked them about it they would have denied it because they would have persuaded themselves that they could never do something like that. And in normal circumstances, they probably couldn't. They weren't bad boys, Inspector. It was as if they were possessed.'

'And you?' Wesley asked gently.

Francis looked Wesley in the eye. 'I could never blot it out. I've been doing penance for it since I was sixteen.'

'There's more isn't there? What happened after you'd . . . ?'

Francis looked away. 'Charlie said if she wanted to be one of us, she'd have to undergo the ritual. He pinned her down again so she couldn't move and he cut her wrist with the knife. She started to bleed a lot and she was crying. That's when we got scared. We all ran off 'cause we knew it had gone too far. We thought she was going to die and we were terrified.'

'What about Charlie?'

'He stayed.'

'Did you talk about it afterwards?'

'Never. Nobody breathed a word. It was as if it had never happened.'

'And the girl?'

'She went away. We never saw her again.'

'Surely her parents called the police,' said Wesley. 'Surely there was some sort of investigation.'

Francis shook his head. 'No, it was never mentioned again. She disappeared.'

'So her father quit his job as caretaker?'

Francis thought for a moment. 'No, I don't believe he did. But she left and nothing was ever said.'

'So everyone closed ranks. The school covered it up.' Gerry Heffernan said, full of righteous indignation.

But Francis shook his head again. 'I don't think the school knew what had happened. I think the girl had been too ashamed to tell the truth.' He hesitated. 'That's one of the things I asked her when . . . She told her father she'd had an accident. Her mother was dead and her father kept his distance. She'd been adopted and they weren't close.'

'Did she say how she tracked you and the others down after all these years?' This was one of the things that had puzzled Wesley.

'The Belsinger website has details of what old boys are doing now. We were all on it. Mortimer Dean made sure of that. She did her homework.'

'Did she say how she administered the hemlock?'

'She told me everything . . . made her confession. I suppose she didn't think I'd be around to give away her secrets.'

'Well?'

'She'd had a part-time job doing market research at one

time and that gave her the idea. She called round at the victims' houses with samples of malt whisky – irresistible to the likes of Charlie Marrick. They readily volunteered to give their verdicts on the different samples – only the whisky contained hemlock. Once they'd drunk it, she produced a questionnaire and chatted until the paralysis set in. Then she made them bleed to death . . . just as they'd left her to bleed to death. She told them who she was as they lay paralysed and helpless. Said she enjoyed seeing the look in their eyes as they realised . . . as they remembered that night.'

'Where is she now, Francis?' Wesley asked gently.

There was no answer.

Wesley stood up and Gerry Heffernan watched him expectantly. A nurse entered the room with a clattering trolley and Francis slumped back on his pillows, looking almost relieved.

'So you took part in what happened at the beach,' Wesley continued, ignoring the nurse. 'You went along with it all. You could have told Mortimer Dean. You could have gone to the headmaster . . . the matron. You could have told someone.'

The man in the bed shook his head sadly. 'It was against the code of honour to tell tales. I sinned and now I can't live with myself. I wish you hadn't found me, Inspector. I wish I'd been allowed to die.' He swallowed hard. 'I wanted her to kill me. I was ready to pay for what I did to her.'

'For what Charles Marrick did, you mean.' Wesley looked into Francis's tear-filled eyes. 'Did she tell you where she planned to go?'

Francis said nothing.

'Please. We have to find her.'

After a few seconds Francis spoke, almost in a whisper. 'She said she was going to go back to where it happened.'

Heffernan leaned forward. 'And where exactly was that?'

As soon as Francis told them, Wesley, ignoring the hospital's ban on mobile phones, pulled his from his pocket and made a call.

Steve Carstairs stood at the office door, blocking Trish's way. She avoided his gaze, like someone face to face with a bereaved relative who found themselves lost for something to say.

He caught her arm. 'What the fuck's going on, Trish? Why won't anyone tell me what's happening?'

Trish stood for a few moments, wondering how much she should tell him. The boss hadn't actually said that he should be kept in the dark indefinitely. Besides, she had just heard that it was almost over. The search was on now – all the manpower they could spare – and it wouldn't be long now until the arrest was made.

She looked around. The office was buzzing. She needed somewhere more private. She grabbed Steve's hand and led him out into the corridor. Then she turned to face him and looked into his eyes. 'Look, Steve, the boss is afraid you won't be able to keep your mouth shut. But I think you need to know.' She hesitated. 'Cheshire police sent a photo of Christopher Grisham's girlfriend, Jenny – I recognised her and so did Barty Carter. He'd seen her in Tradmouth.'

'What's all this got to do with . . . ?'

She took a deep breath. She was trying to break this gently. 'She called herself Jenny Pringle up in Chester. Her dad was the caretaker at Belsinger. She's down here using a different name.' She paused. 'She's calling herself Joanne.'

He shook his head. 'I don't believe you.'

'She's just tried to kill Francis Duparc – Brother Francis. He's in hospital now and he's made a statement. Joanne's the Spider, Steve. She killed those men.'

Steve stared at her as though she'd struck him.

'Didn't you suspect anything?' she asked warily.

'Of course I didn't. It's impossible. There's been a mistake.

Where is she? Does anyone know? I've been trying her mobile number but . . .'

'They think she might be at the beach at Littlebury . . . just east of Monks Island.'

Steve turned. 'I'm going over there.'

Trish clutched at his sleeve. 'No. The boss said . . .'

'The boss can fuck off.'

He shook off Trish's clinging hand and marched out. But Trish followed him, her mouth set in a determined line. There was no way she was going to let him go there alone.

It was raining now and she stood barefoot on the sand staring out to sea. The sound of the waves brought back the memory of that night. Relentless, pitiless like the boys who had violated her body. She had never let a man touch her in that way since. Even Steve. However much she liked him, she felt no desire, no temptation. The very thought of physical contact – of giving herself – made her want to vomit.

When Marrick had stabbed the blade into her arm and laughed, she had prayed for death. They were alone then, her and Marrick – the others had run off like frightened animals. Marrick had whispered in her ear. 'You enjoyed that, didn't you? Now I'm going to watch you die.' She lay sprawled there on the sand beneath the cliffs, paralysed with terror as he leered down at her.

Then suddenly she'd found herself alone, knowing that death was close as her life blood drained away on to the damp sand. She'd felt faint, as though the world was drifting away, but then she'd sensed a sudden pressure on her arm. Someone was kneeling by her side, binding it with cloth very tightly to stop the bleeding. She'd looked into Mr Dean's face and saw he was crying. And he was telling her to say nothing. It had been an accident. She'd slipped and cut herself. She didn't want to ruin the future of the lads in his charge, did she? It would be better to say nothing. Nobody would believe her anyway.

He'd been kind, Mr Dean. He'd carried her back home and told her father some story about an accident. She could tell by the look in her father's eyes that he didn't quite believe it but he was in no position to argue. And since her mother's death in a road accident, she had never been able to talk to him about anything deeper than trivialities so she kept her silence. Even when she was sent away to live with her aunt 'because it would be better', she'd never told. She'd been ashamed and nursed the secret that had festered inside her soul, unseen and suppressed. But when she'd met Chris Grisham up in Chester, the horror of that night had flooded back.

She'd been calling herself Jenny Pringle by then – she'd adopted her aunt's surname and her father had always called her Jenny so Chris had had no idea who she was and at first she hadn't recognised him either. It was only when they got talking, trading their backgrounds, that he told her he'd been at Belsinger. Then the memory came back to her slowly, seeping like blood from a wound. She recalled his face – much younger then and ridden with acne. But she'd said nothing. She let it carry on and when he became impatient with her refusal to sleep with him, she finished it, saying she'd rather be friends. She even told him that she thought she preferred women and he had made a coarse joke but accepted it. You win some, you lose some.

She had had to use all her self-control to keep up the act, the pretence. And although he seemed quite amiable, she couldn't allow herself to see him as a human being. He was one of the boys who'd destroyed her life, left her emotionally paralysed; unable to form relationships with men like the women around her did. She was petrified of physical contact. Dead to love. And she'd wanted him to die. To be helpless as she had been helpless. He had to know what it was like – what he'd done to her.

The first time had been hard. She had made the hemlock – she knew all about preparing herbs from her aunt who'd been keen on that sort of thing. She'd found the plant growing wild by a riverbank and had chopped up the leaves, put them in a blender and covered the pulp with best malt whisky – the kind Chris liked – before straining it and rebottling the poisoned drink. She knew it would paralyse him. She knew she'd be able to reveal her identity and tell him what he'd done to her as he lay there helpless. And when she'd pierced his throat with the knife, he had had to lie there just as she had lain there on the sand, while his life blood drained away. It had been sweet, that first death. And the others had been easier – almost enjoyable. She had become Nemesis. The avenging angel.

She had called on the others – on Charles Marrick and Simon Tench – in her market research role, armed with official-looking clipboard and small sample bottles of adulterated whisky. Funny how men can never resist the flattery of being asked their opinion . . . especially about something like a fine malt whisky. She flattered and joked and they had no idea who she was. It had been so easy. She was sorry about Mortimer Dean, but he'd known the truth and he couldn't be allowed to betray her.

Now it was over. She could hear the sea, pounding relentlessly against the rocks at the edge of the beach. She had brought death to her tormentors and now it was her turn. This was how it had to end.

She began to walk towards the sea, staring ahead. But suddenly she heard a shout above the noise of the gulls. Someone was calling her name, running towards her, getting closer. She began to move, her eyes still fixed ahead. They wouldn't take her alive.

But she couldn't resist looking round and she was relieved to see that he'd come alone. Steve Carstairs was getting nearer, his progress hampered by the soft sand. If she was going to do it, it had to be now before he could stop her. She began to run towards the waves. Then into the water, gasping as the cold waves hit her warm flesh. She waded out, frustrated at the weight of sea slowing her steps. She was up to her shoulders. Her neck. She walked on. He wouldn't save her. It was over. It had to be.

She could still hear him shouting. He was in the water too, up to his waist now. The current knocked her off her feet and she let the water take her, going under for the first time then bobbing up for breath.

She turned towards the shore but she couldn't see Steve. Maybe he had given up – she hoped he had. Suddenly she spotted his head and arms thrashing about in the water. Then he went under. And she did the same.

When she surfaced again there were sirens. Police cars on the beach. And figures in wet suits coming after her, swimming strongly.

The next thing she knew she felt rough hands on her body, dragging her up on to the sand as she fought, coughing and spluttering. They were pulling at her arms, hurting her. Just like those boys had hurt her years ago.

Her head began to spin as the effort of the fight became too much. Someone – the woman called Trish she had seen once at Steve's flat – was putting a blanket around her shoulders. And someone was shouting, asking where Steve was as she slumped back, shuddering, and vomited on to the damp, golden sand.

Gerry Heffernan and Wesley Peterson had hardly said a word on the journey back to Tradmouth. Both men felt numb, stunned. And both experienced a nagging guilt that in life they hadn't really liked Steve Carstairs. In death, they both knew, Steve would become a fallen comrade. A hero. *De mortuis nil nisi bonum.* Nobody would ever speak ill of Steve again.

It was Heffernan who broke the stunned silence. 'Those currents are bloody lethal, Wes,' he said softly. 'He was an idiot to go in there. He didn't stand a chance.'

'She did.'

'She was bloody lucky for once in her life.'

'I doubt if she'd see it that way. She's got a life sentence ahead of her.'

'Or a spell at Her Majesty's pleasure in a secure psychiatric hospital. Under the circumstances . . .'

Wesley shook his head. 'She planned it so carefully. There's no way any jury's going to believe a plea of insanity. And she killed Mortimer Dean just to cover her tracks.'

Gerry Heffernan didn't answer. Wesley, he knew, was probably right. 'Didn't you say you needed to see Neil?'

'Yes. It seems he's done our job for us. He's found out the truth about this skeleton business.' He gave Heffernan a brief outline of the facts.

The DCI gave a low whistle. 'That's a turn-up for the books. Fancy going to see him now?' he said like a parent trying to give a child a treat to distract him from something unpleasant.

But Wesley hardly felt in the mood for Neil at that moment. Steve filled his thoughts. Steve whom he had never really liked. Steve who'd given him a hard time. Steve whom Gerry had threatened to return to uniform as soon as the Spider case was over. He could hardly believe he was dead. That he wouldn't slouch into the CID office in that leather jacket like Jack the Lad, fancying himself.

'I'll have to go and break the news to his mum,' Heffernan said quietly. 'Say what a fine officer he was and that he'd died trying to rescue someone.' He sighed. 'Why is it I feel like such a hypocrite, Wes?'

'Can't you leave it to CS Nutter?'

'No, Wes. I've got to do it myself. He was part of my team. Why don't we see Neil first thing tomorrow, eh? See what he's got to say about those bones in the woods.'

'Barry Ickerman

'What?'

'The skeleton's name. Barry Ickerman. Sex offender of the parish of Luton or thereabouts.' He sighed. 'We've cleared up two cases today. Why is it I don't feel like celebrating?'

Gerry Heffernan touched his sleeve. He knew exactly what Wesley meant.

Wesley was silent as they drove out to Stow Barton the next morning with Heffernan by his side. He parked by the gate and both men made their way to the excavation. The first person they came across was Norman Hedge. He smiled nervously at Wesley who greeted him solemnly.

'Any progress, Inspector?'

The two policemen looked at each other. There was no harm in giving the man the bare facts. After all, he'd suffered at Charles Marrick's hands too. 'We've made an arrest, Mr Hedge. A young woman who used to live at Belsinger School. She was the daughter of the caretaker there – a Janet Blincoe.'

Hedge looked surprised. 'I remember her. She was a nervous little thing – terrified of her own shadow. She disappeared suddenly – went to live with her aunt or something. Surely you've made a mistake.'

After a few reassuring words, they went off in search of Neil. They found him talking to Lenny. Lenny looked bored: Neil's archaeological and historical findings were clearly still at odds with his imaginative version of what went on at Stow Barton. Blood rituals are far more compelling than the uncomplicated – if old fashioned – medical procedure of blood-letting. Who needs the facts to get in the way when you've already decided on the story? It was a good job Wesley was used to keeping an open mind or Carl Pinney would still have been behind bars for Charles Marrick's murder.

Neil spotted the two detectives and beckoned them into the site office. Wesley noticed that he looked pale and drawn.

Not his usual self. He sat on a rickety office chair by a makeshift desk while Wesley and his boss perched on a pair of upturned milk crates.

'Are you okay?' Wesley sounded concerned. He'd rarely seen Neil so agitated, playing with a trowel that had been lying on the desk, turning it over and over in his fingers.

'Not really.'

'Sorry I couldn't see you yesterday but . . .'

Neil looked up at him reproachfully.

'So what happened?'

'Diane tried to kill herself.'

'Is she . . . ?'

'Still in hospital. But she'll be fine.'

Gerry Heffernan cleared his throat. 'Wes tells me you've found out who killed our skeleton in the woods. After my job, are you?' he said, his mind only half on the question. He knew he had to see Steve's mother and he wanted to do it sooner rather than later . . . to get it over and done with. And there was his father too at Burton's Butties. He'd almost forgotten about the father.

'So tell us about it,' Wesley said gently.

Neil scratched his head. 'Okay. Where do I start?'

'Try the beginning.'

'Well, Diane was just a kid at the time. She was on holiday at Sunacres and she was playing in the wood when this man tried to attack her. She had a penknife with her and lashed out, I suppose. It was an accident – self-defence at worst.'

'She didn't tell anyone?'

Neil shook his head. 'She was scared stiff. She just left him there and tried to pretend it never happened. You can understand it really. Terrified kid. Bad man. It must have been awful for her, keeping that to herself all these years. What a thing to have to live with . . . no wonder it sent her over the edge.'

'I'm sure no charges will be brought,' said Wesley. 'But we'll need to speak to her.'

'Yeah, I know.' He reached across the desk and picked up a pile of papers. Photocopies. 'Annabel found these. Extracts from the Comperta – the report John Tregonwell, Henry VIII's commissioner, made about Veland Abbey.' He paused. 'Diane found the abbot's journal in the cathedral archives in Exeter too and something in it reminded her of what happened . . . brought it all flooding back. Here, take this copy. I've got another. It makes for interesting reading.' As he handed the papers over to Wesley he looked from one man to the other. He'd been so engrossed in Diane's problems that he hadn't noticed until now that the two policemen seemed more subdued than usual. 'What's the matter? You look as if you're off to a funeral.'

'Steve's dead . . . DC Carstairs. He drowned trying to rescue a suspect.'

Neil's mouth fell open. 'Bloody hell,' he muttered. 'That's bad.'

Annette Marrick passed the man in the High Street. She almost didn't recognise him dressed like that. Last time she'd seen him he'd been wearing shorts. On the day she'd found Charlie dead he'd been walking across the drive of Foxglove House with a woman. She stared back at him for a second then turned away.

If he'd witnessed anything, he would have told the police. And, if she was honest, she didn't really care any more. Charlie was dead and she was glad. It saved the expense of a divorce and this way she kept the house.

But something made her pick up the phone and dial DI Peterson's number. She'd rather liked him. And, since Petronella had gone back to Bath, she wanted someone to talk to.

The atmosphere in the CID office was tense. One of their own was dead. It didn't matter if he'd been an awkward bastard. He was one of them. His mother and father had been told. His father had also been informed about the involvement of his assistant, Joanne. He'd said he didn't believe she was the killer they'd all been calling the Spider but he didn't do much arguing. Steve was gone and the world and its priorities had changed in a moment.

Janet Blincoe was safely under lock and key. She'd be notorious for a while then she'd drop from the public's radar only to be resurrected from time to time in true crime books. Wesley had told Heffernan he felt a bit sorry for her. But the DCI had replied that he was too soft. Always had been. Had he ever considered a career as a social worker?

There seemed little to do now apart from tie up the loose ends. Wesley had a headache coming on after comforting a sobbing Trish Walton. The depth of her grief surprised him. He suspected it surprised her too.

He needed a distraction so he picked up the papers Neil had given him and began to read. First he tackled the report of King Henry's commissioner, John Tregonwell, into the state of Veland Abbey with its intriguing remark at the end about an event so terrible he could not speak of it. Then, before he could make a start on the abbott's journal, his phone rang.

It was Annette Marrick. She had something to tell him. It probably wasn't important but she'd seen a couple walking away from the gates of Foxglove House on the day her husband died. She'd thought they were just out for a walk so she'd forgotten all about them. But she'd seen the young woman since in that sandwich bar on the High Street in Tradmouth. And she'd seen the man today – that's what had triggered the memory. Wesley asked her to describe him and Annette was happy to oblige. In fact she sounded eager to talk. It must be lonely, he thought, in that rambling house alone with the bloodstains and the memories.

He thought about the call as he began to read the extract from the abbott's journal.

Then he told Gerry Heffernan he was going out. He had something to do.

Father Joseph left them alone. He answered to a higher authority than the police but he didn't believe in rocking the boat. If an inspector wished to see Brother Francis that was okay by him.

'How are you?' he asked as Francis sat down opposite him in the plain little visitors' room with the large crucifix in the centre of the wall.

'Shaken. She is all right?'

'She's been taken into custody. But I'm afraid one of our officers drowned trying to rescue her.'

Francis looked shocked. The colour drained from his face as he made the sign of the cross and muttered a prayer for the dead. 'I'm so sorry,' he said, his head bowed. And he sounded as though he meant it.

Wesley decided on the element of surprise. 'What were you doing with Janet Blincoe at Foxglove House on the day Charles Marrick died?'

The monk looked stunned. Then he put his head in his hands.

'She didn't work alone, did she? I was wondering how she came to know about poisons. You work in the gardens here, don't you?'

Francis nodded. 'Yes, but I assure you that Janet's knowledge of poisons didn't come from me. She already knew all about hemlock. The aunt who took her in was a keen herbalist. She'd taught her a lot.'

'Whose idea was it to get your revenge on Charles Marrick?'

There was a long silence. 'Janet got in touch with me via e-mail. She'd found out where I was through the school website that Mortimer Dean so assiduously kept up to date and suggested that we meet. She said she had something to tell me. This isn't an enclosed order, Inspector. I was able to go up north to meet her. She was living in Chester and we met halfway, in Lichfield . . . in the cathedral. She said she'd met Christopher Grisham . . . and then she told me she'd killed him. I was shocked, of course, but I understood. I can never forget what happened that night. I told her she had to go to the police and make a full confession but . . .'

Wesley looked the man in the eye. 'You never raped her, did you? And she didn't try to kill you today. The hospital said your wounds were only superficial. When you heard us coming you wounded yourself to make it look convincing. If we hadn't arrived, Janet would have just gone away. Left the area and taken up a new identity, am I right? You met her to say goodbye.'

'If that's what you believe . . .'

After a few moments of silence Wesley spoke again. 'Janet wasn't the only person Charlie Marrick raped back then, was she?'

His mouth fell open and the colour drained from his face. 'I don't know what you mean.'

'Marrick raped you too.'

Francis looked up. There were tears welling in his eye, trickling down his cheek. 'I've spent my life trying to come to terms with what happened; doing my best to forget. My faith told me quite clearly that I should forgive but somehow I never could, however hard I tried. Marrick scarred my body and my mind, inspector. I kept quiet about Janet's rape because Charlie threatened that if I didn't, I'd be next. I did as I was told but he . . .'

'He did it anyway?' Wesley suddenly felt deeply sorry for the man sitting there before him.

'You don't know what he was like. He was evil.'

'So you helped her to kill him,' Wesley said gently.

Francis wiped his eyes with his sleeve. 'It was a terrible thing to do,' he whispered. 'Even to the man who . . .'

'What about the others – Simon Tench and Mortimer Dean?'

He swallowed hard. 'Janet killed Simon – he'd been one of the ones who . . . She'd seen him on some property programme, she said, with his smug wife – her words not mine.'

'And Mortimer Dean?'

The tears welled again. 'Mortimer had always known exactly what happened, you see. Janet gave me some of the poisoned whisky she'd prepared. Mortimer was very partial to single malt. I took it round as a present. He was delighted. I wanted him to die happy, you see.'

'But why?'

'Because he knew too much. Janet said he couldn't be allowed to betray us. I didn't want to kill him, honestly. But I knew she was right. As he lay there I told him how sorry I was . . . asked his forgiveness.'

Wesley recited the familiar words of the caution and then led Brother Francis gently away.

CHAPTER 15

From the journal of Abbott Thomas Standing 11th October 1535

Brother William came to me this hour weeping and sore afraid. I assured him of my protection even though he killed a man. I told him that man was corrupt, a devil, and he has asked forgiveness of Our Lord who died for our sins on the cross and pardons all that truly repent, so his soul is in no peril.

Brother Silas was ever a corrupter of souls like the serpent in Eden. And when he tried to force Brother William to submit to his unnatural lusts – as he had forced other novices I have since learned – Brother William stabbed him at the seyney house with the lancet the brother infirmerer uses for the blood-letting. It seems that the leisure of the seyney house inflamed Brother Silas's desires. It may be that the rule is too lax there. By some misfortune the blade struck Brother Silas's throat, in a place where the blood flows freely and cannot be stopped. Brother William was sore afraid and his tormentor bled to death as it was night and in a most private place so there was no help to be had.

Brother William confessed all to me and I absolved him of his sins. Perhaps I too am guilty as I feel no pity at this man's death. Brother Silas lies in the chapel tonight and the brothers keep vigil. I have told Brother William not to touch the corpse *lest it begins to bleed again as murdered corpses are wont to do in the presence of their murderer. He will be buried tomorrow in the brothers' resting place and I pray that will be an end to the matter.*

I hear tell that John Tregonwell will report upon our house to Master Thomas Cromwell very soon and I fear our community will not survive if the King has his will — which our King always does. I must pray and forget.

A week later Wesley walked into Gerry Heffernan's office. Since Steve's death the place had been considerably less cheerful than Colin Bowman's mortuary. And today things were even worse. The funeral was to be held that lunchtime. And everyone would be there, from the lowest DC to the chief constable. Wesley was dreading it.

'I've been doing some digging,' he said as Heffernan looked up. The DCI looked tired. He hadn't slept, he said. And Joyce was busy visiting her mother in hospital so there was no comfort from that quarter either.

'Diane . . . Neil's friend. The one who's confessed to killing Barry Ickerman.'

'What about her?'

'I've found out she was married at university to a Paul Lowe — and divorced soon after. Then I looked up her maiden name. Guess what it is?'

'Surprise me,' Heffernan said wearily.

'Ickerman.'

Heffernan raised his eyebrows.

'I finally managed to trace the couple who used to run Sunacres Holiday Park at the time Barry Ickerman disappeared. I know we should have checked this out before but . . .'

'We have been rather busy.'

'The couple live in Morbay now and I sent someone to have a word with them. They remembered the Ickermans: they stayed for a fortnight but the father left after about ten days. It's a long time ago but they remember the mother telling them that he was called away on business. The woman remembered him because she thought he was a bit creepy and she was glad when he left. She said the little girl was sweet though. Diane her name was.' He allowed himself a small smile of triumph.

'So Diane didn't kill a random flasher in the woods. It was her own father and her mother helped her cover it up. Poor kid.'

'Are we going to take it any further?'

Gerry Heffernan hesitated then he looked him in the eye. 'Nothing's been written down officially, has it?'

'Not yet.'

'She was only a kid and I don't think there's anything to be gained by raking it all up, do you?'

Wesley thought for a moment. Colin's postmortem was inconclusive so there was no actual evidence of murder. What would really be the point of alerting the CPS and putting Diane through the ordeal of making statements and the threat of court proceedings? Not to mention the waste of taxpayers' money. His eyes met Heffernan's in silent understanding.

'I think we can safely forget it, don't you, Gerry? Case unsolved. It won't do our clear-up rate much good but . . .'

'Good man, Wes. Least said soonest mended as my old granny used to say. And I don't like men who do that to kiddies.' Heffernan examined his watch. 'Better tell everyone to be ready in five minutes.'

Wesley left the DCI's office and returned to his desk. Absentmindedly, he opened the top drawer. The travel brochure was lying there. Carcassonne with its ancient walls and pepper pot towers glowing in the French sunshine. Pam would love it. And come the end of term she'd need a break badly. Just as he did. Life went on.

When he looked up, Gerry Heffernan was emerging from his office, his face serious above his black tie.

It was time to go.